Sacred Scars

ALSO BY KATHLEEN DUEY

A Resurrection of Magic:
Skin Hunger

A RESURRECTION OF MAGIC

Sacred Scars

KATHLEEN DUEY

Atheneum Books for Young Readers
NEW YORK   LONDON   TORONTO   SYDNEY

Atheneum Books for Young Readers

An imprint of Simon & Schuster Children's Publishing Division

1230 Avenue of the Americas

New York, New York 10020

For information about special discounts for bulk purchases, please contact

Simon & Schuster Special Sales at 1-866-506-1949 or business@simonandschuster.com.

The Simon & Schuster Speakers Bureau can bring authors to your live event.

For more information or to book an event, contact the Simon & Schuster Speakers Bureau at
1-866-248-3049 or visit our website at www.simonspeakers.com.

Book design by Michael Rosamilia

The text for this book is set in Meridien.

Manufactured in the United States of America

2 4 6 8 10 9 7 5 3

Library of Congress Cataloging-in-Publication Data

Duey, Kathleen.

Sacred scars / Kathleen Duey.—1st ed.

p. cm. — (A resurrection of magic ; [bk. 2])

Summary: In alternate chapters, Sadima works to free captive boys forced
to copy documents in the caverns of Limòri, and Hahp makes a pact with
the remaining students of a wizards' academy in hopes that all will survive
their training, as both learn valuable lessons about loyalty.

ISBN: 978-0-689-84095-1 (hardcover)

[1. Magic—Fiction. 2. Schools—Fiction. 3. Fantasy.] I. Title.

PZ7.D8694Sac 2009

[Fic]—dc22 2008056044

FOR GARRETT AND SETH

~ 1 ~

Sadima sat cross-legged on the cold stone, just out-side the cage. She was holding her slate so the boys could see the symbol she had drawn. Most of them were trying to copy it. Two stolen lanterns hung from the iron bars above their heads, held in place by some Market Square merchant's missing tarp hooks. The rest of the vast cavern was dark.

Sadima pulled at a loose thread in her ragged skirt, listening for the sound of Franklin's footsteps in the long entrance passage on the far end of the big chamber. Somiss had no coins to spend, and they needed *everything,* so Franklin had become a thief. He left the cliffs at dark and returned at dawn, carrying sacks of stolen goods, swaying like a farm mule under the weight. He was nearly always exhausted when he got back, ready to collapse on his blankets.

Sadima pushed her hair back over her shoulder, wishing Franklin would come, trying not to imagine him running, king's guards close behind him. Thieves were often hanged. If the guards realized who he was, it would be worse than that. Much worse.

Sadima tucked her skirt between her bare feet and the cold stone. She had shoes, but they were buried in a box in the woods. She had meant to go get them long ago, before winter closed in. But Somiss had forbidden her to leave the dark passages inside the cliffs, and she knew that if she disobeyed him, he wouldn't punish her. He would punish Franklin. Sadima lowered her head to keep the boys from seeing her fear—and her anger.

Somiss was clever. He was used to servants, silk, delicate pastries, the endless round of entertainments in his father's royal house. So was Franklin, in his own way. Neither one of them had understood what it would mean to live in the caverns and tunnels they had found inside Limòri's cliffs. Neither one had even thought of *blankets*.

Somiss had been violent at first, raging at Franklin, at the cold, the darkness, his own hunger and thirst. But night by night, Franklin had robbed the rich of their heavy woolen comforters until there were enough for all to sleep upon and under. Then he had brought lanterns, water buckets, food, paper, ink quills—and everything else.

Sadima looked up. Most of the boys had stopped drawing. "Let me see what you've done," she said quietly. Six of the ten turned their slates toward her. Four had fallen asleep sitting up, chalk wedged between their fingers or dropped on the floor.

Jux's copy was nearly perfect, and when she smiled at him, he sat up straighter. "You're all getting better," she lied, looking one by one into the faces of the boys who had at least tried. Most of them avoided her eyes. The biggest boy, Mabiki, lay down, yawning and dull eyed. His dark, curly hair was filthy and tangled and when he reached to push it off his forehead, his slate skidded sideways. Jux leapt up and grabbed it, then passed it through the bars. Sadima set it aside, glad it hadn't broken. *Jux and Mabiki.* None of the others would tell her their names. Jux had explained it—only the king's guards and magistrates had ever wanted to know. It scared them.

Sadima wiped her slate and drew another symbol. She held it up and the boys started over. At first they had jostled and argued; it had been hard to make them sit still for their lessons. Now they barely spoke, barely moved. They had come from hard lives; they were street orphans. It hurt Sadima to imagine that. No warm suppers. No one ever looking out for them. She was sure none of them had ever held so much as a lump of charcoal to draw a game of jump-and-stop on a boardwalk. Still, somehow, Somiss expected them to learn to fair copy.

Jux was looking at his slate, correcting a line. He was the only one who could draw the Gypsy symbols accurately— and he was by far the fastest at Ferrinides letters. Sadima smiled at him again and he smiled back, lifting his chin. She nodded, then looked at the other boys in the cage to keep from staring at the terrible rose-and-putty-colored scar that crossed Jux's throat and disappeared behind his ear. How old was he? Seven? Eight? Someone had already tried to cut his throat. And now Somiss had put him in a cage.

Sadima thought she heard a sound and turned, hoping to see Franklin's lantern, a tiny amber star shining from across the darkness of the big cavern. But he wasn't back. Not yet. She drew another symbol for the boys to copy. Then another.

It was a long time before Franklin finally returned, his back bent under the weight of the supplies he was carrying. Sadima jumped up and walked toward the light of his lantern, leaving her own behind to have both hands free to help him. He kissed her. She closed her eyes to feel the touch of his lips more clearly. He would sleep all day, then be gone again at dark. Dawn and dusk; these were the only moments they had together now. *I miss you.* She started to say it, but he spoke first.

"Has Somiss come out of his chamber?"

Sadima took one of the heavy bags from him, hitched it over her shoulder. "No."

Franklin nodded. "Good. He's angry about something."

"At you?"

He shrugged. "I don't know."

But he *did* know. She could tell.

– 2 –

I wiped my aching eyes. The history book was dull as
dirt. I was sick of reading about the brilliant Founder—and
our little chamber was filled with acrid lamp smoke. The
stone walls were coated in oily soot. I slammed the book
down.

Gerrard flinched. "Be quiet, Hahp."

I glanced at him across the narrow aisle that separated
our cots. He was cross-legged, facing away from me as
always, studying. He reached up to rub his eyes. How long
had it taken the wizards to realize that soot-clotted lamps
could torture students? Three years? A century? And of
course they were doing this to us now, when we had to read
constantly to memorize the songs.

It was like the sackcloth robes that had rubbed our skin

off in bloody patches, like never getting to eat enough, sleep enough, make a friend, or anything else that would have eased the constant fear. Everything the wizards did fit together as precisely as the bronze and copper pulleys on my father's collection of crossbows. The wizards made it hard to study, nearly impossible to learn. I was starting to wonder how long it had been since anyone had graduated from the Limòri Academy. Ten years? Fifty? I felt the familiar rush of fear and anger, mixed, and glanced at Gerrard again.

His hair was tied back with a twist of threads he had pulled from his robe hem. He had been the first to do it. I had tried to make scissors four or five times and couldn't. I don't know if anyone else had tried, but I had given up. Most of us tied our hair back now.

Gerrard's shoulders were squared. I knew what it meant. I had spent so many hours staring at his back, afraid to interrupt him, trying to figure him out. He wasn't like anyone I had ever known. He wasn't like any of the rest of us. He was so intent on being the one to graduate that nothing the wizards did seemed to distract him for long.

They had lined up all ten of us on the first day, as our parents were leaving, going back through the enormous doors and out into the daylight. Then the wizards had marched us through the maze of stone passages to our chambers: two rooms of four students each, and one room with Gerrard and me. Four boys had starved because they couldn't learn how to make food. *Four.* Every time I thought about it, I started to shake. Four dead, six alive. Somiss had made it very clear: One would graduate—or none, if no one merited it. I believed it now. They didn't care if we all died. Somiss acted like he would prefer it that way. He might get his wish.

None of us was a great student. Me; Gerrard; poor Will, who had lost all three of his roommates; Luke, who hated me; Levin, the only one I had known before coming here; and Jordan, whose dark eyes had been merry at first. None of us did everything well—we all struggled to keep up, to stay alive.

I lay down on my cot and closed my stinging eyes. Gerrard was so serious about studying that he almost never spoke to me. I barely knew any of the other students— except Levin, because we had gone to the same school, a real one, before my father had brought me here. But we didn't speak now. No one did, not before or after class or in the food hall. Somiss had forbidden us to help each other on our first day. We were all scared of him.

Gerrard had said once that the wizards didn't listen to us in our rooms. He had said a lot of things he couldn't possibly know. For the hundredth time I wondered why the wizards hadn't just put each of us in a room alone. Maybe to keep us from going mad sooner than they wanted?

One thing I was sure of: The wizards had worked out all of this over centuries. None of us knew where the others' rooms were in the wormhole maze of stone passages. Our classes were in different places almost every time, and a wizard we had never seen before woke us up every morning. If we had class, he led us there. If not, he walked away once we shouted to let him know we were up. None of them ever spoke to us.

Besides our roommates, we saw each other only in class or in the food hall. At first Somiss had hidden in the shadows there. A few times he had just walked in suddenly, scaring the piss out of all of us. He terrified me. His eyes were expressionless and so light they looked clear. His voice was graveled, rough and deep. I missed Franklin, now that his classes were over. He hadn't kept anyone from dying, but he wasn't as crazy as Jux or as cruel as Somiss; he didn't seem to *enjoy* starving and scaring us.

I had heard his voice inside my head a few times, encouraging me, telling me he had waited for a student like me to come along. I knew I had probably daydreamed it, but it hadn't mattered. It still didn't. Whether it had really happened or not, thinking I was important to Franklin had helped me live through the first year. If it really had been a year. That's what he had told us, in his last class.

"How long do you think we have been here?" I asked Gerrard.

He didn't answer.

"Three years?"

He pretended not to hear me.

"Three years?" I repeated. "Have we been here about three years?"

He turned to look at me, and I could see that he hadn't really heard me. I knew the feeling. The things we studied required a strange, complete concentration. I repeated the question.

"At least two," he said. "But it doesn't matter."

"It does to me," I whispered.

He didn't say anything. I turned over and faced the wall. We were all much taller than when our parents had left us here, that was obvious. Our bodies were changing. We would all turn into men in these dark, smelly tunnels, if we lived long enough. Thinking about it that way brought the usual heavy, cold feeling into my stomach. I got up and went to piss in the slops bucket, then began the third breathing pattern while I washed my hands and splashed my face at the basin. I touched the spigot to stop the water, then just stood there, breathing. It had seemed stupid at first, going to Franklin's breathing classes. But it helped. Sometimes it was the only thing that did. That and the secret.

Gerrard and I had made a pact: to help each other even though it was forbidden, then to destroy this place. Maybe the wizards already knew about it and were just waiting to punish us. I hoped not. I wanted to live, and I wanted Somiss to die. And my father—for sending me here. He had known he would probably never see me again. He had known that would break my mother's heart. He hadn't cared about either of us.

I pushed the thoughts about my parents out of my mind and downward, into my feet, where I could barely hear them. Then I looked at Gerrard again. I was hungry. Was he? His back was straight, his chin was up, and he was completely absorbed in studying. But his shoulder blades poked against his robe like broken wings. We were all stick thin.

I rubbed my raw eyes again, then picked up my song book. *Songs of the Elders*. We didn't sing them. If there were tunes, no one was teaching them to us. Reciting the words was hard enough. I sat on my cot and flipped the pages. With Gerrard's help I was keeping up—barely. With my help, he was catching up with the parts of Franklin's class that had been hard for him. He was learning to move his thoughts. I already could. So maybe we would be all right.

Maybe. Maybe. May Bee. Maybe. Maybe. MAY bee.

The word, repeating itself inside my skull, got louder. This had happened many times before. I used the fifth breathing pattern, slowing and silencing my thoughts the way Franklin had taught us. It was possible Gerrard and I could destroy the Limòri Academy, if we worked very hard, kept our secret, and survived long enough to learn enough. It was just barely possible, but not *im*possible.

I had a favorite daydream about going home. My father would be startled and scared, seeing me in a black robe. Wizards scared him. They scared everybody. I could not stop imagining him sweating and scared of me. I had to believe that day would come—I had to. I realized I was breathing hard when Gerrard turned and glanced at me. "You all right?"

I nodded, and he went back to his reading. Soon the only sound was Gerrard's quiet breathing and my own, both of us using the sixth pattern. I closed my eyes. They changed the length of our days all the time, but I was pretty sure I had time to sleep.

— 3 —

Sadima woke in complete, silent darkness. It still surprised her that somehow—without the sun, birdsong, the shouts of Limòri's Market Square vendors, or the gritting of carriage wheels on the cobbles—her body had learned. She knew it was almost morning.

She sat up, her night's dream still vivid—the usual one about her father's farm near Ferne. In the dream, her brother Micah had been so glad to see her. He had taken her into the hills and they had walked for hours, talking, marking their route with the little piles of stones all the country people used. But when they had gone back to the farmhouse, Papa had been silent, still immersed in grief and anger. And all the joy of the dream dimmed. Just before she woke, the caged boys were there too, all scrubbed, rosy cheeked. Micah and his wife were their parents now.

As the dream faded into the still, captive air of Sadima's little stone chamber, she stared at the darkness. Her father was dead, buried in the meadow. And what about Micah? Did he have children now? Did he still hate her?

Sadima reached out, brushing her fingers over the stone until she touched the cold iron of her striker. Then she got up and lit her lantern and winced. Her quill-hand was sore. Somiss was in constant need of fresh copies of the old songs. She spent most of her waking hours rewriting his marked-up pages. The night of the fire, he had said he would begin a school, that the boys would learn the magic as he recovered it. He had lied, she knew that now. He wanted forced-labor fair copiers—caged orphans no one would miss—not students.

If only Franklin would see there was no point in staying here. Nothing he could do would make Somiss more honest—or kinder. Sadima bit her lip. She knew why it was so hard for Franklin to understand. He had been barely three years old when Somiss's father had bought him. Three years old. And from that day on, if Somiss caused trouble, Franklin had been beaten. He had spent his whole life trying to keep Somiss calm and happy. He had never learned to do anything else.

Sadima set her lantern down and went to wash up. There were two oak buckets standing against the far wall. One for clean water, one for slops. Franklin filled the water buckets—hers, Somiss's, his own, and the ones for the boys in the cage—every few days. He emptied the slops buckets almost as often. Sadima wanted to help, but the spring and the slops pit Franklin had dug were in the woods below the cliffs. Somiss would never trust her to go outside alone. He would never trust her with the key to the cage.

Shivering, Sadima pulled on her dress, jerking at the sleeve when it twisted. Somiss was supposed to be translating the long, strange words of the old songs into Ferrinides now. So he said. Was it true? He had the book of Gypsy symbols, she was sure of that much. She had seen it before the fire. It included a few pages written in Ferrinides— translations he could work from.

She wrapped her shawl close around her shoulders. They had all hoped the Gypsies could help translate. Now Somiss thought the words were from some ancient language that had been lost—that the Gypsies had just copied the symbols generation after generation, knowing they were important, but not what they meant.

Or so he had told Franklin.

Sadima carried her lantern to the overturned fruit crate that served as her desk and took a few slow, deep breaths. She leafed through the pile of Somiss's papers that Franklin had brought her the night before, on his way out. These were the old songs, sounded out and written in Ferrinides—much easier to copy than the ones written with Gypsy symbols. She had copied these so many times she knew some of them by heart. There were hundreds.

Somiss had transliterated songs for almost three years, all collected from country people who had come to him as the word spread that he would pay a copper or two for each old song they could sing. Most of them had known what the songs were for—to ease bellyaches, or hard births, or nightmares, for protection when lightning came too close. But Somiss hadn't asked them until she suggested it, so most of them weren't titled.

Then Hannah, the beekeeper, had brought one she claimed had lengthened her mother's and grandmother's lives. Somiss had hidden it and replaced it with a fake. Sadima was sure he would have kept it for himself if she hadn't seen him and made her own copy.

Humming the tune of Hannah's song, Sadima stretched, then inked her quill and began. Her eyes flicked back and forth from the old copy to the fresh sheet of paper—and her hand flew. If Somiss ever found out she was using the song for long life, he would kill her for it. If he found out what she had buried in the woods the night of the fire, he would kill her for that, too. If he knew she could read, if *anyone* ever found out . . . Sadima took two more deep breaths and finished the copy. Then she started the next one.

The winter storms would end and the snow would melt. She would convince Franklin somehow and they could be long gone by late spring, safe somewhere in a farm village, teaching the songs to rosy-cheeked farm children and to the boys in the cage—who would be rosy and happy by then too.

Franklin would love living on a farm. Once he was far away from Somiss, he would remember how to laugh. Or, if he had never learned, she would teach him. They would not be afraid to kiss, to love each other.

Sadima inked her pen again. If she copied fast enough, if she kept up, Somiss would forget about the boys in the cage, and he would have one less reason to be angry at Franklin. And spring would come.

It would.

All she had to do was wait.

— 4 —

Three days later, if they were days, not hours, or years, I was flat on my cot again. My eyes were closed because it hurt like fire to keep them open in the fog of lamp smoke that filled the room. I was listening to Gerrard whisper as he practiced the songs—he was at least three or four ahead, I was pretty sure. Maybe more. I had one hand on my song book, waiting for him to read the one the rest of us were learning so I could hear the five pronunciations I had missed. I wanted to pass when Somiss decided to have a class again. I was hungry. I had failed my last recitation, so I couldn't make food.

I had never heard the language the songs were in before coming to the academy. The words were incredibly long, and hard to figure out how to pronounce. I had no idea how Gerrard had learned it. All I knew was that he could read the songs cold and pronounce all the words correctly. The rest of us had to guess—the letters were Ferrinides letters, but the pronunciations were a thousand times harder.

We recited in class, with Somiss interrupting every time we made a mistake. He would correct us, then we were supposed to go on, but most of us couldn't just go on from where he had interrupted us. We had to start over. It was painful; a ridiculous way to make us learn. Gerrard pretended not to know all the words, of course, but he did. I was grateful. Without his help, I would have died of starvation long before.

Gerrard began another song. I went into the corridor and ran a little ways, sucking in the cleaner air; the cold-fire torches never dimmed or smoked. Then I ran back. Gerrard was still reading an unfamiliar song in a whisper.

I sank onto my cot and waited again. He studied relentlessly. He wanted to graduate more than he wanted to live. I had never wanted to be a wizard. I still didn't. I had used my hiding places when the men in black robes came to Malek Manor to ease my mother's terrible headaches, to sell my father good weather for his ships, to train the ponies to fly, and a hundred other things. My father was always nervous, talking to them. He paid them what they asked. Everyone did. No one haggled price with the wizards, not even my father.

Gerrard cleared his throat, twice. I jerked around, grabbed my book, and began reading along with him as he read, clearly, slowly, and a little louder than he had been. I ran one finger beneath the words. They looked so odd to me, even after staring at them for so long. Most were five to twenty syllables long.

Gerrard read the song through six times. Then I coughed once to let him know I was finished, that I had it. He went back to his own work. I closed the book. Were these songs the ancient words the wizards used to heal, to raise wind into ships' sails, to light cold-fire, and all the rest? Wizards had been in my father's house often, but they never let anyone watch them make magic.

I rubbed my eyes. Maybe, I thought, this wasn't a real language at all. Maybe the songs, and the words in them, were nonsense, and Somiss was just training our memories. Maybe the graduate, if there was one, would be taught the real songs. But if it wasn't a real language, how could Gerrard have known it before coming here? And if it was real, why—

I shut off my thoughts and recited the song slowly and precisely, my mouth shaping each word carefully. I recited it with the book open to check myself one last time. Then I put the book on my desk and lay down, keeping my thoughts quiet.

After a while, Gerrard switched to the fifth breathing pattern. That meant he was practicing moving his thoughts from his mind to his belly again. I had explained to him what it felt like, how I did it—and I had reminded him of everything Franklin had said in class. I hoped he could do it soon, there was no other way to survive most of Jux's classes. But it worried me too. Once Gerrard could move his thoughts, would he keep reading the songs to me? He got impatient with me sometimes.

I squeezed my eyes shut. They really hurt. Fucking lamps. If I could just picture what the insides had looked like before they were covered in lumps of soot, maybe I could make what we needed. But oil lamps were used only in the farmhands' shacks at home. In the house, we had cold-fire. Not simple torches like the ones here. Ours were encased in colored glass lamps that kept themselves polished. I had no idea which servant changed the wicks—or if there even *were* wicks.

A familiar daydream began in my mind. Malek Manor, midsummer, on a reception night: All the windows are bright, music sifting out the open windows onto the lawns, into the rose gardens. I see my mother so clearly, lovely and kind, flitting from the guests to the kitchen, then back. She is laughing, her eyes lit, as she makes sure all are welcomed, fed, tended to. The lamps burn bright. The serving girls run back and forth, carrying trays laden with Celia's amazing food. After the food is gone and the conversations and the music have dimmed, my mother stands waving as the carriages roll back down the drive. She stays there, calling out good wishes until the last pony pulls the last carriage full of waving guests into the sky.

Then my father begins to shout at her. Her dress fits too close, her hair is wrong. She forgot an important guest. She talked to a ship's captain, a colonial magnate, a magistrate's wife, an old friend, too long. It is the music of my childhood. My father shouts and my mother cries. I hide.

Celia spots me crouching behind a door, lost in the echoing ballrooms of the west wing. She leads me into the kitchen and gives me a place to hide beneath her baking table. She gives me cocoa, and a pastry with heavy cream.

My father sees me when I try to sneak to bed. I run from him, up the stairs and out my window onto the roof. This time, in the daydream, he follows me. I know the stone walls, the dozens of chimneys, every slick patch of moss. I run just fast enough for him to keep me in sight. If I push him off the peak, near the spire where I always crouch to look out over the river toward South End, it would be high enough. He would break like a wine bottle dropped from a balcony. In my mind, I can see him standing there, looking out over his house, his land, his ships lined up on the docks across the wide river. I can picture the silk of his shirt, his dark hair, every detail as I double back and come up behind him. I raise my hand and push him. . . .

And then I sat up, gasping, and turned to the wall to hide my face. The daydreams often felt more real than the stone passages, than my own flesh. I bit the inside of my cheek and breathed Franklin's fifth pattern long enough to shove away the images of my father falling—of blood and murder splattered across the cobblestones.

I moved my thoughts into my belly. I let them pause, then I pushed them again, sliding them farther away, along my left leg and into my toes. From there, they dimmed until I could ignore them. I put out my lantern, lay down on my cot, and cried. The tears stung my raw eyes like vinegar, but I didn't care. I had gotten good at crying silently; I didn't want Gerrard to think I was falling apart. Crying felt good. And, as usual, it put me to sleep.

Sadima got up. It was cold. There was a new stack of Somiss's papers just inside the entrance to her chamber, as usual. Franklin always spoke with Somiss before he left at night, and Somiss always had the papers ready so Franklin could carry them back through the tunnels and leave them for her on his way out. But there was a ream of new paper beside the stack too. So Franklin was back earlier than usual, safe. Sadima's heart lifted, then sank. Maybe he was asleep already.

As she soaped her hands and face, Sadima felt the familiar ache, low in her belly. It wouldn't be long before she bled again. This would be the sixth time, the sixth new moon. They had come here in late summer, so most of the winter was over and gone. When it warmed up, Franklin would be spared the torture of bone-numbing cold on his nighttime prowls, and she would begin to talk him into leaving.

Sadima set the little sliver of soap on the flat stone she used to keep it up out of the floor grit. Before long she would have to ask Franklin for more. She was glad that he had not had to help her with the most intimate things, at least. Rinka had told her where to buy the little cotton cloths—and she had brought them here with everything else that first night, wrapped in her old shawl.

Sadima rinsed, shivering at the touch of the cold water. She dressed, brushed out her hair, and thought about Rinka and Maude. She missed them. She missed Mattie Han. And Micah. Especially Micah. Her brother had been both father and mother to her. She blinked back tears, remembering how angry he had been, how the window shook when he slammed the kitchen door. And if he could see her now, he would be even angrier.

Sadima picked up her lantern and went out into the passageway, turning left. Walking fast, her bare feet silent on the cold stone, she came to the entrance to Franklin's chamber and stopped, lifting her lantern just enough to see that his pallet was empty. Happy that she hadn't missed him, she ran back to her own chamber.

Today's papers were almost all wrinkled and soiled. She lifted them close to her face. The smell of smoke was unmistakable, even after more than half a year. Somiss had carried everything in makeshift bed-linen sacks the night of the fire.

Sadima was glad to see the rumpled pages. She would be able to finish her day's work in half the usual time because there were no changes to make. Somiss just wanted new, clean copies. She arranged the papers so that if Somiss happened to come past her chamber on his way to Franklin's, it would look like she had already begun.

She left her chamber once more, this time turning to the right, walking down the narrow tunnel toward the main passageway. When she reached it, she turned to the right again, walking fast, toward the big cavern. As she entered it, she could just make out the grayish light coming in through the rough, pear-shaped hole set high in the stone wall. Dawn was close. She looked across the chamber. There was no sack of bread beside the cage and the boys were all asleep, the lanterns still turned low. So Franklin was still walking back and forth, carrying in whatever he had brought from Limòri.

Sadima smiled and started forward, then stopped. Little Jux was awake. He was lying on his back, playing some game with his hands. No. It wasn't a game. He was using his index finger to draw in the air. He was practicing the Gypsy symbols. His fingers were slender as twigs. The boys were all too thin. For the hundredth time, Sadima wondered if she should tell Franklin about the coins she had saved up, so he could buy better food than he was able to steal. But she couldn't leave the cliffs, and she couldn't just tell him where to dig. She had buried more than her coins and shoes beneath the rampike pine.

"Sadima?"

She turned. Franklin's whisper had come out of the darkness on the far side of the huge cavern, somewhere down by the long, narrow tunnel that led outside. She smiled when she spotted the tiny flicker of his lantern flame in the darkness. Twenty heartbeats later, she could see him. He had a sack over one shoulder and when he bent to kiss her, she could smell warm bread. Her mouth watered and she turned aside, ashamed of the urgency of her hunger. The boys never had enough to eat. Never. Nor did Franklin. He had always been lean. Now he was bony.

"Help me?" Franklin whispered. She nodded.

Quietly, working together, they broke the loaves in half, then halved them again. Sadima folded the sack and added it to the pile by the stone wall. Then Franklin woke the boys. They always jerked upright, and most of them brought their fists up until they realized who it was, where they were. Then they yawned and stretched, staring at the bread. Jux pretended to awaken with the rest of them.

Sadima got the dipper and handed full cups of water through the bars. She helped Franklin dole out the bread, too, then stood back, listening to him chide the boys to eat slowly and not to fight. Once they had bread in their hands, they all sank into a crouch, glancing at each other, softening the bread with water to get it down faster.

Sadima hated to watch them tear at their food, elbows out, eyes wary. But it was not something they had begun doing here, because of the cage. She knew that. It was the way they had eaten all their lives—choking the food down, ready to fight to keep it. They were almost like animals.

Just behind that thought, Sadima felt a strange onrush of feelings, not her own. She was used to flashes of feelings like this from animals, from horses and goats, even wolves a few times. But from boys? She turned to hide her face from Franklin. The torrent of images in her mind exposed their lives, their scarred hearts. She felt the beatings, heard people shouting curses, then the sound of cartwheels on cobbled streets, someone crying. She heard the scraping of armor, and fear shook her whole body.

Overcome, off balance, Sadima's breath caught. She clenched her fists and fought to free herself. The feelings and images dimmed a little, but for a few more agonizing heartbeats, she was trapped in a raw, wordless understanding, the kind she had felt all her life—from animals, never like this.

The images began to recede. Sadima's pulse was tapping at her temples, her wrists. Why had it happened? The cage? Because the boys were fed like animals, were being kept like animals? She turned to look at Franklin. He was leaning on the cage bars, waiting to make sure the boys didn't fight. His eyes were closed; he was pale and exhausted.

"Franklin?"

He opened his eyes and turned. "Are you cold?" He came forward and put his arm around her shoulders. She knew he could feel her trembling, and she wished it were a chill. But it wasn't this time.

She stepped back. "Remember your promise?" she whispered. "The night of the fire?"

His eyes widened, and he picked up his lantern. Then he

nodded, gesturing, leading her away from the cage. "But things are getting better," he breathed, leaning close.

She stared at him. "Better? How? Those boys are in a *cage*."

"Sadima," Franklin said, touching her cheek. "Please." Even in the ruddy lantern light, his face was the color of ashes. He was barely managing to stand up.

Sadima looked into his eyes. "I just have to know you meant it." She could still feel the boys' fear and pain crouched at the edge of her thoughts. "Spring is close," she said. "We will be able to leave soon. With the boys. And—"

"He will never let me leave," Franklin whispered. And she could tell he hadn't meant to say it, not like that.

"Then I will find a way to put an end to Somiss," she whispered. "I just need to know that you will keep your promise, that you won't try to stop me. Because I—"

"Sadima!" Franklin cut her off. He glanced past her, then peered into the darkness that separated them from the main passageway. "Yes," he whispered, close to her ear. "I remember what I said. I remember it every day. But Somiss says he is barely making progress. There will be enough time to persuade him about the boys."

He leaned back, and his eyes were so full of pain that it touched Sadima's heart. Then the boys started shouting, arguing over the last bits of bread. Franklin turned, starting back to stop them before they began to fight. She caught his sleeve.

"If he hurts them," she whispered, "if he tells you not to

feed them, if he hurts *you* . . ." She lifted her lantern so she could search his eyes. "Promise again. Say it, all of it."

"I promise," he said. "If Somiss has to be killed, I can't help you, but I won't stop you."

"If that's the only way to free you," Sadima whispered, "the only way to save the boys—"

"But there's no need to even think about all that, Sadima," Franklin interrupted. He pushed her hair back over her shoulder. "I saw Somiss's mother last night."

Sadima nodded, wary. If Regina Ferrin could start giving them silver coins again, things would be better. There would be more food, more of everything—waiting for spring would be much easier. "But we still have to get them out of that cage," she whispered. "As soon as the weather warms. We have to get the key."

Franklin nodded. "I know." Sadima watched him force a smile. "Just a little longer," he said. "You'll see."

Sadima nodded and saw the relief in his eyes. They would argue again, she was sure. And she would tell him about the feelings that had flooded into her. But not now, not when he was blind-tired.

Once he had the boys settled, he kissed her forehead, then walked around her, his step heavy and slow as he headed back toward the long entrance passageway to get the next load of his night's work.

Sadima began the boys' lessons as Franklin plodded back and forth, carrying bags and bundles down the main passageway toward Somiss's chamber. By the time she went back to her chilly little chamber, sank to the floor in front of her fruit-crate desk, and began her day's work, Franklin was sound asleep. Still, she waited. The quill fit her hand perfectly, and she wrote so fast the first sheet was finished before the ink had dried.

After she had copied ten pages, she left her chamber without her lantern, turning left this time, walking in the dark, trailing her hand on the wall until she came to Franklin's chamber. His lantern was out and he was asleep; she could see him breathing. Sadima longed to go lie beside him, to wake him, to apologize for adding to his burden, to explain how the boys really felt in the cage, to kiss him, to beg him to help her plan their escape. Instead she sang the song of long life over him as she always did—using just enough breath to shape the melody, careful not to awaken him. Somiss had meant to outlive them both, Sadima knew. But if the song worked, he wouldn't. She wanted to tell Franklin that there would be enough time to make a life together beneath the sky, where sun and wind and rain were not shut out. But she was afraid to.

– 6 –

A wizard pounded on the door. I jerked upright and swung my feet to the floor, then waited until I was awake enough to stand up. I pissed in the slops bucket, washed my face with my last sliver of soap, and moved aside to tie back my hair while Gerrard washed. It had been two days since Somiss's last recitation class, so this was about the right interval, unless the wizards had thought up something worse. I would pass this time, if I was careful and didn't get nervous. I squeezed my eyes shut to ease the stinging and waited for Gerrard.

Opening the door was scary. It always was. But it was just another wizard I had never seen before, ready to lead us to class. He had a face like an old city magistrate, stern and somber.

I repeated the song to myself as we followed the wizard straight down the passageway, breathing the long, ridiculously convoluted words until he veered down a branching tunnel. After that, I had to memorize the turns. There was never anyone to lead us back to our chambers. There never had been.

I glanced at Gerrard. His face was intent. I had no idea how he remembered the routes, but he had been able to do it the first day—long before I could—and he had let me follow him back to the room at first. I was grateful. But Levin was the one who had saved me, by pure chance. I had overheard him whispering to himself, making a sentence out of random *r* and *l* words—right and left. That had saved my life. I used only *r* and *l* words at first. But they had led us on longer and longer walks. It had taken more than a year to work it all out, but I did it without thinking now.

This morning, or night or whatever it was outside the cliffs, the wizard turned right three times, then left twice, and right again. So: *Rainwater irrigates the garden and the lettuce entices the rabbits* was my first sentence. I used all the letters in both "right" and "left" to begin the words now, except the repeated *t*, of course. And I used words with different numbers of syllables to keep track of the passages we passed. *Rainwater irrigates* meant we passed three passages and turned right at the fourth. If the turns were too far apart, I just used the number. *Twelve rings* meant we had passed that many tunnels, then turned right.

The wizards leading us always left the instant we got where we were going, without speaking a word. They all walked fast, faster than seemed possible, their black robes swirling around their ankles. Half the time we ran to keep up.

When the wizard had gone, Gerrard and I stood apart from each other in silence, like we always did. I met Levin's eyes when he walked up with Jordan and Luke. Levin gave me the barely-there nod that meant he was all right. Jordan let his eyes flick across mine, then the corners of his mouth turned up so slightly that it would have been invisible to anyone outside this place. Good. He thought he would pass. Luke was staring into the dark. That was fine with me. Will arrived, following a wizard with a face cast from stone. And then we were all there, the stench of fear sweat hanging over us.

Except Gerrard. He looked calm, as always. I had gone through a lot of theories about who he was and how he had ended up at the Limòri Academy. The best three: He was the son of some Orchid Coast prince who had sent him, disguised as a Limòri beggar boy; his father was some wealthy, strict Eridian merchant who had forbidden him to come here, and the disguise had been his own idea; last—and most recent—he was the son of some embittered Ferrin Hill family that hated the wizards and wanted their royal line to reclaim the throne.

Gerrard said he had grown up in South End, hungry all the time, fighting for food with other street children, all of them dirty, cold—and watching wealthy people glide past overhead in carriages pulled by ponies that flew. That explained everything except who had paid his tuition and how he had learned to read Ferrinides and the weird song-book language that none of the rest of us knew. Which is to say that it didn't explain shit.

Gerrard had been amazed at the water spigot his first day here; he had turned it off and on, like a toddler playing with magic for the first time. He worked harder at studying than anyone else ever could, and he wanted to destroy the academy as much as I did. Or more. Whoever he was.

I glanced around the circle again. I hated it when Somiss was late. It was hard to stand like this, without talking, avoiding each other's eyes. Levin finally decided to go into the chamber and we all followed, silent and stiff.

Somiss arrived moments later, a smoky and wispy wraith for the first instant; then he was solid and real. He always brought a chair with him. This morning it was an Omberglass lacewood chaise—an antique one with the usual bubbled glass knobs on the chair back. My mother had a few dozen of the new ones in the biggest ballroom in the east wing. The antiques were too expensive, even for her.

Mr. Omberglass had seven sons. They were an odd family, the tenth generation of furniture carvers. I had gone to school with two of them, both the most somber boys I had ever known. Learning to carve wood into lacelike patterns from the time they could hold a knife had made them exacting and serious. I had played tricks on them, trying to make them laugh—and never could.

Thinking about the life I had lost hurt so much that I closed my eyes and breathed the third pattern until I was sure I wasn't going to cry. The strange thing was that I hadn't loved my life. I had hated it.

"You."

Somiss was pointing at me.

I looked down and started reciting, slowly, concentrating on the pronunciations, feeling the familiar prickle of nervous sweat on the nape of my neck. I didn't even glance at Somiss. I never did when I was reciting. When I was finished, I exhaled, relieved. I had passed, I was almost sure of it—he hadn't interrupted me to correct anything. But when I looked up, Somiss's eyes narrowed, like he was angry with me. I held my breath until he nodded. Then, when Levin passed, I saw the same reaction on his face. Gerrard passed, of course, then Luke, then Jordan. And though he spoke slowly and hesitated a little on one word, so did Will. All of us had passed. So we could all eat.

Frowning, silent, Somiss faded into nothingness, taking his chair with him. We all sat quietly for a moment. My belly growled and no one laughed, or even glanced at me. I looked from one face to the next as we stood up. Everyone's eyes were bloodshot and watery. So no one had figured out how to fix the lanterns.

I knew why I couldn't, and it was true for everyone. Most of us had grown up with servants who made our beds and washed our backs in the bath and tended the cold-fire lamps and the hearth fires and everything else—and there had been no oil lamps in our houses. If Gerrard was telling the truth about growing up in South End, begging, he had never had a chance to study the construction of oil lamps either.

Out in the passageway, we separated without speaking, without really looking at each other, in case Somiss was in the shadows between the cold-fire torches, watching. Gerrard went back to the room to study. I turned toward the food hall.

Walking alone, as we always did, I watched Levin. He was twenty or thirty paces ahead of me, his dark green robe billowing with every stride. The robes they had given us the day we arrived had been rough sackcloth the color of shit. We had worn them until they were stiff with sweat and dirt. We all had pink, shiny scars where the cloth had rubbed. The green robes were much softer. I was still ashamed at what a joy that had been for me; with four boys dead, I had been so happy about getting a better robe.

I glanced behind myself. No one else was close. It was hard to imagine why Somiss would follow us or use magic to hide from us, but I knew sometimes he did. I would walk the perimeter of the food hall, and if he wasn't there, maybe Levin and I could exchange a word or two. It was absurd how much that thought lifted my heart. Was it always going to be like this? If we learned all the tuneless songs, learned to make our lanterns work, survived every beast Jux had in his fake forest, memorized the stupid history book that no one ever had time to read, would they give us black silk robes and let us talk and laugh again? Or would there be only one of us alive by then? Or maybe, long before that, we would all be dead.

Levin was walking fast, and he seemed strong. I was

glad. I glanced behind myself again, expecting to see Will and maybe some of the others, but none of them were there. They probably wanted to wait until the food hall was empty. We all did that. It was easier not to talk to anyone if we kept apart. I slowed my step, dropping farther and farther back. When I finally walked into the food hall, Levin had already made his dinner and was sitting far off to one side. He did not look up when I came in. That was an unspoken signal too. He didn't want to talk.

I tried not to let it upset me too much. I liked the food hall. I had been the first one who had managed to make anything to eat: apples, the gold and red ones from my father's orchards. Now I could make almost anything. Hiding from my father's rages in the kitchen, I had grown up watching Celia cook. I could remember fifty different dishes, or more. When I passed the recitations and was allowed to eat, I ate well.

I crossed the big cavern, skirting the immovable tables and benches that had been carved, whole, out of the stone when the chamber had been made. I was hungry, and with every step I was imagining Celia's omelets. I had eaten dozens of them, all kinds. This time I chose morel mushrooms, with a creamy, sourish, herbed cheese called Ferne White, after the little village where it was made. I decided on thick slices of summer tomatoes on the plate, covered with chard, chopped fine as grass blades and marinated in dark vinegar, honey, and pepper.

I held the food in my mind the way I would hold the plate in my hands, firm and careful. I could see the cheese bubbling where it leaked from the layers of whipped eggs. I could smell the sharp, mineral tang of the chard and see every wrinkle that held an extra drop of the vinegar-and-honey mixture. Only then did I glance up at the ship-sized gem on its dark stone pedestal. All of its tiny, uncountable facets were winking in the torchlight.

For an instant, the beauty of the stone distracted me, and I closed my eyes again to sharpen the image of the food in my mind, the mixture of scents, *everything*. Then I took a single step, reaching out so that the palms of my hands pressed against the ice-cold surface. The faint crying-wind sound and the flash of light told me, before I opened my eyes, that it had worked. The food was at the front edge of the pedestal, steaming, on a plate identical to the ones that my mother used.

Levin left before I was finished. He set his plate on the floor, and it sparkled and faded into nothingness. Then, walking past, he greeted me with a barely perceptible nod, unnoticeable to anyone watching. I nodded back at him, a motion that lowered my chin the length of a rice grain. He squeezed his eyes shut, then opened them and frowned, very slightly. He touched his stomach with one hand, in a motion that looked like he was straightening his robe. He lifted the corners of his mouth a tiny bit. I curved my own mouth and turned so he could see my reddened eyes for an instant as he went by.

It wasn't an exchange of greetings that anyone outside this place would have appreciated, but here, it was a whole conversation. Levin was glad that I was managing to eat.

I was glad that he was eating and looked well and strong. We liked each other and we both remembered a time when we'd had fun together. His eyes hurt. So did mine. Neither of us had found a solution for that yet. All that had been communicated, and more.

I made bath soap before I left, imagining the kind my father's servants made. I had never seen them make it. I had no idea how it was done. But once I had the scent and the feel and the weight and the color and the shape of the soap in my mind, I touched the stone. The soap appeared on the pedestal exactly where my food had appeared.

Leaving, I ran until I was out of breath, placing my feet exactly to minimize the bruising. I had learned to run lightly when my feet were still tender, but even now that I had thick calluses, it was better this way. And much quieter.

I slowed to a walk when I saw Will coming toward me. He was thinner. But he smiled at me, a tiny, almost invisible smile, as he got closer. I smiled back and touched my heart as he passed to let him know that I was glad he was managing. I made sure he saw the soap. His eyes widened. If he hadn't made any yet, I was sure he would try soon.

Then, alone again, I felt bad. I was passing Somiss's recitations because I was cheating. The guilt turned cold and brittle in my stomach. If Somiss suspected it, I would not live much longer. Neither would Gerrard. And on the heels of that thought came another one, familiar and terrible. I tried to stop it, but I couldn't. I never could.

Tally, Rob, Joseph, and the boy whose name I had never learned—had the wizards buried them? The Limòri Academy had been teaching magic for nearly two hundred years. Was there some cavern deep in the belly of the cliff full of rotting flesh and boys' bones?

— 7 —

Three mornings later, by the time Sadima finally heard Franklin's footsteps, she had finished the boys' lessons and was back in her chamber, copying. They had barely spoken since she had gotten angry about the boys in the cage. She unknotted her hair, ran her fingers through it, then twisted it back up and waited.

Franklin stopped just outside the arched entrance of her chamber, holding two parcels of paper beneath one arm, a baker's bag in his left hand, and his lantern held high in his right. He smiled at her, then murmured something that she couldn't understand. His eyes were vague, and she could see him shivering.

"Are you all right?" she asked, already certain that he wasn't. She took the lantern from him, turning him around as a mother would guide a sleepy child; he was shivering so violently that his whole body was vibrating.

"Bbbbbbbbread," he said, stopping midstep, turning to face her, holding out the bag.

She took it from him and set it down. "You have to get warm."

He started to argue, then leaned on her as they went down the passageway. Standing beside his pallet, he dropped the reams of paper and collapsed. Frantic at how pale he was, Sadima pulled off his battered shoes and rubbed his feet, then managed to get him onto his pallet. She covered him with his blankets and slid in beside him. He clung to her. He kept talking, telling her he loved her, thanking her, crying. His hands, his cheeks, were like ice. She rocked him, holding him close, until he was warm enough for his rigid body to stop trembling. And in that instant, he was asleep. She put her feet against his and pressed his hands on her belly until they were warm. And then she waited, counting Franklin's breaths until they slowed and deepened. Only then did she slip from beneath the covers, crawling in a circle around his pallet to tuck in the blankets.

She stood beside him for a long moment before she could whisper the song for long life over him. Close to tears, shaking with anger, she snuffed his lantern, setting it where he always did, beside his striker at the head of his pallet, so he would be able to find it when he woke.

This had to stop. Franklin was going to get sick, or worse, trying to do the impossible. And Somiss wouldn't notice or care unless Franklin fell over dead—and then only because there would be no one to run his endless errands.

Sadima turned to leave and stumbled over the parcel of paper. She still had plenty in her chamber. So this was meant for Somiss. And he would be upset with Franklin if he did not get it.

She carried the heavy reams back with her and set them beside her makeshift desk. If Somiss came looking for the paper, he would have to pass her chamber. He scared her, but she was going to tell him what he was doing to Franklin. If he didn't care, if he got violent, she would let him think he had silenced her, then she would start planning how she would kill him.

Sadima pulled her shawl around her shoulders and forced herself to work. It was Gypsy symbols this time, with corrections, so her other thoughts faded as she began to concentrate. After fifteen songs had been finished, leaving out the symbols Somiss had crossed off and adding the ones he had written in the margins, she turned to the stack that was written in Ferrinides.

She flew through the pages, then set down her quill.

Carrying a stack of finished work and the reams of paper, she walked to the main passageway and turned left. It felt odd to go that way; she could not recall the last time she had. She walked fast, to get it over with. Maybe Somiss would be asleep. If he was, she could just leave the paper and her work where he would see it and tiptoe away. Maybe.

She had been inside Somiss's chamber only once, before

he had claimed it as his own. He was convinced they were in the true home of magic now, because his chamber wasn't just a miner's chamber, like hers and Franklin's, or a natural one, like the big cavern. Franklin had discovered it, and he had shown her first. There were shelves cut into one stone wall and a stone platform for a bed. Best of all, there was a slit high in the east wall so that a little sunlight and fresh air came in. But it was all rough-hewn—nothing better than a miner with a pickax and enough time might have fashioned.

All the passages Sadima had seen were the same. They all had rough surfaces and chunks of stone scattered at the base of the walls. Franklin had said the ancient steps that led up the face of the massive, soaring cliffs were hand-hewn too. She wondered if he had ever gone all the way up them, but she was afraid to ask. He would know why she was interested; he would know what she was thinking. Was there a way out besides the narrow, vine-covered tunnel they had found in the woods?

Sadima lifted her lantern and walked faster, passing tunnels that opened onto the main one, counting them to keep her bearings. She didn't stop until she came to the entrance of the long passageway that led to Somiss's chamber. She squinted. Was there a faint glow from his lantern at the other end? Maybe. Maybe not.

Sadima was unsure what to do. Franklin had told her once that Somiss had forbidden him to enter even the far end of this passage, for any reason, without shouting down the tunnel first. So when Franklin had to tell Somiss something, he probably stood where she was standing now and yelled until Somiss yelled back.

Sadima stood uncertainly. If she called to Somiss, the way Franklin did, would he punish her—or Franklin—for the interruption? He might. Would it be worse if he ran out of paper? She stood still, staring into the darkness. Then a low, dim shape caught her eye and she took three or four steps toward it, lifting her lantern high.

It was a crate, bigger than the one she used as a writing table, positioned against the wall. She crept forward, listening for footsteps, her stomach tight. She held her lantern closer. There was a book in the crate. The gold Ferrinides royal seal was printed on the cover. Sadima reached to touch it, then heard Somiss's voice.

She jerked back, but he wasn't close. He was in his chamber, somewhere far up the passageway, reciting the words of the songs, as he always had, in a loud, precise voice. She stared at the book. It was finely made, beautiful. She longed to pick it up, to find out what was in it. But she was afraid to.

She hadn't meant to learn to read. The Ferrinides letters had just been shapes to her when Franklin taught her to copy them. She had used the quill to draw them the way she had painted the shapes of flowers back on the farm. Then, one day while they were working side by side, Franklin had written her name for her, then Somiss's. She had stared at the paper, realizing that the first letters were the same because the sound was the same: *Sssss*.

She glanced up the stone corridor, then back at the

book. Once she had known which letter made the sound that began her own name, it had become impossible not to notice all the letters and the sounds they made. She had memorized a few of the songs and recited the long, strange words, staring at her fair copies, running her finger beneath the letters as she recited. Then she had begun to practice on the shop signs along the north side of Market Square, sounding out all the words she could. Commoners' shops had signs painted with pictures of cheeses, bolts of cloth, sheaves of wheat and corn, and round red apples— whatever was inside. She had slowly gotten good enough to read the lettered signs on the shops that catered to royals. Ferrinides words were much easier to pronounce than the words in the songs.

Somiss was still reciting. Sadima set her finished copies and the paper in the crate. Then she bent to touch the book, sliding her fingers over the heavy flaxen cover, the ice-smooth seal. She had never told anyone, not even Franklin, that she could read. The old King's Laws were clear: Any commoner caught reading would be hanged. Somiss had hired a scribe to alter Franklin's ancestry and sign it, attesting to its accuracy. She hoped Somiss had paid the scribe well and she pitied the man if the magistrates ever looked into it. If Franklin's real lineage was exposed, they would both be hanged.

Somiss abruptly fell silent.

Sadima stood straight, lowering her lantern and turning to shield it. Had he seen her? She whirled and walked fast—not back toward her chamber, but going farther into the cliff, almost running, turning into the first branching tunnel she saw. If Somiss hadn't actually seen her—and she was almost sure he hadn't—it would be all right. Franklin had been almost delirious. He wouldn't remember whether he had taken the paper and her finished work to Somiss or not.

She came to another passage and paused just long enough to stack a few rocks into a wedge shape that pointed the way back. Then she ran again, turning twice more and marking the turns with little stone cairns like the first one. Then she stopped, afraid that even one more turn could make her lose her way back. And only then, because she was so far into the maze of the stone tunnels that Somiss could not possibly hear her, did she allow herself to cry.

— 8 —

One morning, if it was a morning, the wizard beat his fists against the door like a man trying to escape a fire. I sat straight up and blinked in the darkness. My eyes stung. My thoughts were slow, cloudy. How long had they let us sleep? Three hours? Three days?

"We're awake!" I shouted.

The pounding paused, then started again. Maybe it was Jux? His classes came at odd intervals—I hadn't had one in a long time. And he loved to scare us. Or maybe it was Somiss.

I felt myself sweating as I lit my lantern. Gerrard was already up. He pissed and washed, then I did the same. My thoughts were circling. I had passed the last recitation easily. Too easily? Did Somiss suspect that Gerrard and I were helping each other? What if it *was* him out there, his eyes colder than snow-shadows? Would he kill us both, right now? If that was it, I wanted to be first. I didn't want time to think about it, and I didn't want to watch Gerrard die. I forced one foot forward on the cold, gritty stone, my right hand raised, reaching for the silver fish-shaped door handle.

"Wait!" Gerrard hissed at me.

I turned and saw him shoving what looked like a slender blue book beneath the mattress on his cot. I blinked and felt my whole body go rigid. A *book*? How? I stared at him.

"Open the door!" Gerrard whispered as he straightened. The fear on his face unlocked my body. I whirled around and jerked the door wide.

It wasn't Somiss. As always, a wizard I had never seen before leaned in, his eyes scanning the room and our faces. Then he turned and walked away fast, without looking back, the way every wizard had, every time we had been led to class.

My pulse slowed a little, but I glanced at Gerrard as we followed. We had been given two books each, both thick and heavy—the song book and *The History and Purpose of the Limòri Academy*. Where had Gerrard gotten another one? There was no library here, no visitors, no way in or out.

I balled my hands into fists. *Shit*. If he got caught, our pact was meaningless. Even if Somiss didn't punish me, too, what would I do without Gerrard? How could I survive? My thoughts jangled with fear, and it took me a while to realize where the wizard was leading us—to the food hall. Why? We hadn't had a class in the food hall since Franklin had showed us how to use the stone.

The others were already there. Levin turned when we came in, and I saw my anxiety reflected in his face. I scanned the walls and saw no trace of an extra shadow, no one hidden and watching. The massive gem stood silent and waiting on its dark stone pedestal.

"Feed yourselves."

It was Somiss's graveled voice. Behind us. I caught my breath and turned. We all did. He was standing with his arms crossed, his angular face half-light, half-dark because of the torches. He looked disgusted. "Who among you is too thick-witted to understand two simple words? Feed yourselves."

I couldn't stop staring. No one moved. Would the one who obeyed first be the only one who got to eat? Sometimes Somiss seemed to favor boldness. More often, he punished it. I started to take a step and Luke barged past me. I just stood there, pissed off, as Gerrard followed him, then Levin and Jordan. Then Will.

I wiped my watering eyes on my sleeve, feeling foolish. This made no sense. We had all passed our last recitation. So we would all be able to use the stone. Maybe it didn't matter who went first. I started across the chamber, glancing at Somiss. I didn't care if I was last, unless he did. He was looking at the ceiling, and I angled away from him so he couldn't see the fear on my face.

Luke stood in front of the huge stone, his eyes closed. I stepped to one side to see better. The massive gem was always so beautiful, clear, the endless facets reflecting the torchlight. Luke was holding perfectly still. Was he trying to make something difficult? Maybe, if this was a test, I should try to make something complicated too. I could make Celia's braised salmon with crushed mint and a pomegranate-and-honey sauce. Just thinking about it made my mouth water. But maybe Somiss would be impatient by the time my turn came. It was possible that he just wanted to make sure that we could all *make* food, that no one had been cheating all this time? If that was all he—

Luke's scream jerked me out of my thoughts. There had been no flash of light, and there was no plate of food. Luke was gasping, bent forward, staring down at his hands. Then he stood upright, white faced, his eyes oversized circles of pain and shock. He stumbled backward, reached out to steady himself on one of the tables—and cried out again when his hand touched the stone.

"Next?" Somiss said quietly.

I stared. Luke had slumped onto one of the stone benches, cradling his hands. I exhaled, trying to take it in, trying to think. Had Luke done something wrong? What? Made sure he went first? Or was Somiss punishing him for something else and had wanted us all to watch? I fought a familiar tightness in my throat—both fear and anger. But I was last in line. If I could just figure out what—

"Next!"

Gerrard inhaled deeply, then stepped forward and widened his stance, hunching his shoulders as he closed his eyes to imagine the food he wanted. I knew it would not be fancy. He had told me the story. A woman who had pitied him, a dirty, skinny little orphan boy, had bought him a bowlful of fish stew from a cheap vendor's cart. He had been so hungry, so cold, that he remembered everything about the stew, everything about the woman, the sky, the South End dogs that circled while he ate. He had no other childhood memory that vivid.

Or so he said.

Gerrard suddenly straightened and stepped back from the stone. "May I ask one question?" he said clearly, turning to look at Somiss.

We all stared at him. But Somiss *smiled*. "Only one," he said.

Gerrard lifted his chin. "Is there any way to avoid being burned?"

Somiss hesitated—it was clearly not the question he had been expecting. He shook his head. "No."

Burned? I closed my hands into fists and looked at Luke. His head was down; he was rocking back and forth. He whimpered, and I noticed blood trickling down his forearms. No, not blood, something paler, more watery. I swallowed hard and made myself look at Gerrard again. He was changing his stance. At first I thought his courage had faltered, but then I saw that he was locking his elbows and putting his feet closer together, very deliberately. When he finally leaned forward, stiff kneed and straight armed, he fell, palms flat, against the stone.

It took me a few seconds to understand that his weight had pinned him in place so that the jolt of pain couldn't make him jump back as Luke had. So his fish stew appeared on the foremost part of the stone pedestal, with the usual little flash of light and the faint sea-storm sound as Gerrard bent his knees and lurched backward. He did not fall, nor did he cry out. He made no sound at all as he retreated to the back of the room, carrying his little bowl full of supper more or less between his wrists. I saw his face as he passed me. His lips were pressed together, his teeth clenched. But his eyes were not full of pain or fear. He was proud of himself.

"Next?"

Somiss sounded angry. Why? Because Gerrard had managed to eat?

Levin stood a long time before the stone, stepping forward, then back. He was scared. So was I. When he finally tried, he screamed and flinched as Luke had, jerking back so quickly that no food appeared.

Jordan didn't scream, but he couldn't make himself leave his hands on the stone long enough to have food appear either. Nor Will. And Will very nearly collapsed as he was walking away from the stone. His face was ashen.

And then it was my turn. As much as I was scared of burning my hands, I was more afraid of starving. Somiss had told us to feed ourselves. That was the assignment. So only Gerrard had passed. Or maybe this was our last meal for a while because our hands were going to be so painful.

I imitated Gerrard exactly, forcing up an image of Celia's griddle cakes, the first meal I had managed to make, the one that was engraved deepest on my memory. Then I extended my arms, fingertips pointed at the ceiling, and rocked forward, letting my weight carry me.

The stone was usually cold as ice. This time, the pain was like fire, and it spread from my palms up my arms in a single heartbeat. I had meant to bite my lip if I had to, to keep from crying out, but I was too slow. I screamed, high, quivery, and silly sounding. But the griddle cakes appeared, and I used a handful of my robe hem to pad my hands so I could carry the hot plate. I walked as fast as I could, fighting down the pain-nausea. It hurt so bad I was afraid to look at my hands. I was afraid I would faint. If I did, Somiss would laugh. And Luke, no matter how much his own hands hurt.

But I didn't faint. I sat down at a table not far from Gerrard. I opened my right hand. It was a red mass of blisters and scorched skin, oozing blood and a clear fluid that would have filled the blisters, I was sure—if the skin had not been so ragged.

I looked up. Somiss was gone. I glanced at Gerrard and he met my eyes for an instant. After so long in silence, we were learning to understand each other. We would talk later, maybe, where no one would hear or see. Not now. Not a word.

He went back to eating, his wooden spoon held awkwardly in one clawed hand. I stared at my plate. I knew Gerrard was right to eat, in spite of the pain, and I knew I should. If Somiss had made it so that we would be burned every time . . . the thought was so terrifying that I pushed it out of my skull and kept pushing it down and down, moving it the way Franklin had taught us. I shoved it into my right foot, hard, where it would be nearly silenced. Then I just sat still, breathing, until I could pick up the fork.

I could barely hold it, but I speared and lifted one griddle cake and ducked to get a bit of it in my mouth. Then I heard footsteps and glanced up to see Luke and Jordan leaving, walking toward the arched entrance. Neither of them glanced at me. Then Levin stood, his wrists crossed in front of his chest. He nodded, like a friend at a normal school, letting me know I had played a good game of chess or something. Holding his gaze, I slid back on the bench a little, then leaned forward, letting my weight carry my body forward so that my forearms bumped against the edge of the table, my back stiff. Like all of our gestures, it was scaled down, barely noticeable to anyone but us. His eyes widened slightly, and I knew he had understood. When Will walked past, his skin milk white, his step slow and uncertain, I wanted to show him Gerrard's trick too, but he didn't look at me.

Gerrard wolfed his food, then rose and left. I stayed and ate, slowly, doggedly, until every crumb was inside me. Then I leaned over my plate and licked up every drop of the sweet maple syrup. I went back to the room. It was almost impossible to open the door. I finally managed with my left elbow and the back of my right hand.

Gerrard was reading aloud, whispering, just loud enough for me to hear. I practiced the new song with him, my lips barely moving. He read it ten or fifteen times. The pain in my hands was terrible, and my eyes hurt. I learned only the first four or five lines. But I was grateful to him for setting the example. He was right. Nothing had changed. We had to study or we would starve.

When I heard him switch to the fifth breathing pattern, I knew he was practicing moving his thoughts, and I was glad that I could already do it. I lay down, so tired that I fell asleep in spite of my throbbing hands.

I had a wonderful dream that night. I saw the wizards running, but not fast enough, as flames roared down the passages. It was like my father's field hands pouring lamp oil on an anthill, then setting it afire. Before long, the wizards were gone, the whole nest of them, dead forever, once and for all. I wasn't burned. I kept walking and found the huge doors my father had led me through, the first day here. I shoved them open and went out onto the pasture-sized niche that had been cut into the cliff face. My father's carriage was there, waiting. Gabardino helped me in, then let the white pony have his head. He cantered straight for the edge, leaping upward, pulling the carriage into the sky as he always did. Gabardino half turned. "Home," I told him. "I need to see my father."

9

Sadima had watched Franklin get thinner and weaker.
She pleaded with him every day to eat more. "Do you
think Somiss would do for you what you do for him?" she
whispered one day, when they were walking back to their
chambers. "Do you think he cares about you at all?"

As they turned from the main passage into their own,
he stopped and set down his lantern and kissed her, a
long kiss that made her press against him. He held her
close for a long time, then stepped back, shaking his
head. "No," he said. "He would never do for me what I
do for him. But you are wrong about the rest. I am his
only brother, and if he could love, he would love me.
You have no idea what his father did to him, to both of
us. Somiss can't—"

She shook her head to make him stop. This was an old argument, one she knew she would never win.

"If you want to leave now, Sadima, I understand. I will help you."

She stared at him. "I want to leave together. With the—"

He put his fingers on her lips, looking into her eyes. "I want that too," he said. "More than you can know." He started to say something else, then stopped. "I will do all I can to make it true," he said, meeting her eyes. "I promise you." Then he turned and walked toward his own chamber.

Sadima smiled, watching him go. He had never said it that plainly before. Later, when she went to sing the song for long life over him, she saw that he had fallen asleep with his boots on. His blankets were askew. She straightened them without waking him.

That evening she stayed up late, working. Franklin left without saying anything to her—which meant he had tiptoed past her chamber while she was working. It made her both sad and angry. The next morning she gave the boys their lessons, trying to encourage all of them. It scared her to see how listless they were.

Franklin hadn't returned before she left the big chamber and went back to her own. Sitting at her makeshift desk, she lifted the first soiled and rumpled paper on top of the stack. She read it through three or four times and was almost certain she had never seen it before. Five copies later, there was another unfamiliar one—and she remembered what Franklin had told her. Somiss had claimed he wasn't making much progress. Was he lying? What better way to hide new work than to make it look old? Maybe he was writing up new translations, then soiling the papers and putting them in with the old ones until they stank of smoke too.

The next morning Franklin came back from a night in Limòri, tired as always, carrying a sack full of bread and cheese—soft, white cheese! And it was a bigger sack than usual.

"Somiss's mother?" Sadima whispered, hoping it was true.

Franklin didn't answer. He began breaking up the bread. The boys put both arms through the bars, pushing at each other. Sadima faced them. "There's enough for everyone," she said quietly. Jux stepped back. When none of the others budged, he stepped forward again.

Sadima felt the fear and the anger that lay beneath their hunger, but she forced the feelings away before they exploded inside her. Taking deep, long breaths, she stood still for a long moment. When she looked up, Franklin was watching her. "Are you all right?"

She nodded and started to help him divide the bread, but found that she could only stand very still, fighting to keep her mind closed. She took five more slow, even breaths. Franklin kept glancing at her. When the cheese had been given out, he leaned close and whispered in her ear. "Can you *hear* them?"

She nodded.

He put his arm around her. "Does breathing like that help?"

Sadima nodded again. Franklin held her hand until every speck of the food was gone, until there was no further reason for any of the boys to start a fight. Then she walked beside him, their lanterns held high, their steps in perfect unison, toward their own chambers. Once they had turned down the narrow passageway, he put his arm around her shoulders and they slowed.

"Somiss has forbidden me to practice silent-speech," he said. "It's like trying not to breathe. It's hard for me, and my gift is nothing like yours. It must be almost impossible for you."

Queasy, Sadima leaned close to him, grateful, as always, that he understood. No one else in her life ever had. But she was furious that he would let Somiss tell him what to *think*. Once they were inside her chamber, she faced him. "No more than three or four of those boys stand any chance of learning how to fair copy in Ferrinides," she whispered. "Only Jux and Mabiki can do the Gypsy symbols at all, and only Jux is good at it." He started to answer her, but she shook her head. "Three of the boys are nearly witless. The darkness, the cage . . ." Her eyes filled with tears.

Franklin nodded wearily. "I will be able to bring more and better food now," he said. "Somiss has needed so many things that I could barely—"

"Franklin?" she interrupted him. "If they can't copy, what will Somiss do with them?"

He shrugged. "Maybe they can help me. They can—"

"Learn thievery?" she cut him off. "They probably know more than you do."

Franklin shook his head. "A few will learn the copying. The others can help me carry. They will be fed, and warmer and safer than they would be on the streets of Limòri until I can talk Somiss into setting them free."

Sadima just looked at him.

He rubbed his face with one hand. "I know, Sadima," he whispered. "But at least Somiss is preoccupied. The Gypsy book isn't helping at all. He thinks the symbols must be out of order. He's working constantly. And he seemed calm enough last night."

Sadima bit her lip to keep from screaming at him. Franklin was aware, every second, of Somiss's moods; that was how he had survived a lifetime of Somiss's rages. She watched Franklin glance at the entrance before he lifted her hand and kissed her fingers. "We have a year at least. There are thousands of papers, and Somiss wants them all recopied."

Sadima blinked. A year? "Aren't there copies of everything in the safe box at the moneylender's?" she asked, trying to whisper so quietly that Franklin wouldn't glance at the entrance, but he did it anyway.

"Almost everything, yes." His lips barely moved. "But he's afraid to go there—or to send me. Or even you. Because—"

"Because of the king's guards," she said, before he could.

"He fears his father more now," Franklin breathed. "Because of the fire. But when the king finds out, he will—"

Sadima looked aside, and Franklin stopped midsentence.

They'd had this argument before. Somiss had always said his father and the king would do anything to stop him from recovering magic. But it made no sense to her. If magicians could heal the sick and feed the poor, wouldn't kings be glad? "I know what he tells you," she said quietly. "But it is possible that Somiss hired the men who set the fire, not his father. He could have paid a coachman to leave one of his father's fancy carriages close by. He led us straight to it."

Franklin was watching her, and she saw fear in his eyes. "Don't ever say anything like that where he could hear it, Sadima."

"He was tricking the boys into coming here before the fire," she said. "You know that. He was ready to leave Limòri." She closed her mouth and kept the rest of her thoughts to herself. Somiss loved the idea of being a persecuted scholar, the one man who could change the world. It was like a boy's hero-game to him. He didn't care—or even notice—who he hurt.

Franklin was looking at her.

"We just need to leave," she whispered. "Soon."

"When we can, we will," Franklin said. "But if Somiss finds the old magic—"

"I know," Sadima said, to make him stop. Heroes and villains. Revolutions and battles. Somiss imagined he was the hero of a hearth tale—

"No," Franklin said.

Sadima stiffened. He had caught her thoughts. She turned to walk away, but he grabbed her wrist. "The battles are a matter of scholarship, not legend," he said, speaking as quietly as a sigh, his eyes fixed on hers. "There are books, recopied by generations of scribes. Four hundred years ago, magicians could do every-thing—*anything*. And they dragged the kings from their thrones. Wicked kings. Drunkards. Kings stupefied by orgies and intoxicants. And simple-minded ones, like our next king will be. And they let the people starve to pay for their whims. The magicians raised an army of dirt-floor commoners and changed their desperation into murderous rage. They killed all the kings, everywhere, all within a single year."

Franklin went into the passageway to look and listen, then came back. "Listen to me," he whispered. "Two hun-dred years ago, the bitter descendents of those kings killed almost all the wizards, with axes and poisons and bricks and knives and fire. And the Ferrins became royalty again. And now, every day, Somiss's mother bathes in goat's milk and virgin's blood. His father has a three-year-old girl he is training like a dog." Franklin stopped, his eyes full of tears.

Sadima stared at him, shocked into silence.

"There are twenty-five thousand people in Limòri by the king's last count," he told her. "Most of them have too little to eat. The orphans. You know how many there are, how they starve in the winters. The royalty is rotting again. Everywhere. In every land. Exactly as it is written in the books. But there are no wizards this time, no one to lead the farmers and the blacksmiths and the vendors. The Eridians hate all this, but even the ones who want to recover magic and share it according to their doctrines won't fight. So there's no one to help the commoners. Not yet."

Sadima took a long breath. "And you have read these books? Yourself?"

Franklin went out into the passageway again, his lantern held high, whistling softly. He walked ten or twelve paces in each direction, then came back.

"The books are hidden within the king's library, in gold boxes, for his eyes only, and his advisers, if he so chooses."

Franklin glanced out the door. She waited for him to look back at her. "Is Somiss's father one of the advisers?"

Franklin nodded. "So are two of his uncles. We began reading the history books when we were nine, sneaking them out of his father's study. Sadima, the ancient magicians were real. The wars were terrible. First the kings were killed, then, generations later, the wizards. Back and forth, fighting with armies raised among the poor. And the kings in every land know this."

"Is that why they—"

"Shhh!" Franklin stopped her. "No more. Please." He shook his head, glancing past her at the dark corridor outside the entrance to her chamber. He opened his carry-sack and handed her a loaf of bread and a ball of the cheese. Sadima set both on her crate-desk and thanked him, her spine and her voice stiff.

He leaned close so suddenly that it startled her. "Somiss says the wars will end when magicians master magic and become true wizards. Then they'll be invincible." He kissed her cheek, then inhaled slowly, his lips against her skin.

She felt his breath trace the line of her throat when he exhaled. She closed her eyes.

"Someday the king will realize what we are doing. You must leave before that," he whispered.

"You have to come with me."

Franklin stepped back. Sadima saw how pale his cheeks were, the dark circles beneath his eyes. "Go to bed," she said, and stood on her tiptoes to kiss him good night. He smiled, then walked away, disappearing into the passage.

"Sadima?" he whispered from the darkness. "You are the sun and the moon to me."

10

When the wizard pounded on the door, I sat upright,
shoving the blanket off, and stood, then sat down again,
hard, rocking back and forth as the sparkles receded from
my vision.

"We're awake!" I yelled, but the pounding went on.
Class again?

I could hear Gerrard fumbling, trying to light his lamp.
I got up and raised my right arm so my robe sleeve would
slide back. Then I slid my forearm carefully across my desk
until I felt the cold iron of my own striker. But I could
not pick it up. The blisters and blood had congealed into
thick scabs overnight. Flexing my fingers, even a little, was
almost more than I could stand. I heard Gerrard curse and
knew there would be no light this morning.

The wizard pounded on the door again.

"Coming!" Gerrard shouted, and the pounding stopped. I heard a little squeak, like he had moved his cot, and I remembered the book. What had he done with it? And then I had a terrible thought. Did Somiss know? Had we all been burned as a punishment for Gerrard's book?

I heard Gerrard moving, then the sound of him pissing—he was squatting over the slops bucket, I was sure. I waited until I heard him moving toward the door, then I eased forward until my bare toes found the oaken bucket. I straddled it, hoisting my robe out of the way as best I could. It was terrible to feel so helpless. Once I was finished, I straightened up, my heart thudding—and had no idea which way to go. There is no way to describe how dark it was.

"Where are you?" I whispered.

"Here," Gerrard answered, barely breathing the words. "By the door."

I took two steps toward him and stopped. "Go ahead. Can you open it?"

"Come this way first," he whispered back, and this time his voice came from behind me.

Behind me.

I turned around and took three steps toward his voice, my hands out, aching, tense with fear. This had happened on our first day. We had raked the darkness with our fingers, turning over and over, counting our steps aloud, desperate to find each other, a wall, a bed—shit, *anything* in what felt like endless darkness. Then the wizard had opened the door, and the room that had seemed endless was really very small.

"This way," Gerrard whispered. His voice came from off to my right now.

The wizard pounded on the door again, and the sound came from the same direction Gerrard's whisper had. So I turned to walk toward it in the dark, sliding my feet, my heart beating hard at my ribs. I was afraid to lower my hands, but equally afraid I would bump into something and tear the scabs. I took ten steps and stopped. Our little chamber was about six paces long. They were doing it to us again. Why?

"Here," Gerrard whispered. He was on my left. I turned, and he began whispering, "I am here," over and over until I finally bumped into him, my extended right palm scraping the wall on my last step. I doubled over to breathe through my mouth so I wouldn't cry out. The wizard began pounding at the door again. I heard Gerrard gasp and knew he was trying to turn the door handle. I forced myself to stand up straight. "Can you do it?"

"Yes," he answered, and the door suddenly swung inward. The light from the wizard's torch shone into our tiny little chamber, just as it had that first day. Was this punishment for the book? For something else? Or just to remind us that we were helpless?

I followed Gerrard out the door, my wrists crossed against my chest, my hands throbbing. The wizard was a tall man with jowls and white hair. Was this Jux's class? Or Somiss's? Or something worse? I noted the turns, the tunnels we passed, as always. The pain in my hands made it hard to concentrate. The wizard stopped abruptly and pointed. I looked through the arched entrance of the chamber. It was Somiss's class. He sat, his back to us, in a wide, sky-colored velvet chair this time. It had a high, tufted backrest, a heavy, ebony frame, and a braid of carved snakes, real enough to make me look twice.

Gerrard and I watched the wizard walk away, then glanced at each other. I lifted my eyebrows a little. He shook his head, paring the motion down until it was almost imperceptible. I nodded. Neither of us wanted to be in there alone with Somiss. We would wait for the others to come.

I held my hands a little higher to ease the throbbing, then looked into the chamber again, wondering if Somiss knew we were there—and if he cared, one way or the other. I shivered, feeling light-headed.

This wasn't a school. Real schools had real teachers and real classes, and all the ones I had ever attended had roofs. If there had been a wide, interesting one here, I would have known how to escape, where to hide. And Levin would have gone with me. I had introduced him to roof-running back in fourth form. He had been scared at first, but he learned to love it. The school's roof wasn't as big as my father's, but it was steeper and more angled. There were four trees that offered both entrance and exit. In the winter we had wrapped scarves over our ears and noses when we'd gone up to sit in the snow and watch the stars. The headmaster had heard us walking up there more than once. The teachers all suspected us. But they had never caught us. We were too good for them.

There is no way to explain what that last thought did to me. I breathed the first pattern, fighting a swoop of sadness. I remembered what it was like to laugh, to get away with a prank. . . . I had been happy then. Why hadn't I known it?

I turned aside to hide my watery eyes from Gerrard— and found myself staring through the entrance at the back of Somiss's chair again. The snakes in the carvings were truly remarkable. It was as though living serpents had been turned into wood, their muscles stopped, their skins hardened, between one breath and the next. I stared at the chair. Was that *possible*?

Gerrard made a quick, nearly inaudible clicking sound. I turned back to look at him. He tipped his head: footfalls. The others were coming. We went in. We were used to sitting down, cross-legged, on the stone floor. I had never once thought about how I'd had to arrange my loose, long, idiotic robe as I got settled. With our hands burned, stiff with scabs, it was almost impossible. Gerrard somehow managed, but the rest of us had to try over and over.

I knelt, then sat, and had to get back up because the cloth had bunched beneath me, pulling tight against my neck. On my fourth try, I finally hitched the hemline up high enough, but I broke a scab. I pressed my hand against the hem of my robe to stanch the bleeding.

Levin, Jordan, and Luke came in like servant-children for sale. They held their hands against their chests, cupping inward, their wrists crossed as though they were bound.

We had all realized that the aching was worse when our hands hung by our sides. On his way past, Levin lowered his brows slightly and tipped his head toward Luke. I nodded—a tiny, hairbreadth nod—then curved my mouth a little to thank him. I was always watching out for Luke. He was taller and heavier than I was, and he hated me. He said my father had cheated his. Maybe it was true.

Once we were all seated, uncomfortable on the stone, Somiss looked at us. I was so afraid that he would point at Gerrard and ask him about the book. Or that he knew Gerrard and I were helping each other. But he didn't. Class began as it usually did.

I was so glad I had studied in spite of the pain, and I was grateful when Somiss pointed at Gerrard first. I closed my eyes and recited silently along with Gerrard and then with Will. They both passed. Then I did, then Jordan and Levin. Luke missed five words.

When we were finished, Somiss disappeared, chair and all. We left in silence. I walked slowly, letting Luke—and everyone else—get ahead of me. I don't know if anyone else went to the food hall. I certainly didn't. My hands already hurt so much I was nauseated—and we had all gotten used to being hungry.

When I came into our chamber, Gerrard had somehow lit our lamps. He was switching breathing patterns, lost in the effort of moving his thoughts. I read the history book for a while, wading through more pages about the wars, reading about the kings who plundered each other's lands, the endless killing they had caused for generations beyond counting—and the amazing Founder of the Limòri Academy who had put an end to all of it.

When my eyes were too full of lantern-smoke tears to read any more, I closed the book, hating Somiss. Usually, when we passed a recitation, we got a day or two to eat normally, to study, to rest, and feel a little safer. Not this time. He had stolen that. Maybe he would never let us rest again. I felt heavy and weak, thinking that. I was probably going to die here, no matter how hard I tried. Why not sooner than later? But how? Maybe I could lay my body against the stone, let it burn me enough to kill me. I could feel my pulse in my swollen hands as I tried to think of some other way, one that would hurt less.

I forced myself to close my eyes and listened to Gerrard breathing, timing mine with his, changing patterns when he did, then quieting my thoughts the way Franklin had taught us, then moving them from my mind into my belly, then farther away, into my feet. It always helped me feel a little better. But it didn't *change* anything. It was only going to get harder here.

When Gerrard finally finished practicing, I sat up again. "Where did you get that book?" I whispered. "Is it still in the room?"

His back straightened a little. But he didn't answer me. I balled my fists without thinking, then flinched and loosened them when the scabs bent. Were the wizards making sure we couldn't fight? Had they thought of that?

"Whatever it is, get it out of here," I whispered. "Are you trying to get us killed?"

He still didn't answer. He didn't respond in any way, not even an invisible nod, some small shift of his shoulders that would have let me know he'd heard me.

"I mean it," I breathed. "You have no right to—"

"Be quiet," he interrupted me.

I stood up. I meant to hit him, to shove him to the floor, to do *something*, even if my hands bled all night.

"Go to sleep, Hahp," he said, not whispering, but in a normal voice, and it stunned me into silence. I glanced around the room.

"You said once that it's safe to talk here," I began, still whispering. "Is it?"

"Go to sleep," he said again, and there was a weariness in his voice that scared me. I opened my mouth to argue and couldn't. I was tired and hungry and my hands hurt almost more than I could stand. And because Gerrard had told me to go to sleep, I wouldn't. For a long time I sat on the edge of my cot, rocking, trying not to cry, trying not to scream. I could hear Gerrard breathing the fifth pattern, then the seventh.

I finally blew out my lantern, lay down, and turned to face the wall. I tried to summon one of my daydreams— Somiss and my father, both of them afraid of me. But it didn't work, I didn't feel the rush of shameful pleasure, the daydream wouldn't start in my mind. So I curled up around my hands and tried to cry, but I couldn't even do that.

I dreamed about rats. They were in the tunnels, so many that they were clawing up and over each other's backs, trying to get out. But it was impossible. The passages just went in circles.

11

Every morning Sadima woke in the darkness, in the silence. Her first thoughts were for Franklin's safety, then for the boys in the cage. The sham of the lessons she tried to teach them lay heavier and heavier on her heart. Nothing had changed. Even with more food, nothing was truly better. The boys were caged and they hated it—a dull, hopeless hatred that seeped into her and settled in her belly and made her feel ill.

After the lessons and, sometimes, a few sweet moments with Franklin, she worked the rest of her waking hours alone, copying Somiss's soiled, wrinkled papers. Only a few were in the convoluted symbols from the Gypsy book; the rest were in Ferrinides. So most of her work was easy, mindless and dull.

Sadima felt herself sinking into a joyless stupor; she felt her own hope dimming. She missed Franklin so much. He was the only person in her life who had ever understood her. Their walks in Limòri, their quiet talks, seeing his face light up because she had made a good supper, or given him a clever idea, or made him laugh—those things had been the best part of her whole life. She loved Franklin. If he had only been a kindhearted farmer's son instead of the whipping boy for a royal heir, she would have been dreaming about her wedding, not an escape and a murder.

Late in the day—which she had learned to judge by the tightness in her shoulders and hands—she sometimes went to the big chamber a second time, to make sure the boys were all right. They were usually napping, and she took care not to wake them. The pear-shaped opening in the wall let in light that was sometimes colored by the sunset. Seeing it always made her feel a little better. The world was out there. It had not disappeared. It would be waiting.

One afternoon, as Sadima lifted an inked sheet and set it aside to dry, she noticed the silence in a way she never had before. It was so deep, so complete, that for an instant she imagined that she could hear time passing, an odd thrumming sound deep in the rock. It scared her. A few days later, listening to the roar of the silence again, she thought she heard something else, far away and indistinct. Voices? She blinked, sure she was imagining it. She put her fingers in her ears—the faint sound disappeared.

Sadima stood up and walked to the entrance of her chamber to listen. The vague sound of voices was gone, but after a long moment she thought she heard footsteps. Leaving her lantern behind, she went down the corridor and stopped a few paces before it met the main passageway. There. The smallest sound of stone grit beneath a shoe. Then a whisper. She pressed her back against the wall, trying to tell which direction the footsteps were coming from. Franklin should be asleep. She had sung the song for long life over him; he wouldn't rise until evening. It had to be Somiss.

She held perfectly still. It wasn't one person. It was two, and they were whispering. She strained to hear. Only the rhythms were audible—but she recognized both. Somiss and Franklin were coming closer, walking toward the main cavern. Somiss was doing most of the talking, as always. As they got closer, they stopped whispering and quieted their steps even more.

Sadima tiptoed back toward her chamber, far enough from the main passage so their lantern light could not reach her. She watched as they walked past, both of them turning to look down the passageway into the darkness that hid her. She held her breath, waiting until she was sure they were past to exhale. Then, after a long moment, she tiptoed back to the main passageway and peered around the corner.

They were walking side by side, each one carrying a lantern, the ruddy light sliding across the stone walls. Sadima slipped into the passage, following them, listening. Halfway to the big cavern, Somiss turned to Franklin.

"You arranged for a woman before the meetings?"

"She'll be waiting when we get there," Franklin said quietly.

"Dark hair?"

Sadima couldn't hear Franklin's response, but Somiss said, "Good." And then they were silent.

Sadima stopped and watched their lanterns dim with distance. Of course Somiss would buy sex and of course he would make Franklin arrange it. Would Franklin hire a woman too? *No*, she told herself. He had said he loved her.

In the distance, she could see the arched entrance of the big cavern as Franklin and Somiss went through it, and the light from their lanterns touched the walls. They didn't turn toward the entrance passage. Would they go to the cage? Was this the day that Somiss would find out that only two of the boys could copy? How angry would he be?

Hoping desperately that they wouldn't turn around and start back toward her, Sadima hurried, walking fast, one hand trailing on the wall to guide her, watching as they crossed the huge chamber. She turned hard left, pressing her back against the wall, hiding in the dark, staring across the cavern at the cage.

She couldn't hear all they said—not even half. But it was easy to see that Somiss was upset by whatever Franklin told him. Then Franklin had Jux draw a Gypsy symbol. Somiss said something and slapped Franklin's shoulder and seemed pleased. He gave a slate to Mabiki and repeated the test. He didn't slap Franklin's shoulder, but he nodded and reached through the bars to tousle Mabiki's hair. The boy took a step backward, ducking Somiss's hand.

Sadima stood still, scared that Somiss would make all the boys try, but he didn't. Franklin must have been honest with him. She watched them walk away, disappearing into the darkness that hid the far end of the big chamber and the long, narrow passageway that led outside. Sadima held herself very still. They were leaving the cliffs, going somewhere. To talk to Somiss's mother? Or the Eridians?

Sadima looked up at the opening in the wall. It was deep blue. Evening was coming. She felt her throat tighten. Wherever they were going, Somiss would see the woman, then he had meetings. They would almost certainly be gone for a long time, maybe until morning. This was the chance she had hoped would come before the weather changed. She might never get another one.

She hurried back up the main passageway in the dark, feeling her way along the wall until she came to the much narrower tunnel that led to her chamber. Then she ran again. Once she had her lantern in her hand, she hesitated. If some unpredictable reason brought them back, if Somiss found her . . . she was so scared her body felt stiff, unwilling. But the opportunity to find the key to the cage might never come again.

Sadima started walking, faster and faster, pushed along by the thudding of her frightened heart. She glanced back every few steps, ready to shield her own lantern if she saw the distant wink of theirs, but she didn't stop until she came to Somiss's passageway. Then she stood frozen for a long moment. There were a few side tunnels, she remembered that much. But she had no idea if they were dead ends or where they led. If Somiss did come back when she was in his chamber—or the passageways around it—no clever explanation would save her.

Sadima forced herself to look; the crate was empty. Where was the book now? Still in Somiss's room, or had Franklin taken it back to Somiss's father's library? Or the king's? She began to walk, counting her steps. Somiss's chamber was on the right. She was sure of that much, but she had been here only once, and she wasn't sure how far it was. After sixty paces, she saw an arched opening and walked into it, holding her lantern high. But it was just another corridor. She went on, looking into one more empty passage before she thought she smelled food—no, not just food. Meat. It had been so long since she had eaten anything but bread and cheese that the odor was almost overwhelming, faint as it was. She turned into the next opening, then stopped, lifted her lantern, and stared.

Somiss had a real desk, a big one, with a real chair. How? Franklin must have taken the desk apart and carried it through the narrow entrance passage a few planks at a time, then rebuilt it here. But where had he stolen it? How had he carried it all the way from Limòri to the cliffs?

Somiss had left a reading lamp burning low. That made her nervous until she realized he probably left it on all the time. He had never in his life had to worry about a short supply of lamp oil or anything else. There was a box beside the lamp, and Sadima heard a scrabbling sound as she leaned to look inside. Mice? She could feel their utter contentment, and it startled her. Animals almost always hated being confined. She looked closer. They stared up at her, entirely without fear. There were little chunks of cheese and an old ointment tin full of water in one corner. But the box wasn't as deep as she had thought. She lifted it carefully and it separated from a second box—or half box really. There was no lid, just miniature partitions that would make a mouse turn this way and that, trying to guess the way. Sadima set it back.

Somiss would never keep mice for amusement. He had some other reason. In Limòri he had stopped eating for days at a time and had made Franklin do it too, because he thought he learned faster that way. She looked at the mice and allowed their thoughts to come into hers. They were not hungry. They were all plump. So this was something different.

Somiss had spread out his papers in uneven stacks as he had back in Limòri. But here, along one wall, there were three or four dozen wooden boxes, mostly empty. There were Ferrinides words painted on each one, in Somiss's precise hand.

"Fever," Sadima read, whispering. "Weather, Heartbreak, Sadness, Trust, Love, Crops, Youth, Fear, Longevity." He was planning to separate the songs by purpose. She looked at the single sheet in the box marked "Longevity" because she didn't know what the word meant—and instantly recognized the song for long life. Somiss had made three small changes. She memorized them.

Then she lifted the front row of boxes, one by one, looking beneath them. The key wasn't hidden there. She turned and saw the soft featherbed that topped the stone platform, the fine woolen blankets folded across it, the linen-covered bolster. She took a step to feel the wool between her fingers and realized there was a thick, woven rug alongside the platform too, that she hadn't seen because she was holding her lantern high. A rug.

Somiss had kept Franklin busy providing him with luxuries while the boys were half-starved and cold. And, she thought, as she set down her lantern and felt beneath all the stacks of Somiss's papers, Franklin hadn't argued or disobeyed. He was scared, like she was, that anything he did would only hurt the boys more. Or her. Oh, how she hated Somiss. She couldn't wait for the morning he woke and found no one here to wait upon him, no one to scream at, no one to threaten. Or maybe, on that morning, he would not wake up at all.

Careful not to disturb anything, Sadima kept searching. There was a bowl of fruit on the desk, and her mouth watered. She made sure the key wasn't beneath the oranges, then put them back in place. She picked up the rug, then replaced it. She slid her hands beneath the blankets, then reached beneath the featherbed. Nothing. There were clothes, folded neatly on one of the stone shelves that had been carved out of the wall. They looked new and smelled clean. Sadima made sure there was no key hidden in the fabric. Then she stood straight and looked around the chamber.

Nothing could be hidden in the floor or the walls, unless the person who had made the cavern had chipped hiding places out of the rock. She ran her hands over the stone, from the floor to the limit of her height. Nothing. Where would Somiss put the key? Sadima turned in a slow circle, scanning the room. The rough-hewn shelves on the back wall held four rows of books. The key could be between the pages of any one of them.

She walked into the corridor without her lantern and stood in the dark, listening. When she went back into the room, she took each book down and held it spine up, shaking the pages back and forth. There were two dozen books with a Ferrinides seal. But there was no key.

There was another wooden crate behind the desk. Four oil lamps stood inside it. Four. And they were fancier and finer than any she had ever seen in her life. Somiss was not straining his eyes to read. Sadima lifted the box very carefully, set it back, and took the lamps out one by one.

Sadima found herself glancing at the entrance every few seconds, her stomach tighter and tighter. Where else could she look? The walls were bare. The shelves hid no hooks, no key-sized boxes. On an impulse, she pulled the desk chair out and knelt to slide her hands along the underside of the wooden desk. Nothing. She exhaled. Maybe he kept it with him all the time? Or hid it somewhere else? She ran her hands over the chair itself. Nothing. Standing straight again, she scanned the chamber. There was no place left to look. Sadima pushed the chair back in and bit her lip, fighting tears.

She looked up at the ceiling, then back at the floor. The bottom shelf was about a hand-span above it. On her

KATHLEEN DUEY

knees, sliding her hand along the stone, she worked her
way backward, and she finally found it. Not the key, but a
small curved iron spike, driven into the rock. Somiss had
taken the key with him? Of course he had. But now she
knew where he kept it.

Sadima hooked her lantern bail with three fingers and
stood up, then walked around the room again, holding the
lantern high, carefully straightening everything she had
touched. Then she ran. She didn't slow until she was ten
paces from her own chamber, breathing hard. Her heart
was flying.

– 12 –

The scabs on my palms had thickened so much that I couldn't close my hands. I managed to light both our lamps one morning, then we left them burning in the corridor when we weren't using them, so the smoke wouldn't thicken unbearably. They didn't run out of oil, and I was amazed that I had never once thought about it before. Either the wizards had been filling them, or they were magic. They didn't *seem* magical. Strikers and oil lamps were used by anyone who couldn't buy cold-fire—and that was almost everyone in Limòri.

Somiss left us alone for a time. It was wonderful. At first I was careful not to wipe my eyes with my fingers. The tear-salt seeped into the edges of the scabs and stung. But with every day that passed—even though the days felt very short to me—my eyes hurt a little less and my hands began to heal.

It felt like we were barely sleeping. Gerrard studied like he always had—constantly. He wasn't bothering to go to the food hall. I don't think anyone was. He wasn't reading the mysterious little book in our room, either, and I hoped he had found another place to hide it. I asked him, but he didn't answer. It pissed me off, but the last thing I wanted was a fight.

I studied too, turning the pages of the song book by licking the back of my hand, then dragging it across the paper. And because Gerrard's hands were even worse than mine, I found out that my suspicions were true. He didn't need the song book. He recited without opening it, whispering the next song aloud once or twice a night—if they were nights—so that I could learn it. I followed the text as he recited and then practiced in a whisper.

I passed the next recitation and wondered if it would mean I could eat soon. But Somiss was imperious and distant and didn't say anything beyond what he had to. His chair was like an ugly, ostentatious throne for some story-book king. Truly. There were *gems* set into the wood. I was giddy with hunger, and it was all I could do not to laugh.

Leaving, I saw Will stagger, then catch his balance. He looked terrible again, skinny as a reed. He had passed the test too, not that it mattered. I slowed down. As he went past me, he lifted his hands—his palms weren't just scabbed. They were raw and bloody. Had he tried to eat? He ducked his chin in one of our invisible nods. I tipped my head in the general direction of the food hall, then lowered my brows and my shoulders so he would know I had been hoping that the stone wouldn't burn us anymore, then touched my heart to thank him for telling me—for saving me the pain of trying. I touched my belly and raised my brows, hoping he had at least managed to eat. He lowered his eyes. So he hadn't. I exhaled so that he could hear how sorry I was as he lengthened his step and went past.

I went to the food hall three times over the next three days and just stared at the beautiful, faceted stone, wondering if it made sense to make enough food for a few days, cheese and apples, something simple. If I starved, would it matter that my hands healed? The last time I went, my belly was hollow and aching, but I still could not force myself to burn my hands again. What if I jerked back and it was all for nothing? What if I was so dizzy and weak that I *couldn't* step back? Would my flesh burn all the way to my bones?

Later I sat on my cot, listening to Gerrard breathe. He was working with the seventh breathing pattern now.

"Can you do it yet?" I breathed. "Can you feel your thoughts moving even a little?"

"Almost," he whispered.

"Good," I whispered back.

He didn't answer, but I knew he had heard me. I could only hope he was grateful. Jux hadn't come for him nearly as often as he had for me—most of Jux's classes would be impossible until Gerrard could move his thoughts. But once he could my worst fear might come true. He wouldn't need my help. Then I would be alone again.

To keep from sinking into a round of worrying, I stood up and lifted the history book awkwardly between my elbows, then dropped it on my cot. I used my right wrist to flop the book open, somewhere past the middle. The heading was "The Eridian Uprising." I fumbled at the pages, turning back to read the introduction. It took five pages just to say this:

A few years after the Founder had begun his work, there had been a young, dull-witted Ferrinides king whose chancellors hated magicians. They had hunted them down. In Limòri and every village in the kingdom, soldiers found magicians in the marketplaces and hanged them before cheering crowds. Many of these people were not really magicians, and none had mastered more than the most trivial magic. Their incompetence had caused the hatred of the populace.

The dull-witted king had died young, and his chancellors found an ambitious half-blood heir to wear the crown. He hated magicians too, for a different reason—there were rumors about the Founder and his work. The half-blood king feared real magic. He knew, as all kings do, that people who have real magic don't need or want royalty.

For three more generations, the Founder's students hid. They studied inside the cliffs, recovering secrets from the writings of ancient magicians. During the dotage of the Ferrinides king who was called Daniel, the Last King, magicians came back into Limòri, quietly, working with the merchants and magistrates who really governed during Daniel's disastrous reign.

Because of the Founder, this time they came as true wizards; they had been taught infallible magic. They could help the sick, bring rain where it was needed, make the cold-fire that gave light without heat. The powerful families of Limòri paid a great deal for all these things and came to depend on the wizards.

When the wizards finally wore their black robes into the city, common people mobbed them, begging for healings and other magic. They helped many of the poor and were beloved and welcomed by all except the Eridians, a sect of zealots whose prophet was a magician who condemned magic. They rioted, stoning the wizards and the crowds who had come to see them, killing people, including a mother and her sick child. The magistrates drove the murderous Eridians from Limòri at sword-point, forcing them into the countryside, where they had stayed, becoming farmers and fishermen.

I looked up from the book, astonished. Eridians rioting? Could that be true? Everyone knew about King Daniel and his unfinished building and how the magistrates took over once and for all when he gave up the throne. Magistrates had governed Limòri since my great-grandfather was a boy.

But it was almost impossible to imagine Eridians rioting. They had one odd festival that irritated the Ferrinides—but I had no idea why. Eridians didn't use magic much, and most of them wore plainer clothes than my parents. But if someone in a wealthy Eridian family was ill, they sought a wizard's help. Everyone did. And if Eridians encountered wizards in the city, they nodded politely like everyone else. A lot of them owned enormous farms—my father shipped their produce everywhere. A lot of them were Servenians, known for hating violence because of the constant wars in their homeland. I had never heard anyone talk about the Eridians ending up in the countryside because they had been driven out of the city. I put the history book back on my desk, wondering what was true, as always.

At the next recitation class, I passed again. Gerrard did too, of course, and Levin and Jordan. Will and Luke did not. After Somiss disappeared, I heard Luke laugh. He was staring at the wall, cradling his hands against his belly, until he noticed me looking at him. Then he frowned. I turned away, my face blank, as though I had not noticed. He laughed again, louder, his voice cracking into his new, lower range. It made him sound half-mad.

What was so funny? The idea that the ones who passed still wouldn't be able to eat? I turned to glance at Gerrard, but he had already gone. Everyone had. I was alone in a chamber with Luke, who hated me. I stood up, tripping on my robe, and started for the entrance.

"No need to hurry, Malek," Luke said behind me.

I lengthened my stride and heard him run a few steps to catch up.

"Are you afraid of me?" he taunted as we started down the passageway.

And it struck me funny, all of a sudden. I was. Why? If he hit me, it would crack open his scabs and hurt him as much or more than it hurt me. I stopped and faced him.

Then I laughed. It sounded idiotic, even to me, too high, and too loud. But if he was dumb enough to hit me with burned, scabbed hands, I wanted to know. If he was that stupid, maybe I could stop worrying about him.

Luke cleared his throat but didn't speak. I turned and started off again. He caught up. For a long moment we walked almost side by side. Then he dropped back and kicked me, hard, his calloused bare foot catching my right hip and making me stumble and fall as he ran off. I just sank to the floor, loose bodied, instead of trying to catch myself, so I saved my hands at least. But my right knee slammed into the rock, and my hip hurt. I got up, watching Luke disappear into the patches of darkness between the torches until I couldn't see him at all. *Kicking.* I hadn't even thought of that. Gerrard would have.

It hurt, but it was such a small hurt compared to my hands and my fear-weighted thoughts that I just stood up and went on my way, reversing the sentence I had made up. I was glad all the others—including Gerrard—were already out of sight, because I started giggling. It was shrill, breathy, not like my own voice at all, and I couldn't stop until I was nearly back at the room.

I stared at the silver fish-shaped handle, breathing to calm myself for a long time before I wound my robe hem around my hand a few times and opened the door. Even that much pressure hurt.

It was bright in the room. Gerrard had brought in both lamps and turned up the sooted wicks. A haze of acrid smoke hung in the air. Blinking, I expected to see him sitting cross-legged on his bed, studying, or maybe reading his mystery book, but he wasn't there. I stood still, staring, trying to understand. His bed was gone. So was his desk. Oh no. Oh no. Oh, shit, *no*. Had he been caught with the book? Did they know about our pact? Had they killed him?

My knees were shaking. I sank onto the edge of my bed and felt something jab the underside of my thigh. I used the back of my right hand to push the thin blanket to one side. It was Gerrard's book. So they hadn't found it? Or maybe they were watching me, right now. I shoved it back under the covers and felt tears in my eyes.

I would never be able to learn the songs. I would starve, even if they had just moved him to another room. And he would die in Jux's classes without my help. I blew out both lamps and lay down in the dark, the book on my belly. I knew I should hide it, but I couldn't move.

Gerrard had always been here. Through everything else, he had been here. Even when he had acted like an ass, when he had hated me, he was *here*. Was he dead? Or maybe he was in Will's room, moving into one of the empty beds. Maybe this was my punishment, not his. My gut got so tight that I could barely breathe.

Oh, please. Please. Not this.

I did not want to be alone in the dark.

– 13 –

Sadima lay awake that night and three more, listen-ing, afraid Somiss would do something awful to the boys who hadn't been able to copy. When he didn't, she began to worry that he might yet find some tiny sign that she had been in his chamber. She had been careful, but she had moved nearly everything in his room.

And every waking moment, she hoped that Franklin would tell her where they had gone and what had happened. But he didn't, and she couldn't ask without admitting she had overheard them—and that she had known she was alone in the cliffs that night.

Franklin seemed preoccupied with something. When she asked about it one night on their way up the main passage, he shook his head. "Nothing is simple."

"Is Somiss's father really looking for him?" she asked.

He nodded.

"What would happen if he saw you?"

Franklin smiled wearily. "I would find a hole, like a rabbit does."

"A hole?" She made a face at him, and he laughed.

He took her hand once they had turned the corner and were in the narrower passage that led to their chambers. "We Marshams are hard to catch," he said. He looked into her eyes. "Even if we could somehow get Somiss to release the boys, if we all left, it wouldn't stop him. Limòri is full of orphans."

She nodded. "But that doesn't mean we shouldn't—"

"I know," he interrupted her. "I just wonder who would help the new ones."

Sadima nodded. She knew he was right. "Have you spoken with Somiss's mother?"

He nodded. "There will be better food for us all soon," he said.

Sadima couldn't look at him. Somiss had better food *now*.

Franklin kissed her and held her close. Sadima collapsed against him, hating Somiss, wishing his father would kill him, or that someone else would. That would free all of them.

Franklin swayed, as though they were dancing, breathing into her hair, whispering that he loved her. When he finally drew back, he was yawning. "I need to sleep."

Sadima watched him turn to leave, hoping he hadn't

heard her thoughts. "If I can't stay," she breathed, "will you come with me?"

He hesitated, then spoke. "I want to. But the magic—"

"If we could take it with us?" she interrupted, thinking about her secrets, buried in the woods.

Franklin shrugged. "How? Neither of us can do what Somiss is doing."

"But if we could?"

"There is nothing I want more than to be with you— and free of him," he whispered. He kissed her again, soft and slow, then left, walking like an old, tired man. Sadima closed her eyes, remembering the first time she had seen him, the sound of his laugh, his long stride, his smile. If she could convince him to leave, he would smile again.

That night she fell asleep with hope in her heart and woke up making plans. She had to wait for warmer weather but it wasn't that far away now, one cycle of the moon, or two at most. She would have to get the cage key. And it would be best if she could find another way out of the cliffs, so they could start off in a direction Somiss wouldn't anticipate.

That day Sadima began looking. And every day that followed, after she finished with the boys and her copying, she walked the passages, exploring. She was careful, marking her paths with little wedge-shaped cairns made from the loose chunks of rock that lay scattered along the walls.

She couldn't venture very far at first. The darkness felt endless and the complete silence when she stopped walking was almost more than she could bear. But every morning the boys looked a little worse, even though Franklin brought extra food more often. So Sadima forced herself to take longer walks, to explore farther than she ever thought she would be able to, carrying her lantern carefully and watching constantly for her cairns.

One morning Sadima watched Jux and Mabiki copying, competing to see who was better. They might still be all right when the weather warmed. But what about the others? Six of the ten boys were asleep. Two more sat slumped, staring at nothing. Looking at them, she realized that it had been a long time since their feelings had come to her. She closed her eyes and *tried* to hear them. There was nothing to hear, not even from Mabiki and Jux. Sadima felt physically ill. The cage *was* killing them. Her hands were shaking as she drew another symbol.

There had been a winter calf on her father's farm, abandoned by the cow. They had raised it by soaking soft rags in milk and letting it suckle the cloth. Her father had built a stanchion to hold it motionless so they could keep it covered in blankets, keep it warm enough to survive. It fought at first. Sadima had begged her father to let it loose in the stall. He refused, afraid it would freeze unless they kept it wrapped up.

Sadima had known that he was right, so far as he could see. But she could feel how frantic the calf was, how terrified, how his legs ached. Her heart had been filled with the calf's misery, but she'd had to hide it. She knew her father would only get angry if she tried to tell him the truth, maybe angry enough to slaughter the calf to end the argument.

Eventually the calf wasn't scared. It lifted its head when they fed it, then lowered it again. Sadima's fear had subsided too; the aching she had felt from the calf dulled, then dimmed. And the calf had lived. But it never galloped around the pasture on a misty morning; it rarely raised its head. It spent its life standing alone in a corner of the pasture in sun, wind, rain, and snow, until her father sold it.

Sadima looked at the boys again. Mabiki and Jux had closed their eyes when she stopped drawing symbols for them. Would they still be alive when she and Franklin were finally ready to leave? Or half-alive, like the calf?

She had lived through hungry winters on the farm, some of them starvation winters, with snow piled up over the windows. She had sat—side by side with her father and brother—in the cramped sitting room. Blankets hung over the hall doorway and the windows to try to keep the warmth in. But the only truly warm place was close to the fire. So they sat, day after day, staring into the flames, listening to the storms howl, while Micah told stories.

Sadima arranged her skirt better, tucking the cloth beneath her bare feet. "Do you like stories?" None of the boys looked up. "Would you like to hear one?"

Jux opened his eyes. Mabiki nodded. The others didn't react at all.

"There was a king who had a coward for a son," she began, speaking slowly and dramatically, the way Micah always had. "So he went in search of a boy to raise who could follow him on the throne. Since he did not want to steal anyone's child, he went into the poor parts of the city to search among the beggar children."

Mabiki sat up straighter. Several of the others were listening, she could tell. She raised her voice. "He found a brave boy, one who smiled even when he was hungry, even when he was scared. And the king was so impressed by his courage that he adopted him."

The boys exchanged glances. Sadima kept going, explaining all the little details the way Micah had when he'd told her stories—the boy's rough clothing, his fair hair, his sore heart. By the time she got to the part about the legitimate son being made to learn from the good deeds of the beggar boy, they whispered to each other. When she described the adopted prince using his wealth to build a place for street boys to sleep, safe and sound, with full bellies, they smiled. Jux and Mabiki cheered.

"Do you know another story?" Jux asked.

Sadima nodded. She told them about the ancient circles of stacked, rounded stones that lay in the fields around Ferne, where she had grown up—and the odd people who had lived there when the circles were upright and whole, each stone squared with perfect edges.

"How can anyone not leave footprints?" Jux asked when she finished.

She shook her head. "I don't know. The stories say they could fly, too. Higher than birds." That made them all laugh a little. The sound skittered over the dark walls and made the lanterns seem brighter.

"How'd the stones get to be round?" Jux asked.

"Rain," she said. "A thousand years of rain." And she thought about the weather-worn steps cut into the stone, zigzagging up the cliff face.

"Rain can't wear down rocks," one of the other boys said. Sadima looked at him. His eyes were shaped like pumpkin seeds, and his skin was dark as strong tea. Wherever he had been born, his parents had lost him or left him in Limòri to live on the streets however he could.

"I think it can," she said. "Just very slowly."

He met her eyes for the first time. "Do you know my mother?"

Sadima shook her head. "I wish I did. She must be very beautiful."

He looked down at his hands.

"What's your name?" she asked him.

He answered, without looking up. "Jess."

The pale boy sat up straighter. "Wren. My name is Wren. Like the bird."

"Hello, Jess," Sadima said. Then she smiled at the pale boy. "And Wren."

Then, before anyone else could speak, Franklin came in, his back bent beneath two heavy sacks. He had cheese this morning, and apples. Apples? He had not found apples in Market Square, not this time of year. Had he robbed some royal family's root cellar? Sadima watched the boys eat without arguing, their faces a little brighter than before.

She walked back to her chamber with Franklin. He was tired as always, dragging his feet. She wanted to talk to him about the boys, her long walks looking for a way out, about how much she loved him, but she didn't. She would wait. They talked a moment about nothing and kissed. Then he turned to leave, and she sat down before her makeshift desk.

"Sadima?" She glanced up to see Franklin still standing in the entrance, a weary sadness in his eyes. "Somiss says he thinks the Gypsy book is a fake," he whispered. "That it's something his father paid them to give us, that it's full of symbols that don't mean anything."

Sadima caught her breath. Was that possible? Then she shook her head. It didn't make sense. "Why would Somiss's father pay to have him use a fake book, then burn down the building we were living in too? If he was going to kill us all, why—"

"It's complicated," Franklin whispered. "Somiss thinks his uncles probably convinced his father to talk to the Eridians after Somiss had the book and—"

"I have to work now," Sadima interrupted him. "I am a little behind." The truth was she didn't care if Somiss lived or died. She didn't care about the Gypsy book or the king's secret library or any of the rest of it. None of it mattered to her. She just wanted to leave and take Franklin and the boys with her.

Franklin was staring at her, and this time she hoped he had heard her thoughts. He exhaled, a long, sad breath. Then he shuffled out, on his way to sleep.

Sadima refused to look up, to call out to him. And she did not go to whisper the song for long life over him after enough time had passed for him to be asleep. Instead she worked furiously and copied the whole stack of papers, ignoring her cramped hand.

Only then did she stand, picking up her lantern. She walked down the main passageway, tiptoeing past the turnoff to Somiss's chamber. Then she turned at random, and built a cairn to mark the way back before she went on. Before long she made another turn, building a second cairn. Then she went on, building cairns in wedge shapes that would point the way to her little chamber, or, if she found a way out, the way to freedom.

"I wish you could come with me," she whispered, pretending that Franklin could hear her. "This would be much less scary." She walked on, keeping to the same passage because it was wide and the walls were a little smoother— maybe it actually led somewhere. "If you *were* here," she whispered, "we could talk in our real voices again, like we did in Limòri when Somiss wasn't around."

Sadima kept walking and found herself whispering fast, in time to her long stride. At first she told Franklin how much she loved him and what it had meant to her to have had a reason to leave the farm, to leave her father's melancholy and anger behind, to be with someone who didn't think she was crazy, pretending she could feel what animals felt. "I want to save your life the way you saved mine," she whispered.

And then she started talking about Somiss, telling the cold, deaf stone how much she hated him for his cruelty to Franklin when they were boys, for beating him and bullying him until he couldn't think about anything except making sure Somiss didn't get angry. She hated Somiss's father, too, and all the royal family, for letting children starve in Limòri's streets while they planned entertainments and voyages and parades and their own children grew into monsters.

Sadima was walking faster and faster and might have begun to run, but a rock rolled beneath her foot and she fell, wrenching her ankle and barely hanging on to her lantern.

For a long moment she just sat still, her chest rising and falling in time with her heartbeat. Then she set the lantern down very carefully. How could she do something so stupid? If it had broken, if she had been without light, she would never have found her way back. She took three long, deep breaths and noticed that the air smelled different— fresher—almost like she was standing outside. Could there be an opening in the stone?

Sadima picked up her lantern and went forward very carefully. The ground was littered with rocks. Wary, going slow, she stopped to build cairns every ten steps, the reach of her lantern's light. Beyond the fifth cairn, she could no longer see the opposite wall or the ceiling, not even with her lantern held high. Was she in a cavern now?

Three cairns later she saw a glimmer, a shine, when she lifted her lantern high. She threw a small stone as hard as she could—and heard a splash. Water? She slowed her step even more, advancing until she stood within an arm's length of the water's edge. It looked black in the small circle of lantern light, infinitely calm, still and silent, a dark mirror.

Sadima threw a second stone—a bigger one—as far as

she could. She heard animals waken—the way she had always heard animals, not with her ears but somewhere between her heart and mind. And as sorry as she was to have disturbed them, she was so glad to feel the startled thoughts of something small and wet. A toad? Yes. And a newt, unhappy and astounded that water was rippling into its pebbled bed. There was a stirring overhead. Bats woke just enough to wonder if the clumsy intruder was in the water or along the shoreline. They did not worry either way. The water would drown anything that did not belong here, and the shore was both far away and far below.

Sadima smiled. So the lake was big—maybe really big—and at least part of the chamber had a high ceiling. For an instant she wondered if Franklin would risk coming here with her. They could sit and eat, then swim—like sweethearts did, back in Ferne. A picnic without sun or breeze, but a picnic nonetheless. Somiss would never find them here. Sadima blushed at the thoughts that followed that one.

She set down her lantern and inhaled the scent of wet stone, then knelt and put one hand in the water. It was cool, and when she brought it to her lips, it smelled and tasted sweet. If there was water here, it came from somewhere outside the cliffs. And the air was fresher. Maybe she was close to finding another way out?

Sadima held very still, realizing that neither Somiss nor Franklin was likely to find this place for a long, long time. She could start making extra copies of each song, and she could hide them here somewhere. With a set of the corrected songs, and the early copies she had buried, they could have a real school somewhere. She drank another mouthful of the water, then stood up. She felt odd, light-headed, then recognized the feeling.

Hope.

~ 14 ~

When the wizard pounded on the door, I sat up in the darkness and shoved the blanket back the way I always did, then sucked in a breath, cradling my hands. "Can you light your lamp?" I whispered to Gerrard. And then I remembered. Or had it been a dream?

I used the back of my hand to find my striker and forced myself to grip it hard enough to make it work. My hands were shaking as the flame rose and started smoking. The light revealed the empty space where Gerrard's desk and bed had been.

The wizard pounded again, louder. I used the slops bucket, feeling unbalanced by the empty side of the room, as though the floor slanted away from me. I touched the spigot and water rushed into the basin. Trembling, I rinsed my hands. I could smell my own sweat. I stank. How long had it been since I had washed? How many days had passed since Somiss had burned our hands? My eyes filled with tears and it made them sting. I was sick of hurting.

The wizard pounded again. "Coming!" I shouted.

Then I went to my bed and fished the little book out of the covers. Holding it between my wrists, I turned in a slow circle. Should I hide it? No. Why pretend it was mine when it wasn't? But where should I put it? Lay it on the floor on Gerrard's side of the room? What if he had somehow smuggled it in here? Maybe it was the pronunciation guide for the songs? If he had hidden it in my bed to help me . . . ?

I tried to think. Maybe they had just separated us because they thought we might be cheating. Other schools did that, all the time. And if that was it, he would want the book back—and I wanted to read whatever was in it when I could. Or maybe that was the test. And if I didn't read it—

The wizard pounded once more.

"I'm *coming*!" Sweating, I finally laid the book on the floor, an arm's length past the door hinges, in the darkest shadows of the room. Probably the dumbest thing to do, but there *wasn't* anywhere to hide it except my bed or my desk, and I was afraid to have them find it in my things. If they looked. If they cared.

When the pounding started again, I padded my palm with a handful of my robe and reached to open the door. Maybe this time it would be Somiss, and I could stop being scared once and for all.

But it wasn't. The wizard was frowning and when he walked away, I followed him. I raised my hands to my chest, and it helped a little. Then I put my arms up, straight over my head. It was wonderful, the relief that brought.

At the first turn, I started building the sentence that would get me back to the room. The wizard turned again, then again, then four more times, and then the tunnel slanted gently upward. Jux's class, then? After a few min-utes, the air changed, and I was certain even before we got to the steep switchback passages.

So. Was Jux going to be my executioner, or one of his snakes? Or the bear? Whatever he had planned for me, I felt my heart lift a little, in a ridiculous way. I just hoped it was daytime outside. Maybe I would at least see sunshine one last time, through the slits in the stone above Jux's forest.

I had fallen a few paces behind, and I ran to catch up before the first hairpin turn of the steep tunnel. With every step, the air smelled better—and I pulled in long, delicious breaths as I always did on the way to Jux's classes. Even after most of us had made soap, the tunnels below had heavy, stale air, and our room had always smelled from the slops bucket. The acrid fog of lamp smoke was just the newest torture.

By the time we were at the top, I was out of breath and still holding my hands above my head to soften the throb-bing. "Thank you," I said, without meaning to. The wizard had already turned and was walking away. He glanced back at me, and then almost ran down the slope.

I smiled, watching him. Why had I spoken to him? I wasn't sure. Maybe because this might be the last day of my life? When my father had brought me here, I had thought over and over about jumping out of the carriage, just to die instantly, to be free of him. Now I just wanted to die and be free of the Limòri Academy. Fast, slow, it wouldn't matter—and it wasn't my decision.

I stared at the round copper door. Had I ever been the one to open it? The handle was a silver half moon. I didn't recall that. Bending closer, I saw that its edges were sharp as a hunting knife. I exhaled and sat down, cross-legged, thinking. I could probably gather up my robe and wrap my hand well enough. Any pressure would hurt, but I was pretty sure I could open it without cutting myself. But was that what they wanted me to do? It seemed too simple.

Or maybe they wanted a simple answer this time. Jux had scolded me once for figuring out an elaborate thought-moving process to keep ants from eating honey. That was the assignment; keep them off the honey. When Jux had come back to see what I had done, he just dropped a handful of dirt on it and told me not to waste magic. I stood up and padded my hand as well as I could and tried to ignore my thoughts. They were getting louder.

Jux's classes were almost always harrowing. Maybe I could run back down the tunnel, all the way to the food hall, then past it. I could hide in the little chamber where I had hidden food during the first year. I had felt so safe there—

"Stop it." I said aloud. "They knew where you were."

And they had known I was hoarding food, too, because when I finally found the courage to try to help the starving boys, the food was gone. I had never been safe in the little chamber. I wouldn't be now. Not there, not anywhere.

I looked at the door.

"Just go in," I said. Then I shook my head. "And stop talking to yourself."

Awkward, wincing, I unwound the robe from my hand and wrapped it again, a little tighter. I pulled the door handle slowly, carefully, scared that the blade might be so sharp that it would slice the fabric and my hand before I could react. The door was heavy, but I got it open and ducked through, then unwound the cloth. When it fell free I looked up, and for a sickening instant I was bent almost double, staring over the edge of a cliff at the ground far below.

I staggered backward, startled shitless, breathing in gasps. Where was the forest? Nothing looked like it had before. The gentle hillside was gone. All the crazy glass enclosures where Jux had kept his animals were gone. Shaking, I looked over the edge again. The land just dropped off. The trees at the foot of the cliff looked like toys. If I had taken one more step, I would have been dead. I had survived starvation, fear, loneliness, and constant exhaustion, just to take one unlucky step and die? This was how the wizards picked which one of us would graduate? Why? Were they all crazy?

From the day Sadima found the lake, she felt its presence. The water lay dark and sweet, motionless inside her. When she began to suffocate from her fear or her anger, she reminded herself that it was there, waiting for her. Then she could go on with her work. And it *was* her work now.

She began making double copies of the songs she didn't recognize and hid them in the deep shadows of her chamber, beneath the stack of her ragged clothing. When she had three or four, she walked to the lake and hid them on a flat-topped stone she had found, covering them with stones she had washed in the lake.

Every time she added to the pile, her heart was lifted. It made her so happy to be doing something *real*. She longed to tell Franklin, to take his hands and pull him along through the passages and show him what she was doing. She wanted to make him smile the way her brother had when Laran had taken his hands at Winterfeast, laughing, pulling him into the celebration dance.

Usually Sadima brought her papers to the lake, then hurried back. But sometimes she stayed awhile. She found an egg-shaped boulder as tall as she was—with a flat niche where her lantern could perch, safe and high enough to see from all sides. She began to walk along the edge of the water, both in the dark and carrying her lantern, always listening with her heart and mind for any creature that she might harm. Or that might harm her.

As she got to know the toad, the bats, and the few salamanders, she learned that none had been born there. The bats had been fleeing a storm. There was a crack in the stone somewhere that they squeezed through to come and go. The toad and the salamanders had all been pushed along by rain somehow. She felt them sliding over the rock, tumbled along in shallow water, against their will. Only the bats knew how to get back out. Sadima loved having animal friends again. Once they came to know her, they understood that she meant them no harm.

She began wading, leaving her striker beside her lantern. The water was cool, but not cold. She went up to her ankles at first, then her knees, the hem of her skirt lifted in both hands. The bottom sloped very gradually for a long way out. She had no fear of the water—it was the darkness that stopped her from swimming. She could see the amber glow of her lantern on the rock, but she couldn't see more than a hand's span in front of her face.

Then one day she slipped and fell sideways in the shallows. Even though she had known, had often scraped her bare feet on the stone bottom, it was still odd to feel solid rock beneath her instead of mud or river sand. She stood up dripping, her dress soaked almost to her shoulders.

She pulled it off and wrung it out, then waded ashore to drape it over another boulder, this one as big as a plow horse.

She knew her dress would not dry quickly in this sunless place, and if by chance she encountered Somiss on the way back, he might notice her wet clothing. She stood naked beside her lantern, listening to the bats' sleepy complaints, staring at the dark, still water for a long time before she touched the cloth again. It was still wet.

Walking slowly, her hands out from her sides for balance, she waded back in, feeling the water deepen bit by bit, rising on her thighs, covering her bare belly, then her breasts. She bent her knees and ducked beneath the water, then swam.

Giddy with the rush of the cool water across her skin, her hair floating behind her, tickling her back, Sadima swam in a big, lazy arc, keeping her lantern in sight. She stopped and treaded water, thinking about Micah and the creek where he had taught her to swim. As the water streamed between her legs, her fingers, her toes, she tipped her head back and laughed.

The sudden sound of her own voice was so out of place

in the silence that it jarred her into swimming to the shallows, then wading out, shivering. She stayed ashore, swinging her dress over her head to dry it faster, humming at first, then singing louder and louder until the sound of her own voice stopped scaring her.

After that, Sadima worked faster than she ever had to finish her day's work long before Franklin woke every evening. On her way to the lake—once she had tiptoed past Somiss's corridor—she explored at least one new passageway each day. One or two were long and straight, and dead-ended in a wall of black stone. Most branched off, curved, seemed endless. So time after time, she ended up retracing her steps, afraid she would lose her way if she went on. None of the passages smelled of fresh air or pine trees, or gave any other sign of leading her out of the cliffs.

Once she was at the lake, she swam sometimes, or just stood knee-deep in the water, her dress hem lifted with one hand, her eyes closed, breathing slowly, feeling safe from Somiss, from everything. Hidden. Unfindable.

One day she decided to walk the shoreline as far as she could, to get some idea of how big the lake was. She began by building a big cairn close to the water, directly across from the stone where she always set her lantern. Then she started off, walking slowly inside the little globe of light her lantern cast. Beyond that light was endless darkness. It felt strange to leave the little bit of the shoreline she had come to know. The silence was complete but for the sound of her bare feet on the stones—an eerie clicking, soft and uneven—and her own breathing.

Twice she stopped, wondering how far above her head the stone ceiling was. She listened for the bats, but they were gone, or sound asleep. She stretched up, holding her lantern as high as she could. Then she set it down and jumped, raking at the empty darkness with her fingers. She tossed a stone almost straight up. It didn't hit anything before it fell.

She moved a few steps away from her lantern, to see if there was light coming from a crevice or a passage that opened to the outside. Then she walked a few more steps. Had the people who had carved the passageways and the shelves in Somiss's chamber known about this lake? Had the magicians, if ever they were real? If they had, they would have carried their water from here—to avoid being seen outside the cliffs, to keep from being discovered and attacked.

A tiny rattling of pebbles made Sadima fetch her lantern, then lift it, holding her breath to listen. She was sure it was a salamander or some other sleepy, small creature. But there were no images, no feelings in the air at all. What else could have made the sound? There was no wind here, no rain.

Sadima was suddenly uneasy, feeling the cool touch of the enveloping darkness that began at her skin and went on forever. She veered off to her right, building little cairns every ten steps, until she had made her way around the place where, somehow, pebbles had rattled without anything living touching them. And she kept walking.

After four more cairns, she came to a wall of dark stone.

She walked along it and found an arched opening—a passage like all the others. Still marking her way, she went into the tunnel, intending to go just far enough to see if others intersected it, then start back to her chamber.

But the passageway was different from the ones she was used to. It was straight, the floor was smoother, with only a few loose stones, and it led uphill, gradually at first, then more steeply. The air was fresher and Sadima kept going, excited, hoping to find a gap in the rock where the sun shone through. But when the passage leveled out again, she slowed. She had already been gone a long time. If Somiss or Franklin tried to find her and couldn't . . .

She turned to go back, then stopped, startled by a faint sound that seemed to come from the rock itself. Her skin prickled; she kept walking, but she could still hear it, coming from behind her now. A voice? She turned, walking uphill again, silent and tense. The sound became even fainter, then silenced.

Doubling back, taking smaller steps, she heard it again and stopped where the muted voice seemed to drift out of the stone. She lifted her lantern high, then lowered it to knee-level three times before she realized that what looked like a shadow was a hole where the wall should have met the floor. When she crouched and peered into the dark opening, the voice got a little louder. She drew in a breath. Somiss. She recognized the cadence. He was reciting one of the Gypsy songs Rinka had taught her—the one for holding close loved ones who had died.

Sadima bent to hear better. Could there be holes in

the stone—rain-worn passages or cracks—that carried his voice this far from his chamber? What else could it be? She crawled through the low, narrow entrance, her lantern held before her in her right hand, the stone scraping her back. She could only half stand inside the little chamber, but Somiss's voice was a little louder here.

Sadima turned in a circle, lifting her lantern, running her free hand over the stone. She couldn't see any openings, but there had to be one. She set her lantern on the floor and moved along the base of the wall, using both hands to search the deep shadows. She was more than halfway around when her fingertips found the gap. She brought her lantern closer. There. It was a narrow, arched opening. She measured, using her hand and forearm as a height-stick. She could get her lantern through without tipping it far enough to risk putting it out. Barely. She crouched to listen. Somiss's voice was louder, more distinct—but it was still impossible to understand more than a word here and there.

Sadima rocked back on her heels and thought about it. Somiss's chamber was somewhere below her, and far away. This was some accident of the stone and the way sound carried, like the echoes in the valley back in Ferne. There was no danger that Somiss would be able to see her lantern light. But he might be able to hear her. She would have to be careful.

She looked again. She could fit, but she would have to lie flat and wriggle forward. And she would have to either push her lantern through first, or set it as close as she could to one side in this chamber, crawl into complete darkness, and reach back to get it once she was through—if there was enough room on the other side *to* turn back. Either way was terrifying.

Sadima finally set her lantern to the side, then crept, hands first, far enough through the gap to pat every inch of the stone that she could reach. The passage, wide or narrow, high or low—she couldn't tell—was steeply slanted. But there was a smooth, perfectly flat place just to the right of the opening. Had it been carved that way as a lantern-perch?

Shivering, she pushed herself back out, then passed the lantern through, slowly, so scared that she had to stop twice to breathe for a moment and steady her hands. Once her lantern was steady on the flat rock, it took all her courage to let go of it. Then she lay on her stomach again and belly-crawled forward, her chin brushing the stone until she had her torso through the low-arched gap. For a few seconds she rested, craning her head back. Her lantern's light fell in a circle that touched the far wall. The passageway was narrow.

When she was finally through the arched opening and lifted her lantern, Sadima was careful not to make a sound. Inexplicably, Somiss's voice was coming from above her now. Hesitating, scared, she started up the sharp incline. It wasn't a passageway, not like the others, anyway. It got narrower and narrower as she went. At the top, she stopped and stared at an ornate silver grate. She could feel the constant, soft passage of air. The shaft's purpose was clear. It had been built to carry fresh air into the tunnels. Maybe there were a hundred like it—or maybe it was the only one.

She leaned forward and touched the silver grate. It was more finely wrought than anything she had ever seen, so beautiful that it took her a moment to realize that she could make out every word Somiss was saying.

There was a sudden silence. Sadima waited, sure Somiss would begin to recite again soon—he had practiced for hours at a time, back in Limòri, before the fire. Sadima swallowed. Would this be the day he came looking for her? A sheen of sweat dampened her forehead.

The silence went on.

Sadima fled back down the steep incline. She skinned her chin wriggling out of the vent shaft and back into the little chamber. She hurried back down the long tunnel, slowing only to make her way around the lake. Then she followed her cairns. She forced herself to pause before Somiss's passageway, stilling her breathing, her heart, her fear—and she heard him reciting.

Back in her chamber, Sadima found herself dancing, happy. The vent shaft was even safer than the lake. Neither Franklin nor Somiss could fit through the opening into the little cavern. No man could. Not a thief, not a king's guard. And even if they somehow managed that, they could never fit through the hole she'd had to drag herself through on her belly. As soon as she could, she would bring in what she had buried in the woods. And she would carry her new copies of the songs up there too. All her secrets would be safe.

— 16 —

I backed up, then turned to leave, but nothing was there: No wall, no copper door. There were pine barrens as far as I could see. A cliff with two days' journey of wasteland beyond it? How? Could magicians make *land*? Where had the stone wall gone?

The sun was muted, but it was almost bright. Almost. I looked up, trying to see where it was coming in, but I couldn't, even without the trees. The sky was blue. Blue like any summer sky I had ever seen.

A buffeting wind hit me. I lost my balance and stumbled backward, my hands locked against my chest, sitting down so hard my teeth clacked. I heard a hawk's cry and looked up, then stood up and turned in a circle, hoping, stupidly, that the door would still be somewhere nearby. A flash of red caught my eye. A kite? And there was a boy—

Gerrard?

He was out of shouting distance and facing away from me, flying the kite. I was so glad to see him. If he was still taking Jux's classes, then—

I watched as a gust of wind lifted him off his feet and set him down again. I winced, imagining how much it must be hurting his hands, waiting for him to drop the string. But he didn't. When the wind ebbed, he ran backward, dragging the kite with him, fighting it, trying to get farther away from the edge. I felt clammy, almost sick. Maybe this wasn't Jux's class. Maybe this was Gerrard's punishment for the book. And mine was to watch him get dragged toward the cliff, a pace or two at a time, until he finally fell?

The kite jerked him upward again, his feet leaving the dark stone. The instant the wind eased and the kite came down, he ran backward, gaining every bit of distance he could before the force of the wind lifted him again. I watched as it happened twice more. And it took me all that time to realize that Gerrard wasn't holding the kite string. He was tied to it. I glanced around. There were rocks everywhere. I could find a small, sharp-edged one, pad my hand again, and cut him loose. And our combined weight—

It was only then, when I tried to stand up to go help him, that I realized my own hands were bound. I turned, scared, and the next gust came. A mound of gritty pine needles scattered on the stone in front of me and I saw a yellow kite, dirty from being buried, skittering along the ground when the wind got beneath it. A stronger gust came, and the kite lifted a little more. I felt the tug on my wrists.

I could step on the kite string, I thought, and break it. But it wasn't string. It was a stout, woven flax cord, fastened to the rope that bound my wrists together. The knots were big, complex, impossible. So I just stumbled backward, pulling hard, and the kite lay on the ground again.

In the sudden stillness, I strained at the rope, trying to loosen the knot, even a little, but the wind came again, and this time when I jerked on the cord, it only kept the kite steady so it rose again. The next gust lifted it higher. The one after that dragged me forward—pulling much harder than any kite should have been able to.

I braced for the next gust, setting my feet, my knees. I was so rigid that I toppled straight onto my face and the kite dragged me over the ground for a few paces. There was a lull between gusts. I managed to get up and stagger backward. The scabs had been rubbed off my right palm, and the rope shackles were slick with blood. The wind was getting stronger. When the next roaring gust hit, I pitched forward again. This time I managed to keep my hands and head up, but it still moved me a few paces toward the edge.

When the next buffeting wind came, I screamed and raised my hands above my head to shake my fists. I felt myself leave the ground and closed my eyes until I felt the stone beneath my feet again. Then I scuttled backward, away from the edge, shaking, breathing hard.

The next gust came almost immediately, and it picked

me up again. I twisted to look at Gerrard. He was farther back now—much farther. He was moving *away* from the cliff's edge. How? He had let the wind pick him up too, but when it ebbed, and I fell, I saw him land like a cat, turn, and sprint—with his hands up to keep the rope out of his way. He ran like a madman on his long, skinny legs, hands high, running forward instead of scrambling backward. Of course.

I tried it his way and gained more ground that time and the next, and the one after that. I kept glancing at Gerrard. If our strength held, we might both get far back enough to find a sharp stone or some other way to cut each other free. If I got loose first, I would help him.

When the wind came again, I shouted at him—not words, I knew he would never be able to understand anything above the screaming wind—just a loud whooping sound. I wanted him to know there was hope, I guess. Or to convince myself.

Gerrard yanked at his kite cord, pivoting around toward me—and I was sure in that instant that he hadn't seen me before, that he had been too focused on staying alive. I shouted again, and he ran toward me after the next gust. I angled my sprint toward him. I was glad not to be alone. And if this was my last day alive, I was glad to be here, in the wind and the sunlight with Gerrard, instead of starving to death alone in the stinking tunnels.

The wind got even stronger. We were in the air longer, sailing toward the cliff's edge five and six paces at a time. And the moments we had to run back seemed fewer. Still, every time the wind paused, we were a few steps closer to each other and only a little closer to the edge of the cliff.

The cord was grinding across my left palm because of the angle now, tearing the scabs sideways. I was stupid with the pain, gasping in long breaths, managing only to land, run, and wait to do it again. So when Gerrard got close enough to run up to me, I was expecting an awkward embrace, some kind of good-bye.

But instead of a farewell, he ducked under my kite cord and then ran behind me, his arms up, passing his cord over mine. "Tangle them!" he screamed at me as he veered off at an angle, forcing the cross in the lines to skid upward.

I ran backward, widening the distance between us to force the twist even higher. Then I knelt after the next gust; he managed to run the circle a second time before the wind hit us again. I glanced toward the cliff. We were drifting closer to the edge.

"Just run back next time!" I shouted at him as the wind rose.

He nodded, and we used the break between the next two gusts to regain most of the distance we had lost. Overhead, the kites began to circle each other. We increased the angle again, widening the space between us. The next gust barely pulled me forward. The kites began to spin faster and faster, slanting into the wind, dropping lower and lower until they fell out of sight, over the cliff. I began to cry, smiling, shaking. Gerrard looked at me and grinned. The wind stopped.

It took us a long time to find an outcropping of rock with a sharp enough edge to cut the ropes. It hurt so much to saw the rope back and forth over the stone that I felt half-dizzy. But I managed it, and when I looked up, Gerrard was waiting for me. He looked into my face and said, "Don't be afraid." Then he pointed up into one of the scrub pines. I saw a sack hanging an arm's length above our heads.

Gerrard climbed slowly, bracing himself with legs and shoulders, guarding his hands. And when he came back down, the cloth clenched between his teeth, I could smell warm bread. He broke it in half, and I ignored the pain in my hands and ate it like a wolf, like a skinny stray dog on a South End dock, tasting my own blood, or maybe his. At first my stomach writhed, then I felt strength come back into my limbs. I closed my eyes, so grateful I was afraid I might cry again.

And then I heard a wizard pounding on the door. I sat up and rubbed my eyes. My hands hurt and I was sure I had torn the scabs on the blanket—then I remembered. But I could hear Gerrard pissing in the darkness, and I closed my eyes.

So it had all been a dream. All of it.

I gritted my teeth. Gerrard had his back to me, lighting his lamp. The wizard outside the door pounded again. Furious, I hit my desk with a loose fist as I turned, opening my mouth to yell that we couldn't go any faster. Stupid, stupid, *stupid*. Gulping air like a fish in a net, I stared at my own hands in the lamplight. My palms looked like raw meat. All the scabs were gone. And the rope burns on my wrists were perfect, bloody circles.

Every morning Sadima gave copying lessons to Jux and Mabiki. Since she had begun telling stories, Wren and Jess had started trying again. The other boys sat up straight when she came, then waited quietly for the lessons to end and the tale to begin. She always smiled at all of them and said good morning. Sometimes even the six boys who had never spoken to her smiled when they saw her.

Sadima had named the orphan boy in the story Micah, after her brother, and each day she made up another tale about him, the kingdom, and the beautiful girl named Laran who became his friend. And every day she stopped the story at a place that gave the boys something to wonder about. When she walked away, they were usually talking, arguing about what would happen next. If she looked in on them before she went to the vent shaft, they weren't always sleeping. Sometimes they were talking or playing a game. Maybe, by the time the weather turned, they would all be able to recover themselves.

Franklin came and went. They kissed and stood close, and when he wasn't exhausted, she rested her head on his chest and listened to his heart beating and timed her breaths with his. But they talked less—mostly because she had stopped pressing him to help the boys. He was doing what he could for now, and the stories were helping. Franklin would do his part soon enough, she reminded herself. The boys would be far more likely to trust a man to lead them safely away from the cliffs.

She had asked Franklin for more quills and ink. He hadn't questioned her. From every ream of paper she used, she put aside twenty or thirty sheets and carried them to the vent shaft. And she told Franklin a lie—that she had dropped her lantern and broken it, stumbling over a rock on her way to her chamber. Again, he didn't question her. She told herself that he would forgive her the small lies when she explained that they really could leave, that they could have a life together. When she went to the vent shaft, Sadima lit her old lantern and left the new one burning in her chamber, papers arranged as though her work had been interrupted, not stopped.

Sadima loved sitting next to the silver grate on her folded shawl, careful not to make a sound, listening to Somiss recite. When he paused, she sharpened her quills and swirled her ink pot. Because he was practicing, he read the same song a number of times. She was already familiar with most of his transliterations, so it was easy to manage a new copy—including all his newest revisions—before he was finished.

One day she recognized the song the beekeeper had said was for bellyaches—it was one she had memorized, then repeated to Somiss, so she knew it well. It hadn't been in her stack of papers to copy in a long time. And as Somiss began to recite, she was amazed how many changes he had made. When he was finished, she reread it and stood up, furious.

In Limòri he had switched the real song for long life with a fake. She hated him for it, but at least it made sense. He wanted to live longer than anyone else. And she had known for a long time that he was hiding new work in the smoky, soiled copies Franklin brought her every day. But there were a dozen new changes in this one, not a few. Why would he hide his progress on a song for *bellyaches*? It had to mean he was hiding *everything*.

Sadima paced silently down the vent shaft, then turned back and went uphill again. This meant that most of the double copies she had made were worthless. Of course. Somiss had told Franklin he wasn't making much progress, that the songs were impossible to translate, that the Gypsy book wasn't helping, had turned out to be a fake. He had been fooling both of them.

Sadima sat down when Somiss began to recite again. She would stop making extra copies of the papers Somiss had Franklin bring to her chamber. Instead, she would make three copies of everything she heard him recite here—one for the Eridians, to teach and share someday, one for herself and Franklin to take when they left, and one copy to leave here, in the vent shaft, safe and dry, like the seed barley her father had stored each year—always more than they would need, just in case.

A few days later Somiss was reciting the same sentence over and over, changing the pronunciation only slightly, and Sadima picked up a stack of her copies to leaf through to see if he had recited the same song recently. She scanned the first twenty or so words of each one, looking for a match, and she noticed something else.

There was a little string of words in all of the first five songs she looked at. She looked at five more and saw the words in every one of them: *Nikamava resporet telan.* Sometimes the phrase was near the beginning, sometimes elsewhere, but it was always there. Were there other repeated words she hadn't noticed?

When Somiss began reciting again, Sadima continued copying. Whatever the words meant, it had to be important. She wrote quickly, keeping up, until Somiss finished the song. Then she laid down her quill and waved the paper to help it dry faster. Did Somiss know what the words meant? He would never tell her, or Franklin. It wouldn't matter. They would have the rest of their lives to figure everything out.

As the days passed, knowing that the songs she was copying in her chamber were almost certainly falsified, it became very hard for Sadima to make herself work as carefully as she always had. But she knew she had to. There might be only one real song out of every fifty that she copied, but Somiss would notice if she got careless. Then he might begin to check on her, begin to notice what she was doing. He might set Jux and Mabiki to work—and that was the last thing she wanted.

Sadima continued to hide both her uneasiness and her hope from Franklin. When they talked, she didn't bring up anything that would upset him. They kissed and whispered as they always had, and she dreamed about the day they would be together and free from Somiss. Until then, she knew she had to keep her secrets. She would tell him about the shaft, the duplicate sets of papers, and everything she had buried in the woods, all at once.

Sitting at her crate-desk, she daydreamed about their escape, walking at night so they wouldn't be seen, finding barns and ditches and plum thickets so they could sleep, hidden, by day. She imagined, over and over, using the coppers she had saved to buy a little farm.

She was daydreaming when she noticed the silence. She looked up sharply, as if it had called out to her. And once she had noticed it, she couldn't stop. The quiet was so complete she could almost *hear* it; it filled the chamber like water poured into a cup. She longed for the sound of wind in trees, birds chittering, rain, voices. And then she heard the thrumming sound again. It was louder this time and it unnerved her. She could almost feel it seeping into her skin, sliding along her bones.

Sadima stood up, got her old lantern from its hiding

place, and almost ran to the lake. Hearing the bats and the salamanders with their complaints and worries soothed her. She swam. And by the time she went to the vent shaft, she felt hopeful again, and calm.

But the thrumming came back the next morning when she was telling the boys a story. She ended the tale as quickly as she could, forced her mouth into a smile, then snatched up her lantern and walked toward her chamber. She meant to go whisper the song for long life over Franklin before she began work. Instead she stopped in front of her own chamber and turned around. It didn't matter which way she walked. The thrumming was getting louder.

She went back to the main passageway and turned toward the big cavern, retracing her steps. She held her lantern low, draping her shawl to shade it, acutely aware of the sound in the stone under her feet. When she got close to the big cavern, she stopped and blew out her lantern, then went on, through the arched entrance. She turned left, walking along the wall, glancing across the cavern at the boys in the cage. They had not heard her. None of them looked up.

At the mouth of the narrow entrance tunnel she hesitated, but only for an instant. She did not slow down until she could feel the chill and hear the air rushing through the pines. She stood at the end of the passageway almost outside—obeying Somiss's edict by a finger's length. She was giddy, shivering, breathing in the scent of the forest and the earthy smell of wet spring snow. The wind topped the trees, and the thick tangle of leafless vines overhead rattled against the cliff face.

Sadima heard sparrows and nuthatches waking up, cheered because they had found grubs in the pine bark. It was all she could do to make herself go back up the passageway. But she did. She didn't tell Franklin what she had done, and she promised herself that she would never do it again. But she knew she would.

~ 18 ~

Keeping track of the turns was hard because I was so uneasy, my stomach tight. I took deep, long breaths and it didn't help; what would Somiss do if I threw up in his class? I had vomited on the docks once, with my father. He had never taken me back there. Only Aben. I swallowed over and over, trying not to think about my father or my brother.

Gerrard and I were the first ones to arrive for class. We went in and sat down. I was clammy and sick, hoping we would not be alone when Somiss came. But he appeared moments later. He didn't bother to look at us. He was pre-occupied with something in his right hand. Abruptly he tossed it straight upward, then looked away. Whatever it was, it didn't fall to the floor.

The chair was made from some dark strong-scented wood this time, carved to look like a kneeling monster, scaled, hideous, its tail wrapped around the chair legs. It looked as real as the snakes had, and the smell was overpowering. Somiss was staring at nothing, stroking the carved monster as though it were alive and he was soothing it.

I looked aside, breathing through my mouth, hoping the nausea would subside. Levin and Jordan came in next, and I saw each of them glance at me, then glance again. Was I that pale? Luke came in, then Will. He raised his eyebrows a little, just enough for me to see. I lifted the corners of my mouth to let him know I was all right. Or I would be, anyway.

"You," Somiss said, pointing at Will the instant he sat down.

Will rocked back and forth, trying to straighten his robe without bending his fingers much. Then he closed his eyes and recited. He missed a dozen words. I looked away. He was crying.

Somiss pointed at Jordan. He stared at the floor as he spoke, and he made no mistakes. Once he was finished, he didn't look up until Somiss had pointed at me. When I recited, Somiss interrupted me twice in his rusty-hinge voice. Somehow I was able to start where he stopped me, and go on, instead of starting over. He was looking at me when I glanced up at the end; then he gestured at Gerrard.

As Gerrard began to recite, I was happy. Only two words

wrong. Shaky and sick, I had almost passed. Gerrard *did* pass, and I hated him for his steady voice and his straight back. I hated everything about him for about ten heart-beats. Then I reminded myself that he had saved my life. I would never have thought of tangling the kites. Luke and Levin missed one word each and then it was over. When we stood up to leave, I followed Gerrard out into the corridor.

I waited until we were back inside our stinking, smoky room. "What happened?" I whispered as I closed the door. "How did we get back here?"

He looked puzzled. And as much as it hurt to close my fingers on anything, I reached out and yanked up his sleeve to see his wrist. Then I leaned so close my nose nearly touched his. "Dreams don't cause rope burns. Who put the bread where you could find it? Jux?"

Gerrard exhaled. But he did not speak. His eyes were steady, calm, infuriating. I knew I would pass out from the pain if I hit him. Or vomit. I also knew he could beat the shit out of me. I thought about driving my shoulder into his gut anyway, then didn't because I was afraid I would fall and hurt my hands if he stepped back. And he probably would. My father had paid for boxing tutors, young men from house-servant families. Gerrard said he had learned to fight for food on Limòri's docks, to stay alive—probably a much better prep course for the Limòri Academy, if it was true. When I looked up, Gerrard was watching me.

"Where did you get the book?" I asked him.

He didn't answer me.

"What's in it?"

His eyes widened.

I hesitated, then told the truth. "I was afraid to read it. I thought maybe they had killed you for having it."

Gerrard shrugged and sat cross-legged on his cot.

I stared at his back. "Where were you last night? Your *bed* was gone."

He shook his head. "None of that matters." Then he cleared his throat twice. I turned and picked up my book. As he recited, pronouncing every word perfectly, I read along with him, beginning to memorize the next song. I studied until the lamp soot was more than I could bear, then I went to sleep.

And things just went on. The pain in my hands was almost unbearable for two days—if two of Somiss's classes and two stints of studying and sleeping added up to two days. I was pretty sure it didn't or we would have all been much weaker with hunger by now. On the third day, we had class again and I passed. So did everyone else. But, of course, we couldn't eat. Or at least I couldn't. My hands weren't better—they were worse. New scabs had formed, but there were still patches of raw flesh, the rope burns on my wrists stung, and ugly bruises had bloomed around the raw skin. And, of course, my eyes still ached. Hardly the worst pain, but endless and maddening.

I wanted to kill someone. Somiss would do. Or maybe myself.

The next day, while Gerrard studied, I walked the passageway to escape the lantern fumes, pacing back and forth, whispering the next song until I had it about half memorized. I dreaded going back in. Then I realized I could bring my lamp out; the smoke rose almost straight up and drifted down the passageway along the invisible ceiling beyond the torchlight. It was simple and obvious, I could study in the passageway.

I set myself up against the wall, knees up to hold the book to spare my hands, my body at an angle so the lamp-light would shine on the book. At first, every time I moved, even a little, the book slewed sideways and I had to stop it with my elbows, then get back to the right page, which was painful and slow and left little bloodstains on the paper. But I got better at it.

When I started to ache from sitting on the stone floor, I went back in and got my blanket and managed to fold it, more or less, into a makeshift pillow. It helped a lot, for a little while. Then my back started to hurt. I had no idea why the wizards had to make everything an ordeal. But I knew Gerrard was right; it didn't matter. I had to study: If I didn't, I would starve.

I got the book open again, read through the next song, then closed my eyes and recited, whispering, until I got lost. I opened the book again, reread the song, and started over. My belly growled and cramped and I tried to ignore it, reminding myself that I had eaten bread with Gerrard. Had there always been food hidden in Jux's classes and I had never noticed? I shook my head to stop thinking and went back to the studying.

After a while, my stomach growled again, longer and

louder. I wanted to go eat. But when I tried to imagine pressing my raw, half-skinless palms against the stone and letting that shock of hot pain sear them, I knew I couldn't do it. Not yet. Maybe when I was truly half-dead from hunger, horrible pain for food would sound like a fair trade.

I was so sick of all this. I opened my mouth to scream—or something—but nothing came out. It wasn't fair. I was passing recitation classes, I should be able to eat. I tried to rearrange the folded blanket and almost knocked over my lamp. Without thinking, I jumped up and hurled the book at the opposite wall. It smacked the stone and fell to the floor. I kicked it down the passage, making noises like a dog in a fight.

I was still breathing hard, my teeth clenched, when I finally picked it up. Many pages were wrinkled. None had torn. None were loose. I was relieved and pissed off, all at once. I was so sick of studying in choking smoke, being hungry. . . . Tired of sitting on the floor, I looked down the passageway. I didn't need to go to the food hall for the usual reason—but there were tables there.

I put out my lamp. While the glass chimney cooled off, I threw my blanket back on my bed, fit my striker between the book pages, and figured out how to push my sleeve up so I could hold it under my arm without it slipping. I ended up carrying the lamp to the food hall with both hands, gently, a wad of my robe hem between my ragged scabs and the glass oil reservoir. The song book was clamped beneath my left arm. The awkward arrangement hurt, but not more than I could stand. And it was worth it.

The tables and benches had been made when the chamber had been made; they were all extensions of the dark stone. So they weren't soft, but they were smooth. And in the huge chamber, the smoke just rose and disappeared. I could set the lamp close. I could lay the book on the table and turn pages with my knuckles—and not drop the book. I could study.

Once I had the song memorized, I got up and paced the long perimeter of the chamber just to stretch, but I found myself standing in front of the faceted stone. I had wondered a thousand times how it worked, but as soon as I wondered this time, I heard Gerrard's voice in my head. *It doesn't matter.*

My belly rumbled and I looked at my palms. The pain this time would be worse than the first time. On the raw patches, I had no skin left to burn off. Would it work to just slap the stone—barely an instant's contact?

"Probably not," I said, talking to myself. "Or it would have worked when Levin and the rest of them flinched."

My feet instead of my hands? I exhaled. That was equally stupid. I'd be lame, even if it worked, and it might not. The bastards. There had to be a way to make food without crippling ourselves. Or maybe that was the test? To be able to stand the pain long enough to eat, every time. Or maybe we were supposed to stand the hunger until we healed.

I tried to think. Had I ever seen a wizard with burn scars? Not bad ones, or I would have noticed. Maybe they already knew none of us was good enough to graduate. Was it possible they were just amusing themselves, like boys who pulled the wings off stable flies?

I clenched my fists in anger, then gasped in a quick breath. What an idiot I was. I lifted my hands over my head and splayed my fingers, blowing out quick, short breaths, waiting for the pain to subside. Both palms were still oozing blood and amber-colored water in places. My fingertips were a little better. All ten of them. The skin was starting to heal over.

My fingers. All ten.

I stared at them.

We all pressed our palms against the stone, both at the same time, because that was what Somiss and Franklin had done when they had shown us how to make food.

But . . . would one hand do?

Or one fingertip?

Holding my breath, I imagined the meal that was easiest for me to make—Celia's griddle cakes. I imagined them with love and longing, every detail in place, perfect. And then I pressed the tip of my left index finger against the stone. And there was a flash, the sound of a rising wind through weeping willow trees, and then the food was there. As it always had been.

The tip of my finger was burned, and it hurt. But by the time I finished eating, it hurt a little less, and there was a taut blister forming on it. I was so happy.

It was always like this: Whenever I finally understood something, when I figured out whatever the wizards wanted us to figure out, I felt joyous, light. It never lasted, and I knew that more terrible things would happen. But for the time it took to carry the lamp and the book back to the room, I was full, relieved, smiling. I could eat. Studying would get easier, and my eyes would heal if I studied in the food hall. Everything was going to be all right, for a little while. That was enough.

I held my breath, wadding up my robe to open the door. But Gerrard was there, asleep in the dark. He had put out his lamp. I felt my way to bed, happy, careful of my hands, especially the newest burn. I fell asleep before the little rush of relief and false joy passed. I did not cry and I didn't dream. It was a good day.

19

"Sadima?"

She looked up from her work, startled when Franklin whispered. "Why aren't you asleep?" she asked him. "Is everything—"

"Somiss is going to Limòri," he said. "I've been carrying notes back and forth for days, and—"

"Is he meeting with the Eridians?" Sadima interrupted, careful to speak as quietly as he had. "Or just with his mother?"

Franklin looked past her, shrugged. "He has another errand for me."

"You haven't slept at all, have you?"

He shook his head. Then he looked down the passage-way, before he looked back at her. "I just wanted you to know that things are going to get better. By midsummer, maybe sooner." He paused, then looked into her eyes. "If you ever hear shouts or voices or . . ." He trailed off, then started over. "If you ever hear what sounds like king's guards or men hired by Somiss's father, just run farther into the passages and hide."

Sadima stared at him. "Has someone found out we are here?"

He shrugged. "Somiss said it was possible." He looked at the floor, then back at her. "Sadima, I don't know. If you hear anything, run and hide. Don't go to the main cavern, and don't worry about the boys. No one will hurt them. Just hide and I will come back and find you." He took her hands in his, and she thought he was going to say something else, but he didn't. He just sighed, then turned and walked out, headed for the main passageway.

Sadima finished the song she was copying, and then stood up and went out into the narrow passage that ran past her chamber. Staying well back in the shadows, she waited and watched the main passage. Somiss went by first. He was wearing a fine woolen cloak and boots that came up to his knees, and he carried his bright lantern. Five heartbeats behind Somiss, Franklin walked by. He glanced up the passage, but Sadima knew he could not see her in the dark. Once he was gone, she leaned against the wall and tried to think.

Somiss was entirely selfish. Entirely. He had known that Franklin would warn her. Was he just making sure that she wouldn't dare leave the cliffs? She waited for a long moment, telling herself that Somiss could have had ten reasons or more to scare her and that none of them mattered. The day the weather warmed, she had to be ready.

She tiptoed to the end of the narrow corridor and peeked into the main passageway. Far in the distance, she saw two specks of light, one brighter than the other. They were just entering the big cavern. She held her breath. Somiss turned left, heading for the entrance passage—not the cage. Sadima exhaled. Good.

Once she was convinced they were gone, she went back into her chamber and arranged her things to look as though she had only stopped work for a moment—just in case. Then she went out, leaving her lantern behind. She didn't want the boys to see her, and she was going to need both hands free.

Wrapped in her old shawl, Sadima walked close to the wall of her little corridor until it ended. She stopped and listened, then went on, hands out in front of her, straight ahead until she touched the far side of the main passageway. She smelled scented soap in the still air. Somiss had bathed—so he was meeting with someone he wanted to impress?

She walked all the way to the big cavern, following the wall to turn left, trailing her fingers on the stone as she tiptoed toward the entrance tunnel. The darkness pressed against her, and she was afraid the thrumming sound would start, but it didn't. At the far end of the narrow entrance passage, in the muted light that sifted through the thick vines, she saw Somiss's lantern and striker next to

Franklin's, waiting for their return. The air was chilly, but there were winks of sunlight so bright it hurt her eyes.

Sadima took four cautious steps, then stopped at the cascading wall of bare vines. They would bud before too much longer. She inhaled, deep, hungry breaths full of pine scent, and forced herself to move, to walk out into the open. She felt her heart beating as though she was facing death, exposed, like a woods mouse crossing a meadow.

The sky, the trees, everything felt bigger than she remembered it. She heard a hawk in the distance and looked up. Somewhere it was flying free. A rustling in the bushes startled her; it was a vole, scuttling deeper into its nest. It had heard the hawk too. Sadima found a sturdy deadfall branch, then ran into the forest.

There were banks of dirty snow in the deepest shade, but most of the ground was bare. She ran across the pine needles, ignoring the tiny stabs at her bare feet. She knew exactly where her little crate was buried. The charred top of the rampike pine was easy to spot.

She stood beneath it, breathing hard, relieved to find the dirt undisturbed and exactly as she had left it, except for a layer of wet brown leaves. She dug at the damp soil with the stick, loosening dirt, then scooping it out with her hands. Finally she dragged the crate free. The waxed flax-cloth had kept her papers dry, more or less. A few of the top sheets were smeared. She had been frantic the night she had brought it here, the night after the fire. She had stopped twenty-odd times to rest, barely making it back inside the cliffs before Franklin and Somiss had risen from their uncomfortable sleep on the bedclothes Somiss had used as makeshift bags to carry his papers. Sadima shivered. It felt like that dark, starry night had been ten years before—and it hadn't even been one.

She glanced around, listening, feeling a dozen small animals around her. There was a squirrel, happy, glad to be warmer, waiting for full spring. She heard jays arguing over a bark beetle. So there were no strangers nearby. Good. If Somiss came back and saw her outside, she had no idea what he might do. If he caught her carrying these secret copies—there were a few hundred pages—he would know how long she had been betraying him. For an instant she remembered the blood spattered on the walls of their Limòri apartment, and the terror on the Marsham boy's face as he ran from Somiss.

Sadima crouched by the crate and thumbed through the papers. She had made many of these copies the same day Somiss had written them down for the first time, when he was guessing at the spelling by the sound of the words. If Somiss's work was wrong and some other scholar wanted to start over, these rough copies might be valuable.

Trembling, Sadima took everything out of the crate and shook the waxed cloth bundles to get rid of the damp dirt. Then she bound them in her shawl, along with the knife she had taken from Rinka's cheese shop. She had used it to cut the thick layers of waxed flax-cloth, then decided to steal it. It wasn't big, but it was very sharp. And Sadima knew she might need it one day.

Sadima refilled the crate with her few keepsakes, her

shoes, and her honey tin full of coins, then reburied it, scattering leaves over the damp dirt. The shawl-bundle was heavy, but she managed to hoist it onto her shoulders. Going back inside, Sadima was bent almost double under the weight of the papers, stooping to keep from scraping herself where the ceiling was lowest. When she came into the big cavern, she stopped and slid the bundle off her shoulder, catching her breath. Then she picked it up again and walked as fast as she could, staying close to the wall. She glanced at the cage as she started to turn toward her chamber, dreading the long zigzagging route to the lake and the vent shaft. She stumbled to a stop.

Jux.

Little Jux was out of the cage. He was the smallest one—small enough to squeeze between the bars. He was dancing, or playing at something, running a few steps in one direction, then back, his arms in the air. Sadima stood, unable to move, shaking with urgency. He looked toward her across the darkness. Could he see her? Sadima held her breath, watching him walk to the edge of the lighted area. Then, instead of stopping, he came closer. And closer.

"Lady? What is that?" Jux whispered.

"Nothing important," she said. Then she swallowed. "You need to go back . . . inside."

He stopped and tipped his head. "But you hate us being in there, me especially."

"I do," Sadima said, trying to think. What if Somiss and Franklin came back and saw her? What if Jux told Somiss what he had seen? Before she could say anything, Jux lifted his chin.

"Somiss left too. And Franklin."

"Did they?" Sadima asked, her right hand starting to shake with the weight of the bundle. If she dropped it, if Jux saw the papers . . . "I'll come back soon," she said, and started walking.

"Lady?"

She looked at him over her shoulder.

"I smell pine trees," he said. "Is it pine boughs?"

Sadima didn't answer. She kept walking. When she glanced back at him again, he was staring at her. No, he was staring at the bundle with the keen eye of a lifelong thief. He could tell how heavy it was. He knew she was hiding something. She forced herself upright, both hands clenched around the ends of the shawl.

"Where is your lantern?" Jux called.

"I'll be back soon," Sadima repeated over her shoulder, keeping her voice steady, calm. And she walked away with what she hoped looked like a light step, without hurry, and without looking back.

Oh, she had been foolish. If Jux told one of the other boys, if any of them awakened, they would talk about it. Somiss might even have told Jux to watch for her, might have promised him extra food. Sadima turned up the main passageway, sick at heart. Everything Franklin had suffered, everything she had tried to do—might all be for nothing.

20

At our next class, Will missed sixteen words. Everyone else passed or came close. The class after that, he looked ill. His cheeks were flushed, his eyes hollow, and he missed seven words. I passed and had been eating, sacrificing one fingertip each time, so the palms of my hands were healing and I was gaining a little weight, but only because Gerrard was helping me. If he hadn't been, I knew I would have been right there with Will—starving.

Will was the smallest and youngest of all of us. He had started out scared, begging the rest of us for food. But somehow he had found his courage. He had helped all three of his roommates walk to class when they could barely stand, even though Somiss had forbidden us to help each other. The rest of us had just watched, too scared to do anything.

And we were still cowards, filing out, pretending we didn't see how weak Will was getting.

Starting back to the room, I saw him stumble. Jordan stepped close to steady him, but Will shook his head. He didn't want to get Jordan in trouble. I felt sick. I liked Will. I didn't want him to be the next one to die.

That night I had dark, confused dreams that made me wake up feeling like I hadn't slept at all. The only part I could remember began with all of us standing in a field full of flowers. All ten of us were there, even the boys who had died. My feet were stuck to the earth somehow; I couldn't move. None of us could. And there was a man in a black robe with a scythe, swinging it in wide arcs, coming closer, the flowers falling before him.

The next day we had no classes. In the morning I tried to get Gerrard to talk about the kites, but he just looked blank. It pissed me off. I asked him about the book again too. He just shook his head, looking puzzled, like I was a child, making things up. I went to the food hall to study. It made it better for Gerrard, too, I was sure. If I wasn't in the room, the lamp smoke was cut in half.

Late that evening, when I was back, reading the history book, Gerrard cleared his throat twice and began reciting the next song, whispering, saying each long, convoluted word slowly and precisely. I opened my book and read along with him.

"Can you move your thoughts yet?" I whispered when he finished.

He nodded, without facing me.

I lay on my back, wide awake in the dark that night, thinking: Somiss had made it so that passing the recitations didn't really matter. No one could eat, so far as I knew, but me. Why? It almost seemed like he wanted us all to starve faster. Maybe the idea was to figure out how to eat. If it was, I had already passed the test.

And then, out of nowhere, another thought came. I wondered how old I was now. Thirteen at least, close to fourteen, if Gerrard was right. I was growing fast. There was hair in my armpits now, and more and more on my legs— and between them. I almost smiled, suddenly remembering jokes my brother and his friends had made about missing the toilet basin in the morning and who was bigger, teasing each other about girls they knew. Girls. Aben was lucky. Our father had loved him too much to send him here. Was Aben angry with our father for sending *me*? Maybe not. He was older than I was, and we had never been sent to the same schools. We barely knew each other.

I closed my eyes and tried to sleep, but I kept thinking about Will. I didn't want him to die. And after Will it would be someone else—or maybe two or three of us at once, like before. I felt my eyes fill with tears. I was never going home to scare my father, to make him be kind to my mother. I was never going to go home at all.

I lay still with that thought for a long time. Then with this one: The wizards could not make me become like Somiss. They could kill me, but they couldn't make me a heartless asshole. Lying there, staring into the darkness, listening to Gerrard's soft, even breathing, I decided I was going to help Will and anyone else I could, for as long as I could. Then, when the wizards killed me, when I died, my whole stupid life wouldn't have been useless.

Gerrard and I got to our next class a little early. He stood outside, but I went in and stayed near the front, so that I could try to sit next to Will. But when he came in, his eyes dull, walking slowly, he moved so far back it would have been too obvious. So I sat near Levin. Not too close, but a little closer than usual.

I caught Levin's eye, then looked away. He stared straight ahead, but I knew he was watching me. We had all learned to use the edges of our vision. I rubbed the back of my hand against my robe, as though I was relieving an itch. But I left my hand in that position just long enough to extend my fingers so Levin could see the new burn-blister on my index finger, surrounded by healing skin everywhere else. Then I closed my hand, licked my upper lip, still staring straight ahead, and tugged at my robe, smoothing it downward, chest to belly.

I knew Levin had seen me, but had he understood? I counted to a hundred before I let myself glance at him. He nodded, a movement so small it could have been a simple exhalation, except that he scratched his stomach a moment later, then rested his thumb for an instant on the center of his chest, over his heart. He had understood, and he had thanked me. Perfect. He would find a way to show Jordan and Luke, too, I was sure. Had other classes done this? Had they found ways to help each other?

When Somiss finally appeared, he was sitting on a Trissand settee. I knew what it was because my mother had one. They were rare and expensive. Somiss's was covered in moiré silk the color of honey. My mother's was red velvet.

I pictured her for an instant and tried not to wonder if my father was shouting at her for crying over me. I knew he probably was. He always had. I fell into the first breathing pattern Franklin had taught us; it was simple, deep, calming. The third pattern would have made it easier to push the thoughts out of my mind into my belly, then to my feet, where they became small and dim—but I didn't want anyone to notice. Especially Somiss. So I let them slide, slow and soft, until they finally quieted.

Somiss snapped his fingers, and we all looked up. He pointed at Will. I held my breath and listened carefully, hoping. Will spoke slowly and precisely, and he passed. I ducked my head to keep from smiling. Gerrard was staring at nothing as Levin and Jordan recited, his lips moving slightly, as though he had to practice. They both passed. I did too.

I watched carefully, trying to glimpse the others' hands. They were all still heavily scabbed, but the scabs were a little smaller now. Still, I couldn't imagine anyone wanting to touch the stone yet. At least Jordan and Levin would know how to save their hands. And Luke. He missed three words right at the start, then got nervous, going so slowly that Somiss stopped him midsentence and pointed at Gerrard.

Gerrard stumbled a little and missed two words in the middle. Impossible. I glanced around the cavern, trying to see if anyone else found it odd. Luke was wearing his pissed-off-dangerous expression, and he was looking at me. Gerrard was clever. He didn't want Somiss to suspect anything, and he wanted to keep Luke jealous of the rest of us—not him.

When class ended, I was the first one out the door. I heard Luke laugh, but I walked slower and slower until he went past, shoving me aside, his shoulders too squared and his chin too high. Levin and Jordan went by without looking at me. Gerrard and Will were last. I slowed a little more. Gerrard caught up to me and went by me like I didn't exist. Then I glanced back.

Will was walking slowly, smiling a little. He was glad to have passed, even if it didn't mean he could eat. I kept my pace just fast enough to stay ahead of him until the others were almost out of sight. Then I pretended to stumble, smacking my elbow to save my hands. It really hurt; the sound that came out of my mouth was genuine.

Will ran a few steps to bend over me. "Are you all right?"

As he came closer, I showed Will my hand, palm up. He stared at it. My hands were less healed than anyone else's because of Jux's kites; my new scabs were thicker, and the skin around them was inflamed. I twitched my index finger, once, to make Will notice it. Then, when he glanced at me, I licked my lips and brushed my robe front with one hand. He met my eyes for an instant, then looked away. He had understood.

"Thank you," I said, as we both pretended he was pulling me up, his bent arm hooked through mine to keep from using our hands. I walked past him and did not look back.

I felt so good about helping that I carried my lamp and the history book to the food hall and studied longer than usual. While I was there, Will came in and ate. So did Levin. I did not watch them. I frowned as though they were annoying me.

When I went back to the room, the smoke was terrible. Gerrard was on his cot, facing the wall, as always. He gave no sign at all that he had heard me come in. I longed for a window to open and found myself staring at the door. We always closed it, even though it gave us no real privacy, no real protection.

I stood up and opened it. It slowly swung back and closed itself. So I used the song book to prop it open. Gerrard didn't turn, didn't seem to notice. But it helped. A lot of the smoke flowed into the passageway.

I studied for a while, then glanced up at Gerrard's back and realized that he was angry. I didn't know much about his life, or his opinions, or if he liked music, or any of the things that real friends would have learned by now. But I had spent a lot of time staring at his back. I knew his posture, every tiny change in the height of his shoulders, the angle of his neck. It was like the imperceptible nods and smiles, all the ways we had learned to communicate. Tonight the set of his shoulders told me everything.

Maybe he hadn't gone around the corner when I

thought—maybe he had stopped and watched. Maybe he had seen me showing Levin my hand. Maybe he had peered into the food hall without me seeing him. "I can't stand to see anyone else starve," I whispered.

"If you want to die here," he answered, without turning to look at me, "you can. But I can't. Somiss won't tolerate what you are doing. And then he will figure out what *we* are doing."

"What about the book?" I hissed at him. "I'm not the one who is going to get us killed. You are."

He took a long breath. "Learn the songs yourself."

"I can't," I said. He didn't answer.

For an instant I was scared, but then I noticed the ridges of his ribs moving against the cloth of his robe where it was pulled taut. I stood up and went to the spigot and washed my face. Then I made a little sound of pain, and when Gerrard looked up, I whispered to myself, "Shit." I arched my palm open and leaned toward him as though I was using his lamplight to look at the new blister. He glanced at me, at my hand, then looked away, and I was sure he had understood. But his back stayed rigid. I was afraid to piss him off, so I didn't say anything more. I just read the history book until I couldn't stand another pompous, boring word about the Founder of this filthy place.

After I blew out my lamp and lay down, I exaggerated my breathing just loud enough so Gerrard could hear it slow down. I turned over once, then did it again, breathing soft and even, as though I was falling asleep.

I finally heard Gerrard moving around, settling into a

more comfortable position. I listened closely. He started with the fourth breathing pattern, then the sixth, then the third, then the fifth, and I knew: He had lied. He hadn't managed to move his thoughts yet. He was still experimenting. I am ashamed to admit this: I was glad.

21

Staggering beneath the weight of the papers, Sadima
constructed a lie. She would say she had been gathering
stones in the big cavern to weight her crate-desk to keep
it from sliding when she bumped it, and that Jux saw her
carrying them. She would say she had noticed a scent of
pines in the big cavern—that it must have been a trick of
the wind coming up the long entrance tunnel.

Carrying her lantern and the shawl-bundle on her back
was awkward. She stopped four or five times to switch
hands. The steep incline made her slow to an uneven stagger, but she did not stop again until she had the papers and
the knife safely in the vent shaft. Then she hurried back
down the steep passageway, slowing her pace only as she
went around the lake, then ran once she was back in the

tunnels. Just beyond Somiss's passage, she slowed enough to fill her shawl with as many stones as she could carry. Finally back in her chamber, she piled them in her crate-desk and replaced the top.

Then she paced, trembling, until she could work at copying. Having the crate steady and immovable really was helpful, and she was relieved to have a logical story. That didn't mean Somiss would believe her. As she worked, she listened, her skin prickling, for footsteps. Near evening she heard Franklin coming; his heavy tread was unmistakable. He came into her chamber, his eyes bleary with fatigue. "I'm going to start bringing enough bread for six or seven days," he told her, before she could ask him anything. "You will have to give it out each morning."

She nodded.

"Somiss wants me to do other errands," he added, whispering.

"Errands? Now?"

Franklin looked aside. "Not tonight. I have to sleep first."

"Something awful?" she breathed.

He shook his head. "Messages. Back and forth."

"So I will almost never see you?"

He swayed on his feet and nodded. "For a while."

She kissed him and held him close, sorry she had sounded so selfish. She wanted to tell him what she'd done, but she didn't know where to begin. "I am sorry, Franklin," she said. "I didn't mean to—"

"You haven't done anything but work hard and give me

a reason to stay alive," he whispered. And then he released her and walked out, his weariness breaking her heart.

Once he had gone, Sadima lay down her quill and got under her blankets. For a long time she lay awake, hoping Somiss would be angry with her, not Franklin, if he ever found out what she had done. Franklin's life had been a long procession of unfair beatings. She would never forgive herself for adding another one.

The next morning Sadima watched Jux copy—ten times faster and more accurately than any of the others. He smiled at her when he held up his slate. When she told the day's story, he sat with his eyes fixed on the darkness outside the little globe of lantern light that enclosed the cage, absorbing every word. If he had told Somiss anything, if he planned to, she couldn't see it in his face. Perhaps he hadn't. Perhaps he wouldn't.

The morning after that, Franklin brought two big bags full of bread and cheese. He leaned one against the cavern wall, well out of reach of the boys in the cage. He opened the other one, and she helped him break the bread, then walked with him back to her chamber. Twice, he took a breath like he was about to say something, then didn't. He gave her two apples, then kissed her. Sadima watched him leave, his feet dragging. Then she picked up one of the apples.

The boys were asleep by the time she went to give them lessons. She pulled a loaf of bread from the bag by the wall and broke off a big chunk. Tiptoeing, she went around the cage, silent and careful. Jux's right hand was within her reach and she touched him.

His eyes flew open, but he didn't make a sound. She smiled at him and lifted the food so he could see it, then walked past the cage, and hid it in the shadows. Then she woke the others and gave them their copying lessons and told a long, fanciful story.

The next morning she checked. The bread was gone. Jux winked at her, then copied the symbols faster and better than he ever had before. She knew she was bargaining for his silence and his friendship. He was bargaining for hers, and for the extra food.

And so three days passed.

Then five.

And Sadima's fear eased.

Franklin brought home two more sacks full of bread and cheese and said nothing about Somiss's errands. When she finally asked him, he glanced around the big cavern and started to walk away. She fell into step beside him. "Did he find help?" She whispered it, barely shaping the words. Franklin didn't answer. He walked to the other end of the cavern and came back, carrying three reams of paper and another sack of food. She could smell roasted meat. So he was on his way to Somiss's chamber. Sadima fell into step beside him again.

He smiled at her when they got close to the passage that ran past their chambers, and he led the way around the corner. Then he set everything down and turned. He lifted her hair back over her shoulders and kissed her cheek, then her mouth. "Thank you," he whispered. "No one has ever been as kind to me as you are. No one has ever forgiven so much."

Before Sadima could say anything, he picked up the paper and the food sack and walked away, headed back toward the main passageway. Sadima ran to catch up.

"Somiss won't like it if he sees us together," Franklin said quietly.

Sadima hooked her arm through his and stopped. "If you love me," she whispered, "you will answer me. Who has he talked to? The Eridians?"

Franklin nodded wearily. "But it's more complicated than you think it is," he said. "The Eridian leaders argue constantly about Erides's teachings—they all tell the stories differently."

"Do they all believe that everything should be shared?" she whispered.

He nodded.

"Will they help?" Sadima asked. "Franklin, I need to know," she said when he didn't speak.

"Somiss hasn't told me anything," he whispered, but he did not meet her eyes.

"Don't lie to me," Sadima said.

Franklin looked up the corridor. She watched him closely. There was nothing but resignation on his face and in his eyes. And she realized that he could not imagine being free of Somiss. It wasn't that he would not. He *could* not. His whole life had been spent keeping Somiss calm, happy, occupied, flattered, convinced of his own brilliance. And it would kill Franklin if Somiss *didn't* bring magic into the world—because if he didn't, all the beatings, all the years of misery, everything he had given up, would have been for nothing.

Sadima reached out to grasp Franklin's hand and pulled him forward. "Come with me."

He let her lead him along for a dozen steps, then stopped. "You can't come all the way to Somiss's passage. If he sees us—"

She nudged him forward, hating how afraid he was of Somiss. "A little farther. I want to show you something."

That was enough to get him walking again, but when they came close to the passageway that led to Somiss's chamber, he jerked free and stopped. "What are you doing?" he whispered. "If he sees us now, he will—"

Sadima put one arm around his neck, pulling him so close their noses touched. "Call him," she breathed, her lips brushing his, "like you always do. If he comes out, talk to him. But when he is gone again, when you can, walk past his corridor. And just keep walking, straight ahead, farther in. I will be waiting for you." She released his hand and backed away, staring into his eyes. Then she turned and ran past Somiss's corridor.

When she glanced back, Franklin was still staring at her, his lantern lifted. Knowing he was watching, she ran a long way, then ducked into a narrow passageway and followed it far enough to hide the light from her lantern. Breathless, hoping, Sadima pressed her back against the stone. After a moment, she set her lantern down and touched her bodice to make sure she had her striker. Then she waited.

Somiss had called her a field girl once, with disgust in his voice. He still thought of her as a thick-headed farm girl, she was sure. He was right. She had grown up herding goats and planting barley. She had watched her brother and her father slaughter chickens, pigs, and cows for the stew pot a hundred times. They were kind, quick, and accurate with the knife. She would be too, if Somiss hurt Franklin or any of the boys. He wouldn't suspect what was coming. He would not be tortured by fear or pain.

It took Franklin so long to shout to Somiss that Sadima had begun to wonder if he ever would. She couldn't hear the answer at all, if there was one. Then, for a long time, there was no sound at all. Were they talking? Maybe Somiss had sent Franklin on some errand—or maybe Franklin was walking back to his chamber, too afraid to disobey Somiss.

It felt like an eternity before she heard footsteps and peeked around the corner to see the faint glow of his lantern, then ducked back into the darkness. He was looking over his shoulder when he passed the tunnel she was in and the light from her lantern caught the corner of his eye. He turned and came toward her.

When she took his hand, it was cold. He was terrified. She kept him moving, pointing out the cairns, the turns, showing him how she had marked the way. It didn't help.

"Breathe slower," she whispered. "Deep and slow."

As they walked along the intricate path, she could feel his fear easing a little. When they had to slow to walk across the rocky ground, she released his hand. And when he could see the black water, he turned to her, silent, astonished. Then, after a long moment, she saw tears in his eyes. She knew why. He was realizing, as she had, that Somiss could not find them here. Ever.

"A lake?" he whispered.

"Yes," she said, leading him to the flat-topped rock. She set her lantern on its shelf and set her striker beside it. "From the day I found this place," she told him, "I have wanted to bring you here. I was afraid to."

He nodded, then wiped at his eyes and turned a slow circle, holding his lantern high. "Oh, Sadima. Thank you." It wasn't loud, but it was his voice, not a whisper.

22

It didn't matter that I had shown Gerrard the blister on my fingertips or that he couldn't move his thoughts yet. He had meant what he said. He stopped reading the songs so I could hear how he pronounced the words. He avoided me when he could and ignored me when he couldn't.

"Somiss will know," I whispered to him the next night when he was pretending to be asleep. "He'll know you have helped me all this time, because I won't be able to recite all of a sudden."

There was a small silence. Then Gerrard jerked back his blanket and stood up. He grabbed the front of my robe, dragging me up out of bed. He reached out and touched my face. I couldn't see him in the dark—or his fist. He hit me, hard, twice, one for each eye, then two more to make sure, and then he let go.

I fell sideways onto my cot and curled up around the pain. My face felt broken. It was all I could do to keep quiet. I wasn't sure I could see out of my left eye. There were weird sparkles in the darkness that came and went, but I was afraid to light my lamp, or go out into the passageway. I was scared I might be blind in that eye.

I must have eventually fallen asleep, because when the wizard woke us up the next morning, I tried to open my eyes and couldn't. They were swollen shut, pounding with pain that filled my skull when I sat up. Clever Gerrard. The asshole. Now Somiss would not wonder why I suddenly couldn't recite, and he wouldn't care at all who had hit me. I hoped Gerrard's scabs were broken open.

Once Gerrard had washed and left for the food hall or wherever the fuck he was going, I sat up. I had been staying out of the lamp smoke, my hands had just begun to hurt less, and now the pain in my face was almost more than I could stand. I struggled to open my eyes into squinty little slits. Gerrard had left his lamp burning on his desk. I covered one eye, then the other. I could see.

I flopped back onto my cot, relieved enough to be bent on revenge. I spent a long time thinking of ways to kill Gerrard, then sat up and got my song book. I wasn't going to kill him, I knew that. And I knew this: I had to learn, because he would let me starve if I didn't. Our pact no longer meant anything to him—maybe it never had.

Peering through the swollen slits of my eyes, I stared at

the next song. Every word in it was a mass of Ferrinides letters—but I knew they wouldn't all be pronounced like standard Ferrinides. The combinations were ridiculously long. None of them made sense to me. I had memorized Gerrard's pronunciations, not the words in the book.

At our next class, when I stumbled through the first song Gerrard *hadn't* helped me with, my eyes were barely open. I missed more than forty words. Somiss barked the corrections at me, and I had to start over more times than anyone else ever had. He said nothing about my eyes. Luke made sure I could hear him laughing after Somiss had disappeared. The others made tiny gestures of sympathy, and I just tried to open my eyes wide enough not to get lost going back to our chamber.

At the second recitation my eyes were only half-shut, but I still missed thirty words. That night, my empty stomach grinding, I silently rehearsed an apology. I would promise Gerrard never to help anyone but him again. I would tell him I knew he wasn't able to move his thoughts yet and offer to help him more. It had to work. If it didn't, I wasn't going to live much longer.

Twice I took a deep breath and meant to speak, but something stopped me. The rigid straightness of his back, probably. Then, as he shifted and exhaled, I caught the faintest scent of fish stew. Had he used one finger? Probably. So he would take help from me, but not give it?

"I need you to read the songs," I breathed.

"No," he whispered back. "You don't."

I stood up, furious, and the pounding in my skull came

back, duller, but still there. "Will it matter to Somiss whether you give help, or just take it?"

He didn't answer. I kicked him and he spun around, on his feet with his fists up faster than I could blink.

I stared into his face. The last thing I wanted was more pain. But I would fight him, for the pleasure of hitting him at least once. I opened my mouth to tell him I thought he was a selfish coward, but that isn't what came out. This did: "Keep the pact. Please. I can't stand all this without it." My voice was shaking, and I knew it was the deepest truth. *Hope*. I needed to hope.

He lowered his hands. "Then practice," he said, jutting his chin out. "Learn." He sat down again and put his back to me. I saw him change breathing patterns, the seventh, then the fifth. His shoulders were high, stiff. I understood him perfectly.

He was admitting his lie about moving his thoughts—and explaining his anger. He had taken my help and was working constantly to learn to move his thoughts. But after all this time, I hadn't even tried to learn to read the songs on my own. Not once.

"Gerrard?"

He lifted his head, and for a moment I thought he was going to turn, but he didn't, and I knew what that meant too. I could almost hear his voice in my mind. *I am not one of your servants.*

"I'll try," I whispered. I put the song book under my arm and carried my lamp to the food hall. All the way there I tried to figure out why I had assumed Gerrard would read every single song to me, all the way to the end of the book. Because boys like him had cleaned the grounds at Malek Manor and worked in my father's soap shed and on his ships and in his stables and fields? The first time I had seen—and smelled—Gerrard, I had been sure he was someone's hired messenger, a dock-boy earning a few coppers by climbing the endless zigzagging stairs cut into the cliff face.

Opening the book, I began by reciting the songs I knew, looking carefully at the words and paying attention to the pronunciations. After a few hours, I could sight-read one word in twenty, and I was exhausted. I went back to the room.

Gerrard wasn't there. For an instant my stomach tightened, but his desk was against the wall, and his cot. I tried to think where he would have gone, and couldn't. Maybe he ran in the tunnels sometimes, like I did. Or, more likely, he had been in the shadows at the food hall, waiting for me to leave so he could make his fish stew. Or Jux had come for him.

I didn't want to go to sleep, not until he was back. So I stretched, then walked up and down the passage and came back in, awake enough to study again. I left the door open to keep the lamp smoke from getting thick.

This time I flipped back and forth between the songs, looking at those I knew, trying to find letter sequences similar to the ones I was trying to sound out. Then I had to recite each song from the beginning to remember the pronunciations. It was clumsy, and incredibly slow, but it worked. And I knew, with time, that I would be able to do what Gerrard—and all the others—could do. Of course they could. They had studied, instead of depending on getting help.

Like some little kid showing off, I wanted Gerrard to come back and hear me reciting before I had to stop and sleep. He didn't. But he was there when the wizard woke us up. He didn't say a word to me. He didn't even glance at me. We didn't have a class with Somiss, so I studied in the food hall all day. Jordan came twice while I was there. The second time, he brought his book and his own lamp and sat as far from me as he possibly could. We exchanged a single glance. He blinked twice and then closed his eyes for an instant, and I knew his eyes hurt—so they hadn't figured out the lamp-wick problem either.

From then on, I spent almost every waking moment in the food hall, studying. The swelling around my eyes subsided a little each day. And as I worked, more and more of the letter combinations became familiar to me.

The day I noticed the repeated words, I looked up sharply, then back at my book. I turned the pages, staring. *Nikamava resporet telan*. In every song, the same three words appeared, always in that order. And in all but seven of the songs, the three words were near the beginning. Had Gerrard noticed? Probably everyone had, long before.

I wondered if Gerrard understood the weird language, if he knew what the three words meant, but I was afraid to ask him. He was still acting like I was empty air, and I just wanted to prove myself. I wanted him to say we would destroy the wizards one day, together. I know that sounds like something a five-year-old would want, but it was all I thought about when I wasn't studying. I wanted to believe it again. I needed to believe it.

At the next class, I missed four words. The one after that, I passed. Gerrard glanced at me, and his mouth was curved, very slightly. I looked aside and breathed the first pattern to keep from grinning.

After that, I found a rhythm. I would pass a song, then study hard on the next one, eating like a pig for the two or three days before we recited again. I burned as few of my fingertips as I could by making piles of cheese and fruit to carry back to the room. My first try at recitation always failed, so after the next class, I ate much less, most of it cheese and apples. Once in a while, I needed a third class to recite the new song perfectly—so I fasted. We all took two or three classes to get it right, even Gerrard, because he pretended to have trouble.

Will was the exception. He always struggled. But as his hands healed—all but his fingertips, anyway—he ate good meals when he could, and he started to look better. Everyone did, including Gerrard. And it brought me more joy than I can explain. I hid my hands in Somiss's class. We all did. It was impossible to know whether he realized what I had learned, what we all were doing to eat more often. If he did, he gave no sign.

It helped that we had no classes with Jux for a long time. They had never been often, or regular, but this time I began to wonder if his classes were over. Franklin had announced the ending of his, but I knew there was nothing logical here, no reason to think one class would resemble any other class. Gerrard and I had survived the kites and the terrible wind. Maybe everyone had done something like that and we had all passed some kind of final exam?

"Do you think we're finished with Jux's classes?" I whispered one night.

Gerrard put his lamp outside, came in and stretched, then looked at me. "We have barely begun."

The next day, after Somiss's recitation class, Jux was waiting for me. Just me. He gestured at Gerrard, a quick, dismissive wave of his hand. I saw Gerrard's face change, then snap back into a bland, disinterested expression. Was he pissed? Scared? Maybe both.

I was only scared.

23

Sadima stared at the dark, still water. She heard Franklin take a long breath, then the stone grating beneath his boots. She knew what he was doing. After his first few moments of joy, he was looking around, wishing that he could see farther, that he could be completely sure that no one was near.

She caught his sleeve. "It's safe. I've listened as hard as I can. There are salamanders and newts, a toad, and a few bats. Nothing else."

He nodded. When he spoke, it was quiet, but not a whisper. "How did you find this place?"

She told him, then touched his cheek. "What happened in Limòri?"

Franklin was silent so long she was afraid he wouldn't

tell her, not even here. But then he cleared his throat. "Somiss was angry the whole time." He lowered his voice. "Angry and scared. He told me if anyone tried to harm or capture him, I was to prevent it, or if I couldn't, to follow and see where he was taken, then to go to his mother."

Sadima sighed. "If Somiss isn't kidnapped at least once, if no one ever tries to kill him, he will die a bitter old man."

Franklin lifted his chin, and she thought she saw him smile. But he shook his head. "There is real danger, Sadima," he said. "Everything I told you is true."

Sadima nodded but said nothing, wishing he would kiss her here, now, where there would be no reason to stop, no reason to be afraid.

Franklin looked out at the little stretch of shoreline dimly revealed by their lanterns, then back at her. She wanted him to tell her that he loved her, but what he said was this: "About half of the Eridians want nothing to do with magic. The rest want him to share his work, all of it, with them, the royal scholars, every literate person in the city, everyone."

Sadima nodded. If Somiss ever did share his work, it would be false copies.

"The Gypsies won't trust him," Franklin said. "They believe the magic was real once," he added quickly. "But they believe it was entrusted to them, that one of them will bring it back. I don't think they know the Gypsy woman gave Somiss the book he's using, but—"

"She intended it for you," Sadima interrupted. "You're the one who kept her son from harm."

"Somiss will never remember what I have done. Or your help." He reached out to touch her cheek. "It feels very strange not to whisper."

"It's wonderful," Sadima said. "Will we at least have enough food, Franklin? Just until the weather warms up?" When he didn't answer immediately, she began to hope that he knew what she was saying and that he was considering it, even without knowing about the copies she had made. But then she saw him smile, a crooked, wry smile.

"Somiss's mother gave him a bracelet."

Sadima blinked. "And you sold it somewhere? What if people think you stole—"

"I sold it to my cousin," Franklin told her. "He buys stolen things every day, but this was a gift. Somiss's mother will tell his father that she lost it, if he ever notices."

"But . . . a bracelet?" Sadima shook her head. "Just that? Nothing else?"

Franklin smiled again. "It was set with icestones, small ones, but perfect. I got enough to feed and clothe us all for a year. Perhaps more. And my cousin will double the price he paid."

Sadima stared. "Will Somiss's father believe she lost it?"

Franklin nodded. "She has a hundred bracelets, or more, most of them much finer."

Sadima hid her astonishment, then lifted her lantern to see his face. "As soon as it's warm, I want to leave," she said. "With you and the boys."

He nodded and sighed, and she knew what he was

thinking. What if Somiss kept the magic for himself, or gave it to his family to impress his father, or the king? Or something else that was even worse? "Even if you stay here, he might never—," she began.

"I know." Franklin stared out at the water.

"You will have given up your life for nothing."

He didn't answer.

"And mine. And the boys'."

She expected Franklin to say that Somiss intended to teach magic, that the old wars would stop because of Somiss's school—everything she had heard so many times. But he didn't.

"What happens to the magic will never be up to me. Or you," he said. His voice was leaden.

"If it could be, would you leave with me?"

He blinked. "What?"

"Would you leave with me if the decision about magic was up to us?"

He nodded, very slowly.

Sadima took his hand and led him along the shoreline, then uphill, and into the passageway where she had first heard Somiss reciting. She showed Franklin the little chamber, then ducked through the opening. Because he was thin, he managed to crawl inside too and sat beside her, his knees beneath his chin. When she pointed at the hole at the base of the wall, he contorted his lanky frame, trying to see it.

"Just listen," she said.

Franklin tipped his head. "Listen for wh—?"

The sound of Somiss's voice made him stop.

"Beyond that opening," Sadima said quietly, "there is a narrow, steep vent shaft. At the top of it is a beautiful silver grate. Sitting beside it, I can hear every word he says. Every word. Perfectly."

Franklin's eyes widened, but he didn't speak.

"I write it down," Sadima said. "He has made lots of changes, Franklin, that he isn't including in the copies you bring to me. He's lying about his work, more than I ever imagined."

Franklin struggled upright, dragging himself across her legs to get out of the tiny cavern. She followed and felt him trembling when he took her hand.

"I write down what I hear," she said. "I sound out the words very accurately so I can read them back." She paused to let him realize what she had said.

He looked at her, fear in his eyes. "I have wondered," he whispered. "But you must never tell anyone else that you can read. A commoner was hanged in Market Square not long after we came here, because he stole a book."

"Could he read?"

Franklin shrugged. "The king's magistrate thought so."

Sadima nodded. "I will be careful. Always. But this makes it our decision, Franklin. I want to give copies to the Eridians, maybe others. We can decide."

"Our decision," Franklin whispered. "Not his?"

"Yes."

Franklin shook his head. "I can't believe it."

"I know," Sadima said. "But I do. And I will convince you. We will—"

Franklin suddenly pulled her close, stilling her voice, and he held her for a long time. "I love you, Sadima Killip," he whispered in her ear. "For this and a hundred other things."

− 24 −

Jux walked fast, as usual. I ran to keep up and was
out of breath at the top of the long switchback incline. He
walked through the door—without opening it—and left me
alone in the passageway. This time the handle was shaped
like an animal that existed only in storybooks, an almost-
horse with a single long horn. The artist had been excep-
tional. It almost looked alive, leaping, its body forming a
curve. Had Jux meant to echo Somiss's chairs with another
imaginary animal? Did it mean anything?

I was afraid to touch it. I leaned close, peering at the
handle. I couldn't see any sharp edges. Maybe the door
would open normally, and the joke was inside. Another
cliff. Or a sea of fire. My skin prickled.

I heard Jux laugh. It was clear in my mind, as though

he were standing beside me. And it made me just angry enough to step forward, my heart thudding, and pull open the door; the familiar slope was there again, and the sunny forest.

"Are you afraid of doors now?" Jux asked.

I whirled around—he was, somehow, behind me, his back to the now closed door. Had I walked *through* him? He lifted his chin, and the sight of his horrible scar made me uneasy—it always did. He laughed, then just looked at me, an almost friendly expression on his face. No. It was sympathy. I met his eyes, something I almost never did with anyone anymore. He just looked back at me.

Jux was a teacher, not just someone who led skin-and-bones boys to class. "Were you a student here?" I asked him, expecting to be ignored or punished.

He nodded. "In a way, yes."

Then he turned and led the way uphill. I followed, looking up into the trees, wondering if there was food hidden there. I really wasn't very hungry, but if there was food, I would eat it. I had learned that much here—food was never to be taken for granted. Hunger was.

I stopped when Jux did, and my thoughts scattered as we stood in front of one of the glass enclosures. It held the biggest wasp's nest I had ever seen, hanging from a tree limb. It was nearly as long as I was tall. The wasps were milling around the entrance, flying in and out.

"They can kill you," Jux said.

I exhaled. He had said that about most of the animals.

"One sting," he said, "can kill you." He paused, and I felt

the familiar, crawling nausea in my belly. Maybe he was lying, but probably not. He opened the enclosure door and gestured. I stepped inside.

"There is something in the center of the nest," Jux said from behind me. "When I come back, you must tell me what that is."

Before I could respond, he shut the glass door and walked away. Must? I looked up. Had he ever said that before? *Must?* I couldn't tell if there was a glass roof. If there was, it was high overhead, taller than the tree, invisible. I lowered my eyes and stared at the nest again. How could I possibly find out what was inside it? I slid into a sitting position as far from the nest as the glass walls allowed. A wasp's nest was like paper. It'd be easy to tear apart. But I would get stung a thousand times.

The sound of the buzzing rose a little. Could the wasps sense my thoughts? I closed my eyes and breathed the way Franklin had taught us, quieting myself. Then I sat very still and tried to figure out what to do.

I had pushed my thoughts into the snake that very first time, to tell it that I meant it no harm. But it hadn't worked until it had touched me. Same with the ants. I tried to tell them honey was bad for them, but it only worked with the ones that were crawling on me. The hummingbirds had been harder, but I had managed to move my thoughts into them without touching them, guiding them out of the enclosure. That same day, waiting for Jux to come back, I had *played*, pushing my thoughts into the trees. I had made a flower bloom, and I hadn't done it since. Why? Because I was too busy just trying to stay alive? It was hard to imagine playing at anything now, even for a moment. I hated the wizards for making everything a do-or-die riddle. And they always—

I jerked my thoughts to a standstill and stared at the nest again. Wasps were crawling around the funnel-shaped entrance. Could I make them all leave the nest so I could look inside it? My father's apiarist had shown me the countless little chambers in a beehive once. Were there that many in a wasp's nest? I glanced upward, then down again. Even if I talked them into leaving the hive, the glass enclosure would be full of angry, buzzing wasps. One sting, Jux had said. One.

I moved a little closer and picked out a single wasp to watch. It was climbing up the side of the nest. I had guided the hungry Servenian hummingbirds to a hole in the enclosure so they could get to a honeysuckle vine outside it. I had told them the truth, and they had wanted out. But I had lied to the ants, putting my thoughts into the honey, convincing them it was dangerous. I had touched the ants at first—they had touched the honey after that. I couldn't do that with the wasps. Had I touched the flower? I couldn't remember.

I was sick of stupid conundrums. I glanced back at the door. There was a handle on the inside this time. Sometimes there wasn't. I breathed the third pattern and nudged my thoughts toward the wasp. Maybe I could convince it to tell the others there was danger, to fly straight up to safety. If there was no ceiling, or one that was high enough, maybe

I could look in the hive before they all came back down. I tried to think of something else, and couldn't.

I pointed at the single wasp and pushed my thoughts down my arm to my fingertips. Suddenly I heard the buzzing of its wings, loud, as though it was clinging to the rim of my ear. Then I felt an odd sensation, like a door opening, behind me, and I could see myself through the wasp's eyes.

I was a big, blurry shape, sprawled, lying at an awkward angle, my shoulders and head against the glass wall. Had I fallen? I kept breathing, slowly, holding the third pattern, trying not to panic. This had happened with the snake and the hummingbirds for a few heartbeats; then I had been able to see through my own eyes again, and I had pushed my thoughts gently into theirs.

But this time it didn't end. I blinked and wiped at my eyes, then closed them. It didn't matter. I still saw what the wasp was seeing; I saw the papery shell of the nest, mottled gray and brown, and the wasp's own dark, barbed legs. I could still see myself, too, lying in the dirt. Then I slid out of sight as the wasp continued its climb.

It crawled toward the entrance, and I could feel its stiff little legs as though they were my own. When it passed through the papery door, the sunlight blinked out and there was only darkness. The wasp kept walking, picking its way down a passageway. It was glad to be home. Its gladness was perfect. Complete.

I tried to sit up straighter, breathing hard, trying to free myself. I opened my eyes and saw darkness. I closed them and nothing changed. I felt high-pitched vibrations in my bones. An odd, sharp odor slammed into me and then a strange nausea. I retched, forcing myself to vomit, but it was something sticky that came up. Something sweet. I felt a wiry scrape around my mouth. Antennae?

Terrified, I listened to a murmuring and a steadier, rustling sound. I knew what it was. Babies. I had fed one. There were thousands more, and they were all hungry. So I was climbing again, inside the nest, my brittle legs bent, hinged, my wings pinned tight so that I could pass the others in the narrow passage. I needed to do the work I was meant to do.

I heaved again, bringing up more food for another baby in its papery cell-cradle. Then I went on, both sharing and taking food from others' mouths. I knew, in a faint, distant way, that I did not belong in the hive. But nothing seemed more urgent than feeding the babies. Nothing. And as I went about the work, I began to feel peaceful. No. I was far beyond simple peace. I felt inevitable, sure, deeply, completely certain. I was doing what I had been born to do, what needed doing, and I knew exactly how to do it. It was wonderful. Incredible. I was so *sure*. I was so happy.

"Hahp?"

I recognized the voice: Jux. But he meant very little to me.

The heaving of my abdomen and the sweet taste were familiar now, part of the dance of my life. What mattered were the papery cells, the babies, the eggs that did not yet need food but soon would, my silk-winged brothers who brushed against me on their way to do what they had been born to do. We were connected, each of us, all of us. The thrumming of the nest was a song we were all singing together, an anthem, a communion. I had known both of those words half my life, from school lists. I had never had a reason to use either one before. But here they were perfect. I was perfect.

I heard a shout. A word I could not understand. Not close. Distant. A searing pain in my forearm made my brittle legs click together, then soften. My antennae went numb. I was terrified, trapped in a huge, sprawled body, weighted, pinned to the dirt, helpless. I was frantic to get back into the hive. But I couldn't move my wings. The pain stopped me.

"Hahp!" That was the word. My name. Jux was saying my name. I opened my eyes and saw blood darkening my green sleeve, dyeing it black. Dyeing? Was I dying? There was a roaring in my ears and I twitched, my legs jerking in a spasm timed to the thrumming of the hive. I closed my eyes again, trying to lift my wings and work my legs. The babies were hungry.

A second sharp pain ended the roaring, and my legs spasmed again. I felt myself peeing and couldn't stop. I opened my eyes once more and saw Jux kneeling beside me. I opened my mouth. No air came out and none went in. Jux shoved both hands against my chest and I felt my lungs collapse, then fill.

"Franklin said not to save you if you got too far lost," he whispered against my ear. "Tell me quick. What did you find?"

"Everything," I said, or thought I said. "Beautiful certainty."

"Good answer," Jux whispered.

I felt him grip my shoulders. And then I felt nothing at all.

25

Sadima's hands were cramping and her eyes were weary. She was so tired of doing what she knew was mostly useless work. And Franklin had brought her a huge stack of papers. He was gone for longer and longer stretches, and that made everything worse. She missed him. He had said that she gave him a reason to live. She wanted to be his reason to *leave*. But after everything they had said at the lake, he was still doing what he had always done— whatever Somiss told him to do. And it absorbed every second of every day.

Sadima stood up suddenly, her heart beating too fast as she walked in the dark to the opening at the end of the entrance tunnel. It was a cool day, but not cold, and she pulled in one deep breath after another as she always did, almost tasting the scent of the pines. There were brown-green bumps on the vine stems. Spring really was close. This time, like all the others, seeing the sky, thinking about the day she and Franklin could leave, was a pleasure so deep that she shivered.

Going back in, Sadima walked quickly, silently. The boys were sleeping, except for Jux. He had squeezed between the bars again and was out of the cage, getting extra bread from one of the sacks by the wall. Would he try to run away on his own? Limòri wasn't that far, just a long morning's walk through the woods to Ferrin Hill, then down the road back to Market Square.

Or maybe, she thought, Jux didn't know where he was. Maybe Somiss had blindfolded the boys and walked them around in circles, like a child's game of Darkest Night. She almost hoped so. If Jux went missing, it could ruin their chances of leaving. Somiss would be frantic, dangerous.

Back in her chamber, Sadima considered telling Jux her plan, but knew she couldn't. She finished her day's copies, then headed for the vent shaft to begin her real work, carrying her unlit lantern until she passed Somiss's passage. But when she stopped to light it, she decided not to. The decision made her shiver and smile. She walked slowly, savoring the sharpness of the fear, bending to touch the first two cairns as she came to them.

The instant she was confused, she relit her lantern, but the next day she tried walking without lantern light again, and she made it farther before she needed light. Every day after that, she practiced. She trailed her hand on the stone, counted her steps, and memorized the textures of the wall, the turns, the smell of the air.

At the lake, she walked within inches of the water to mark that part of the way, touching the cairns with her bare toes to be sure where to leave the shore—and relighting the lantern every time she wasn't positive. The tenth day—with Franklin gone for the last six—she walked the whole way without lighting the lantern at all. She could not stop smiling. The darkness was hers now, a dangerous friend.

Franklin stared at her when he came home the next morning, his arms full of fresh paper and a sack of apples. He struggled to set his lantern down. "You look happy," he said.

She smiled. "Because you're back."

It was true. She was very glad to have him there. But part of her happiness came from the darkness. It was hers. Like the lake, like the pine-scented air. She turned away and set her thoughts on dividing the bread.

"Has something happened?" he asked once they were walking back up the main passageway.

"Nothing important," she lied. "I miss you," she added, leaning close. "We could walk to the lake."

He kissed her and then shook his head. "I haven't slept for two nights."

She tried to hide her disappointment, but couldn't. "Once we leave here," she whispered, then stopped, not because there wasn't anything to say, but because there was too much.

"I know. I think about it all the time," he said. And then

he left to go to Somiss's chamber. When he came back, he was carrying another towering stack of papers. She hoped it didn't mean he would be gone for a long time again.

The next morning, after the boys had eaten and heard a story, Sadima cajoled Franklin into going to the lake with her. She carried a lantern for him but walked fast. It felt stupidly dangerous to be so visible. She had gotten used to the safety of the darkness. But she knew it would scare him at first—and she had no idea when they would have time together again.

As they stood beside the water, Franklin kissed her, and for the first time, it was a deep kiss, long and sweet and hungry. They both stepped back, breathing the same quick rhythm.

"Not here," she whispered.

"Soon?" he asked.

"Soon," she echoed. "When we are far away from here, from Somiss."

He nodded.

"Swim with me?" she asked.

Franklin raised his eyebrows, but he followed her to the edge of the water, then stripped off his tunic and laid it on the stones. She turned away. "Tell me when you are ready."

"Now," he said after a moment. She turned. He was waist deep in the dark lake, facing away from her. Through some trick of water and lantern shine, his shoulder blades were framed by faint crescents. His spine stood out; he was so thin. Three drops of water clung to his skin, shining like stars between the crescent moons. She pulled off her dress and looked again as she waded into the water. The illusion was gone.

When she was close enough, she slapped the water, hard, spraying him with droplets, then dove deep and swam away from him. When she surfaced, she could hear him laughing. The sound echoed off the stone.

They swam close to each other, far out into the lake, then back again, slowly, stopping to tread water, to talk in little bursts of words that seemed out of place against the silence of the lake.

Getting out, they took turns facing away from each other.

"You seem almost happy," she said once they were dressed, their clothes blotched where the water had soaked through.

He nodded. "I am. I just wish I could believe that we will be able to—"

Sadima touched his lips. "I believe it, Franklin." She whispered it, then raised her voice and repeated it aloud. "I have copies of almost everything now," she said. "We will make sure the magic is used for good."

Franklin kissed her, then held her close, warming her. "I forget what I am supposed to be doing, Sadima," he said quietly. "I carry food and water and paper and ink and blankets and new tunics for Somiss and I deliver messages, then I sleep and start over. It seems endless to me."

Sadima leaned back to look into his eyes. "It isn't. You will soon leave here, with the boys, the magic, and me."

He smiled. "And we will sleep together and wake up together."

"Yes," she said. "And I will be able to cook again, and have a garden and goats. And there will be sunlight and wind and rain."

They walked back, shrouding the lantern with Sadima's shawl as they passed Somiss's passage, even though they could hear him reciting. Franklin went to the crate and showed her the day's work, a huge stack of papers—almost twice the usual amount.

"He will give the Eridians false copies," she whispered as he gave her half the stack to carry. "They will end up hating him."

"I know." Franklin sounded like he had the whole winter, tired and sad, and so she didn't say more. Once he was settled under his blankets, he reached up and pulled her close. "Someday," he said, and kissed her.

She sat beside him for a while, whispering, telling him about Ferne and the farms there, and the little road that led into the mountains where the Gypsies lived. Once she knew he was asleep, she sang the song for long life over him.

Smiling, Sadima went to her own chamber and copied as fast as she could, until about a third of the stack was finished. She knew she was missing half a day or more of Somiss's recitations, but she was afraid to fall too far behind at what he thought she was spending all her time doing. Midday she arranged her papers, left her new lantern burning, and carried her old one, unlit, to the vent shaft.

Once she was seated on her folded shawl, waiting for Somiss to recite, she allowed herself to remember Franklin's last kiss. His mouth was warm, and his arms around her shoulders had made her feel beautiful. He loved her. And they would—

The sound of Somiss's voice stopped her thoughts. But he wasn't reciting. He was talking to someone. Franklin? Had Somiss awakened him and noticed that she wasn't in her chamber? Sadima leaned forward to hear better, then began rocking, her hands balled, her wrists crossed over her chest. Not now. Oh, not now when they were so close.

"Do you want an orange?" Somiss asked, his voice light, almost playful. "It's from Servenia."

Sadima froze, her whole body rigid, listening.

"Yes, please," came the answer. And it was a boy's voice, unsure and soft.

Jux.

26

I woke up in my own chamber. It was dark, but I instantly knew the feel of my cot, the sound of Gerrard's breathing, the sharp stink of lamp soot. Within a few heartbeats, I remembered the wasps, Jux bending over me, the blood. And then I remembered the happiness of knowing what I was for, what I needed to do. Or had it been a dream? It had *felt* like one.

A wizard pounded on our door. I shouted that we were awake. And when I rose to wash, I smelled piss. My robefront was damp. So it had happened. I had found the center of everything, and had been forced to leave it. The pounding began again. Gerrard shouted this time as I rinsed the robe in the basin as well as I could without taking it off, wrung it out over the slops bucket, then splashed my face.

Gerrard waited for me. Neither of us said a word. When I opened the door, I was looking down at the handle, placing my scabbed fingers carefully to pull it open. Torchlight spilled inward—and I saw the slit in my sleeve. There was a dark bloodstain around it. But there was no wound, no mark at all on my skin.

"Hahp?" Gerrard said.

I glanced at him. He gestured with his chin. There was no wizard outside the door. We walked out, and just stood there, looking down the passageway in one direction, then in the other. It was empty.

I turned to Gerrard. "No class?"

"But we are supposed to do something," he said.

I looked at my arm again, then back at him. "What?"

He didn't answer me, but he pointed, and I saw a speck of light in the distance, between the rows of wall torches. "Is that a lamp?"

He nodded. "Maybe. What did Jux have you do?"

I glanced at him. Did he really expect an answer? After all the things he wouldn't tell me?

He tipped his head. "The wasps?"

I turned to face him. So he *was* ahead of me in Jux's classes? But if he couldn't move his thoughts . . . or was all of that a ruse?

"I'll go see what that light is," he said.

Before I could react, he walked away. After two long, shuddering breaths, I followed him, more because I didn't want to be alone than any other reason. It was probably a wizard with a torch walking someone else to Jux's class.

My legs felt wrong, too long, too heavy. My vision was strange, blurred. The light looked like it was close at first, then I was sure it was near the first turn on the way to the food hall. As I walked, I felt my gut grinding on itself, cramping the way it had in the beginning, when I first had to go four or five days without eating. Why? I couldn't be that hungry.

When we got close, the light winked out, but we could see it again a moment later, farther down the passage that ran past the food hall. Gerrard didn't pause and I followed, noticing every small thing, the feel of the stone beneath my feet and the sliding cling of my wet robe.

As we passed the food hall, I slowed my step just long enough to see that wizards were eating, sitting in groups at the tables. The huge stone had a line before it—wizards were waiting to make food. I saw Somiss and Franklin standing close together, laughing. Somiss had his arm around a woman's shoulders. Her bodice was loose.

I ran a few steps, grabbing at the back of Gerrard's robe. "Did you see them?" I pulled him to a stop.

He nodded. "They're always in there."

I stared at him. "I've never see them before."

"Franklin must be winning," he said.

"There was a woman, and—"

Gerrard smiled. "Somiss is a Ferrin, after all, born bored and sure that whatever he can reach is his."

I wanted to ask him a hundred questions, but this one came out first: "Who are you, Gerrard?"

He didn't answer me. But he pointed again. The light

was moving, side to side, like someone swinging a lantern. He raised an arm and waved back.

I stared. "Who is it?"

Gerrard glanced at me. "Who are *you*?"

I wanted to punch him. I wanted to put his nose next to his ear with a bloody furrow marking the path. I clenched my right hand. The old burns stretched and stung, but they were mostly healed. I lifted my fist.

And then I woke up.

This time I was in the dark, by myself. No. Not by myself. I saw Franklin, just for a few heartbeats, standing beside me. He said, "You must learn what the songs are for, Hahp." Then he was gone.

I covered my face. I was going mad. If I couldn't tell the difference between my dreams and what had really happened to me, then I did not want to live. I let out a breath so long that it hollowed my chest and my belly and I had to curl up to keep from collapsing in on myself.

They did all this to us on purpose. I was sure of it. Franklin was winning, Gerrard had said. Were the wizards placing bets on us like men in my father's clubs did on dogfights, on the weather, on whose ships would return first? I felt a weight in my stomach like I had swallowed a stone. There was a sudden roaring inside my skull.

Then I woke up.

Gerrard was there. He opened the door and let my father come in. There was a knife on my cot and I picked it up. My father lifted one hand like he was going to slap me. I took a step toward him. "Why did you send me here?"

He laughed. He *laughed*. And I lunged, jerking the knife upward to stab him in the gut. He made a little noise and I smelled something foul—and then he doubled up and fell. I stood back. He was dead. My father was as still as the stone.

And then I knew that it wasn't real. None of it. My father would never die that easily. He would never have come down into these passageways without his guards—and he would have set them on me, like a South End merchant setting his dogs on beggars. He would have fought me if the guards were slow. And he would have won. He always did. Always.

I threw the knife down, disgusted. It was all still a dream. I hadn't really been in my room or staring at wizards in the food hall or talking to Gerrard. And I had not killed my father. I was sure of it. I was dying in the glass enclosure, in the chamber that opened to the sunlight. Knowing that calmed me completely, and a heartbeat later, I could hear voices.

Jux and Franklin were still bending over me. I couldn't move or speak or see, but I could hear them talking.

". . . give you the answer?" Franklin was asking.

"Yes," Jux said. "He understood."

Franklin let out a long breath. I felt it flow across my forehead, warm and soft. "Then it's time," he whispered, and I knew he was talking to me, not to Jux.

I felt a weight on my chest again and knew it was Franklin's hands, old and strong and sure. I felt my heart begin to beat and I realized, only then, that it had stopped.

Every beat shook my whole body. I sucked in a breath. Then another.

And then I woke up one last time, gasping like a newborn.

A wizard was pounding on the door. Gerrard got up. I swung my feet to the floor, then just sat while he washed. Walking up the passageway, my empty belly wrenched and my body ached and it took everything I had to memorize the turns. My robe was still damp against my legs. It smelled. I sat against the back wall, shaking, waiting for the chamber to dissolve or for bats to fly in with bloody teeth. But nothing happened. I saw Gerrard glancing at me. He nodded, just a little. I nodded back, the same way. He looked aside. That seemed funny to me, and I almost laughed.

Gerrard recited, then Will, Luke, and Jordan. They all passed.

I was trying to repeat the song in my mind while they recited, but I kept plucking at my sleeve. The tear was gone. But I knew it had been there. The damp cloth of my robe front was real. It *felt* real. So did every pattern in the stone, every sound, *everything*. I found myself staring at my own hands, turning them back to front, just looking at my amazing fingers, with their pink, blistered tips.

"You."

I looked up to see Somiss staring at me. The ice blue color of his eyes was beautiful. I noticed a tiny sound, now that the chamber was silent. A pulsing sound. A thrumming. The wasps?

"Recite."

I closed my eyes and began. I missed six words. Somiss stopped me on each one, pronounced it correctly, then made me start again. Luke was smiling. Somiss looked pleased to see me struggling. I knew that without opening my eyes. When I was finally finished, I looked down and marveled at the texture of the stone again. I wasn't worried. I had known the song before Jux's class. I had. I would pass next time.

I glanced up and was startled to see Somiss looking at me while Levin was reciting. I looked away. Levin passed. Somiss and his fancy brocade chair disappeared.

We stood, stretching, getting ready to leave. Levin glanced at me, and I saw concern on his face. Jordan managed to catch my eye too, and he nodded, trying to encourage me. I was glad they cared enough to risk making any gesture at all, but I was not discouraged. I was newborn and I was hopeful.

Walking back, I could not stop feeling the cool, gritty, uneven stone beneath my bare feet. I watched the others walk past me, leaving me behind because I had slowed to a toddler's pace. There were faint odors in the air, mostly nasty—our slops buckets and our sweat and my piss-damp robe. But there were others, wisps so small I couldn't identify them before they were gone. I had no idea Luke was behind me until he stepped on my heel, jabbing his overgrown toenails into my skin. I whirled around and faced him.

He spat and hit my right foot.

"I hate you, Malek. And your father."

"I know," I told him. "Please don't do anything like that again. It hurt."

He laughed, but I just kept staring into his eyes without saying another word. He leaned closer. "You think I'm scared of you?"

His eyes were so sad. And the stiff way he carried his wide shoulders was a real effort, something he made himself do. He was terrified of the wizards, of this place, of Somiss, of almost everything. He lunged forward, trying to startle me into stepping backward. But I didn't flinch, so he had to dance awkwardly to regain his balance, then he stood up straight, his shoulders back and his head up. And I was abruptly certain of one thing: We were all the sons of fear and hatred here. Which made us brothers.

When I didn't speak, or try to run, I saw something new flicker in Luke's eyes. It was dawning on him that if I wasn't afraid of him, things had changed. And they had. I heard the tiny pulsing sound I'd heard in the wasp's nest. Was it coming out of the stone and I had just never noticed it before? It didn't matter whether it was real for everyone, or only for me. *I* could hear it. And I wanted to find out what I was supposed to do. Once I knew that . . .

"You think you can beat me in a fight?" Luke whispered.

I smiled at him. "No," I said in a normal voice. "But I could find some way to kill you." I knew it was true. So did he.

He opened his mouth to say something, then closed it. I

wondered if Luke's father was angry and mean like mine. Luke drew back his right fist like he was going to hit me. I just waited until he lowered it. He finally walked off. As I watched him leave, I began to think about Gerrard.

Gerrard was certain he had to be the one to graduate, no matter what—he had never lost that certainty for an instant. I envied him. I would look for what I *had* to do. Then I would find a way to do it.

27

Sadima sat transfixed, listening.

"I never ate an orange before," Jux said.

Somiss laughed.

Sadima heard the scraping of grit beneath his shoes, then paper rustling.

"What's that?" Jux asked.

"It's a song," Somiss answered. "After you finish the orange, I am going to read it to you."

"Read?" Jux's voice was tight, uneasy. "What's that? Does it hurt?"

Somiss laughed again. Sadima heard the sound of his desk chair being pulled over the stone. "Sit there, Jux." There was small silence, and then Somiss spoke again. "No. Here, let me peel it." Sadima could picture Jux eating the way he always did, too fast, wary.

"The lady says that I copy very well," Jux said suddenly, and Sadima could tell his mouth was still full.

Somiss didn't respond for a long moment. Then he said, "Wipe your hands on this."

After another silence he said, "Copy that. Quick as you can."

Sadima pressed against the gate. She could hear the faint scratching of the quill.

"Good," Somiss said when the sound stopped.

"Can I have another orange?"

Sadima could imagine Jux's sweet little smile.

"Listen to this first," Somiss said. "Sit still."

"I just slid a little." Jux sounded scared.

Somiss began to read.

Sadima recognized the song—it was a short, simple one. She had heard it fifty times or more and had recopied her version every time Somiss made changes. She leafed silently through her papers and found it, then sat on her folded blanket and followed along, holding her breath.

Somiss was saying the words slowly and precisely. It was easy to keep up. Her copy was identical to his until he got to the words that were in nearly every song. The word *nikamava* was still there, but the three words that followed it were entirely different. She wrote them across the top of the page, then read on with Somiss. Everything after that was exactly as she had it.

"Did you like the song?" Somiss asked when he was finished.

Jux didn't answer. Sadima leaned forward, listening as the silence continued.

"Did you like it?" Somiss asked sharply. "Franklin says you are clever. Is he wrong?"

"I didn't understand the words," Jux said. He paused. "The lady thinks I am clever too."

Sadima winced, hoping Somiss would not respond, but when he did, his voice was full of false warmth.

"Does she? Do you like her?"

There was another long silence.

"Jux? Answer me. Do you like her?

There was something in Somiss's voice that made Sadima open her mouth wide to still even the tiniest sound of her own breath so that she would be able to hear the answer. If Somiss got Jux talking, if Jux told him about seeing her with the heavy sack, if he said anything about the stories, even, anything at all . . .

"She is very pretty," Jux said.

"That isn't what you were going to tell me."

Sadima heard the chair scrape the stone, a short, quick sound.

"Sit down," Somiss snapped.

The chair scraped again.

"Now tell me what you meant to say."

"She is very pretty and very kind."

Sadima heard caution in his voice, and knew that Somiss would hear it too.

"Is she keeping secrets from me?" Somiss asked sharply.

Sadima covered her mouth with one hand, her heart

thudding in her breast. Poor Jux. And Somiss would keep at this until the boy's courage failed.

"Is being pretty a secret?" Jux asked, and he sounded sincere, timid.

"No," Somiss said. "Where are your parents? Is anyone looking for you?"

There was another pause, and Sadima imagined Jux considering, wondering what Somiss wanted him to say. It was likely he had no idea where his parents were.

"Are you crying?" Somiss asked.

Sadima heard Jux sniffle. "Yes."

"Was your mother pretty?"

Sadima heard Jux's ragged little breaths and she wanted to kill Somiss.

"Jux," Somiss said. "Answer me."

"Yes. She was."

"So. She was pretty," Somiss said. "Was your father handsome?"

"Maybe," Jux said. "My mother said he was."

"Are you lying?" Somiss laughed. "*You* aren't handsome."

"I know," Jux said in a small, sad voice. "Because of my scar."

Somiss stood and paced. Sadima could hear the stone grit beneath his boots. "Do you like me?" he asked Jux.

Jux did not answer.

"Do you want to know a secret?"

Jux didn't answer, but Sadima heard snuffling sounds. Was he crying?

"Franklin hates me," Somiss said. "Almost as much as

he loves me." He paused. "That's the secret. Did you hear it?" Jux murmured something. "Do you have any secrets, Jux?" Somiss asked.

Sadima held her breath. What was Somiss doing? Had she and Franklin ever kissed where Jux could have seen them? She was nearly sure they hadn't. But they had walked close together, had whispered, touched each other. She felt stupid. How could she have thought for an instant that Somiss wouldn't question the boys and—

"Would you like an orange?" Somiss asked abruptly.

Jux was silent again, and Sadima could imagine him squirming. And when he spoke, she expected him to ask if he had been good enough to earn an orange. But he didn't.

"I've never eaten an orange," Jux said.

"Never?" Somiss asked.

"Never."

Sadima caught her breath. What had the song done? Made Jux forget? But he had remembered his mother—or maybe he had made that up.

Somiss read the song again, twice through, with a few words changed, and then asked Jux a third time if he wanted an orange. Jux said again that he had never eaten one. Sadima clasped her hands. Somiss was experimenting.

"I have a secret. It's about Franklin," Somiss said. "Do you know what it is?"

"No," Jux answered, sounding genuinely surprised at the question.

"Tell me, and I will give you a meat pie tomorrow," Somiss said.

There was a long silence, and Sadima could imagine Jux's face, his agony over not knowing.

"I don't know the secret," he finally admitted.

Sadima rocked back on her heels, trying to understand. Somiss was stealing memories from a helpless child, and she hated him for it. But—it had worked. The magic had worked. It was real.

Sadima felt giddy, filled with a volatile mixture of fear and joy. Magic was *real*. But Somiss would use the boys to experiment, no matter what it did to them. She picked up her lantern and the papers and ran, silent, down the steep vent shaft, all the way to the lake. Just past the rocky ground, she blew out the lantern and walked fast, counting her paces, her hand trailing on the wall. The main passage was empty, and once she was past the tunnel that led to Somiss's chamber, she ran again.

When she got back to her own chamber, heaving in long breaths, she waited until Somiss had walked Jux back to the cage. Then she ran to Franklin's chamber in the dark, intending to wake him, to tell him what had happened. But he wasn't there. She ran her hands over his pallet. His blankets were neat, the corners tucked. He hadn't come back yet.

Where had he gone? Back in her chamber, she found herself staring at the papers she had laid out, thinking about what Somiss had done. The changed words had to be the key. But why have them there at all if they had to be changed to make the magic work? No, she thought. It was the other way around. The words she had seen so often had to mean "stop the magic from working." Otherwise, all the practicing would have been working magic. And that was why the words weren't in Somiss's version of the song for long life. He wanted that one to work.

Sadima sat down and went back to work. She made extra copies of the songs she thought might be real, writing slowly and carefully. Until Franklin came back, until she knew they stood a good chance of getting the boys to safety, she had to make sure that Somiss didn't suspect anything.

— 28 —

I passed the next recitation, even though I shook the whole time. Gerrard passed too. Everyone else came close. Except Will; he missed eleven words. We filed out in our usual silence. Will's shoulders were slumped, and he was unsteady as he headed back to his empty room—wherever it was.

I kept watching the others as they walked, wondering if Jux had made anyone else go into the wasp's nest. I couldn't tell, but I didn't think so. Maybe Will. Maybe that was what was distracting him. Or he was just smothering in the silence. I had wondered before: Had the wizards left all the empty cots in his room? Or had they moved them out one by one as his roommates had died? I had no idea how Will had survived this long.

I hoped, desperately, that Jux wouldn't come for me again. Ever. I wanted the certainty I had felt. I wanted it so much that it scared me. And I couldn't—

"Stop it," I said aloud, to myself. Then I glanced around. I was in the food hall. How long had I been standing there, thinking, asking myself questions I couldn't answer? I pushed my hair back off my face and realized I had forgotten to tie it back. Why hadn't I noticed before? Maybe I had, and had just forgotten? Maybe. Maybe, *maybe* . . .

"Be quiet," I whispered. "Just. Stop." I was sweating. I was very close to crying or screaming or something worse. Gerrard would never renew our pact if I acted this way in front of him. I wanted his friendship—or whatever it was. The pact had never made me feel like being inside the wasp's nest had. But it was better than this. Anything was better than this.

I still wanted to go home and see my father. I pictured him shouting while my mother cried, and clenched my fists, ignoring the pain in my burned fingertips until the image faded.

When I opened my eyes again, I realized that while I was daydreaming, I had crossed the big room and was standing before the huge faceted stone. I was hungry, and the relief I felt at having something real to do, to think about, made my knees weak.

Grateful that I had passed, that I could eat, I imagined Celia's chicken and dumplings. Building the image was easier than it ever had been, so easy that I stepped back from the stone and shook my head, wondering why. Something to do with the wasps?

I forced myself to imagine a whole roasted pheasant, with a sauce of lemon-sugar and mangosteen, and sweet autumn squash, buttered, with honeyed pecans. The complicated image came so quickly that it startled me. So I tried again: Celia's roasted venison. I imagined it, then added the tickle of rising steam, the savory scent of the dilled shallots, the bright sweetness of the sautéed cherries, the peppers, all in a heartbeat. I lifted my right hand, my fourth finger extended.

Then I lowered it without touching the stone.

The wasp. I hadn't touched the wasp at all—it had been like the hummingbirds and the flowers and rocks from so long ago. Was that the lesson I was supposed to learn from the wasps? Maybe it wasn't the perfect certainty? Was I supposed to learn how to make the stone work without touching it so I wouldn't have to burn myself at all?

I heard the thrumming, faint at first, but it got louder. If that *was* the lesson, I hadn't helped anyone by showing them they could use one finger. I had just given them—and myself—a way to miss the lesson altogether. Again. Somiss had said it, back in the beginning—that giving and taking help would make us all weaker.

Disgusted, I walked to the benches and sat down. So what was I supposed to learn from the lamp soot? Had I sidestepped that, too? I had, unless the lesson was to study here, in the food hall, and of course it wasn't. Should I have managed to make a lamp wick by now? Or something more ambitious—like trying to replicate the cold-fire torches in my father's house?

I can't describe what I felt. Not that I am too ashamed to tell it, I mean I really can't. It was like drowning, like being suffocated by contradictions and riddles. I had meant to help and I had hurt myself and everyone else. *Shit.*

I finally lifted my head and stared at the stone on its huge pedestal. What would happen if I tried to move my thoughts into it? It wasn't a hummingbird, or a tree, or a rock, or a wasp. It wasn't like anything else. Maybe the first one who took the risk would find out that the stone had some permanent effect. Like the wasps, but a hundred times more intense. Or maybe, if we opened our minds to the stone, it would kill us. If wasps had changed me so much, what would the stone do to me? Maybe the lesson was to master the hunger, to be smart enough *not* to try it.

Why couldn't they just *tell* us?

I paced the perimeter of the food hall, wondering if I cared whether I died tonight. Or today. Or whatever time it was outside the fucking cliffs. After a long time, I decided I didn't care. So I went back to stare at the stone. But what if I didn't die, and just stayed lost inside myself, unable to tell what was real? What if?

I finally touched the stone to make griddle cakes, and sat at one of the shadowed tables near the entrance. I ate quickly, then bent double to put my plate on the floor. It sparkled and disappeared. I was about to straighten up when I heard footsteps, soft ones, someone hurrying into the food hall. I waited until the footsteps were past me, then straightened up, just enough to see.

It was Gerrard. I moved to stand against the wall, where the shadows were deepest, a heartbeat before he turned to make sure no one had come in behind him. I meant to leave then, silently, but he sat at one of the tables and put his head on his arms. Was he sick? Had he just come to get out of the lamp smoke for a while? No . . . no, it wasn't that. I could hear him breathing, a complex pattern that I didn't recognize. We hadn't learned anything like that. Was Franklin tutoring him or was he making it up?

I flinched when the wailing-wind sound began, louder than usual. The flash of bluish light snapped into being at Gerrard's table. His *table.* I jerked my eyes to the stone and back. Gerrard's food had appeared beside him, not on the stone's pedestal. It was fish stew, I could smell it. But there was bread, too, and something that looked like yams. He began to eat. So. Gerrard had not missed the lesson.

I slid along the wall, breathing quick, silent breaths, then stepped into the passageway when Gerrard bent over his soup. Then I tiptoed down the corridor, heading away from our chamber, away from everything, toward the little cavern where I had once hidden food. I wanted a place to hide, or at least to pretend that I *could* hide.

Once I was beyond anyone hearing my footsteps, I ran a long way down the passage before I slowed and started watching the wall on my right carefully, looking for the shadow that was really an opening. And when I spotted it, I smiled.

I had grown. I could barely fit inside and was so cramped that I couldn't stay there very long. Squirming around to crawl back out, I noticed something I never had before. The farthest interior wall had an even smaller opening at the base. I wriggled around to see how big it was. There was cooler, fresher air streaming through it.

I crouched low and listened, but there was no sound. Did it open onto a passage that led outside? The idea made me feel giddy, but there was no way I could ever fit through the opening. I finally lay on my belly, my knees bent, my bare feet in the air, and tried to see, but there was only darkness on the other side of the wall.

I took slow, deep breaths of the fresh air. I couldn't hear anything. I slid my hand forward and felt the rough floor become smooth. My fingertips brushed something cold and I jerked back, but there was no sound, no scent, nothing. I breathed the first pattern, gathering my courage, then reached in again, with both hands this time. My fingers touched metal, then glass, then a slim curve of wire.

I closed my hands around the cool metal and gently pulled at the lantern, tilting it just enough to bring it out. Then I backed up, carrying it into the tunnel, into the light of the cold-fire torches.

The lantern was very old. It wasn't rusted or dented, I don't mean that. But I had never seen anything like it anywhere but in storybooks about princes and milkmaids. The metal was dull and the chimney glass belled out and had little bubbles in it, like my mother's antique fruit bowls. I wondered who had left it behind and how long ago. The wizards had been in the cliffs forever. Maybe one of the students who had died a hundred years before had used my little chamber.

I exhaled and peered at it. The wick was a thin flax rope, more or less, and there was another part I had never noticed in a lamp before, a tiny netted piece, held up by thin wire, wider at the bottom to fit around the round piece that held the flax wick. All the pieces were clean—they looked new. The netted pattern was intricate and almost pretty. The little wire armature was simple enough.

I stared at it for a long, long time, turning it every which way. Then I slid the lantern back through the opening and walked away. I had spent hours in that little chamber the first year. Why hadn't I ever seen the little opening in the back wall? Because I had been small enough to fit without so much crawling and wall bumping?

I passed the food hall and went back to the room to get my lamp and striker. Gerrard was studying, and he ignored me as usual. It took six tries, and six blistered fingers, but the seventh time I got it right. A new wick and the netted piece, the perfect size to fit over it. And the whole time I was picturing the little armature—changing the size a little, the angle of the little wire frame—I could hear the thrumming, and I felt wonderful.

When I lit the wick, the flame sprang up clear and bright, the little netting glowed and there was no smoke at all. I made another set, then placed the soot-ruined wick on the floor. Like our plates and silverware, it sparkled into nothingness. I was happy. I hadn't copied something I remembered. I had *made* something.

When I walked into the room, I put the new wick and armature on Gerrard's desk, then got into bed. I was tired. Really tired. And the thrumming, faint but close, was a lullaby to me. If the wizards didn't kill me for what I had done, there were other things I wanted to try to make. If they did, I could stop worrying about everything. What could be more certain than that?

29

The next morning Sadima gave the boys their food and their lessons, then told them a long story. There were two more big sacks of food leaning against the wall. How long was Franklin going to be gone, now when she desperately needed him here? She went back to her chamber, copied a third of the stack of papers, then ran to the vent shaft.

Somiss recited for hours. Uneasy, Sadima copied everything, resting her hand when he chanted the same song over and over. And she listened, hoping that she would not hear a boy's voice, and she was grateful when she didn't. But when she hurried back to look in Franklin's chamber, she almost wept. He was not there. Sitting at her fruit-crate desk, she stared at the paper before her without seeing it. She was awake most of that night, listening, but Franklin did not return.

By the fourth morning, trying to give the boys their lesson, Sadima was frantic. She could not ask Somiss where Franklin was—or anything else. She thought about showing Jux the way out, giving him coins from her honey tin. But she knew that if Jux was by himself, he would go back to the life he knew. If he did, Somiss would find him and bring him back. Or kill him. Sadima felt her eyes stinging, but she refused to cry in front of the boys.

Sadima had broken the bread into smaller pieces after the third day, just in case, so there was still a little left on the fifth. But the boys' water bucket was almost empty, and the slops bucket in the cage was overfull and stank horribly. She thought about explaining that to Somiss, asking him for the key, but she knew he would never trust her with it, not for a moment. And asking would make him wary.

The next day Sadima woke and tiptoed to Franklin's chamber, carrying her lantern, holding her breath. Then she stood at the arched entryway and fought tears when she saw his empty bed. Maybe he was never going to come back.

Walking to the big cavern, she was trembling, but she forced herself to think—to try to plan. Maybe she could get the key from Somiss's chamber somehow. If Franklin was gone another day or two, she and the boys could be ready when he returned. They could all be headed for the mountains before Somiss found out he was alone in the cliffs.

Midday, sitting in the vent shaft, Sadima made copies of two songs as Somiss recited them. Then he went silent. Waiting, she reread them both. They were familiar, but changed. The last three lines of each one were identical, clearly meant to be repeated. She was still studying them when she heard Somiss talking. "Sit there."

"Please, sir, I—"

Jux. Sadima leaned forward, her forehead resting on the grate, furious with herself. Somiss's cruelty could be terrible, dangerous. She should not have waited for Franklin.

"Sir, I—"

There was a thud, and then Jux cried out. Sadima stood up, one hand over her mouth. This was her fault. She grabbed her lantern and sprinted down the long, slanted shaft, crawled through the small chamber, and then ran down the steep passageway. She slowed as she crossed the stone-littered ground by the lake, then put her lantern out and ran in the dark, counting steps and turns until she stood at the head of the passage that led to Somiss's room. Breathing hard, she cupped her hands around her mouth. "Somiss!" she shouted. "Please! Come quickly!"

The instant she heard his footsteps at the far end of the passageway she ran again, in total darkness and near silence, all the way back to her own chamber. There she lit her lantern and hurried back into the corridor.

Somiss was coming toward her, walking fast.

"Hurry!" she called to him, then ran toward the big chamber. By the time Somiss got there, she was standing beside the cage, breathing hard, her lantern lifted high.

"He's gone," she cried out as Somiss got closer. "The little one. Jux. He's gone! He's not in the cage with the others." She gestured. "I've looked everywhere!"

Somiss stared at her. Sadima hoped he would get angry, shout and pace, maybe even hit her. If she could keep him here long enough, Jux would have a chance to slip past, to hide.

But Somiss turned and looked intently into the cage, from one boy to the next. Mabiki was near the front, the tallest of the unnamed boys standing beside him.

Somiss pointed at him. "You. Come with me." The boy looked up. Somiss pulled a ring with three big, ornate keys from his pocket and fit one of them into the lock, then opened the door just wide enough to stand sideways in the opening. Sadima stared at the keys. What were the other two for?

"What's your name?" Somiss asked.

The boy looked down again.

"He won't tell," Sadima said. "They are all afraid of constables and—"

"He never talks," Jux said from behind them. Sadima turned; he looked into her eyes for an instant, and she saw his gratitude and his fear. But he hadn't hidden. He had come to help her.

"Perhaps he will tell me his name," Somiss said, reaching for Jux's arm to drag him forward and shove him into the cage. Then he gestured at the tall boy again. "It will be better if you don't make me pull you out."

The boy came forward, his head down, his shoulders

hunched. Sadima wanted to scream at Somiss. She couldn't. It would help nothing and harm everything. An instant later the nameless boy lurched forward. It almost looked like he had stumbled, but he shoved Somiss back one step and then kept going, sprinting, disappearing into the darkness beyond the lanterns—all in the space between two heartbeats. Somiss spun around, shouting at Sadima, but the boy was already past her. Mabiki whooped and the others cheered.

"Quiet," Somiss shouted as he fumbled with the keys. "Not one more sound!"

The boys in the cage stared through the bars, their eyes wild and their fists clenched, looking in the direction the boy had run. Sadima listened. There was no sound of footfalls. There was no sound of breathing. Had the boy been clever enough to run a few steps, then slow, walking silently to the far wall? If he followed it to his right, he would end up in the narrow entrance tunnel—he would find his way out. If not, he could get lost forever.

Mabiki leaned against the bars. "Sir?"

"Shut your mouth," Somiss spat.

Without speaking, he pointed at Sadima, then himself, and motioned with both hands, drawing curved lines in the air. It was clear enough. They would walk parallel paths, then curve toward each other near the passageway at the far end of the big chamber. She nodded.

"Hold your lantern high," he murmured.

She nodded again.

Her heart aching, Sadima did as she was told, walking

as slowly as she could, trying to think. There would be no good end to this. If the boy went back to Limòri, Somiss would find him and kill him. Or maybe the boy would tell someone they were living in the cliffs, and the king's guards would come and arrest them all. Somiss's work would end up in the king's library, and all of this misery would be for nothing, unless she left soon enough and got away, taking her papers with her.

"Faster!" Somiss hissed at her.

Sadima obeyed, gathering her skirt in one hand. Somiss's boots scraped on the stone. She tried to make her own footsteps louder, sliding her bare feet over the grit. If the boy was trying to stay clear, any sound she could make would help him.

Thirty steps later, nearing the far wall, Sadima stepped on something soft. She was startled, but managed not to react. She took three longer strides and held her lantern even higher, counting to five before she glanced at Somiss. He hadn't noticed. She exhaled, glad the boy had lain flat and held still—and that she, not Somiss, had been the one to step on his hand.

"Can you hear anything?" Somiss whispered. It sounded like a shout in the silence.

"No," she answered.

Moments later they were at the mouth of the narrow exit passage. Sadima stared at Somiss. His pale skin had become chalk white from living in the darkness. His eyes looked colorless in the lantern light. He jabbed his finger at the darkness and whispered, "He's here. He didn't make it out in the dark." Then he raised his voice. "Show yourself. You will be sorry if you don't."

Sadima swallowed, pressing her lips together, hoping the boy's nerve would hold.

"Speak!" Somiss shouted.

"I don't think I have ever heard him talk," Sadima said.

Somiss looked down at her, lifting his lantern close to her face. "What?"

She met his eyes and spoke louder so the boys in the cage would hear. "That boy. I never heard him speak. Not once."

"Lady," Jux called out. "He's a mute. And you kept asking his name!" All the boys laughed, whooping and jeering. She wanted to kiss them all for their quick wit and their courage. They were jostling each other, slapping each other's shoulders, raising a din to give their friend a chance. Somiss shouted at them, but they pretended not to hear. When the laughter ended, Mabiki bumped Wren and they started arguing, yelling at each other. Sadima wondered how well they had known each other before the cage, how many times children like these had saved each other's lives, risking their own.

"Be still!" Somiss roared.

Then, in the sudden silence, he reached out and gripped Sadima's arm so hard that she almost cried out. "Find him," he hissed. "If you don't, I'll chain them all to the bars."

Sadima stared up at him, dumbstruck. He shoved her to the side and walked away. She waited, listening, until his footsteps faded. Then she crept forward, turning along the wall, walking until she could peer down the main passage-way. He was going back to his chamber. Once the bright speck of his lantern winked out in the distance, Sadima went back to the cage.

Mabiki was leaning through the bars. "Tegrid?" he called softly. "Are you here?"

There was no answer. He said it a little louder. And then they all heard the scream. Sadima set down her lantern and ran, but by the time she was standing in the dark at the entrance to Somiss's passageway, there was only silence.

Had Somiss killed the boy? Or had he run, terrified, into the passageways? She walked past Somiss's corridor in the dark and kept going, turning into every branching passage, whispering the boy's name, begging him to answer, promising him she could show him a way out. There was only silence.

Coming back, Sadima heard Somiss reciting.

Walking slowly, she wept. She had let the days slide past, waiting for Franklin. And now one boy was lost, or dead, or bound in Somiss's room.

30

A wizard pounded on the door, and I jerked upright in the dark. "We're awake!"

Another class with Somiss so soon? Not likely. My stomach tightened as I watched Gerrard lighting his lamp. I could tell the instant he noticed the wick and armature I had made. He glanced at me and set them carefully on the floor beneath his desk. Then he washed, pissed, and waited for me to finish.

The wizard walked even faster than most, but we were still the last ones there. The chamber was so small that we all had to sit cross-legged in a circle, our knees touching. There was only one cold-fire torch, high overhead, and its light didn't reveal the ceiling. We all kept glancing upward. I didn't know what anyone else was thinking, but I was afraid that Somiss and one of his chairs would appear and crush us. But Somiss didn't come. No one did. We all just sat there, afraid to talk, afraid to leave, afraid to do anything at all. Will looked sick. His eyes were half-closed and rimmed in shadows.

I started to worry. Did the wizards know I had fixed the lamps by experimenting instead of remembering? Did they know I had made extras for Gerrard? I glanced at him. He looked uneasy too. Maybe he was worried about the book. I tried to catch his eye, but he aimed his gaze straight across the circle, over Will's and Jordan's heads, at nothing. He kept it there.

"Could we be in the wrong place?" Will finally whispered.

No one answered. I met his eyes and lifted my shoulders just a little more than my next breath would have. How could any of us know? He lowered his chin in an almost invisible nod. I watched him from the edge of my vision. He was so thin. He was the one who would probably die next—and yet, somehow, he was the only one who'd had the courage to speak, to question what the wizards were doing.

"Line up."

Somiss's rough voice startled all of us. I looked upward first, expecting to see him descending in a chair. We all did. Our knees bumped, and there was a sound of indrawn breath. But he wasn't there. He was standing in the corridor. We stood up and shuffled ourselves into a line and filed out. There was another wizard with him. He was a tall man with dark, curling hair and an expressionless face. He was wearing a white robe. White?

Out of habit, we lined up beside our roommates. Gerrard was first, so I stood beside him. Jordan, Levin, and Luke made the next group. Will was last. Somiss looked at Gerrard and me, then gestured at the other wizard. "Go with him."

The others left, following Somiss. I swallowed hard, wondering what was going to happen to us. The wizard yawned. "My name is Mabiki," he said quietly, and walked away. We ran to keep up.

My thoughts were churning. With every step, I tried to remember if I had ever seen a wizard here or at my father's house, or on the docks casting for good weather, or any-where else in Limòri, wearing a white robe. I was sure I hadn't. But I had never seen the green or shit-brown ones we'd been given either. Only black. Was he a student? He had told us his name. Only Somiss, Franklin, and Jux had ever done that.

The wizard turned abruptly, and the robe belled out like a ball gown. Silk? White silk. Did it mean something? It had to. Everything meant something here. This man might be an executioner, and the others had gone to Somiss's regular class. But would a wizard who was going to kill us tell us his name? I glanced at Gerrard. His face was closed, hard as the stone walls.

The wizard turned abruptly to the right, then twice to the left, all within ten or twelve paces. I made up a sentence as I always did, but the branching passages were so close together that I could barely keep up. I stole another glance at Gerrard. His lips were moving slightly, and I could only hope that between us we could find our way back. Maybe it meant we weren't going to be killed, though. Why would they bother to confuse us like this first?

I tried to hear the thrumming and was relieved when I could, or thought I could, anyway. It was faint. Gerrard glanced at me and nodded, in the barely visible way we always did. I lifted my eyebrows a little to tell him that I didn't know what he meant, but he was already looking straight ahead again.

Suddenly we were at the base of the long incline that led to Jux's forest. I immediately felt less afraid. If it was Jux's class, we had a chance of surviving. I only hoped it was snakes or tigers—anything but wasps. Every day I longed for that feeling of certainty. It was a physical ache, stronger than hunger. If I ever felt it again, I might be lost forever.

Halfway up the second leg of the incline, Mabiki stopped abruptly. He lifted his right hand and gestured at the wall, then the floor. The wall blurred, and he walked through it. I had seen it before, of course, but it was astounding to watch from so close—we were only a step behind him. He passed into the black rock wall like water would seep through cloth. We could see his silhouette for a heart-beat because his white robe seemed to show through the stone—then it darkened again. He was gone.

Gerrard was staring.

"He pointed at the wall, then the fl—," I began.

Gerrard lifted one hand to silence me; his eyes moved over the stone below our feet, then the wall, then back. The stone floor suddenly became soft as river sand. I stepped sideways and sank in to my ankles, then my knees. It was so cold. I gasped, lurched backward, and sank to my waist. Instantly I was in up to my chest, my breath coming in desperate gasps as I slid lower. Gerrard was trying to escape, his arms in a desperate windmill, but he was sinking too. I tried to think.

Had the wizard been casting his thoughts into the stone, coaxing it into becoming soft for his exit, so it would swallow us? Even if we managed to make it hard again now, it would crush us. I flailed, trying to stay afloat, to swim upward, but it was like swimming in a winter fog. I kept sinking, until the clammy stone-mist enclosed me completely. It flowed into my lungs.

I felt Gerrard's hand on my back, pulling at my robe. Frantic, terrified of suffocating, I twisted and grabbed at his arm, but he jerked free. And it was only then that I realized: I *was* breathing. I was surrounded by impossible liquid stone, and somehow I was still breathing. I could see, too, a little anyway. There wasn't much light. Gerrard grabbed at my robe again, but he couldn't hang on and slid away from me into the murk. I turned, trying to drag my feet forward, trying to walk, to find my way out before the stone hardened and swallowed me forever.

I walked for a long time, cold and scared. I kept squinting, trying to see the light of a cold-fire torch. When I felt a sudden weight on my back, then my shoulder, I reached up—and caught hold of Gerrard's hand. But he was climbing me to get out, climbing me like I was a *tree*.

I was so angry it paralyzed me. He was on my shoulders in a heartbeat, then put one foot on my head. I tried to grab his ankle to drag him back, but before I could, his weight lifted and he was gone. And in the same strange way that I had heard Jux's eerie laugh inside my skull a few times, and Franklin's voice when we were still in his classes, I heard Gerrard's. He said two words: *Stay warm.*

I opened my mouth to scream at him, and the gray mist filled it. I spit and gagged and tried again to swim upward, but I couldn't. I tried to calm myself, but I couldn't do that, either. I gagged again, doubling over, and when I straightened there was nothing beneath my feet, nothing within reach of my hands.

After a long time, I stopped fighting, sad and almost relieved. Maybe I would never have to be afraid again. Or hungry or angry. The cold slowed my breathing, my movements. Even my thoughts. I stretched out one arm, then lowered it. Was this what it was like to be buried? It didn't hurt, really, but I knew it would kill me before long. So, I thought, there was no room full of bones. The dead boys were buried in the stone itself, their bones crushed into nothing. It made perfect sense.

Maybe, I thought, dying wouldn't hurt.

Maybe dying wouldn't.

Maybe dying.

Maybe.

And then I felt something poke me in the back. Hard

and sharp. I twitched away from it. Not far enough. I felt it again and turned. Then the sudden pain was in my shoulder. I jerked to the side and it was in my chest. I reached out to stop it and felt something rough. Wood? Leaves? It jabbed me once more, and I grabbed at it with both hands, wrestling it to the side. But I couldn't get away from it. It was all I could do to hang on to it. And then I realized I was being dragged upward.

When my head broke the surface, I saw Gerrard, leaning backward against my weight, every muscle in his body taut, the tendons in his neck standing out like rigging lines. Slowly, careful not to jerk at the branch, I dragged myself up, hand over hand, until I was out to my waist. Then Gerrard heaved backward, a sound like an animal in pain coming from his lips, and I was on solid stone, gagging, shaking.

Gerrard stood up and stumbled. He tried to steady himself with the stick, but it skidded over the edge and an instant later he fell, disappearing into the stone-fog.

I lurched to my feet, reaching for the branch, trying not to lose sight of him. I was numb with cold, snatching each breath. It took far too long for me to get the branch close enough for him to grab it. But once he did, I walked backward, forcing my knees to bend, my hands to stay closed around the rough bark. I pulled him halfway up, then lost my footing and sat down, jarring my bones, clacking my teeth. I shoved at the stone with my feet, moving backward in little hitches, until he was out, all but his legs. From there, he crawled toward me and I reached out, meaning to help, and slumped sideways. He collapsed facedown.

When we finally stood up, I pointed at the branch, my whole body vibrating with cold. "J-J-J-J-J-Jux's f-f-f-f-forest?"

Gerrard nodded. He showed me his hands, torn and bloody. I could see white at the bottom of the worst cut. Bone? Was the door handle a blade again? I looked at my own hands. They weren't much better. The inclined corridor below us was stone-mist as far as I could see. We were standing on the solid stone ramp that ended at Jux's round copper door. But I didn't want to go up the incline. I wanted to go back to our room and get under my blankets until I stopped shaking.

What was this shit supposed to teach us? I was so angry there was no room for fear. If I could fix a lamp, I could make a stinking rock floor. I remembered what Mabiki had done.

"The wizards will expec—," Gerrard began.

"Fuck the wizards," I interrupted him.

I stared at the stone-fog and imagined the floor the way it had been before—hard, black, rough. I didn't *remember* every gouge and bulge, but I looked uphill and memorized a section of the solid wall as well as I could, then pushed the image down my arm into my right hand. I pointed at the mist. The fog stopped swirling. It settled, it darkened, and it solidified. We were standing in a solid stone passageway again. And I felt hollow. Heavy and hollow and strange.

Gerrard put out his hand, blood dripping from the wound. I understood him. We had saved each other's lives. We were equally grateful. And he was surprised that I had been able to make the stone solid again. So was I. But I needed to vomit. There was a sick, clammy sweat seeping out of the skin on the back of my neck and across my forehead. I walked off a little way and threw up what little there was in my stomach. Then I went back. Gerrard was waiting. He extended his hand again.

I looked into his eyes, my hands at my sides. I tipped my head just enough for him to see it, then I raised my brows the same way. I lifted my left hand and touched my heart, then my own shoulder. I stood straighter, squaring up my stance. And I made my mouth into a perfect line, not curved up or down.

If there was going to be a pact again, I needed it to be certain. Once and for all. I would be a worthy ally this time—not lazy, not assuming anything anymore. But it meant no quitting, no backing out until we destroyed the academy or died trying.

For a long time, Gerrard just looked at me. Then he nodded, and I knew he had understood. I put out my hand and he clasped it, the blood from his wounds mixing with the blood from mine before we let go and stepped back.

And so we walked, side by side, following the usual route, leaning on each other all the way back to the room. By the time we got to our door, my shivering nausea had eased a little. Gerrard's hand had stopped dripping blood. And when we went inside, there were two red robes, one on his bed, and one on mine.

I could hear the thrumming in the stone, steady as a heartbeat.

– 31 –

Sadima blew out her lamp and dozed in the big cavern, sitting up, her back braced against the stone wall opposite the cage. She was ready. She had gotten her knife, then had run all the way to the rampike pine to get the coins and her shoes. It had been hard to rebury her paint box and the papers she had brought from Limòri the night of the fire. She knew she might never see them again. But she couldn't carry everything.

She had the current copies of every song she had heard Somiss recite tied up in her old shawl. Another set was safe in the vent shaft. She had rolled two blankets with her things inside them and torn a worn-out skirt into strips to tie the bundles. There was nothing left to wait for but darkness, and one last chance to take Franklin with her. She glanced at the pear-shaped hole, high in the cavern wall. It would be dusk soon.

Sadima had left her lantern lit in her chamber, some of her papers laid out, so that if Somiss came, she could tell him she was sitting in the dark, hoping to catch the missing boy sneaking back to his friends. She would pretend she hadn't heard the scream. But Somiss didn't appear. Sadima hoped he was finished reciting, preparing to go to sleep.

When she finally heard footsteps coming from the entrance tunnel, she stood up, tears in her eyes. Moments later Franklin was beside the cage, laying down bags of bread and apples. Sadima ran to help him. He was exhausted, barely keeping his balance as they divided the bread and gave the boys their food. Walking beside him as he started unsteadily toward his chamber, a small carry-sack still under his arm, Sadima told him about Tegrid, hoping that would be enough to convince him.

He said nothing until they had turned into their passage-way and walked halfway to her chamber. Then he stopped. "Is the boy—?"

"We all heard him scream," Sadima explained again. "I walked the tunnels and couldn't find him." Her hands were shaking. "Somiss said if I didn't, he would chain the other boys to the bars."

Franklin touched her cheek. "There are no chains," he told her wearily. "I will tell him I can't find any. He'll forget about it." He shut his eyes and rubbed his face with one hand.

Sadima leaned close. "Franklin, we have to leave," she said. "All of us. Tonight."

He shook his head, started to say something, then couldn't find the words. "After I sleep," he managed. "Then we can talk."

"Just go get the key," Sadima said. "Tell Somiss you have to empty the slops bucket in the cage."

Franklin shook his head. "I have been talking with—"

"I don't care," she interrupted him, wishing she could shout instead of whisper. And before he could say another word, she told him what she had overheard. "Jux's memory was gone," she whispered. "The magic worked."

Franklin blinked. His lips parted. "Truly?"

She nodded. "Most of the songs are unmarked—from the years before I came. Somiss intends to find out what they're for by using them on the boys."

She waited for Franklin to look shocked or even just helpless and angry. But he only lowered his head. She put her hands on his shoulders. "There's no reason to stay. I have copies of all the songs. All we need is the key to the cage." She waited for him to look up. "And you."

It hurt to watch the contortions of his face. He was so sad. So desperately tired. He looked into her eyes. "Soon," he said. "I promise. But the Eridians won't help unless Somiss involves their scholars. I still have to talk him into it. After that—"

"No!" Sadima interrupted. "I have copies of everything. *We* can give the songs to the Eridians."

Franklin was shaking his head before she finished. "But Somiss has learned more about the translations than we can possibly know. He's the only one who can explain all that to other scholars. He won't want to, but I can—"

"The boys are all bone thin," Sadima cut him off. She was shaking. "Who knows what the songs are for?" she whispered. "He might kill all of—"

"Somiss's mother gave him more money," Franklin interrupted her. "He's hired cousins of mine." She started to speak, but he took her hand and looked into her eyes. "Sadima. Stop. Just listen to me. There are passages beneath Limòri, three hundred years of smugglers' tunnels and thieves' dens. One runs up to Ferrin Hill. They'll dig a branch from that one and . . ." He trailed off, gesturing vaguely, and Sadima could see how close to collapsing he was. "Food," he said finally. "Food and everything else can be brought underground to a meadow less than an hour's walk from here." He smiled and pushed her hair back over her shoulder. "The boys can help me carry. They'll get to go outside. It will be so much better and—"

"No," Sadima said, pulling her hand free. "It won't. And you know it. Somiss will never let them out of that cage. He will never take the chance of one of them leading the king's guards or his father back here."

Franklin nodded wearily. "Not for a while," he said. "But he won't always be afraid of his father finding out he's here, not if the magic is real." Sadima heard the wonder in his voice when he spoke the last few words. His eyes were full of something she had never seen in them before, and she wasn't sure what it meant. She took a long breath.

"Did you hear me?" she whispered. "He is going to use

the boys to find out . . ." She stopped because Franklin's face was full of pain. But not surprise. "You knew?" she whispered. "Is that why he brought them here?"

Franklin met her eyes. "They are street orphans," he said quietly. "Three or four of them would have starved or frozen over the winter if we hadn't brought them—"

"We?" Sadima interrupted him and stepped back, feeling sick. "You helped trick them?"

"Sadima," Franklin said, "there is so much good to come from all this." He touched her cheek and she saw both shame and sadness in his eyes. And love for her. A crippled, resigned, useless kind of love.

"You won't ever leave Somiss, will you?" she whispered.

"Someday," he said. "Yes. I want everything you want, Sadima."

She stared at him. He was lying. He wanted it to be true, but it wasn't. It never would be. Franklin loved her, but he loved Somiss more—Somiss and the dream of magic they had shared since they were little boys. He knew it. And now, finally, so did she.

"I can convince Somiss to work with the Eridians," Franklin was saying. "I know I can." He fumbled in the sack he was carrying. "Here, I almost forgot." He had brought her a new bar of soap.

Sadima felt sick. Franklin was hoping that a gift of soap would buy him a day or two or three, and that somehow the days would add up to her lifetime, that he could stay with Somiss and help him murder boys and still have her love.

She took the soap and thanked him, swallowing both rage and tears. She lifted her head and squared her shoulders. And then she lied. "Maybe you're right. Maybe we should wait."

Franklin nodded, smiling, his face transformed with relief. "I have to leave again, but not for as long. After that, I'll talk to him about the boys. And—"

"Franklin," she said gently. "You can barely stand up." She guarded her churning thoughts as she touched his cheek. She took his hand and led him to his pallet. He lay down and she knelt beside him.

"I love you," Franklin said. "I am so sorry for all this. I wish I could—"

"So do I," she told him, and kissed his mouth to stop his words. When she leaned back, his eyes were closed. A moment later he was asleep. Sadima stood up. She sang the song for long life over him fifty times, whispering the words, barely shaping the melody, tears on her cheeks. He would stay. And he would be the only hope for the next cage full of boys.

Back in her own chambers, she used her pile of old clothes and a half ream of paper to plump up what was left of her bedding to look like she was asleep. If Franklin just glanced in when he left in the morning, it would work. She picked up her quill and a fresh sheet of paper. She had never written anything but the words of the songs, but she was amazed at how easy it was to write her own thoughts. Too easy. The first attempt was a torrent of anger. She crumpled it and used her lantern flame to burn it. Then she started over.

"Thank you for understanding me," she wrote, "for saving me from a father and brother who never could. I will find a home and give the boys a chance to grow up to be good men."

She stopped and stared at the paper for a long time before she added the last few lines: "Please, Franklin, stand up to Somiss. Protect the ones he tries to hurt. You are all they have." She started to write "I love you," then didn't. It wasn't true anymore. She wrote "I wish you well" instead.

Sadima put the note on the flat-topped rock by the lake, weighted with a stone big enough so that the white edges of the paper didn't show. Franklin would notice the out-of-place stone, if he ever found this chamber again. No one else would, not before the paper was yellow and brittle, anyway. On her way back, she scattered all the cairns, rebuilding them to form a false trail. It was the best she could do.

Sadima asked the boys if they had seen Tegrid, begging them to tell her the truth. They all shook their heads.

"I think Somiss killed him," Mabiki whispered. Jux nodded. So did Wren and a few of the others.

"Are you going to help us?" Jux asked.

Sadima spoke her hopes aloud, as though they were truths, so the boys wouldn't be afraid. "Once we are long gone, tomorrow, Franklin will leave again, like he always does. My bed looks like I am in it, so he won't know. He won't come back for two or three days. If we are fortunate, Somiss won't have any reason to leave his chamber for at least that long."

"You have the key?" Jux asked. His eyes were wide.

"I have to go get it," she said, keeping her voice level. "I won't be long."

"Where will you take us?"

Sadima looked up. The boy asking the question had never spoken to her before. She met his eyes. "I know the way to the farm country near the mountains."

There was a murmuring among the boys.

"What will we eat there?" Jux whispered.

"We will find a farmer who has no children," Sadima told him. "Or a widow. Or an old farm no one is working. I know how to grow everything," she went on. "I will teach you. It will be hard work, but it will be much better than this—and better than it was in Limòri."

They nodded solemnly, and she hoped, with all her heart, that she wasn't making up one more story to keep them from giving up—that she could make it true. "Roll up one blanket each and make the rest look like you are still here, sound asleep," she said. "Be quiet, and be ready."

They all nodded, and she walked back across the cavern to her little pile of belongings, stacked against the wall in the pitch darkness. She took the knife out of her bundle and slipped it into the bodice of her dress. It was ice-cold against her skin as she walked, in the dark, all the way to Somiss's corridor.

There was no sound.

She tiptoed to the arched entrance slowly, silently, fear stiffening her spine. His lamps were out, the darkness was complete. She could hear him breathing, slow and soft. He was asleep. Sadima slowed her own breathing and calmed herself, picturing the room she had searched so thoroughly.

She could hear her own pulse. If Somiss woke, he would kill her and order Franklin to dig the grave in the woods. And Franklin would, weeping. Then he would come back into the passages to see what Somiss wanted him to do next.

Her angry thoughts muting her fear, using her hands to guide her, she crept forward and made her way around the desk. Then she took a long time crossing the small distance to the bookshelves on the back wall. She knelt, carefully and quietly, to run her hand along the wall below the lowest shelf. If she couldn't find the keys, if she had been mistaken, or if he had moved them . . . but her fingers touched the cool silver and she exhaled. She lifted the ring gently from the hook, sliding her fingers between the three keys so they wouldn't jangle against each other. Once they were tight in her hand, she rose, then stood still, feeling the cool metal of the knife against her breast.

It wasn't a big knife, but it was very sharp.

This would be her last chance.

One quick slash and the world would be free of Somiss. After what he had done to Franklin, to the boys, and what she knew he would do to others if he was left alive . . .

She drew the knife out of her bodice.

But then she just stood in the dark, trembling, the keys in one hand, the knife in the other. What if Franklin was right? What if Somiss was the only one who could put magic back together? He had already managed more than she had thought possible. And Franklin would stay, would always be there to absorb Somiss's anger, to watch for the tiny moments when he could be influenced, reminded that he was human.

And Franklin would never forgive her if she killed Somiss. She blinked, ashamed that it mattered to her. But it did. Just enough. Just enough to make her start walking, silent and slow, until she was out of Somiss's room. Halfway to the big cavern, she put the knife back in her bodice and ran, fleet as a deer, in the dark, two fingers on the wall until she was close enough to see the lanterns on the cage.

Her skin prickling with fear and joy, she turned the key in the lock and swung open the iron-barred door. "Not a sound." The boys nodded as she tucked the keys in her bodice.

She walked the nine of them down the entrance tunnel, warning them to duck where the ceiling was low. And then they were outside. The cool night air was stirring. The stars were bright against the moonless sky. Sadima turned to the boys. "We should get as far as we can before morning." They all nodded and followed her into the woods.

32

Gerrard and I didn't talk about what had happened, but there was a difference in the way he acted—not in class, but alone, in our chamber. The set of his shoulders was different, less stiff, less *ready.*

I understood. I might never be his friend—I wasn't sure Gerrard knew how to have a friend. But I was no longer his enemy. When he used a strip of his old robe to bind his hand, I tied the final knot. When I was struggling with a fifteen-syllable word, he whispered the correct pronunciation four or five times one evening, just that single word. Then he went back to whatever he was trying to do, changing breathing patterns every few seconds. It wasn't simple thought moving, I was certain of that now. He was working hard at something else. And he wasn't hiding it anymore. I hoped that meant he trusted me.

The next recitation class was two days later. We were the only two in red robes, whatever that meant. Somiss didn't seem to notice. Everyone else did. I caught Luke peering at me, at my face, and I realized that it was more than the robe. He was looking into my eyes. No. *At* my eyes. They had to be less bloodshot. Our lamps didn't smoke at all anymore. I kept my eyes down. If Luke had noticed, Somiss might. Making the new wicks by using the old lantern I had found could still get me killed.

If it *was* cheating to copy something real, without using memories. All of a sudden, I remembered the soap Gerrard always made. He had used mine as a model—mine was a perfect copy of the soap I had used all my life, made by my father's servants. But Gerrard had added a flowery scent. He had never been punished. Maybe making things up was a lesson we were supposed to learn. Maybe—

"You," Somiss said, jabbing one index finger in my direction. I closed my eyes to concentrate, and I passed.

"Go eat. All of you," Somiss said at the end of our recitations. We all drew a breath at once. None of us moved. Only Gerrard and I had passed. The others had come close, except for Luke and Will. Luke had missed a dozen words, Will only four.

Somiss gestured. "Go."

We got to our feet and filed out. I held my breath as I passed him and stared straight ahead, but when I looked back, Somiss was still sitting there, perched on his chair.

It was another carved monstrosity with seven eyes and a feathered tail that curved around the backrest. As I turned away, I wondered if he had *made* the chairs. What was the difference between a fancy chair and a lamp wick, except complexity? Was that what they wanted us to do? Learn to make anything we could think of? Or would they kill us if we tried? I wanted to just *ask*. How could the wizards expect anyone to graduate if we didn't know what they wanted from us?

We walked silently in a loose group toward the food hall. I kept pace with Gerrard. No one was walking fast. Permission to eat without passing the recitation? Jordan, Levin, Luke, and Will looked worried. They had to be wondering if they should try, or if Somiss just wanted them to burn their hands again. Or something worse. I saw Luke watching me, that dangerous, angry hardness in his eyes. I looked aside, but not fast enough. He spit in my direction, and I pretended I hadn't seen him do it.

I let the line form in front of me, partly because I knew Will and Jordan would be the hungriest, and partly because I wanted to stay away from Luke, who had crowded his way to the front. But mostly, I stood back because I didn't trust Somiss. What would the stone do to us this time?

Luke went first, and he stood still for a long time, his shoulders hitched up high and his stance wide, like someone facing a fight that scared him. At first I thought he just wanted us all to admire his courage, but as the time went on, I began to think he was even more afraid than he had expected to be. I would have been. Any of us would have. That was why none of us was first in line.

Luke finally put out the middle finger of his left hand and touched the stone. The light flashed, and there was the odd, faint sound of trees crying in the wind. Then a plate of food appeared. It looked like roast lamb, and it smelled good, and I realized how hungry I was. Maybe Somiss just didn't want us to get too weak. Maybe no one was being punished for anything. Will went next, and his plate was full of warm bread and gravy. I exhaled. Somiss hadn't lied. He was at least willing to keep us alive in order to torture us longer.

Jordan was next. He stood a moment, making the image in his mind, then he reached out to touch the stone with the smallest finger of his right hand. He screamed. He kept screaming. The light flashed and he fell, his back arched hard. His food appeared, but he was on the stone floor, faceup, his whole body jerking like a fish on a riverbank. Levin dropped to his knees beside him.

"Leave him alone."

Levin leaned back, but he didn't stand up. We all turned toward Somiss.

He was standing just inside the door. "You have all missed a lesson," he said in his hoarse, strangled voice. "Until you all learn it, this will happen to someone." He paused, and I was sure I saw a half smile on his lips. "Sometimes."

And then he was gone.

"Jordan?" Levin was whispering. "Jordan? Can you hear me?"

I turned. Jordan lay still, his skin white as eggshells. Levin was bent over, pleading with him to say something, to sit up. Levin suddenly rocked back on his heels. "He needs water. His mouth is so dry his lips are cracking."

Jordan's eyes fluttered, and he managed to sit up. He stared at Levin, his face spasming, his hands twitching. "Wa-water." It was a rasp, barely understandable.

I glanced back toward the wide, arched entrance, then peered into the shadows along the walls. Somiss was gone. It was silent in the chamber except for the sound of our breathing and Jordan's desperate whispers. I looked at Gerrard. He shook his head, barely, just enough for me to understand. He wasn't going to show everyone what the lesson was. It was up to me.

It was my fault they had missed it. Instead of learning to use the stone without touching it, I had shown everyone a way to avoid being burned. I exhaled. I wanted to make water for Jordan. But I was so scared that the stone would hurt me if I touched it and that it would swallow me the way the wasps had if I didn't. Maybe this time I would go crazy and never come back. That terrified me.

"Stop it," I said to myself, then realized I had said it aloud. Luke laughed. I went to stand before the stone and positioned myself so that everyone could see I was too far back to touch it. I held myself rigid. My heart was banging inside my chest and I was sick with fear, but I imagined a glass of water, clear and cold. I moved the image into my arm, my hand. My knees were shaking.

I was about to point at the stone when Gerrard shoved

his way past Luke and stood in front of me. "Don't," he whispered, then faced the others and raised his voice. "I'll bring water from our room. It isn't that far."

Gerrard clasped my forearm, his eyes warning me to calm down, not to do anything stupid while he was gone. Then he turned and sprinted for the entrance. Maybe he didn't want the others to see me make the stone work without touching it. I had never told him how afraid I was. Whatever his reason, I was ashamed to be so relieved.

We formed a loose circle around Jordan; Levin was still kneeling by him, clasping his hands. He looked terrible, and he kept pleading with us for water. I felt like shit. This was my fault. His eyes were wild, and he was covered in sweat. I wondered if he was seeing us, or twenty wizards walking around who weren't really there. Or maybe they were really there and I just couldn't see them anymore.

I felt almost dizzy and stepped back a little, breathing the first pattern thirty times before Gerrard came back, breathing hard, carrying his clean, overturned lamp glass in the palm of his hand. It was nearly full of water.

I stared, realizing that we had never been given cups, or bowls, that there was nothing in our room except the lamp glass that would have worked. Everyone realized it at the same time. I could hear them exhaling; they were as amazed as I was. Gerrard had washed the glass and was holding the small end tight against his hand, hard enough to keep the water from seeping out.

Jordan sat up a little straighter and grabbed at the water. Levin got a tight hold on both his hands. I held his legs down. Will got behind him, bracing his back so he could sit up straighter. Then Gerrard knelt beside Jordan and held the lamp glass to his lips.

Slowly at first, then in bigger and bigger gulps, Jordan drank the water. All of it. When it was gone, he just sat, staring straight ahead. After a while, he managed to stand up. "Thank you," he said, looking at the floor. He blinked and exhaled. "It was . . . I think I was dying of thirst."

"I'm glad I didn't help," Luke said.

We all turned. He was off to one side, standing by a table. His plate was still in front of him, but it was empty. He had been eating while the rest of us were crowded around Jordan.

Luke shook his head. "I just hope Somiss was watching that."

Levin leapt past me, used a bench and a tabletop like stairs, and hurled himself at Luke, knocking him backward onto the floor. Levin managed five or six quick punches, then straddled him, sitting on Luke's belly, hands on his shoulders. Levin rocked backward, lifting Luke toward him, then slammed him back down. Luke made a sound full of pain and rage and writhed, trying to throw Levin off. But he couldn't. Levin rose onto his knees for an instant, then dropped all his weight hard. Luke's breath whooshed out and he groaned.

"Let him up!" Jordan shouted. "Levin, let him up." He was leaning on one of the tables, his face still sickly and pale. There was blood dripping down his chin. His lips *had* split.

Levin made a noise like a trapped animal, but he jumped off Luke and danced backward as he stood up. Luke lurched upright and started toward him.

"Stop!" Will shouted. "It's the wizards we should hate. Not each other."

Luke turned to face him. "Do you want to fight too, little boy?" He took a step toward Will.

Levin went to stand beside Will, his chin up and his arms loose, ready. Jordan stood by Levin. He was unsteady, but his head was up. I moved closer and finally, slower than any of the rest of us, Gerrard came to stand beside me.

"Fuck off, Luke," Levin said.

Luke didn't answer. He walked out of the food hall with his shoulders up too high and his fists still clenched. I could see how hard it was for him to leave like that, driven out, with all of us against him. But I didn't care.

33

That first night was terrible. It was chilly, and clouds covered the moon. Sadima led the boys through the dark woods along the base of the cliffs. The plum thickets were just beginning to bud, and the stiff twigs scratched their arms and legs bloody. The pine needle thatch that covered the ground prickled at her feet, but she didn't want to put on her shoes when the boys had none. They stayed together and did not complain, and Sadima was grateful, even though she knew it was because they were so desperate, so scared. She could feel their thoughts, a roil of emotions, and she pushed them away, over and over.

Sadima stopped often to let them rest, and every time they immediately sat down. She wanted them to run, but she knew that except for Jux, none of them had walked, except to pace back and forth in the cage, since the summer before. And they hadn't eaten well in all that time, or before it, when they were begging in Limòri. Long before dawn, when they came to the ridge above the bay and turned eastward, four of the nameless boys were stumbling along. She was afraid one of them might fall—the ground was littered with rock.

The night was no more than half gone and they were not nearly far enough from Somiss, still a day or two from the road that had brought her to Limòri, but Sadima knew they had to stop. In the first clearing with grass patches between the rocks, the boys staggered to a halt, ate a little bread, then sank to the ground and slept as they had in the cage, heaped like puppies. Sadima used her shawl and the bundle of papers inside it as a headrest and fell asleep too.

Near dawn, she was jolted awake by a cry of fear. She leapt up. Mabiki was standing, his hands up to protect his face. Then he lowered them, breathing hard. "I dreamed he was here," he said quietly. "That he was here, that he had found us."

Sadima whirled to look around, to listen with her ears and her heart. The woods creatures were upset by the cry and were listening intently, but they began calming themselves when no second cry came and they heard nothing else nearby. Sadima turned back to the boys and realized that there was empty ground where most of them had been asleep. She looked at Jux, Mabiki, and Wren. "Where are the others?"

Jux shrugged. "They wanted to go back to Limòri."

Sadima covered her mouth with one hand. She had meant to save them. "Why?" she whispered. "Somiss will find them there."

"They'll hide at first," Jux said. "They'll change the way they look."

Sadima was ashamed of her stupidity. Why had she thought they would come with her? They hadn't even trusted her with their *names*. She looked up at the sky, then at the boys again. "Did they take food?"

"Two bags," Jux said. "That seemed fair."

She nodded. It was more than fair. They could have taken it all. "Where will they go?"

"South End," Jux said. "That's where they were from."

She stared at them. "They lived there?"

Jux nodded. "On the docks where the river comes into the bay. Geirst said he knows four or five ship's captains who would take them as galley boys or maybe even as swabbies."

"We should sleep if we can," she said, trying not to think about how the boys would make their way in the dockside slum Franklin had described to her.

Jux helped Wren spread his blanket better. Mabiki's was tangled and he shook it out, then lay down and closed his eyes. Sadima shook out her blanket too, marveling at how calm the boys were. They had been in a cage. Now they were traveling to find a place among strangers—trying to escape a man they knew might kill them. Most of their friends had run off, and somehow, in moments, they were all asleep again.

It took her much longer. She lay awake, staring at the brightening sky, breathing the cool, clean air and wishing for a good farm dog. One that would bark if danger came close, and sleep silently if none did. When morning arrived, Sadima shaded her eyes from the fierce orange and gold sunlight that woke them. They traveled until noon, then stopped and napped until the sun set.

The second night's travel was no better. In some ways it was worse. Mabiki's feet were blistered and swollen. Jux's and Wren's were only a little better. She had no blisters—walking on the stone had given her thick calluses. But the arches of her feet were covered with painful little wounds from the pine needles and the rocks. All of their shoulders were rubbed red by the heavy sacks of bread and apples swinging as they walked, and anywhere bare skin showed, it was crosshatched with bramble scratches.

But they kept going. They walked through the woods and across meadows. They crossed a pasture full of weather-stained gravestones. Some had names, impossible to read. Others were set flat in the ground, the lettering completely worn away by gritty soil and heavy hooves. While the boys rested, Sadima walked across the field and chose a big, dark brown stone on the far side of an oak tree. There, where not even the boys could see, she used a stick to scrape out a hole. She buried the silver keys and scattered twigs and leaves over the scar, knowing the next rain would erase it altogether.

They finally found the wide road she had followed coming to Limòri and started down it. They traveled only at night and hid during the day. Sadima began to glance behind them more often. Franklin, coming back from his errands, would see the empty cage. Would he tell Somiss? Maybe not immediately. He would do what he could for her, she was sure of that. She hoped Somiss would not hurt him. There wasn't any logic in it—Franklin had not helped her; he hadn't even been there. But she knew that would not matter if Somiss was angry enough. And he would be. He would be crazed.

There were now ten people who knew where he was, who could lead his father—and the king's guards—to him. If the king's guards questioned any of the boys, for any reason, now or years from now, the truth might come out—or be offered for sale. The boys going back to South End might realize that soon enough.

Sadima shoved her fears aside and kept the boys moving. She thought about her brother every night as they walked beneath the scattershot glitter of stars. They would come close to Ferne on their way. She longed to see Micah, to find out if she was an auntie. But the last thing she wanted was to bring Micah trouble. So they would travel the wide road to the outskirts of the village, then head farther east, up into the foothills.

On the fifth day, as the sky faded from black to morning-gray, they found an old barn to sleep in. There was no smell of manure. The days when it had held livestock were long gone. Its roof was still more or less tight, and it sheltered them from a rainstorm that rumbled through just after sunrise. There were mice, though, rustling through the dregs of an old haystack. Sadima reminded the boys to tie the sacks closed after they ate. They lay down and were asleep in moments in the dim light of the barn. Sadima envied them again and lay a long time with her thoughts, her regrets. But when she did go to sleep, she didn't waken until sunset.

"Could we stay here for a few days?" Mabiki asked when Sadima woke them. He was whispering. They were all still whispering.

She shook her head. "We can't risk it, not yet."

"Do you know where we're going?" Jux asked as he stood up to stretch. There was simple curiosity in his voice, nothing more.

"Far past the farm where I grew up," she told them. "Then as close to the mountains as we can and still find a farm. There are Gypsies up there."

Wren yawned. "How far is it?"

Sadima hesitated. Then she told the truth. "I'm not sure. I've never been there. But it was a fifteen-day journey from my father's farm to Limòri, so it will be longer than that."

"Will that be far enough?" Wren whispered.

Sadima reached out to touch his cheek, and he ducked aside. She apologized for startling him and lowered her hand. "If we don't think it is far enough, we can go farther," she said. "We will decide. The four of us." Wren looked up at her, sidelong, and she felt his confusion. He had no idea what to do with kindness.

Sadima waited for the boys to stretch and eat a chunk of bread; then they set off again. As before, she walked a little in front and they followed like ducklings, talking in low voices now and then, but mostly silent. They covered more ground on the road than they ever could have cross-country, and Sadima hoped that she had made the right decision. She was careful. As soon as dawn lightened the eastern sky, they found a thick stand of ash trees and slept, well hidden from anyone passing by.

By the seventh night, she had gotten used to the flashes of images and half thoughts that came from the boys—and the animals. Once she began listening, in the way she had as a little girl, she remembered the safety of the forests, the fields. Danger was always announced by whoever saw it—or scented it—first. A farm dog barking would only give them away. The field mice and the raccoons and the crows would wake her without a sound if danger came close. She slept better and better and her fear subsided a little with each day that passed. By the twentieth night, she had begun to hope.

34

Gerrard and I were studying in our room again—the way we had before the lamps had begun to smoke. Our eyes got better and better. But neither one of us tried to eat—or I hadn't, anyway, and I was pretty sure Gerrard hadn't either. I wanted to talk to Jordan about what he had felt, what he had seen. Had he been lost like I had? I wanted to know if Jux and Franklin had helped him, too, but I was afraid to ask.

I wondered, over and over, what the lesson was this time. Was it as simple as all of us learning to use the stone without touching it? Or was it that we should never help each other? Gerrard and I were in violation of that. Maybe everyone else was too. Somiss was a cruel bastard and a real genius. He had never taught us anything. He resented every moment he was with us; I could see it. I had no idea why he didn't get someone else to listen to our stumbling recitations. And he kept us in constant fear.

An odd thought struck me. Maybe Somiss was being punished. Maybe he wasn't really the headmaster or whatever they called it here. Maybe he was being forced to run the academy. But they needed new wizards, didn't they, to take over when the old ones died?

Gerrard and I passed the next recitation—so did Levin. Luke sat apart from the rest of us, and he recited perfectly. He had a black eye and cuts on his face from the fight, but if Somiss noticed, he said nothing. Jordan, his lips still scabbed, shadows beneath his eyes, missed a dozen or more words. So did Will.

And the whole time they stumbled and started over and tried not to weep, Luke just stared at the wall, a little smile curving his lips. I saw Gerrard glance at him, and Levin did too, more than once. I don't know what they were thinking. I wanted to hit him until he stopped smiling.

Somiss waved one hand to dismiss us. "You must progress faster," he said. "All of you. Or you will be of no use to me." Then he disappeared.

We all exhaled at the same time, and it was weirdly comforting for me. It reminded me of Franklin's first-year classes, the gentle cadence of our breathing in unison.

"Luke never came back to our room," Levin whispered as we left. The words came from his barely parted lips. We moved away from each other, staring ahead, watching each other from the edge of our vision. I lifted my eyebrows, he ducked his chin. I was astounded. Where would Luke be sleeping? In a passageway? In the food hall? Without a blanket to put between him and the stone?

I slowed my step, then stopped to examine the bottom of my bare foot, as though a callus had cracked and was hurting me. They all passed me, and then I started walking again, gimping a little in case anyone was watching. I kept Luke in sight and felt sick when I saw him follow Will around a corner. When I walked past, I slowed just a little and watched without turning my head. Luke was walking behind Will now, too close. I heard him laugh—a quiet, not-funny laugh.

Of course. Luke hadn't wanted to face Jordan and Levin after the fight. So he had followed Will back to his room and forced his way in. If there were three empty beds in Will's room, Luke had taken one of them. If there was only one, I had no doubt Will was the one sleeping on the stone floor. And was Luke scaring him, shoving him around, maybe forcing Will to make food for both of them?

I tried to remember if Somiss had ever specifically forbidden us to find each other's rooms. I was almost certain he hadn't. He *had* forbidden us to help each other. But the wizards had given us all roommates on the first day. So Luke really hadn't broken the rules as long as he wasn't helping Will. And he wasn't. I was sure of that.

I went into our room, hoping to talk to Gerrard, but he wasn't there. I lay on my narrow bed and stared up at the darkness beyond the reach of the lamplight. What would the wizards do about Luke? Anything? Probably not. What would *I* do? Follow them back to Will's room and threaten Luke? Will would pay for that, not me.

My father had never beaten me. But when he was angry about my school marks or my daydreaming, or anything else, he often argued with my mother. And a few times, when her dressing gown had gapped the next morning at breakfast, or her wide sleeves had fallen when she reached for a top shelf, I'd seen the bruises.

The door opened and Gerrard came in, the red robe swirling around his ankles. I took a breath to ask him if he had eaten, and he held up one hand. "It's done."

I blinked.

"Luke," he said. "I warned him."

"He's been staying in—"

"I know," Gerrard interrupted me. He settled into his usual study position and I stared at his back, getting angrier every time his shoulders rose with a breath. *How?* How had he known? And why hadn't he told me?

I leaned toward him. "If you threatened Luke, he's just going to hurt Will and—"

"No, he won't," Gerrard said.

"I care about Will," I whispered.

Gerrard's shoulders tightened.

I leaned forward again. "I know you think that's stu—"

"More than twenty thousand people live in Limòri," he interrupted me. "How many of them can buy magic? A few hundred?"

I knew he was right. Magic was expensive—but that had nothing to do with Will. "What did you say to Lu—"

"I need to study," he cut me off. "So do you."

I stared at his back a little longer, waiting for my anger to subside. Then I opened the song book and skimmed the beginning of the next song. *Nikamava resporet telan.* The three words leapt out at me.

"Do you know why—," I whispered.

"Shh," Gerrard breathed, pointing at the door.

A few heartbeats later, the sudden pounding jerked me to my feet. I glanced at Gerrard. How had he known? We had just left Somiss's class. This had to be Jux or something worse.

"The book?" I breathed.

"It's gone," Gerrard mouthed, almost no air passing from his lips.

I watched him open the door. There was a short, gray-haired wizard in the passageway. He had a grim expression on his face that emphasized his jowls. As we followed him, I was so pissed off at Gerrard that it took me a long time to realize that the wizard was walking slower than any of them ever had. He even hesitated once, as though he wasn't quite sure where he was taking us.

I glanced at Gerrard. He was watching the wizard as closely as I was. The passage we were in slanted slightly downhill. The wizard turned twice more to the left, and both of those passages had downhill inclines too. Not steep. But constant. Gerrard caught my eye. His face was blank, tense. He glanced back, then forward, and lifted his eyebrows, then his shoulders. I ducked my chin. He was right. We had never been this way before. I would have remembered it too.

After a long time, the wizard stopped suddenly. We were in the middle of a wide passageway. There was no chamber entrance, nothing but solid stone. The wizard pointed at the wall, then turned and walked away.

Gerrard was standing with his knees bent, his eyes flickering over the dark rock all around us. I was tense too, ready to leap, to run, to try to live through whatever was coming next. But nothing happened.

I finally tipped my head toward the wall the wizard had pointed at. Wizards had gestured and pointed at every chamber entrance for every class they had walked us to. I raised my eyebrows just enough for Gerrard to understand my question. He shrugged.

"He seemed confused," I whispered.

Gerrard ducked his chin just enough to acknowledge what I had said. He was staring at the stone, walking closer, running his hands over it. He backed up. "I think they expect us to *make* an entrance."

I shifted my weight from one foot to the other. I didn't want to do it. I didn't want to feel heavy and sick again. Gerrard was going through the breathing patterns. Then he pointed at the stone. Nothing happened, and he exhaled, his shoulders dropping. He looked pissed. "Can you do it?" he asked very quietly, without turning.

"Maybe," I whispered. "But the wizard made it dissolve. All I did before was imagine it solid again."

Gerrard nodded without speaking. There wasn't a trace of uncertainty in his eyes. He walked ten or twelve paces up the corridor, then stood, watching me intently. I closed my eyes and remembered the stone mist—the way it had smelled, the odd, dead, gray color, the way it floated, much heavier and slower than real mist, and how cold it had been. Then I pointed at the stone wall in front of us. Nothing happened.

I exhaled and tried again. Nothing. I was almost relieved.

"Psst."

I looked at Gerrard.

"You have to," he breathed, "get pissed."

I looked at the wall again. I had been angry the first time. I imagined Somiss on the other side of the wall, waiting, sneering, and Luke, laughing at me, sure I couldn't do it. Oh, how I hated them both. I felt something shift inside my mind. I remembered the mist again, the way it had swirled, then I lifted my hand and pointed. I felt the oddest sensation, like something was being pulled out of me, then shoved back. Suddenly the wall collapsed into a roil of mist. It hung in the air, and my stomach clenched. I was afraid I would throw up again.

Gerrard stepped forward. I followed him through the misty gap in the wall into a huge chamber and I wondered where we were—then I saw the tables. It was the food hall, but we were behind the massive faceted stone and off to the side.

"Welcome," I heard Franklin say.

Everyone else was already there. They were sitting at the tables. And they were staring at me, their faces slack with surprise. All but Luke. He was sitting with Will at the table farthest from Franklin's. There was simple hatred in his eyes.

"Please sit down," Franklin said. "Today we begin to chase paradox again." He smiled. "We will go farther than before. Much farther."

I heard an odd, barely audible grinding sound and looked back. Without Franklin looking at it, or lifting a hand, the wall had closed, the stone had become hard and dark again.

35

Once they were past Ferne, deep in the foothills, they began to travel by day. And everything changed. Sadima felt the weight leaving her heart. She saw Wren smiling when a mother hummingbird chased him from the tree that held her nest.

They were not foolish. Sadima kept her hair knotted up and covered it with a makeshift scarf torn from what was left of her oldest dress. Jux hid his scar with a strip of red cloth Sadima found tied around a tree branch—a remnant of some children's game, or the landowner marking a limb to be cut. From a distance, at least, it looked like a real jabot.

They had long since eaten the last of the bread. Sadima showed them how to dig wild celery roots. She wove a little net on a willow frame, and they began eating fish some evenings. After she showed them the first time, the boys loved fishing. Sadima was glad. She had felt, all too clearly, the fear of the fish when she lifted them from the water. In all her years on the farm, she had never questioned her right to kill the extra roosters, to raise a calf for slaughter. But now it felt wrong to kill anything.

Maybe her time away from the countryside had changed her. Maybe it was seeing the boys in the cage for so long, feeling their despair. Whatever it was, she had a hard time eating flesh. They passed Drabock, then Werlin's Creek. The towns were farther and farther apart, and so were the markets. They bought eggs and a little cheese when they could—but it was less and less often.

One morning a Gypsy caravan came around a curve in the road before any of them heard the horse's hoofbeats or the tinkle of the wagon bells.

"Be polite," Sadima whispered. "Stand straight."

The shirtless Gypsy boy holding the reins nodded at them. They all nodded back. Jux mumbled a greeting.

"Their tattoos are different from the Gypsies in Limòri," he said, once the swaying wagon had passed. Sadima nodded. He was right. And the tattoos in both places were different from the Gypsies she had seen in Ferne's market square when she was a girl.

There were two more Gypsy caravans that morning, and Sadima longed to ask where they were going, but she didn't dare. If Somiss—or men he had hired—came looking for them, she wanted anyone who'd seen them to have forgotten them entirely by then. They could almost pass as a farm family, with her as the eldest sister and Jux and Wren her brothers—or cousins—so long as no one saw Jux's scar, or noticed how dirty they all were. But not Mabiki. His skin was darker, and his hair was a mass of exuberant curls. She tried wrapping a scarf around his head, but it was impossible to contain his hair for long.

One evening, when they were all tired and thirsty, walking in silence, Sadima saw an outcropping of milk white stone, with a thick copse of cottonwoods around it, their leaves flashing in the last of the late-day sun.

"Over there," she said, pointing, and as they got closer, she could smell the water. There was a spring-fed rill, barely knee-deep, and for the first time, she felt safe enough to bathe. She showed the boys how to find fine scrubbing sand and let them use her soap. When she got it back, it was smaller and gouged where someone had dropped it, but the boys' faces were radiant. "I have never been this clean," Mabiki said, so solemnly that they all laughed.

Once the boys were off looking for a sheltered place to lay out their blankets, she went to bathe. The water was cold, but washing herself truly clean was a joy. She slept well, and when the rising sun woke her, she felt herself smile. How had she forgotten the beauty of the land, the grace of the changing weather, the way the sky smelled after rain?

"There," Wren said, seven days later. He pointed. "That man needs help."

Sadima followed his gesture. There was an aged man in a wide, weedy field. He was trying to hold a plow steady. His mules looked as old as he did, and as worn. Sadima stood still, conflicted. She had meant to travel farther. But this was exactly the kind of farm she had hoped to find. If a man that old had to plow, he was in need of help. The house was a ways off the road. There was a barn, and gnarled peach and apple trees dying along the fence line.

"Do you think we are far enough away?" Jux asked, and she understood him perfectly; he was echoing her own thoughts.

"I don't know," she said.

Jux tilted his head, the makeshift red scarf hiding his scar. "It would be nice to live somewhere."

Mabiki's lips parted; then he exhaled without speaking.

"Live where?" Wren asked. "Here?"

Their faces were so wistful that Sadima guided them into a wild plum thicket where they could all stand and watch the old man for a while longer. It was terrible. He was far too frail to be doing hard work.

"Wait for me here," Sadima said. "Not a sound, and watch closely." They all nodded somberly, and she walked back onto the road, veering to the other side, hoping that the old man would notice her and wave, give her some kind of permission to come closer. But he didn't. She kept walking, turning up the farm road. He still didn't see her. The closer she got, the more she shortened her steps. The last thing she wanted was to startle him. Finally she stopped, more or less in the path of the mules, and waited for him to rein them in. He didn't.

Sadima could feel the mules' uneasiness, not just at her appearing in their field, but about everything. They were thirsty. They were hungry and scared. Sadima listened carefully. They didn't trust the man to guide them. When he was nearly upon her, she could see the milky haze that covered both his eyes, and she backed up twenty paces as quietly as she could.

"I don't mean to startle you," she called in the most pleasant voice she could manage. He jerked the mules to a stop and turned to face her.

"Who's there?"

"My name is—" She hesitated an instant, feeling foolish. She should have thought of this. "Rebecca," she said, naming herself after the milk goat she had loved best, the one that Franklin had helped her save the day she met him. "Rebecca Franklin."

The old man spat once, then again. "I don't know anyone by that name. You're not a Gypsy, are you? That ain't a Gypsy name."

"No," Sadima said. "My little brothers and I have lost our home."

He shrugged. "I'm sorry to hear that, but I haven't any food to spare." He reached up and scratched his ear. "I've lived too long."

"Is your family—"

"All gone off from here," he said before she could finish the question. "Gone off one way or another. The fever last year took my wife and the only one of our boys who stayed put." He spat again, and Sadima saw fear cross his face. He was sorry he'd said he was alone.

"I grew up on a farm," she said slowly. "And my brothers and I are tired of digging wild carrots. Do you still have a cow?"

"If you're going to steal the cow," he said, "kill me first. I have no wish to starve."

Sadima felt a wash of raw fear from him, and something like joy behind it. It startled her, as it had with the boys. And the old man's feelings were even clearer. He *wanted* to die.

"I know how to make cheese," she said. "I can cook. I can teach the boys to plow. Do you have seed?"

He nodded, warily. "Some. Just take what you want, but do as I said. Don't you leave me to starve."

Sadima walked closer to him. "May I ask your name?"

"Jack Peery," he said.

"We are in a bad way too, Mr. Peery," she told him. "Maybe we can help each other?"

He lowered his head. When he looked up, there were tears on his face. "It's hard without eyes. I could always tell a liar before. I know your name ain't Rebecca."

Sadima took his hand and held it gently. "I lied about my name, but nothing else."

He squeezed her hand, once, hard, then let it go. "Are you running from trouble?"

"Yes."

"Could it come and find you here?"

"I don't think so," Sadima said. "Maybe."

Jack wiped his face and stood straighter. "I hope it don't, but if it does, I won't mind dying very much. Call your brothers over."

Sadima gestured, and the boys came in a ragged line, Jux first, then Mabiki and Wren at the rear. She introduced them as Micah, Matt, and Robin. Jack put out his hand and they each came forward to shake it.

"Your sister tells me you could learn to plow," he said.

They understood instantly what Sadima had told the old man, and they all answered at once, a jumble of eagerness. And Jack Peery laughed. It was small, cramped, rusty. But he laughed.

~ 36 ~

Franklin told us to make food, that the stone was safe.
I don't think anyone questioned it. I didn't. I wanted to ask
him about the wasps, about what had happened to me, but
I was almost sure I would never be able to.

I lined up with the others, and we all made big meals.
Franklin gestured toward one of the tables, so we sat
together. We were all stiff and awkward. I could not make
myself look directly at anyone and kept glancing from one
face to the next. Jordan was fidgeting, but he managed to
smile at me once and I was glad. At least the life had begun
to come back into his dark brown eyes. Only Luke perched
at the end of the bench, as far from all of us as he could
manage, staring off at an angle toward the far wall.

Franklin made a chair, a small, plain one, that he set at

the head of the table. While we ate, he began to talk quietly, explaining what Limòri had been like ten generations back—before the Limòri Academy had opened its doors. His story echoed what the history book said, but Franklin made it much more vivid.

Women had often bled to death giving birth. One, in the countryside near Ferne, died after birthing a daughter because the marketplace magician who was supposed to help her robbed her family and left, telling her husband not to disturb her. "So he didn't," Franklin said, "for a long time. When he opened the door, he and his son found her dead, the baby barely alive. The magician traded cheap silver-plated candlesticks for a life—almost two lives."

We all looked up from our food and exchanged glances.

"The streets were overrun with orphans back then," Franklin told us. "Not just South End—the whole city. Parents were so poor some sold one child in order to feed the rest."

I glanced up, and he met my eyes.

"It was like the flax-brake slavery in the north—or the vanilla plantations on the Orchid Coast—but worse," he said. "Some of the children were just a year or two old when they were sold. And they were never set free. It was for life."

We all caught our breath. We had studied this in school. The magistrates' laws bound slavers to fair practice. Most slaves were immigrants, older boys and grown men working off debts. When their contracts ran out, they were freed.

Franklin paused, and I was astounded to see tears in his eyes. "The street children were pickpockets, cutpurses, prostitutes," he said. "Or they became household pets for the wealthy. Some were taught to sing or cook or fight or whatever else the best—and worst—masters wanted them to learn."

I laid down my fork and glanced around. Everyone had stopped eating.

Winters had been colder, Franklin told us, with winds strong enough to push over farm wagons and tear off roofs. Lightning had sometimes started fires in the woods during the drought years—crops had often failed entirely for lack of rain. Late springs killed seedling crops. Early winters ruined harvests. City families had hard, hungry years when they couldn't afford to buy enough food. Farm families often came close to starving between summers.

Franklin paused and waited until we were all looking at him. "No one thought any of this could ever change," he said. "Most people thought magic was an amusing hearth tale. They could not imagine enough food for everyone, or real help for sickness and pain."

He looked upward into the darkness overhead and stopped talking for so long that we began to shift our weight, to glance at each other. Then he looked at us, one by one. "Most of you could never have imagined hunger like theirs, before you came here. Or the weariness of constant work and little food or sleep. You have never known life without magic."

Franklin looked at Gerrard for a few heartbeats before

he went on. "When the Founder finally proved magic was real, the black-robed fortune-tellers in Market Square were long gone because the last few kings had hanged them. But magicians were still hated, because too many families had stories like the motherless girl from Ferne." Franklin stopped, then noticed we weren't eating. He gestured. "Finish your food."

We picked up our forks and listened. Franklin's lecture had begun like a real history class in a real school. Now it changed. "What you are learning here is what the Founder learned," he said. "It nearly killed him, a hundred times. It has killed some of you already. But if one of you graduates, he will be strong. Strong enough to control magic, and his own heart. Magic can make homes free of the lantern smoke that once blinded old people in the harshest winters and choked babes in their cradles. It can eliminate diseases that come from filth. Clean water fills the city wells. The sick are made whole. Most children have enough to eat."

Franklin was looking at each one of us in turn again as he spoke. "You are all here because the wizards who gave you your entrance tests thought you could be the one to graduate." He paused once more and looked straight at me. "One of you could have the honor of spending your life helping the people of Limòri." Then he looked at Gerrard. "There is still so much work to do."

Franklin pushed his chair back and stood. "Remember that," he said. "Magic is still there to be discovered." And then he left, walking like any teacher, tall and straight, out of his classroom.

We looked at each other, but no one said another word. I left, walking behind Gerrard, thinking. I had never questioned the bright, clean lights in my father's house, until our lamps had started smoking. I had never once wondered about Limòri's mild weather. I had never gone hungry before coming here. None of us had, except Gerrard. But if the wizards wanted to help people, why was magic so expensive? South End was filthy and dangerous and full of beggars and thieves. And I had seen children in Limòri who were like the orphans Franklin had described. Why?

Paradox?

I heard the word whispered inside my mind and slowed, waiting to see if I was sliding back into a dream. I looked at the stone, the cold-fire torches, holding my breath. I didn't feel strange. Then I noticed that Gerrard had lengthened his step and lifted his chin. I looked down the passageway and saw what he had seen. Luke had his arm around Will's shoulders and was shoving him along. Crap.

I walked faster too. Gerrard veered away from me and slowed just enough to match my pace. I understood. We came up behind them, one on each side, and fell into step. Gerrard was on Luke's side. I couldn't hear what he said, but Luke let go of Will. And when Will ran a few steps to get ahead, Gerrard leaned close to Luke and whispered again. Then we both dropped back. Will shot Gerrard a grateful glance, then broke into a run.

Luke hawked and spat, walking slower than usual. He turned down the next passageway. Was he going back to his old room with Levin and Jordan? I kept glancing over my shoulder to see if they turned where Luke had. They didn't. Maybe they had learned a different way back from the food hall, though. I wondered if Gerrard knew another one. I didn't.

Gerrard was frowning. At me? Probably. If a wizard saw me looking around like I was trying to figure out where the other boys were going, maybe he would think I was trying to help someone, or get help. Franklin had just talked about how much magic helped people. But if we helped each other, they would kill us.

"Paradox," Gerrard whispered.

I saw his mouth move, but he was staring straight ahead, and he wasn't watching me from the edge of his vision. I closed my hands into fists, fighting a cold uneasiness in my belly. I didn't want to start imagining things again; I didn't want to hear people say things before they said them. I didn't want anything else to happen that made me feel crazy.

Once we were back in our room, I tried to be invisible. Gerrard had interfered with Luke only because of me, and now it was going to be complicated. He was pissed, I could see it. So I opened the song book and studied. And after a while, I stopped thinking about Gerrard.

Everything Franklin had said made me feel like all this was important, like *I* was important. Feeling almost peaceful, I closed my eyes. I was nearly asleep when I heard Gerrard's voice.

"Fuck Franklin," he whispered. "Stay pissed."

Jack and his wife had raised six sons over thirty years. They were Gypsies—and farmers—like many of their neighbors. The house had four bedchambers. Wren and Mabiki shared the biggest one. Jux and Sadima each had their own. Jack's was the smallest—the house had been expanded in stages, as his family had grown. The first spring rainstorm told Sadima what she already knew about the old man: What he did, he did with care. The heavy timbers creaked only a little, even when the wind roared outside, bending the biggest trees. The storm scared Mabiki and Wren. Sadima found them sitting together on the floor, talking, a candle lit between them. Jux slept soundly through that storm and all the rest that followed.

The boys learned to plow that spring, more or less. They were exhausted every night, but they loved to listen to Jack's stories, and if he needed anything, they fell over each other getting it.

They got the barley in the ground just before the rain started. The furrows were crooked, and Sadima was glad Jack couldn't see them. They would do better next spring.

The first time Sadima walked around to the back side of the barn, she stopped and stared. The midden heap was enormous, and it had rotted down into crumbly black humus. She used the barrow to spread it around the half-dead fruit trees along the road, and there was still enough left to double the size of the old garden patch. There were volunteer seedlings all over. Sadima thinned and sorted them as best she could, using a spoon to lift them into the beds she had prepared. She dug up the walnut-sized potatoes and moved them off to the side into tilled earth, then the broad-leafed squash seedlings, then the corn, then the cauliflower.

Jack gave her melon seeds from a jar in the kitchen closet. She could see that they were more than seeds to him somehow. He handled each one carefully, holding the jar tightly, giving her just five to plant. She was careful with them, and all five came up. When she told him, his face lit and he nodded, over and over, without saying a word.

Weeding around the house, she came across the trap-door to an old root cellar. It was built at a slant and ran back under the house, dry as bones. Jack said it was the first one he'd dug, and he told her where the bigger one was.

Sadima waited until they were all asleep one windy night, then wrapped all the papers she had brought in her oldest blanket. She carried a lantern out to bury them in the old root cellar, as far in as she could go. She used the knife to dig a hole, then plunged it into the dirt, all but the tip of the hilt, to mark the spot. A week later she shoveled two feet of dirt on top of the door and a wide patch around it and planted a flower garden.

The cow's name was Beth. She was good-natured and patient, and she loved Jack. She was starting her second year without a calf, but she still gave enough for a stout cup of milk for each of them every day, and enough left over to curdle for cheese once every two or three days. Once they had green fodder, she gave a little more.

By late spring, Jack was whistling as he felt his way around the place, doing most of his usual chores. There had been a half-dozen elderly chickens in a dirty coop the first day. By midsummer, with a little help from Sadima's savings and a kind farmer on market day, there were twenty more, young and productive, with six hens setting fertile eggs. As the year rolled on, Jack had the boys catch up the extra roosters before they were old enough to tear each other up fighting. He killed them for the stew pot, quick and clean, an instant neck-break that left no time for fear or pain. Sadima watched him twice, and she was sure of that. Still, she could not bring herself to eat the chicken stews she made. The boys and Jack took her share and were glad for it.

Sadima was so happy on the farm that it frightened her. She missed Franklin every day and hoped, with all her heart, that he was well, but she didn't once consider going back. The very idea of magic seemed distant, like something from a story, something wonderful that people didn't really need.

The boys bloomed. Jack had been both farmer and father, and he knew both jobs as well as any man ever had. He asked the boys if they had gotten enough to eat before he took his share. He patted their backs to thank them for small favors. He sometimes put his arm around Wren's shoulders, moving slowly so Wren wouldn't flinch. He was teaching them how to mend a fence, sow a field, hammer planks into a corn bin. Sadima knew what he was doing. He wanted a second family. He wanted them to stay when he died. He was like all the farmers she had ever known. He wanted his farm to outlive him.

Autumn brought enough of a harvest to carry them through the winter. And when spring came again, they planted. That next winter was mild and they had radishes, squash, and kale long into the autumn. But the next summer had little rain, and winter came early and hard. The stock was thin by spring and so were they. All three boys were much taller than they had been when they'd left the cliffs. They needed more food than ever. Sadima was desperate to start the garden early.

She got the radishes and the onions in just as the weather turned warm. She was planting chard while the boys thinned seedlings one morning when she heard distant hoofbeats. She looked up and listened. It wasn't a farm wagon. And it wasn't a farm boy riding back from a friend's house. It was three horses. Or four. Coming at a gallop.

She stood up and looked at the road that ran along the far side of the pasture. She couldn't see well through the line of fruit trees—they were just leafing out—but she could hear well enough, and she winced at the hollow clopping of shod hooves. She listened harder, deeper. The horse leading the way hated its rider. Its flanks were welted from the whip. There were two other horses. One of them shied, afraid of the birds rustling in the plum thicket.

.And then she knew. No neighbor's horse was shod. No Gypsy would beat a willing horse. And no country horse would shy at birds rustling *leaves*. Scared, angry, she ran toward the boys, using their real names. Their heads jerked up from the half-thinned row of onions. "Get Jack out to the barn," she told them. "Hide yourselves in the hayloft and stay there, no matter what you see or hear, until you're sure you are alone."

They ran and were out of sight in an instant. She knelt beside the row they had been working on. She was breathing fast, her thoughts speeding with her pulse. She forced herself to slow her movements, feigning the rhythm of daylong work. There was hope, she told herself.

It might not be Somiss. If it was, he might not notice her. Her hair was covered to keep the dirt out, and she was wearing a dress that had belonged to Jack's wife years before. She glanced up, as anyone would, before the horses were too close. It was Somiss, and two other men. She bent over again, hoping, with all her strength, that they would see her for what she was, a farm girl, weary from tedious work, that they would just go past.

But Somiss reined in, and she glanced up to see him staring at her from the road. She kept thinning the onions, her fingers deft and quick, her eyes flooding with tears. Franklin had told him where to look for her. Why had she left the letter? Why hadn't she at least lied about her plans? She deserved to die for her stupidity. But she had to save the boys. And Jack.

She watched Somiss without turning her head. They were all just sitting their winded horses. Somiss looked at the sky, then said something to the other two. Sadima tensed. Maybe if she ran, right now, straight across the road and into the woods, they would chase her. She glanced up to judge the distance and saw Somiss with one hand cupped around his mouth.

"Sadima!"

His voice was strained, even rougher than it had been.

She lifted her head. Then she stood to face him as he spurred his horse up the little dirt road, the other men coming behind him. He veered toward her, crossing the garden, the horses' hooves churning up the soil, crushing the plants. Sadima lifted her chin and stiffened her spine as he reined in, looking at her. He gestured at the road, the mountains that rose to the south. "I have looked for you for a long time. You have no idea the trouble you have caused me." He sounded sad, not angry.

For the first time Sadima wondered if he had beaten

Franklin—or worse—to find out where she had gone. Her breath stopped. "Is Franklin all right?"

Somiss dismounted, and in one quick stride he was close enough to hit her. Sadima fell sideways. She kept herself from glancing toward the barn as she got to her feet and faced him again.

"Where did the boys end up?" Somiss asked her.

"Limòri," she answered, touching her cheek. It was sticky with blood.

"Limòri?"

"So they told me," she said. "Six of them left while we were still near the cliff. The other three stayed two nights longer. I meant to save them all from you. If I did, I am glad."

Somiss lifted his hand, but she didn't cower, and he lowered it again. "I found six of them," he said. "So I missed three? How odd those three were the ones who trusted you most."

Sadima fought to keep her feelings off her face. "They asked my advice about how to hide from you. I told them to sign on as cabin boys with the first ship that would take them."

"So the little one is alive?" Somiss asked. "The one who could fair copy?"

Sadima shrugged. "If he wasn't among the ones you found, perhaps he is."

Somiss smiled. "You are very clever, Sadima. Who else lives here?"

"One kind old man," she said quietly. "He's at his son's

house this fortnight, visiting grandchildren. That's why he let me stay—so the work would get done without him."

"Look in the house and the barn," Somiss told the men.

Sadima pulled in a quick breath before she could stop herself.

"Wait!" Somiss shouted. The men reined in. He tipped his head and looked at her carefully. "You must come back with me," he said. "I gave Franklin my word. But if all three of the boys are here, I only want the little one with the scar. The other two can stay, once I am finished with them."

"Is Franklin all right?" she asked again.

"No," Somiss said. "He barely eats. He is nearly useless to me. He made me promise not to harm you in exchange for his promise in another matter, or you would be dead now. You have caused me much annoyance." The disgust in his voice seemed real. "Are the boys here?" he asked again.

Sadima shook her head. "I am alone."

"Go look in the house and the barn," Somiss repeated to the men. "Don't break anything. I want no quarrels with the Gypsies."

Sadima looked at her feet, afraid Somiss might see the glimmer of hope she felt. If he didn't want the Gypsies as enemies, he would leave Jack alone. Maybe the boys would run. Once the two men were off their horses and inside the house, she spoke. "If Franklin is ill, you can blame yourself, not me."

"I do," Somiss said.

Sadima was caught off guard by the low, bitter tone of his voice.

"I should never have let you stay," he told her. He glanced toward the house, then back at her. "Franklin is foolish over women. He loved a maid in my mother's house. He once made my father angry enough to beat him senseless so that she could sneak back to her quarters after I was done with her." Somiss looked into Sadima's eyes. "Franklin sees her when he visits my mother; he is always glad when I send him there."

Sadima looked down, trying to breathe, to hide her reaction. When she looked up, Somiss was smiling. "Give me the keys." He put his hand on her shoulder.

"I lost them," she said. "I dropped them in the forest that ni—"

He slapped her, hard. She would have fallen except for his hand on her shoulder. He leaned close and whispered, his lips brushing hers. "Give me the keys or I'll burn the house and barn to the ground."

Sadima held herself still for a long moment, refusing to cry. "I don't have them."

Somiss looked into her eyes, then suddenly pulled off her scarf. She jerked back, and her hair fell free. Somiss wrapped it around his hand, closed his fist, and forced her head back, making her look into his face. "I will kill everything and everyone here if you don't give me the keys."

"If I had them," she said, "I would have already given them up. You know I would."

He tugged at her hair. "I believe you," he said. "And now it is time to leave."

"I do not want to leave here," she whispered.

"But you will, nonetheless," he said. "You and Franklin and his games with the Eridians. What fools you are, both of you."

Then he began reciting. Sadima struggled. She recognized the song, but then it changed, a torrent of words she had never heard before. She tried to run, but Somiss held her against his chest, forcing her to tilt her head so that they stood like lovers, exchanging secrets. He spoke quietly, his lips against her ear. She could see a vein pulsing in his neck. He released her hair and she felt it lifting, rising from her brow like smoke from a chimney. She reached up, but he slapped her hand aside, his words still pouring over her like water. Her whole body felt too heavy, her flesh dragging at her bones. She thought of the repeated words and tried to say them. She tried to fight, tried to scream, tried to run, tried to remember who he was, and why he was hurting her. But in the end, she could not manage any of those things.

– 38 –

In between Franklin's classes, we still had to recite, of course. I kept looking for more repeated words in the songs. I couldn't find any. I asked Gerrard about it one evening. "Just learn all the words," he whispered. "Don't leave any out."

I stared at his back. Had I said I *wasn't* learning them? I started to repeat my question, then got pissed and went out into the passageway for a while because I knew I might cry. I was crying more often, and it embarrassed me. It wasn't because I was any more scared or any more worried about staying alive than I had been. I was angrier. Part of it had to do with everything Franklin had said. I wanted it to be true. I wanted Franklin to be good-hearted, kind. And I knew he wasn't. Not really. He had watched four boys starve. And that weighed on my heart.

Franklin's next two classes were quiet and somber. We reviewed the breathing patterns. It was easy for me, and I left feeling calm. His fourth class was in the food hall. "Make something," he said. "Make the most complicated meal you can." And then he smiled. A real smile; I could see his teeth. After three years of reducing our gestures and expressions, a normal smile looked exaggerated and silly, like the mummer-clowns my mother hired to entertain houseguests' children. And somehow that made everything he had said seem false.

We all stood still as trees.

"The stone will not hurt any of you," he said.

Still, no one moved.

"Complicated? Do you mean difficult to—," Will began, then he stopped.

"Yes," Franklin answered. "The best you can do. Who will be first?"

I was watching Jordan. He was pale, and his eyes were too wide, flicking over the stone wall. Was he seeing things we couldn't? I wanted to tell him that it would get better, but maybe for him it wouldn't. I had nearly lost myself in a wasp's nest. The stone had to be a thousand times worse. Jordan made an odd little sound, and I winced. I knew how hard he was fighting to tell what was real.

Franklin was still waiting. No one had stepped forward. We were all wary of the stone now. And who wanted to be the first to show everyone else the best meal he could make?

We were used to hiding our progress from each other.

Gerrard was staring at nothing. I looked at the floor. Franklin waited without speaking. I glanced up when I finally heard footsteps. Luke was walking toward the stone. He stood before it, and Franklin spoke quietly to him. Then Luke readied himself and touched the faceted gem. The bluish light flickered, and there was a plate of steaming roast chicken on the stone pedestal. I could smell the rosemary, and my mouth watered.

Franklin spoke to Luke again, still too quietly for the rest of us to hear. Luke carried his plate to a table and began to eat. No one else stepped forward.

Franklin looked at us, and I saw something in his eyes. Pity? "I just want to make sure you all get something to eat today," he said. "I want to see how well you use the stone. Nothing more than that."

He said it quietly, and he sounded like a good teacher in a good school—it was like putting salve on wounds. One at a time, we lined up. Levin made a full supper with meat and vegetables. I heard Franklin say, "Very good." But then he lowered his voice again, and I couldn't hear more.

Jordan made a complete supper too, after a long, shaky hesitation. No one was impatient. Everyone understood. Including Franklin, or so it seemed.

Will's meal was stew, but there was a nice sprig of parsley on top and it smelled of garlic and good butter. Gerrard made fish soup with buttered yams on a separate plate. I wondered if it was still the best he could do or if he was just pretending. Then it was my turn.

"The most complicated meal you can manage," Franklin said quietly.

I looked at the tables. Luke had finished eating, and he was watching me. They all were, between bites. I knew this was something Gerrard would sidestep. He tried not to make himself a target for Luke or anyone else, and for all I knew he could make anything he wanted and just wouldn't do it in front of anyone.

"It's important to do your best at this," Franklin said.

I looked at him. His gray hair had grown a little. His eyes were still sad, but there was something else there too. Relief? About what? Or maybe I was imagining it. It had been a long time since we had see anything but emptiness in the eyes of the wizards who led us to class, and cold cruelty in Somiss's. And as angry as I was at him for not saving the starving boys, and even though I knew Gerrard was right about staying pissed, I was glad to see Franklin. Very glad.

"We all missed you," I whispered, barely moving my lips, so low that I thought he might not hear me.

I saw his eyes shine with tears. But he didn't answer me. Instead he said, "Make a wonderful supper, Hahp."

So I did. I made a braised leg of lamb with honeyed ginger carrots, the tiny ones from the spring garden; roasted leeks with ground pepper; summer squash, sliced thin and dressed with thick, hundred-year-old vinegar; and hot, buttered bread. I looked up at Franklin. The tears were gone.

"Your eye is perfect, the colors are exact, every detail

is vivid and good," he whispered. He leaned a little closer. "You can imagine the songs, too."

I stared at him, sure I had heard him wrong. But before I could ask him, he was walking away, out of the food hall.

Without Franklin there to guide us, we sat apart. I ate slowly, tasting every wonderful bite. Then I wondered if Somiss knew we were there. He would hate seeing us like this. I took a bigger bite and chewed faster, thinking about Franklin. He was much older than Somiss. So he must have graduated a long time before him, but every time I had seen them together, Somiss seemed to be the one in charge. Did wizards elect a leader like the people in Limòri elected magistrates? Why would they have chosen Somiss over Franklin?

I turned to look at the tables behind me. Everyone else was finished. Levin and Jordan were leaving. Luke left next, then Gerrard, with Will right behind him. Will touched the center of his chest as he passed me, then ducked his chin and tipped his head toward the entrance. It was a thank-you, meant for Gerrard, but given to me because he knew Gerrard wouldn't want it. I smiled, barely curving my lips.

I swallowed the last few bites, set my dishes on the stone floor, and started back to the room. I walked slowly at first, weighted down by my thoughts. Then I gathered up my robe in one hand and ran. My feet were calloused now, but I always ran light-footed. It had become a habit.

Halfway back to the room, Luke lunged at me from a

side tunnel. His momentum lifted me, then I fell, hard. I scrambled, trying to get up, but he straddled me, pinning me with his weight. "If Gerrard says one more word to me," he whispered, "one more time, just one, I'll kill you."

I wrenched back and forth, trying to roll him off me, but I couldn't. He hit me over and over, pounding at my shoulders and sides. He was almost snarling; a weird animal sound was coming out of his mouth. He leaned down and stared into my eyes. "If he ever—"

I butted my head against his chin.

The animal sound got louder.

I grabbed his hands and held on. "Luke!" I shouted his name over and over, but he just kept roaring, his head tipped back. "What the fuck is wrong with you?" I screamed. "Get off me!"

He leaned back and punched me in the gut. It hurt so bad I could barely breathe.

"Tell Gerrard," he said, between loud, gasping breaths, "if he says one more word, you're dead." His face was contorted with rage. Or maybe he was about to cry. I tried to free myself again, but he was too heavy, too strong. I hated him; I wanted to kill him. And then this thought came to me: The blood in Luke's veins would probably be as easy to change into mist as the stone had been.

The thought terrified me and made me happy at the same time. I must have smiled, because Luke's eyes narrowed and he shoved himself back and stood up. He opened his mouth, and I thought he was going to say something. But he didn't. He just stood there for a long, terrible moment, then kicked me once before he ran. And because I was flat on my back and because he was standing so close when his robe flared out, I saw his legs. They were purple-black with bruises.

It was chilly. Mixed with the creaking of wooden hulls and thick ropes, she could hear voices. Not too close. But not far enough away, either. She was wedged into the space between a dock mooring post and the cargo stacked next to it. Her legs ached, and the cut on her lip was swollen and throbbing. But the warm bread was in her lap, and as soon as she could stop crying, she began eating.

She had learned: The safest place for food was in her belly. The rats were always prowling. The ferocious, underfed dogs hunted them at night, so the rats often found their way into the same hiding places she did. Sometimes they stole her food. But rats and dogs didn't scare her. She understood them, and they liked her. The skinny children were much worse. Every time they saw her, they sang the little rhyme they had made up. *"Who is she, the one with almost no hair? Where did she come from and why does she stare? She won't speak a word, but she howls and she spits. And when you scare her, she runs and she shits."*

It had happened that terrifying first night, in the dark before the roosters crowed. It was her oldest memory, her first one. She had been so hungry, so confused, and sick, too, shaking with cold sweats, her stomach grinding as though she had eaten rotten meat. The children had chased her, taunting her. One tall, mean-faced girl led them along, promising extra bread to whoever knocked the stranger down.

The chase had gone on so long that her stomach had cramped, sharp as knives, and she finally had to stop to relieve herself, hidden behind a trash heap, crouching, her bare feet in her own filth. They had found her by the smell.

The next day a kind old man had seen her crying and had given her bread. "I don't know why you stay in South End," he said. He gestured at all the children sitting along the street, curled up in the doorways.

"South End?"

He had patted her cheek and nodded, pity in his eyes. "Along the river here, all the way up to the marsh at the edge of the bay. South End. That's what it's called." He gestured at the children again. "They're all Marshams, clannish as Gypsies, but dirty and mean. Their parents sell them off, or keep them home and teach them to beg and steal."

She had tried not to wonder about her own parents when he said that. "Why?"

He spat on the cobblestones. "I've heard it a few different ways. A hundred years ago, or two hundred or three, they fought the Ferrin clan over something, and lost."

She looked at him. "Over what?"

He shrugged. "The stories don't match. Some think they were kings way back, or magicians. I've heard it both ways. They're thieves now." He reached out and patted her head. "But you can't cut this short enough to hide the color. They know you aren't one of them. Anywhere else in Limòri would be better for a red-haired girl."

"Thank you for the bread," she said, stepping back so he couldn't touch her again. Her hair was red? She had never seen anyone with red hair. She mumbled something and walked away.

She knew now that he had been right. She didn't want to stay here. She had found four long, narrow alleyways that ended at a wide boardwalk. She followed them all. In the daytime, men and women who smelled clean walked past. They stared at her, disgust on their faces, clasping their children's hands tighter as they hurried by.

And she could not step forward, could not keep walking. She could move backward, or to either side, but when she tried to go forward, her heart spasmed and her knees shook. Sweat rose on her face, and she knew she was dying. She tried again and again. It happened every time, and it scared her so much she stopped trying.

One morning the same old man gave her more bread, then reached out to hold her hand. She jerked back and ran. The street children spotted the bread. She ran faster.

Some of them had sticks and they caught up, whacking at her legs until she fell. They swarmed over her, kicking and biting. Then they were gone, sprinting barefooted over the uneven cobblestones. The next day a kind woman took pity on her. But the street children took her bread, and her dress, too.

The sailors who found her said they had been two years at sea, coming back from Servenia. They took what they wanted from her as well, but one of them bought her another dress, made of soft, old cloth. She was grateful. The dress had big, wide pockets, though. So the children chased her whenever they saw her, to make sure she had no bread hidden in them. Her ankles were always mottled with bruises.

A few nights after that she had a whole loaf of bread, a gift from a sailor too drunk to stop her from running. She sprinted down the dock and found a piling with crates stacked near enough to hide her. She settled in, wedging her feet against the stout post, then shifted her weight a little, careful not to make a sound. She started eating. Then she heard the children's voices. They got louder.

She wolfed the food, shoving the last of the bread into her mouth, chewing furiously even as she made herself smaller, her back against the mooring post, her knees up beneath her chin.

"Do you see her?" The voice was high, sharp, all too familiar. It was the tall, mean girl.

"I don't see anything, Chee," a high child's voice called back.

Chee. Chee *Marsham*?

All the little ones looked up to her, and they all obeyed her. She was smart, and it was very hard to hide from her. But it could be done.

The voices came very close, very close. But none of them, not even Chee, thought to search the tiny space between the crates and the mooring post. If the crates had held fruit, they might have tried to pry one open, walked around, noticed her. But it was a cargo of heavy chains and ropes, the scent of the packing oil thick and sharp in the air. So they walked in circles, whispering, waiting for any small sound, for her nerve to break, for her to run.

Instead she dozed, something she was learning to do in impossible situations.

When the voices finally dimmed, it was more than half-way to sunrise. The stars overhead were sharp and clear, so maybe there wouldn't be fog in the morning—she would need to find a safe place before sunup.

As the moon rose, she held still, sleeping in fits, carefully changing her position a few times to ease one ache, then another. Near dawn she heard sailors waking up, hawking and spitting—and arguing. She'd had all she wanted of sailors. And unlike the children and the thieves, she had no fear of the night-dogs that roamed South End when the shops and dockyards were closed.

So she crept out, cramped and stiff, walking soundlessly in the very last shreds of the night. No one saw her go except a half wolf that snarled at her, then came closer as she assured him she meant no harm. He walked with her a ways, her hand resting on his shoulder, then turned back to guard the brickyard that was his home.

She decided to walk far enough to begin the day at a cheese shop she had discovered. The man there was kind. He had let her wash the window once and paid her in food. She turned down the first alley, then cut across the tannery lot. It was pocked with clay-lined pits full of urine and ashes. Stacks of bloody, raw sheepskins ran along one side. At the end there were piles of coral from the beach that the tanner beat into lime dust.

Her eyes watered from the stench. The finished hides hung on lines strung from the balconies of the buildings on opposite sides. The old woman and her family would be out soon, washing hides, scraping hair and blood off the raw ones, pounding the cured leather with heavy mallets until it was soft enough to dye. And they would be arguing; they were always shouting at each other.

As always, their dog snarled, his ears pressed flat against his head. His name was Murder, and he was unleashed at night. She hesitated long enough for him to catch her scent among so many that were stronger. When he did, his ears came up, and he stood quietly as she came close.

"How are you, my friend?" she whispered, crouching beside him. He sniffed at her fuzzy scalp; he always did. Then he investigated the hand that had touched the brickyard dog. Then he leaned against her, while she listened to him.

He had no new tales. The tannery woman had beaten him again. He never made much of it, but it hurt to know that the family he protected fed him so little and so often hit him when they were angry with each other.

She slid her hand over his coat, gently scratching the places he could not reach, avoiding the bruises. He lay down, and she sat beside him for a few moments. Then she cupped her hand beneath his muzzle and kissed him. "I have to go," she said. "If they see me, they'll chase me, and I'm too stiff to run." The dog whimpered, but he understood well enough; she always left too soon, and he always wanted to go with her. But she was his friend. She always came back.

A door banging open made her flinch and crouch. "Ben? Ben! Come eat your porridge!"

It was the grandmother, standing in the lantern-lit doorway across the tanning yard. She was fat and loud and she knew her business. Ben was one of the stray street children. The tanners had either bought him from his parents, or he had been captured and held by both cruelty and the promise of food. He always had his head down, and he never lifted a hand when he was slapped or shoved. She pitied him, but at least he had a name.

"Ben!"

Still no answer. He was hiding. Good for him.

When the door finally banged closed, she kissed the dog on his forehead, then slid away into the copse of old cottonwoods behind the tannery yard, disappearing into the dawn-dusk.

- 40 -

Walking back, my left side and my back ached, and there was a separate, sharp pain in my ribs. I had to walk with my left shoulder lifted almost up against my ear. I felt sick, probably from the pain but also from this: Gerrard hadn't warned Luke. He had kicked the shit out of him. And he had been careful not to leave marks where they would show. My father's favorite trick.

I shoved the door open and let it bang against the stone. But Gerrard wasn't in the room. My breath hitched, but the furniture was in place, his lamp was on his desk. He had left the food hall and he hadn't passed me coming home, so he hadn't gone back there. Where was he?

His cot was neat, the blankets unrumpled. Maybe he hadn't come back here at all. Had Jux come for him? Or,

my thoughts whispered, maybe he had been caught reading his mysterious little book somewhere.

I just stood there, staring at my bed. It hurt to stand up.
But when I tried to lie down, it hurt even more. So I paced
back and forth out in the passageway, slowly, walking lopsided, waiting for Gerrard. I was so angry with him. He had
no right to beat Luke, any more than Luke had the right to
beat me. It wasn't up to him to define our pact, either. Not
anymore. I was learning the songs. He might be way ahead
of me in other things, but he couldn't make the stone melt,
then turn solid.

"Gerrard, we have to talk," I whispered to the stone,
rehearsing as I walked. "We have to decide. Do we want
to turn into assholes—cruel, filthy assholes—like they all
have?" I turned and paced back the other way, still whispering. "And we have to learn everything they know before
we can *do* anything. We need to help each other more, not
less. I mean all of us. Not just you and me. We all have to
become real wizards before we can destroy the school." I
paused and walked in silence for a dozen steps. The truth
was we probably *couldn't* destroy the school, but I wanted
to try more than I had ever wanted anything.

I started back toward the room, my head down to ease
the tension in my lifted shoulder. "If we all help each
other," I whispered, "think how fast we could learn. And if
we hide how fast we are learning—"

"What are you doing?" Gerrard's whisper interrupted my
own. I jerked around and felt myself blushing. Blushing?

Gerrard looked disgusted and gestured toward the door.

We went into our room. He started to settle into his study position. "Gerrard," I whispered, "we have to talk."

"You seem to do it well enough without me," he whispered back.

I raised my fist, and the pain jabbed at my ribs. Even so, it took every bit of self-control I had left to straighten my fingers and lower my hand. I wanted to talk, not fight.

"You can't beat Luke up like that," I said in a low voice. Not a whisper. In my own voice.

Gerrard turned to face me. "What?"

"I saw his legs. The bruises are awful."

Gerrard looked blank.

I explained.

"I didn't do it," Gerrard said. I was looking into his eyes. His shoulders were loose. He was leaning forward just a little. His eyes were narrowed. He cared what I thought of him, I could see it. And I knew he was telling the truth.

I sat down on the edge of my bed, wincing when my rib popped. When I looked up, Gerrard was watching me. "Gift from Luke," I whispered. "He jumped me." Then I touched the center of my chest, let the corners of my mouth fall a tiny bit, lowered my head a little, and closed my eyes. When I opened them, he gave me a somber, almost invisible nod, accepting my apology.

"I didn't scare him enough," Gerrard said. He ran through the sequence of gestures, and I nodded to accept his apology.

"If you didn't hit him, who did?" I whispered.

He shrugged. "Not Will."

"Not Levin," I said. "I know him from before."

He exhaled. "Jordan is still trying to outlive whatever the stone did to him."

"I just hope he can," I breathed. Thinking about Jordan brought back the shadowy presence at the edges of my own vision. I stood up.

Gerrard looked at me. "Maybe Luke got hurt in one of Jux's classes?"

I sat down again. Of course. I started to apologize again, but Gerrard waved one hand. I met his eyes. "There's more," I said. He didn't respond, so I forced myself to start talking, telling him everything I had thought about. When I was finished, he was still staring at me. I repeated my last sentence. "We have to include everyone."

Gerrard shook his head.

I stood up, and almost cried out when my rib shot a wedge of pain into my side. I sat back down, slowly and carefully, left shoulder high. "It won't work any other way," I said, my teeth clenched.

"I meant to do this alone," Gerrard whispered, looking at the wall.

"But you can't," I breathed the words, trying to soften the insult. It didn't help much. I saw him holding himself still. The air between us hardened. I could feel how much he wanted to hit me.

"We're three words away from a fistfight now."

He exhaled and nodded.

"With everybody included," I whispered. "No one else has to die."

Gerrard looked at me with pity, like I was an amusing but deficient child. "Somiss will see it. Or some wizard whose name we will never know will overhear someone on the way to class, and then they will kill us all."

"We can get better at talking without words," I said. "There won't be anything to overhear."

"Other classes have probably done that twenty times. Somiss knows."

I shook my head. "Maybe. I don't think so. I watch him in class. If he does know, he doesn't care anymore."

Gerrard looked at me for a long moment. "We will have to kill Luke."

"No," I said. "We just have to help him. He's scared shitless. He's sad."

Gerrard shook his head. "He's an asshole."

I braced my rib with one hand, and it eased the pain a little. "Right after the wasps, I saw Luke. I saw what is inside him. He's hurt so deep, it makes him hate everyone." I watched Gerrard's face. "So are you," I said. "So am I."

Gerrard nodded. "But Luke *likes* hurting people."

I leaned toward him to try to convince him, and I felt my rib pop again. When I winced and straightened, Gerrard reached out and slid his hand down my side. "It's broken."

Then he went to the door and looked out into the passage. When he came back, he settled onto his bed with his back to me. "It's a stupid idea," he said. Then I saw his shoulders rise as he began to practice. It wasn't a pattern I recognized. I wanted to ask him if he had made it up, but

I didn't. I knew he wouldn't tell me. And I was exhausted. I hadn't said that many words to anyone in all the time I had been here.

I placed the song book close, then lay down, wincing and grunting. It took time for me to stop hurting enough to concentrate on the next song. And when I did, I remembered what Franklin said. *Imagine the songs.* The way I imagined food? I stared at the page, then closed my eyes. About half of it was there, in the darkness inside my mind. I could almost read it, but it faded quickly. I tried again.

By the time I put out my lamp, I had a whole page in my head, the same way I had so many of Celia's dinners there. If I closed my eyes, I could *read* the words. Not perfectly, but that was only because I had to figure out a few of the pronunciations still. I could see the words as clearly as they were inked in the book.

Going to sleep, I remembered something else. The entrance test I had worked so hard to fail—there had been little drawings, inked in rows. An orange, a knife, a kitten, a cart wheel—everyday things. The wizard had let me look at them for a few heartbeats, no more than that. Then he had asked me to name them, left to right. I had done it exactly, sure that anyone could. Franklin had said the colors of the food I'd made were perfect. There had been squares of colors on the test that I was supposed to match. I had done that part accurately, too, afraid that missing something that simple would be too obvious and they would tell my father. Half the test had seemed idiotic to me, but it had all mattered.

I had a dream that night. In it my father was a wasp, buzzing around my head. I lifted a hand to swat him, but then I remembered the little ones in the nest that needed feeding. I wasn't meant to kill, I was meant to bring life to the babies. So was he. He hadn't loved me or fed me, but that was what he was meant to do. I lifted my hand in friendship, and he stung it. One sting, Jux had said. One.

I slid into the darkness, rolling and flailing, and woke up, gasping, every breath lifting my rib, stabbing me.

"Are you all right?" Gerrard whispered.

I dragged in three or four more breaths before I could answer him. "Yes. Just . . . a dream."

"Are you sure?"

"Yes." Wincing, moving in little jerks, I eased myself flat again, and the sharp pains stopped.

Gerrard turned back over. I could hear his bed creak. Then I heard a faint whisper that sounded like "Good night."

I didn't answer him, in case I was wrong.

She had a route. It wasn't exactly the same each day, but morning almost always started with a walk to one of the alleys to see what she could see. She had learned not to get too close to the end that opened onto the boardwalk or she began to feel the cold fear that seemed to seep into her body from the earth beneath her bare feet.

But from halfway down the alley she could see women in clean dresses with scrub-faced children holding their hands, and boys in sturdy trousers and soft shirts chasing one another. She went often because she loved to watch them go past. They all looked happy. Carriages rolled by, and even the horses seemed content.

But one morning there was a long procession of women in chains, shuffling along. She stared, wondering who they were and why they were prisoners. They wore dark robes, and most of them were weeping. Tall men with long knives in their belts were shoving them along. One of the guards looked down the alley and stared at her.

She turned and ran until she was out of breath, then walked, her shoulders hunched against the shouting and the stink of dishwater and slops water being thrown from opened windows. Chained dogs lunged at her, but she kept on instead of stopping to assure them she meant them no harm. A woman wearing odd, bright clothing grabbed at her wrist but missed, then stood shouting in a strange, sing-song language. A man hawked and spat, and she felt droplets on her arm. Somewhere a baby was crying. As soon as she could, she turned right onto a wider street.

It was quieter. There were shops with clouded windows and children asleep in the doorways, but no one shouted at her, and there were no dogs with spiked collars. The sailors she passed stared at her but didn't speak. It was early. They were still looking for new shirts and something to eat besides ship's biscuits. Wagons of goods rolled past, heading away from the docks. The tinsmith led his donkey slowly and carefully through the crowds. They were both old and both kind.

She turned again, then again, and saw the hanging sign painted with a picture of a round of cheese, one wedge cut from it. She had come to love the cheese shop. Inside it was always quiet. The gentle, sour smell of clabbered milk was always mixed with the scent of lye soap. The cheesemaker kept his sinks and counter very clean. The place always calmed her heart. And the cheesemaker had hired her. He paid her to sweep the shop, the storage rooms, and the boardwalk.

For the hour or so that she was there every morning, she felt almost safe. The cheesemaker was not talkative, and she was grateful. He had never asked her name. Or about her hair. She had no answer for either one. She had no name and no idea why her hair didn't grow past the length of her eyelashes. It just didn't. She always came early, got the broom from its corner, and went to work.

"If you would like to clean upstairs, too," he said, one day, "I could pay you in bread."

She straightened and turned to stare at him, one hand tight on the broom.

"It's dirty. And I have no time for cleaning," he said, carrying a wheel of cheese to the cutting block. He leaned back against the weight as he set it down and centered it. Then he looked at her. "Will you help me?"

She blinked. He had always been kind to her.

"My name is Charlie da Masi," he said. "There are rags up there, and lye soap, vinegar, and three buckets, two full of clean water."

This was more than he had ever said to her. And she could hear something deeper than his words. It was almost like what she felt from the tanner's dog and the old mule that carried the tinsmith's tools. Charlie was honest. He meant well.

"The bread will be fresh and good."

She felt her mouth flood with saliva. "How much?"

He looked up again. "Half a loaf?"

"I'll finish the sweeping, then go up," she said.

"Good." He reached for the cutting form. "If you need more water, just shout down the stairs."

She nodded and went back to sweeping. An impatient banging on the door made her turn. There was a farmer's wagon outside.

"Trey and her daughter bring me milk once a week," Charlie said on his way to help carry in the tall milk cans.

She watched, wondering if she should lend a hand too. But he didn't ask, and the woman and her daughter were both stout and strong, so she just kept sweeping. Once the shop was clean, she edged past Charlie and went up the stairs, scared she would get up there and realize that she didn't know how to clean. Sometimes it happened. Sometimes she didn't know the simplest things.

Walking around the little apartment at the top of the stairs, she was relieved. The floors were sticky-gritty. That would mean a broom, followed by lye soap and a scrub brush. The table and chairs were coated in an odd, oily dust that smelled like cheese and was hard to get off. That would need the lye, more diluted, and rags. There were two windows, and she knew that vinegar water would be best and that she should do them first, with the cleanest water, so they wouldn't streak. For an instant she waited, hoping that she might remember where she had learned to clean. Or her own name. But of course, she couldn't.

Once the windows were finished, she stood staring down at the street. What comfort it must be to have a place to sleep. One with walls that kept Chee and the sailors out. And everyone else. And to be up here, far above the muddy cobblestones and the voices and the chill of the fog. She shivered and knew that once, lost in the times that she couldn't remember, she'd had a place with walls. A room or a house, or something.

She hurried through the rest of the cleaning, wrung out the rags, and was almost ready to go downstairs when she heard a sound from the street. She crossed the little room and looked out the window. There was a puppy, yowling, skinny and scared. She could feel its heart thudding, its hatred for people. Chee and five or six girls had it cornered against the wall of the rooming house across the street. Chee had a stick. A thick one.

Pounding down the stairs, she startled Charlie, but ran past him. "Get away!" she shouted at Chee as she burst out of the door. All the girls turned to look at her. They began to sing the rhyme, but she motioned impatiently and they faltered, then stopped.

"I'll trade you half a loaf of bread for him," she said.

Chee shook her head. "Where would you get that much bread?"

"From the shop." She turned to point and saw the seamstress next door to the cheese shop standing at her window, watching. People on the narrow boardwalk had stopped to stare too. Charlie was in his doorway. He lifted one hand, questioning. She nodded, and he went back in. A moment later he brought her the bread. She went to stand by the pup, her back to the wall, holding out the bag.

Chee snatched it—and ran. The rest of the girls followed, shouting, jumping over the slops puddles, dodging around the people who were just trying to make their way down the narrow street. The pup stood up and barked after Chee and the others, his dark, wiry coat lifted in a ridge down his spine. When they were out of sight, he looked up.

Will you come with me? she asked him without speaking. He blinked like a surprised child when he understood her. She stood straight and turned to go back across the cobbles to the cheese shop, the puppy at her heels. Charlie was still standing in the doorway, watching her. "I finished upstairs," she called. He nodded, and she walked toward him. "The buckets are full. I will—"

"I'll carry the water out," Charlie interrupted her. He looked down at the puppy.

"I thought it might bite you," he said, giving her a little more cheese for sweeping than usual. "You weren't a bit afraid, though, were you?"

She shook her head. "Of him? I am never afraid of animals." And she knew it was true. She held the feeling close, the certainty of that one thing. It was almost a memory.

Charlie walked closer, and the pup bristled and snarled, deep and low.

"He'll get used to you," she said.

But he didn't. The puppy didn't get used to anyone but her. He snarled so often she began calling him Grrur to tease him, but it stuck. She fed him every bit of food she could spare for a while, then he learned to catch rats and grew faster. Charlie let him loose in the storeroom now and then, to keep the rats from getting started inside. Chee was afraid of him. He could smell trouble and danger and Marshams, all from a distance.

Her route changed. Every day she cleaned Charlie's little room and swept the shop for her bread and cheese while Grrur waited outside. Then they headed for the docks, where he could catch his breakfast. She watched from a little way off, calling him back if she saw sailors noticing her. They were not all bad men, she knew that now. But they were all wary of Grrur, and she was grateful.

One day, after she left Charlie's shop, the woman who sewed clothes out of rags in the little building next door asked if she would trade work for a coat. "I need someone to sweep the boardwalk and the workshop and to sort the scraps and threads by color. Pretty dog," she said, bending down.

Grrur growled at her.

"Will he bite?"

"Not if you don't try to hurt me."

"I have no such intention," she said. "My name is Mrs. Jenness." She waited a moment. But when the awkward silence stretched thin, she pointed. "Those are the sorting baskets."

There were only four. One for red, one for green, one for yellow, and one for black and white. It seemed silly. "Do you have any boxes?"

Mrs. Jenness shrugged. "Maybe. This was a fruit-packers' place before I took it over. Look in the back."

The shop door creaked, startling Grrur. He growled, but he followed her into the room. The faint light coming from high windows made it hard at first, but as her eyes adjusted it was obvious that the fruit packers had gone out of business and left in a hurry. There were a hundred crates and boxes, stacked by size and shape. While Grrur found three rats, she found one kind of box—sturdy, shallow, and long—that worked perfectly for the thread. For the scraps, she found several boxes much bigger and laid them out against the wall. Before dark, the scraps were sorted so that the blues became purple on one end and green on the other. The next day she filled a box with green cloth that slowly became almost yellow. The remainder of the scraps sorted out into yellows, oranges and, finally, reds that ranged into purple.

"You have a fine eye for color," Mrs. Jenness said. "It's a pity you don't weave. Or paint." It was meant kindly, that was obvious. But it had the opposite effect.

For the rest of that day and well into the one that followed, even with Grrur walking close, the wondering consumed her. Weaving. Painting. A painter? Was she? If she knew what both those things were, why didn't she know anything about herself?

Walking back to the docks, with Grrur beside her, she found a place to sleep before the moon was up. They settled in, but she stared at the sky. She could feel Grrur breathing. He had begun sleeping with his back against hers. He was growing up. He would never be a match for a midshipman's fists or a thief's knife. But she knew he would try to be, for her. And she would do the same for him. Every night some of her loneliness seeped into his wiry curls, was dimmed by the soft rhythm of his breathing, was eased by his warmth.

– 42 –

We didn't recite for Somiss the next day, or the one after. Jux did not come for either of us, and no wizard took us to Franklin's class. We had nothing to do but study. And starve. I don't know if anyone else had tried to eat without Franklin standing there, promising it would be all right. I wouldn't. I drank more water, kept busy, and ignored my fluttering thoughts until they settled again. And I was very, very careful whenever I moved. My rib hurt more every time I did something that made it pop. I tried not to grunt and groan. It was hard. Gerrard pretended not to notice.

In two days, the bruises on my chest and belly were fading a little and the aching dimmed by half, but my rib hurt so much that it was impossible to sit for very long. Standing was easier. Flat on my back was best, but lowering myself into that position was torture, and getting back up was worse. So I stood up at my desk as long as I could.

I stared at the pages of the song book, learning to take in everything at once, instead of reading the words one by one. When I closed my eyes, I could force up a perfect image of the whole page, the way I had learned to picture food or soap or lamp wicks.

At first the edges of the page were faint, but they got sharper and sharper as I practiced. I can't explain how relieved and happy I was the first time I did it perfectly. I rocked back and forth, my mouth open wide like I was cheering, but nothing came out. If I could make the images clear, correct, and permanent, I could stop worrying about Somiss's class. I could spend the time on other things. I might live a lot longer. Maybe there would be time to make the pact with everyone.

Maybe? Maybe. And that was enough. I decided not to talk to Gerrard about it again. Not yet.

The next morning Gerrard washed up, then went out the door without saying a word. Was he going to try to eat? My stomach was starting to hurt and I felt a little weak, but I didn't want to try yet. I was still terrified of being lost again.

Once Gerrard was gone, I washed and pissed and then stood at my desk with the song book closed, holding my left shoulder as high as I could. I closed my eyes and imagined the song I had worked on the day before. I was afraid the images wouldn't appear. But they did. So I opened the book and began working out the pronunciations of the words I didn't know.

It was hard to concentrate. The aching in my side had abated, but the jabbing pain from my rib still came with each little movement. Every time I leaned forward to turn a page in the song book, I felt it pop again. I lay flat for a while, holding the heavy book up so I could read it. Then I tried, grunting and wincing, to find any position on my side or my belly that wasn't excruciating. I couldn't. I finally just went back to stand at my desk, my left shoulder lifted, the book open before me.

By the end of that day, I had the next two songs in my mind, whole, perfect, identical to the pages in the book. I could see and read the words. It was amazing to me. I wondered if it was something that anyone could do, with practice. Or had the entrance tests picked out the ones of us who would be able to learn how to do it? I suddenly remembered a few questions about daydreaming. I had told the truth on that one, thinking it had to be a trait they wouldn't want.

Wherever Gerrard had gone, he came back in quietly, without saying a word. His back was stiff and straight, his step slightly awkward. Was something bothering him? Had he tried to make food? Then, as I watched, he bent double and reached beneath his robe. He had a length of gray cloth around his waist. He pulled it free. "Take your robe off."

I blinked, startled.

"Hurry. Class is about to start. I saw a wizard in the passageway."

I hesitated.

He shook the cloth. "I'll wrap your ribs. It'll help."

I pulled off my robe, clumsy and slow; it hurt to lift my arms over my head. Gerrard was glancing at the door as I struggled, trying not to groan. He wound the soft cloth tightly around my chest and belly, tucking the end under to hold it in place. When I lowered my hands, the sharp pain was almost gone.

"Thank you," I breathed. "Did you steal this?" I patted the cloth.

He shook his head.

"Did you use the stone to make it?"

Without answering, he shook out my robe and held it up so I could get it on quickly. "Did you run to Market Square and buy it from a Gypsy?" I asked him as I pulled it on. His lips twitched, and I thought for an instant he might laugh, but he didn't.

"I talked to Luke," he whispered. "I think he'll leave us alone now."

"He said he would kill me if you threatened him," I breathed.

He almost smiled. "We discussed that. He gave me his word he would leave you and Will alone."

A wizard pounded on the door before I could ask Gerrard anything. It was another silver-haired man, and we fell into step behind him. Halfway there, I knew where we were going. As we started up the incline, I was grateful for the cloth holding my rib in place. But I was scared, too. Jux's classes could be terrible. If the cloth came undone—

or even if it held and I had to climb something or run—I might not be fast enough.

But when the wizard left—and Gerrard opened the round door, slowly and carefully—we saw Franklin, not Jux. He was on the far side of a meadow, his back to a stand of pine trees. I stood there blinking. I had no idea what it meant. At least it was a sunny day in Jux's forest. I looked up as I always did, trying to see how the light came in. I couldn't.

We were halfway across the meadow when Levin and Jordan arrived. Luke and Will were not far behind them. I slowed, and Gerrard shot me a glance, but he shortened his stride. We were all walking more or less side by side as we neared Franklin. I began to hope, just a little. No one was afraid to sit at the same table or walk closer together if Somiss wasn't around. Maybe Franklin's classes could be our first step toward trusting each other.

"Welcome," he said, and smiled, baring his teeth again. It looked even more clownish in the sunlight. He turned around, and when he faced us again, he had an impossible creature in his hands. It was a miniature lion, as small as an apple. It roared and lashed its tiny tail.

Will laughed, a nervous, chittering sound. Jordan lifted one hand, his eyes dreamy, as though he wanted to touch it. Levin gripped his wrist. I looked at Jordan. Every time I saw him, he looked a little better, but not the same. Not himself. Not yet. Maybe I wasn't either.

"Is it real?" Franklin asked.

No one answered.

Franklin turned around once more. This time, there was a winged girl in his hands. She was lovely beyond words. Green eyes. Her long hair was dark red, her skin pale, her cheeks pink as roses. She evaporated as we watched.

The third time Franklin turned in a circle, a miniature lake of fire burned in his cupped hands. I glanced at Gerrard. His eyes were narrowed, cautious.

"Is it real, Gerrard?" Franklin asked.

Gerrard stared, then finally shook his head. "No, or you couldn't hold it like that."

Franklin swung his hands, throwing the liquid. Gerrard ducked, but not fast enough. He screamed, clawing at his face, stumbling. I started toward him but could not take the second step. Something was holding my left foot. I tried to crawl toward Gerrard, but my foot was pegged to the ground and my rib ached and I could only watch as he rolled in the grass, curled into a ball of agony.

I looked back at Franklin, trying to shout at him, but my voice would not obey me. Franklin lifted his right hand and said five or six of the long, twisted words in the language the songs were in. Gerrard stopped writhing. His body turned in the opposite direction, then he uncurled himself and sprang back to his feet. The fire on his face and chest dimmed, then leapt from him back into Franklin's hands. And all of this within three or four heartbeats.

Somewhere in that same time, my foot had freed itself and I had stood back up and Franklin was looking into our faces, smiling, holding the little lake of fire. "Do any of you think it's real now?"

I glanced at Levin. He was sheet white. Jordan's mouth was open. Will was blinking, shaking his head. Franklin repeated the question. We all nodded, cautiously, our weight on the balls of our feet, ready to run. All but Gerrard. He just looked puzzled.

"And you?" Franklin was looking at him. "Is it real?"

Gerrard slowly shook his head. There was not a single singe on his robe, not the tiniest pink burn on his skin. "No," he said. "But it doesn't matter."

Franklin's hands were suddenly empty. "No, it doesn't. What matters is what you believe. And what you believe is behind the second gate in your mind." He looked into each of our faces, then asked us to sit down. I took longer than the others. Sitting on the edge of my bed had hurt. Sitting on the ground was really painful, even with the tight cloth. It would have been impossible without it. I felt Luke watching me, and I tried not to let it show.

"Thinking and believing are separate," Franklin said. "Sometimes they match. Often not. We all believe, in our skin and our hearts, that fire will burn us. Most of us prove it to ourselves when we are little children, often more than once."

Franklin started breathing the first pattern, and we all joined him on the second breath. I lifted my left shoulder a little to ease my rib as he led us up through all the levels he had taught us. It hurt, but it still felt wonderful. I closed my eyes, the sound of our breathing washed through me like salt water through beach sand. It had always calmed me, all the way to my bones. I had missed his classes.

"There are three gates inside your mind," Franklin said quietly. "Three that I know about. I am sure there are more."

Our collective breath paused, then fell back into unison. He had said something like this before, back when he was just starting to teach us to move our thoughts.

"Good," he said. "You all remember." He paused and looked up at the false sky, then back at us. "The first gate leads to your everyday, careless thoughts," he said, "the ones you have learned to quiet, the ones you have learned to move." He looked at us one by one again. "Have you all learned to move your thoughts?"

I watched Gerrard from the edge of my vision. His back straightened just a little, and my stomach tightened. Maybe he hadn't. Maybe all that complicated breathing was just to fool me.

"Let's practice," Franklin said.

He had us all breathe the first pattern, then asked us to think about whatever made us the most angry. "Here," he said. "Or when you were at home. Or at another school. Choose something that made you angry enough to want to kill something—or someone."

There was a round of shifting and sighing as we all settled ourselves on the grass. I thought immediately of my father—as I had the first time Franklin had guided me into moving my thoughts. But then I thought about Somiss. I pictured him sneering, his eyes cold and dead when he looked at us. I remembered his impassive face when the dying boys shuffled past him. And then, for some reason, I knew that neither my father nor Somiss made me angriest. It was Franklin.

I had never once expected Somiss to give a shit about any of us, to show even the smallest kindness. In his way, my father was just as ruthless. But Franklin was kind. I could see that he was. I could feel it. But he had done nothing to save the boys who had starved. How could he have just watched them die, day by day weaker, paler? How many times had he just stepped around starving boys on his way out of class?

Like I had.

I looked down to hide my face. I hadn't done anything to help them until it was far too late. I had never helped my mother, either. Or anyone else in my whole life. Not really. I was the one. I was the one I hated most of all.

Franklin leaned toward us. "Once you have the thought, push it into your belly. Anger is very comfortable in your belly, more comfortable there than in your mind."

I had moved my angry thoughts a hundred times. But this time I couldn't. I had no idea why. I tried twice more, then looked at Levin. His eyes were closed. Gerrard was breathing in one of his strange breathing patterns, but his back was stiff and worried. Jordan was staring up at the sky, rocking back and forth. Will was hunched over.

"You can move a thought," Franklin said, looking at me, "much more easily than a belief. When we open the second gate, you will know why." He paused, then looked past us. "But before we can go on, Gerrard, Will, and Luke must learn to move their thoughts so they can open the first gate." He breathed in, then out, and I could see his eyes shine with tears. "Practice hard," he said. "Or we will have to leave you behind."

Will started to say something, but Franklin had already disappeared.

In late autumn Charlie got sick with a deep, painful cough. It worried her to the bone. He paid her in coppers when he was too ill to walk to the baker. She would have worked free for him but was glad to have the money.

One day she took enough coins to buy his bread as well as her own, and brought it back to the cheese shop for him. Grrur lay in the corner, polite and hopeful. Charlie usually gave him a bit of bread, then let him into the storeroom to hunt rats.

"What is your name?" Charlie asked quietly.

Startled, she glanced at the door.

"Don't leave, please," he said. "You don't have to tell me."

She shook her head. "I don't know my name."

Charlie stood very still, and his silence somehow freed her tongue. He listened as she explained waking up in South End one morning, more than two years before, how Chee and the others had chased her. She had never told anyone else, and the words just poured out. She told him how she had soiled herself. And then she started to cry. Grrur came to stand beside her.

Charlie waited, patient and sad, until she was finished. Then he came and put one arm around her shoulders. Grrur didn't growl at him. "You could just choose one," Charlie said. Then he stepped back and left her to herself.

He kept coughing. The weather turned, and he did not get well. She began walking new routes, listening to the voices around her, the warm quilted coat Mrs. Jenness had made for her buttoned to her chin. Grrur loved to taunt the half wolves, chained in the daytime, and she warned him over and over. One day she imagined it for him, the chain breaking, the wolf-dog killing him, and her eyes stung with tears. Grrur whimpered, then walked closer to her as they went on.

She finally heard two women talking about ailments. One was on her way to buy a curative. They were old friends, chatting, walking slowly. It was easy enough to follow them. They turned into one of the narrow paths that snaked between the old buildings, leading her to a part of South End she had never seen before.

Chickens pecked at apple peels dumped from a kitchen window. There were black-robed women with small folding tables. They were burning sage leaves, moaning and singing, while weary-faced people gave them half coppers for good-luck charms. She looked into the faces of the people around her. There was both hope and fear in their eyes.

Farther down, she saw men selling little parcels to tall boys wearing cloaks that covered them head to toe. When one of them turned, she caught a glimpse of a white lace sleeve and knew that the boys did not live in South End. They were from somewhere far on the other side of that invisible line she could not cross. What were they buying? The parcels were small, tightly wrapped.

She walked slower, trying to overhear as she passed, but the man taking their money glared at her and raised a fist. Grrur snarled and the man jumped backward. The boys laughed. The man kicked at Grrur, but he was too quick and jumped aside. She called him, and he leapt to catch up and stayed close until they had turned the next corner.

The women had stopped. It was an alley of herb vendors. Artful displays of baskets filled with dried leaves had been carefully laid out. Grrur's nose was twitching at the pungent scents as they walked to the end, then started back.

"Did you find what you need?"

The voice startled her and Grrur. He snarled, but only once. The woman tossed him a scrap of meat, and his opinion of her changed instantly. The woman smiled. "Something to make you more beautiful?" The vendor tipped her head. "Something to kill lice? I have all sorts of herbs."

Blushing, bending over to pat Grrur, she shook her head.

The woman nodded. "I know. We all have to be very careful now, with the king's guards watching us closer and closer." She dropped her voice to a whisper. "These are nothing to do with what the Ferrin Hill families sell. These are bitter herbs, for healing, not for stews and soup." The woman looked around, then leaned close again. "The knowledge is old, old, old. It's from the long ago and all too near." She straightened and lifted her voice. "I do not promise magic. I know none. But I have mixtures of herbs and oils that will help. . . ." The woman stopped suddenly, staring. "Oh, dear. It's for a friend who is very ill?"

Grrur growled low in his throat. He was ready to attack her if she meant harm.

"I won't harm your girl," the woman told him.

Could she hear Grrur too?

"Are you a mute?" the woman asked, looking up.

"No."

"Do you love this friend?" the woman whispered.

"He is kind to me. He's gentle."

The woman smiled. "A kind, gentle man is hard to find in South End."

"I wasn't looking. It was an accident."

The woman laughed. "What's your name, dearie?"

There it was. The question she could never answer. She bent to touch Grrur's stiff, curling fur. When she looked up, the woman's smile had collapsed.

"Where are you parents? Where are you from?"

She shrugged. "I just woke up here."

The woman was watching her carefully.

"That's all I remember," she said. "Waking up. And I was here."

"Were you bruised? Did someone beat you?"

It was another question she could not answer. She had been sore, maybe. But she had been so scared, nothing else had mattered but food and staying away from Chee, and the sailors.

The woman reached out to pat her shoulder. "One day you will be able to remember everything."

"Oh, I hope so," she said quickly. Grrur paced around her legs once, then sat down, leaning against her shins.

The woman opened her leather bag. "All right, then. Does your friend feel too warm?"

"Yes. And he has a terrible cough."

The woman nodded and began searching through her bag. The sound of the glass vials clinking against each other went on for a long moment. Then she looked up. "Here."

It was a tiny vial of a flame-red liquid.

"Put it in your bodice," the woman said. "Don't let anyone see it."

Once the little vial was out of sight, she leaned close again. "Heat a pot of water to boiling, then pour three drops of the elixir into it," she said. "He should stand above the pot, breathe it in. Deep, long breaths until it cools."

"And it will make him well?"

The woman arched her brows. "It will help him expel

the bad humors. Feed him warm food and all the tea he will drink. Do you know any of the little songs?"

She shook her head.

"Here's the one my mother used." The woman leaned close and sang in a very soft, breathy voice. The tune was very simple, and the song was short. But the words were strange and meaningless—a string of sounds all run together. The woman sang it a second time, then a third. "Can you remember that?"

The alley was getting crowded. "Yes. I just sing it to him?"

The woman nodded. "Don't tell anyone where you learned it. They can't hang every farmwife in the kingdom," she whispered. "But you never know. I'm an Eridian. Do you know what that means?"

"No." The copper coins were cold as she held them out.

The woman smiled. "There are a lot of us up where the river runs into the bay. Have you heard of the Celebration of Birth?"

"No." She held the coins higher.

The woman took one, then smiled again. "Come back and talk to me."

"I will," she said, but she didn't want to think about coming back here, she wanted Charlie to get well. She was about to leave when a commotion erupted at the far end of the alley.

"Run!" the woman hissed, and started away.

Panic was rolling up the alley like a wave, the shouts coming closer, more people running, a metallic clanking striking the walls and echoing. Grrur barked and they fled, ducking into the first deep doorway she saw. Grrur pressed his back against her legs and snarled as tall men with sword scabbards clattered past. A moment later there were more shouts. She leaned out enough to see that they had two women backed up against a wall—herb sellers, but not the one she had talked to. Clutching the little packet, she ran in the opposite direction and made her way back out of the twisting paths, onto the cobblestone streets.

Out of breath, she slowed down. Her heart was jumping in her chest. Would the men come looking for anyone who had bought bitter herbs?

Halfway back to the cheese shop, a tall man on a side street looked at her, and his eyes widened. His face contorted with some desperate emotion. He stumbled, then caught himself. "Sadima?"

She walked faster. The last thing she needed was for a drunk to mistake her for some long-lost sweetheart.

"Sadima! Wait!" She glanced back. He was gesturing wildly. He ran into an old man and stopped to help him up. While he was preoccupied, she ran, ducking around one corner, then another, until she had put enough distance between them to be sure he could not follow.

~ 44 ~

Gerrard was gone most of the next day. He studied for a while, then left without saying a word to me. I hoped Franklin was wrong—that Gerrard *could* move his thoughts. I was past simply wanting him to need my help and keep our pact. I needed him to help save us all.

I studied the next song. Imagining it came even quicker. Figuring out the pronunciations took much more time, but once I had it, I had it perfectly. By the time Gerrard came back, I was two songs ahead. I couldn't smell fish stew or anything else, so I wondered where he had gone, but I didn't ask.

The wizards had been making our days shorter and shorter, or so it seemed to me. I was hungry, but still not enough to make me risk opening my thoughts to the stone—or touching it. With every day that passed, my thoughts were a little clearer, and the thrumming sound was quieter. Seeing the faraway stare on Jordan's face had scared me. Maybe Franklin would let us eat without fear again soon. I hoped so. I tried not to think about what would happen if he didn't.

Somiss's next class was the following day—except that Somiss wasn't there. Jux listened to our recitations, standing at one end of a little chamber, his head down, his eyes closed. Levin passed. So did Jordan. Gerrard missed three words—on purpose. Will missed many more than that. Luke did even worse. I recited last, with my eyes closed. I was reading the song from the image in my head, so I spoke without hesitation, absolutely sure of every word. When I opened my eyes, I saw Luke staring at me. And Will. And Gerrard, but he immediately glanced away. Levin and Jordan were staring straight ahead, at nothing, but Levin's jaw was locked and his hands were fists. Was he angry at me?

I glanced at Jux and found him smiling at me. Then he leaned backward, legs straight, shoulders squared, like a child playing at falling backward onto a feather bed. He fell through the stone wall, the soles of his feet silhouetted for an instant, then gone. No one moved, no one spoke, but I was sure we were all wondering the same things. Where was Somiss? Could the ones who passed eat safely? Could anyone? Was *sometimes* still with us?

Going back to our chamber, Gerrard walked as far from me as he could without making it obvious. Once we were inside the room again, he positioned himself on his bed, his back to me.

"I saw you make food without touching the stone," I whispered. "Why did Franklin say you—"

"What?" His whisper was sharp.

"You can move your thoughts. I saw you. The day I made the lamp wicks. I hid and—"

"You hid? And watched?" He turned around and faced me, and I knew my next answer would either start a fight, or prevent one. I told him the truth. "I was bending over when you came in, and you didn't see me. So I was just going to leave without bothering you, but then you—"

"It wasn't me."

I stared at him. "But I saw you. Sitting at a table. And the food appeared beside you, not on the pedestal."

"You didn't see any of that," he whispered. "I can't move my thoughts yet." He lowered his whisper to the barest escape of breath. "Wizards make illusions, Hahp. They know we are up to something. They want us to hate each other."

I didn't answer him. He had long pretended to have trouble in the recitation classes. Maybe he was doing the same thing with me. Or maybe he was telling the truth. "Why would Franklin tell us who can't move their thoughts yet?" I whispered.

Gerrard was silent for so long that I thought he wasn't going to answer me. He finally exhaled and shrugged. "I don't know. Something is wrong."

That caught me off guard. "What do you mean?"

He barely breathed the answer. "The days are too short. Franklin was gone a long time, too long, and now Somiss is gone. And the wizards who lead us to class are always—"

"Old," I said. "It wasn't like that before."

Gerrard nodded. "Franklin is lying about—"

"I told him we had all missed him, and he cried," I interrupted. "And the things he said made me feel like all this matters."

Gerrard looked at me like I had suggested that rain was falling *up*. "He doesn't believe that shit."

"Yes," I said in a rough whisper, "he does." And then I felt stupid because I had no idea if Franklin believed magic should be used to help people. I just *wanted* him to.

Gerrard was shaking his head, looking disgusted. "Why would he tell us who's falling behind, Hahp? What would you think if Somiss had done it?" He turned and began practicing again.

I stared at his back. If Somiss had done it, I would have assumed he was trying to see who would help who, to expose any friendships. I exhaled. Somiss wanted all of us to die so he would be free of us, done with teaching. "I wonder how many classes actually produce a graduate," I whispered. Gerrard ignored me. And then I thought of something that had never crossed my mind before. "Are there other classes here? Two years ahead of us, or two years behind?"

"No," Gerrard said. "Now shut up."

I made myself study. I imagined another song and worked at the pronunciations I wasn't sure of. When I finished, I closed the book and walked to the food hall. No one was there, so I went in and stood before the stone. I knew Gerrard as well as I had ever known anyone. I was almost positive that I had seen him make food—not some wizard's illusion. But why would he lie to me?

"Hahp?"

I spun around at the whisper. It was Will. He walked toward me, and I knew what he was going to say before he said it.

"Would you help me?" he asked once he was close. "Even a little?"

He was thin, and the dark circles under his eyes were worse. I saw his hand tremble when he lifted it to push his hair back from his face. He was hungry. Really hungry. I hesitated about three heartbeats, then I nodded. I didn't care what Gerrard thought. We had to help each other or we would all die.

I led Will out of the food hall, turning left, away from our chambers. I went fast, until I realized that he was having trouble keeping up, then I slowed. A few hundred paces past the little chamber where I had found the old lantern, I made six random turns, then stopped.

My heart was thudding. I was terrified. The wizards had known about the food I had hidden long before, and they would know about this if they cared enough to be watching. But it didn't matter. If they killed me for it, at least I would die hating myself a little less. If they didn't, this was the beginning of the pact. I sat down, ignoring the rib-stabs. Will arranged himself cross-legged before me.

I described the weird, shifting feeling that I got when I moved my thoughts, like I was pushing them along. I told him that starting with angry thoughts was easier. "And you have to expect it to happen, like you do with the stone, like Gerrard with Franklin's little fire. Belief, not thought." I looked at him. "You are moving thoughts, not beliefs. But you have to believe you can do it." That sounded so contradictory and stupid to me that I started over, but Will stopped me.

"I know what you mean," he said. "I do. I have to expect it the way Gerrard expected to get burned." He closed his eyes and began the breathing patterns.

I paced away from him, then stopped about halfway back to the food hall and turned around and went back. Will looked up at me when I got there, and his face was full of panic. "I can't expect it to work. I expect it not to." He shifted on the stone. "It sounds so weird. Can you really do it?" I nodded and sat beside him, wincing a little when my rib hurt. He shook his head. "What if Somiss is seeing who is stupid enough to help the ones who can't—Hahp, I think I'm too scared to be angry."

"I am too, a lot of the time," I whispered. "Just think about Somiss, about everything he has done to us. Picture his little smiles when we can't recite, the way he interrupts us." He closed his eyes, and I waited until I heard his breathing quicken before I spoke again. "Think about your roommates. About every day you spent watching them die." I could see Will's shoulders rise. "What would you do to Somiss if you could? Picture it."

When I saw his face harden into a mask of hatred, I leaned closer. "Anger thoughts are slow, heavy. Push them toward your belly."

Will was very still. Then he went stiff, and after a long pause, he nodded, his eyes still closed. "That feels very strange," he whispered.

"You will get used to it," I told him, and tiptoed away.

Passing the food hall, I slowed. I really was hungry. I went in and stood in front of the stone again, knowing I was too afraid to use it. "I am sick of all this shit," I whispered.

The stone sparkled.

I stared at it.

I hadn't imagined anything and nothing appeared. It wasn't the usual flash of bluish light. It wasn't anything I had ever seen before. My heart started pumping. "What does that mean?" I asked the ceiling, then looked at the stone. "No more fucking mysteries. Please." The stone sparkled again, threads of tiny lights outlining every one of the endless facets on its surface.

I lowered my head and closed my eyes. I couldn't think about anything else—I had no strength left to wonder. I just walked away. Once I was out of the hall, I ran, hard, taking weird turns, until I was so tired I could barely walk. It helped a little. When I got back to the room, I could study.

The herbs helped. But by the time winter closed in, the wind howling off the sea, Charlie's cough came back. She spent every morning with him, prepared the elixir, made sure he inhaled it until it cooled, sang the little song, then swept and cleaned upstairs before she continued her route.

She had shoes this year, thanks to Mrs. Jenness, who wore almost the same size and had an old pair. And because Grrur was so fierce and so protective, she wasn't afraid to walk close to the docks sometimes, in the bright daylight hours. The Marshams were out less in the cold weather; there were fewer children on the street. Maybe their parents had begun feeding them better. She hoped so.

When she found dropped fruit and vegetables on the

docks, she carried as much as she could and took Charlie a share. One morning there were a half-dozen tight, hard heads of cabbage, spilled from a broken crate. She took all of them to Charlie, the front of her skirt gathered like a hammock to hold them all. Chee had followed that day, with four or five others, but Grrur ran them off.

"Do you celebrate Winterfeast?" Charlie asked one snowy morning.

She shook her head. "Is it soon?"

"Tomorrow."

And so they had made the meal together, laughing and smiling, and cooking was like so many things that she knew without being able to remember when or how she had learned. She slept in the cheese room that night and left early, before Charlie was awake.

Grrur found an empty building for them to sleep in not long after that, up along the river, not far from where it drained into the saltwater bay. She had been walking slowly, sure she would soon come to the invisible line, when she noticed a slender cypress tree that had come up through the cobblestones. Grrur slowed with her, then chased a rat through a broken window. She followed.

The building had been a weaver's or a cloth merchant's. The first and third floors were divided into smaller rooms, all the same size. If there had been doors on them, they were gone. The second floor was one cavernous space. There were long bolts of shiny cloth in haphazard piles, each one a beautiful color, almost all different. She found a rusty pair of shears and used a piece of stone to sharpen them. Then she cut two dozen big pieces of cloth, all about the same size. She carried them down and shook the dust out of them. Then she put them one on top of the other for a pallet. She cut ten more for her blanket. It worked well enough, and the colors were a riotous bloom, like springtime and rainbows.

The second-floor windows were mostly broken and the wind blew in, so she slept on the third floor and was warmer than she had ever been in the winter. Grrur lay against her back, his ears twitching, listening even while he slept. She trusted him completely. If anyone came into the building, he would wake her, and he would help her fight if it came to that. She told Charlie about the place, about the bed she had made, and he smiled. Then he coughed.

Worried, she sang the little song, twice through. He was better the next day, and the one after, so she kept singing it to him every morning, hoping she had remembered the words right.

"I know two of those," Charlie told her, "or I used to, anyway. My mother used to sing them. She had one to sleep better and one to make the sun shine. That one never worked." He looked up. "Her name was Anna." He smiled. "Do you know what yours is yet?"

She shook her head, then looked down and fiddled with a pulled thread in her dress. She hadn't told him about the man who had chased her, about the name he had called her. She wasn't sure why. Charlie was still watching her, waiting.

"Sadima," she said without knowing she was going to say it.

He nodded. "It's pretty. It fits you."

She blushed, then felt odd. Could she do that? Could she just choose a name and when people asked her, just tell them? *Sadima.* It was a pretty name, far too good for her. It felt like stealing.

Outside, the wind whined as it hit the stout little building and slid across the bricks. Two customers came in, bringing a single blast of wind with them. Charlie sold the woman half a wheel. She had a servant to carry her parcels, and she wore a fine coat of dark wool. "I can't find cheese this good anywhere else," she said, smiling. "My gardener told me about your shop." Charlie smiled back at her, then turned to the next customer, a young man with restless eyes. Charlie said something to make him laugh. When he lifted his head, she saw an old, knotted scar that ran across his throat and up behind one ear. She looked away before he caught her staring.

Once the shop had emptied, Charlie smiled at her. "You should stay here today, Sadima."

The way he said the name was as kind as a soft touch.

"Maybe you should start sleeping here."

She stared at him.

"Bring your springtime-colored blankets," he said. "Bring them here. It's warmer. There is no reason for you to be cold."

She nodded, slowly, cautiously. Charlie was a very kind man. Did she love him? Maybe. She wasn't sure what love was.

She brought her bedding that day.

"It's all silk," he said, looking at the cloth. "Ten or fifteen years ago, every ship that came up the river was loaded with silk. Then the Ferrinides women stopped buying it. The king made a decree."

She shook her head. "Why?"

He shrugged. "Why do kings do anything? Maybe he was tired of all those Ferrinides coins going to the Orchid Coast."

Charlie helped her carry the stacks of cloth upstairs, coughing, insisting that it didn't hurt him to cough a little more than usual. He had gotten an extra flax-stuffed pallet, like the one he slept on. It looked new, finer than anything South End had to offer. He had bought it for her in some other part of the city and carried it back. She turned to hide the tears in her eyes.

He placed the pallet on the far side of the room, near the window. "Or will the wind bother you?" he asked. "It can rattle the glass."

"I won't mind," she said, looking around the little room. She had scrubbed it top to bottom. She knew every crevice in the planked floor, every speck on the wall. She knew the little woodstove and sideboard where he made his meals. But it was as though she was seeing it for the first time. Walls! She had her own walls, and her own brave dog, and her own dear friend. Charlie looked up at her and smiled as though he understood what she was feeling.

"I lived on the docks when I first came here," he told her. "Like you do, always looking for food."

"Did you just wake up here too?" she asked, and then heard how silly it sounded. But he didn't laugh.

"No. My master got rid of me when he noticed how much his wife liked me. I begged her to stop flirting. She knew how absurd it was. But she wouldn't. It was a way to make him jealous, I guess, without truly risking his anger. I thought he would sell me, indenture me to another family, but he didn't."

"He just brought you here?"

Charlie shook his head. "No. He just shoved me out the door. I started walking and ended up here."

She touched his hand.

"It was almost ten years ago," he said. "I was about fifteen, I guess." He looked up. "Sadima?"

She hesitated, then nodded. It felt very strange to answer to a name. *Sadima*. It sounded so nice the way Charlie said it.

"I would like you to live here, if you want to." He paused, watching her face. "I am not saying . . ." He took a breath and coughed. "I'm not like other men. I can't—"

She put one finger on his lips. "I have always trusted you."

He caught her hand and lowered it, shaking his head. "I was a house servant for a royal family. First cousins to the king. The family had four daughters. My master wanted no chances taken with their virginity. The doctor came one day—there were three of us my master wanted altered."

She felt her eyes go wide as she suddenly understood. "Like farm colts?"

He nodded. "I was four or five, I think. The other two were several years older. They fought and wept. I was just . . . angry. It hurt. Horribly. And for a long time."

She could not stop the tears that came into her eyes.

"I love you," he said. "For all the good that will do you."

She put her arms around him. "Your love has already done me more good than you can possibly imagine."

He held her tight for a long time. When he let her go, he wiped at the tears on his face. "Sadima? Do you want me to try to find out how you got here? I still see the servants from that house sometimes. Some of them are Marshams, so they know everyone on Ferrin Hill. I could ask if anyone knows anything about you."

She shook her head. "It doesn't matter now." And she wanted to mean it. But she kept picturing the man who had chased her. Who was he? Had he known her?

She barely slept that night, listening to the wind, thinking of all the terrible things that might be true. But then morning came and she helped Charlie start two batches of clabber. They salted down a white cheese and carried it to the press. And all day she was astonished at how much she seemed to know about cheese making—in the same mysterious way she had known how to clean and cook, how to listen to the tannery dog. Had she run away and gotten hurt somehow? Was there some royal family looking for *her*?

But as the days went past, one after another, the questions mattered less and less. What mattered was Charlie.

She loved to make him smile. When the next hard winter came and even the walls couldn't keep out all the cold, they slept together, with Grrur between them, or draped across Sadima's legs, or curled up on half of Charlie's bolster. She stitched the pieces of silk together, doubling the width.

The next year they worked hard and made three times as much cheese as Charlie had by himself. And it was better cheese. Trey lowered the price of the milk a little because she liked Charlie and because they were buying so much. More and more people from outside South End began coming to the shop. They told friends and family.

Charlie bought a crate-wagon with spoked wheels to move the heavy rounds of cheese from the back to the storefront and the milk tins in the other direction. They hired one helper, then another. Soon there were more coins than they needed, and they set about buying the building from the landlord. Charlie made his mark on the contract. They paid the moneylender faithfully.

In the summers Charlie's cough almost went away. So when the weather was warm, they forgot about it. Grrur died in the tenth summer and they both wept, then found a place to bury him beneath a cottonwood tree in the open field behind the tannery. Sadima often walked that way, even when she had no reason to, to sit by the patch of earth that held one of the only two friends she had ever had. And one spring day, after seventeen winters had come and gone, the moneylender came and drew up the papers. Sadima was beyond joy. Now the walls really were their walls.

In all those years, and the ones that followed, when it turned cold, and Charlie's cough came back, Sadima went to the herb sellers and bought him herbs and elixirs. She learned three more songs to sing over him, all taught to her by women in the narrow alleyways.

"You are as pretty as you were all those years ago," Charlie told her, over and over. And a day came when he sat her down and looked into her eyes.

"You aren't getting older, Sadima," he said. "Mrs. Jenness has noticed. And others." He went behind the cutting block and carried a slim box over and set it on the floor. He opened it carefully and took out a silvery, shiny piece of glass.

"Have you ever seen a mirror? A looking glass?"

She shook her head. "I know what one is. It can't be so different from looking into a shop win—" and she stopped mid-word, because he had propped the mirror up, then walked back so that she could see them, side by side. She knew what he looked like. His hair had gotten sparse on the top of his head and gray at the temples, and he had wrinkles that fanned out from his eyes and his mouth. His dear, beloved face was staring at her from the mirror. He was an old man. And there was a girl next to him. Her dark red hair was a thick, short fuzz. Her face was unlined, smooth, flushed pink.

"Maybe whoever brought you here did something to you," Charlie said.

She glanced up, then back at the mirror. "What?"

He shook his head. "I don't know. But you look exactly

as you did the day I met you, twenty-seven years ago. People think you are my granddaughter."

"But I don't feel—"

"Listen to me, Sadima," Charlie interrupted her. "The young king is an old man now. He is close to dying and he doesn't have an heir."

Sadima stared at him, wondering why he was repeating street gossip now.

"There's a lot of talk," he said, "about what will happen when he dies. It might not be much different. The chancellors have been running things for a long time anyway. But they hanged the Market Square magicians years back, and some say they are about to bar the herb sellers from the city. The chancellors hate anything that smells like magic to them, even the little farmwives' songs like the ones you sing to me."

She nodded, remembering the chained women in black robes and the day the guards had run down the alleyway, chasing the herb sellers. And she understood what he was telling her. "My not changing might seem like magic to some people?"

He nodded. "You will have to be careful."

They put the mirror away and went back to work and never talked about it again. A few times she noticed him looking at her and knew he wished he could stay young too. She would have given anything to make it so they never had to part. But she couldn't.

They shared five more years of love and laughter, then Charlie died, quietly, on a summer's night, in his sleep, on his side of the pallet. She discovered him in the morning, pale and stiff beneath the silk covers. She cried until she was exhausted, then fell asleep beside him one last time. There was no graveyard in South End. People paid ship's captains to carry bodies out beyond the breakers, out of sight of land, then give them to the sea. Or if they had no money, they carried them upriver and laid them in the marshes to rot.

Sadima had more than enough money; she just couldn't bear the idea of strangers' hands on Charlie's body, the cold sea seeping into his mouth, the fish tugging at his flesh. So she buried him. It took three nights to dig a deep grave beside Grrur's. She hid the hole with branches each morning; then, the night it was finished, she used the wheeled crate-wagon to carry Charlie there. She lowered him as gently as she could, wrapped in some of the silk covers she had stitched together. She spent half the night smoothing and packing the dirt. She rescattered the leaves and twigs carefully. She always visited the graves at night. No one ever knew why she went so often to stand beside the old cottonwood or why it always made her cry.

– 46 –

We had only one recitation class in the next few days—and the days were short. It was Jux again, not Somiss. Luke and Will failed the test by a few words. The rest of us passed, but I don't think anyone ate. We would have to, soon. We were all unsteady, the odd, familiar off-balance feeling. I could barely sleep. My rib was improving a little at a time, but it was hard to find a position that didn't hurt.

More than that, I was thinking too much. Once our lamps were out, I lay awake while Gerrard was sound asleep, breathing slow and steady. I envied him. I was so tired. But my thoughts came so fast that they slammed into each other.

I kept remembering what Franklin had said, and how it

had made me feel. And the longer I thought about it, the more I realized it was a lie. Gerrard was right. It was better to be pissed off. Wizards didn't help the people of Limòri. They served the whims of rich men like my father, and Levin's, and everyone else's—except Gerrard's.

I turned over on my bed, refusing to start thinking about Gerrard. He was still a mystery, but he was a secondary mystery. There were bigger things to figure out. I'd seen wizards all my life, and none of them had looked like the men who led us to class now—or even the silent, meek-looking younger ones who had guided us in the beginning.

The wizards who came to my father's house to train the ponies to fly, relieve my mother's blinding headaches, arrange good weather for Malek ships, and so many other things—they looked more like Somiss: cold eyed, arrogant, straight backed, and sure of themselves. I remembered one or two with graying hair—at least I thought I did. But most were young. Why? And that was just the first question.

How many wizards were there? Twenty? A hundred? A thousand? How many of them were here in the cliffs, and were the class-guides wizards, or just slaves in black robes? Were they failed students, or men who had been trained to lead boys through the tunnels the way the ponies were taught to fly? I had no idea how to find out any of these things, but we needed to know.

And somehow we had to live long enough to figure out how to destroy the academy. That meant we had to learn magic and get incredibly good at it. If we couldn't destroy the wizards, then we at least had to escape them, so we could teach magic to as many other people as we possibly could and come back, reinforced, to try again.

The first step was . . . my thoughts finally slowed, then circled. There were three or four "first steps," and we would have to manage all of them, more or less at the same time. We had to stop competing and start helping each other in order to stay alive. That meant trusting each other. If we couldn't manage that, nothing else was possible. It really was that simple: We had to help each other. We had to. And the wizards knew that was the first step. That's why they worked so hard to prevent it.

That led me to a whirlwind of thoughts about the wizards.

I turned onto my back, wincing. Then I lay still. I could hear Gerrard breathing, and nothing else. The silence inside the stone was complete, final, just like the darkness and the stillness of the air. It was oppressive. *Oppressive.*

I had learned that word in Professor Doohan's class when I was nine. Most of his students had loved him. A few hated him because his class was hard. He had made us write essays, constantly. Writing essays. Such a hard class. Thinking about real schools made me long for a roof again. I kept my eyes closed, thinking about rooftops, about laughing, feeling free. And I went to sleep.

The next morning a wizard woke us, then left when he knew we were up. I waited for Gerrard to wash so that I could. He wrapped the cloth for me again. He was calm, almost kind. It seemed like a good time to tell him that I had helped Will. He stiffened and paced away from me.

"I figured it out last night," I whispered before he got worked up enough to turn it into a fight. "This place. The Limòri Academy."

He shot me a look and then sat on his bed, facing away from me, his shoulders straight as a fence. He began one of his complicated breathing patterns. I leaned toward him.

"A long time ago," I whispered, "maybe the first class they ever taught, or the tenth, or the fiftieth, the students helped each other. Maybe they were more clever than most that year. Maybe they discovered things that the Founder hadn't yet. Or maybe he was just like Somiss and they got sick of him." I paused. "Or maybe they helped each other escape." His shoulders dropped a little, so I went on. "Whatever it was, it scared the wizards pissless. So one at a time, the Founder, and every wizard who has run the school since, figured out ways to make sure the students stayed scared, isolated, hungry, in pain—*especially* once they started to learn real magic."

Gerrard shifted on his cot.

"It makes sense," I said.

He didn't respond.

"You know I'm right," I whispered. "Not helping each other doesn't have shit to do with learning better or faster or ending up as stronger wizards. It's to keep us weak."

Gerrard didn't move.

"We can't do it, just two of us," I breathed. "But if it was all of us, we might have a chance. If we can fool them long enough to learn enough."

Gerrard didn't turn, didn't answer.

I waited until he finished the pattern and started over. "Get angry," I breathed. "Think about who you want to kill. Imagine it in detail. When your thoughts start to make you clench your teeth, when they start to hurt, push them into your belly. Expect it to work." I took two breaths, then raised my voice just a little. "Will did it."

Without saying anything more, I began the third breathing pattern, then switched to the second, then the fifth. Gerrard joined me on the fifth pattern. Then he changed to one of his odd cadences, and I followed him. It was hard to do at first, it was much more complicated than anything Franklin had taught us. But once I had settled into it, I could see why he was using it. Keeping track of the rhythm stilled my stray thoughts.

Gerrard kept breathing the pattern, quicker and quicker, exhaling loudly. I thought I heard the vague shape of Somiss's name in one breath, and Franklin's in the next. Three breaths later, I was sure of it. He was breathing his thoughts aloud. I heard Somiss's name again. And when Gerrard suddenly faltered and I heard a single rush of breath, I knew it had worked for him the way it had worked for Will, and for me so long ago in Franklin's class. Somehow, anger was the key. Anger and belief.

I left the room and walked toward the food hall, meaning to just go past it and find a long, straight passage. I was tired and hungry and I knew I wouldn't run very far. But running would calm me. It always did.

My stomach gurgled and cramped as I got closer to the food hall. I couldn't wait much longer. I went in and stood before the stone for a long time before I imagined griddle cakes and reached out with one finger. Then I pulled it back. Jordan had touched it. Maybe putting my thoughts into the stone was safer. I stood there, getting angry.

There was no logic to chase. There was no way to know. Somiss was brilliant. And an asshole.

They all were.

I had to eat.

I held my breath and imagined the griddle cakes. Then I tapped the stone with one finger. There were no sparkles, no thunderclaps, just the usual crying-wind sound. And the food appeared. I let out a long, grateful breath, then carried the plate to one of the tables along the far wall, between the torches. I chewed slowly, giving my empty belly time to adjust, and I cleaned the plate.

Then I just sat there, thinking about the stone, wondering what it was, how it worked, and why it had sparkled at me. When I heard footsteps, I grabbed my plate and ducked, in case it was Gerrard. If he came, I wanted to watch, to see if he was lying or not.

When I lifted my head just high enough to see, I was glad I had hidden. It was Luke. I stayed low, watching him walk across the big cavern to the stone, his stride easy and relaxed. He closed his eyes a moment, then put his palms on the stone. Both hands. Without an instant's hesitation. Then he turned and went out, carrying an orange. Or maybe it was a peach. Luke wasn't afraid. Not even a little. And he wasn't especially hungry, either. Why?

I took care of my plate, counted to twenty, then went

out into the corridor, peeking first. Luke was walking with Gerrard, fifty paces or more down the passageway. The red robe stood out against the black stone. Why were they talking? They hated each other.

They had turned left, not right. Where were they going? I followed at a distance, always ready to step into the shadows between the torches if either of them looked back. When they turned into another passageway, I ran, my mouth open wide to quiet my breathing, coming down on my heels and rolling my feet forward so that I was very nearly silent. I did not want Gerrard to see me, to know I was spying. But I guess I didn't trust him to tell me what this was about, because I didn't stop.

I stayed back a long ways, and every time they slowed I did, peeking around the corner to make sure I could see them before I went on. The floor became smoother as I walked—a perfect place to run. Maybe they both used it for . . .

I saw Luke try to turn back. Gerrard reached out and grabbed his arm, spinning him around, marching him forward. I had no idea what to make of it. If Gerrard thought he was going to take Luke off into the side tunnels far enough to beat him up, he was wrong. As much as I hated Luke, I wanted him to join the pact eventually.

When they finally stopped, I ran two steps into the dark between the torches and pressed my back against the cool stone. I strained to hear, but they were too far away, and they were probably talking in whispers. I stood very still, trying to decide whether to go on or go back. But I couldn't think of a single reason why they would be doing what they were doing, so when they started off again, I followed.

After two more turns, they went down a long, long incline with no branching tunnels at all. I fell back, barely keeping them in sight as they descended. And then, suddenly, I couldn't see them anymore. I crouched low and went forward slowly. The torches got farther and farther apart, and the passageway widened. And then I heard their footsteps. It sounded like they were walking on gravel. There was an odd smell that got stronger with every step. Rain? There couldn't be rain here.

"I don't want to," I heard Luke say. Gerrard didn't answer. I slid along the wall, breathing silently. My bare toes touched a mat of rounded stones and I stopped, finally sure of the smell. Water. I could feel my pulse. Why would they come this far to talk about something Luke didn't want to do? Were they plotting to kill *me*? Maybe they were the ones who had the real pact.

"Please," Luke said. "I just don't want to."

Still no answer.

I crept forward.

There was a clattering of pebbles and a sudden glow of torchlight in the vast chamber before me. I backed up, out of the light, and stared. They were standing at the edge of an underground lake. The dark water was as smooth as a mirror. And I heard myself thinking: *Drowning would not be a terrible way to die.*

Gerrard had walked to the edge of the water and turned away to pull off his robe. Were they going to swim? "Please," Luke said again. "Please." He sounded terrified.

Terrified and sad. Gerrard turned back. Except now that I was closer and the light was better, I could see that it wasn't Gerrard.

It was Somiss.

I watched for a few more heartbeats. Then I turned and ran back up the incline.

47

Sadima faced the sunrise. After weeks of snow and wind, the weather had turned. The air was soft and warm. Maybe spring would come early this year. Charlie had always loved springtime. She swept the last of the dirt off the porch planks and stepped into the street to sweep the cobblestone gutter along the boardwalk. Levi was stretched out in front of the shop, sound asleep, his paws twitching. She was careful not to wake him when she put the broom away and came back out to wash the new shop window. It had an arched top; there was nothing else like it in South End. The glazier had bartered for cheese.

She was rubbing the glass dry when the door swung open and a boy with black hair and bright eyes stuck his head out. "Sadima? You want the clabber pressed out this morning?" She nodded, and Tapio ducked back inside. He had been a cabin boy at ten. At sixteen he was sick of the sea, and Sadima was glad. He was learning cheese making quickly and was more help than she had expected. She had hired him because he was a sunny-faced kid. Charlie would have liked him.

"Sadima? Do you remember me?"

Startled, she whirled around and stared at the man who had chased her the first time she had gotten the elixir for Charlie. He was old now. His hair was gone, and he held a cane in one hand. She would not have recognized him, but she had never forgotten the sound of his voice.

"I've been back here five times, trying to find you," he was saying. His stance was careful, stiff, like he was trying not to startle a sparrow. He had tears in his eyes. "This was my last try," he said. "It's just too far for an old man to come."

Sadima had no idea what to say.

He gestured at Levi. "That can't be the same dog."

She tried to smile, her heart fluttering. "Same breed. South End terriers, people call them."

"I heard that boy call you Sadima," he said, and there was so much longing in his voice that it made her take a step back. "It's you. I can't believe it."

"I just use that name," she told him. "It isn't mine. Charlie liked the sound of it, and—"

The man gestured to stop her midsentence. "It is your name. After your mother's great-grandmother. Sadima Killip."

She gripped the broom handle. "Do you know me?" It came out a whisper.

He nodded. "I'm your brother. Micah."

Micah. She whispered it, hoping that there would be some memory, some feeling that he was telling the truth. There wasn't. But when she looked up, she could see the joy in his eyes. "I am sorry," she whispered. "For being afraid of you before."

He tilted his head and stared at her. "You still don't recognize me at all, do you?"

"No," she said. "I'm so sorry."

He sighed. "It's been almost thirty-six years since you left the farm. But you must remember me and Papa? And Shy and your goats?"

She could see tears in his eyes when she shook her head. "How old am I?"

"Seventeen when you left. So you're fifty-two now. I turn sixty-two just after Winterfeast." Micah was staring at her. "Your hair was long and shiny. But except for that, you look the same. Like a girl of seventeen. And you remember nothing? Did that man do something to you?"

"What man?" she asked, then held her breath.

He looked irritated. "Carlin? Conklin? Something like that. You only said it once, the day you told me you wanted to leave. I never saw him. I never wanted to see him. I had no use for anyone telling young girls that magic is real." He stared out at the street. "I still don't."

Sadima wondered if he was thinking what Charlie

had warned her about, that not getting older was strange enough to *be* magical.

"Mattie Han lived to almost ninety," Micah said quietly. "Her great-grandmother lived to be a hundred and four. She told me that ten times over the years. A hundred and four. Maybe you are going to live that long." He nodded, smiling. "So it's no wonder you don't look old yet."

Sadima nodded because she could tell how badly he wanted her to, but she knew it didn't make sense.

"You really can't remember the farm?" he asked. "Or Papa? Or me?"

"I'm sorry," she whispered. "There's nothing before the day I woke up here, on the docks."

He glanced at the shop front, then at his own hands, before he looked at her again. "This is your work? Where do you live?"

She pointed. "Here, in the shop. Upstairs. It's mine. Charlie left it to me."

Micah smiled. "Your husband?"

Sadima nodded. It had been true enough.

"Do you have children?"

"No."

"Would you want to visit Ferne? See where you grew up?" he asked. "Laran and I have five children, all but one gone off to their own places in the countryside."

Sadima didn't want to lie, but she couldn't explain her terror of leaving South End, either. "I wish I could," she said, when she realized he was waiting for her to answer. "I can't leave the shop."

His shoulders dropped, and he glanced at the door, then back at her. "Do you want me to tell you about—anything?"

She had given up having memories long ago, and it took her a moment to decide. "Will you come in?" she asked him, then saw the desperation in his eyes and smiled at him. "Please. Come in, Micah."

Tapio helped Micah up the stairs, and Sadima settled him into her best chair, then sat across the table from him. He looked down at his hands. "I don't know how you ended up here, but I do know it's my fault. If I hadn't shouted at you—if I had come back that night to talk, you would have stayed at home." His eyes glistened again. "I have been so afraid I would die before I got to apologize."

"I am sure you never meant to harm me," she said quietly.

"Never," he said, wiping his eyes once more. He took in a long breath and let it out. "Do you want to hear about Mother and Papa, about yourself?"

She hesitated. Then she nodded.

He smiled. His teeth were chipped and worn. "You were a lovely child." His voice was gentle as he told her about their mother, her whimsies, her singing, her flower beds. Sadima listened, still hoping that something he said would light her memories, but nothing did. Then he told her about the day she was born.

"She died?" Sadima echoed. "That old woman just left our mother to die?"

He nodded. "And stole everything that was worth anything out of the room. Papa was crazy with grief, holding Mama, pleading with her to open her eyes. It scared me. I couldn't stand to look at her, all stiff and . . ." He looked out the window. "I carried you down to the barn and made a nest in the hay." He paused and took a deep breath, tapping his cane on the floor before he looked back up at her. "Papa was never right after that, Sadima. He never wanted you out of his sight, and he was strict with you. Too strict. Especially as you got older. He hated to see you painting—wasting time, he called it. He hated the stories you and I told by the hearth all winter. He was so bitter. He was half-alive." Micah cleared his throat. "He made you cry too often. And you were such a sweet-natured little girl."

Sadima sat still, feeling odd as he told her that she had loved the horses, the goats, the chickens, and they had loved her. "You carried your paint box into the woods sometimes. I bought the brushes and pigments in the market square and we hid them from Papa," he said. "You painted the same paper over and over. I still have two of your paintings up on the wall. Just like some fancy town house." He stopped to wipe his eyes, shaking his head. "The stories got us through the winter, you and me. You liked mine, but yours were better, about talking to wolves, to the goats, flying with the birds." He looked up. "At market once, there was a man whipping a gelding, a big, stout horse. It reared, tried to charge him. And you just walked up and looked at that horse for a moment, then led it off." Micah smiled. "You named him Shy. He was just over thirty when he died. Laran took a shine to him, fed him carrots when we had some to spare."

Sadima closed her eyes. She couldn't recall anything he was saying. But she could still hear animals, could talk to them in that silent way. And Mrs. Jenness had said she had a painter's eye. Sadima looked at the man sitting across from her. He was her brother. He really was. And she really was Sadima Killip, who had grown up on a farm near Ferne, wherever that was.

". . . and Papa got so he couldn't abide the magicians on market day," Micah was saying. "By the end, he hadn't left the farm in years." Micah heaved out a breath. "They're all gone now, of course. Not just here in Limòri, but all the way out past Ferne and into the hills. We don't see dark robes at all anymore. The king's guards marched them off, hanged most, and sold the rest into indenture thirty-odd years ago." He nodded again. It was clear he was glad.

"I saw some of them," she told him. "They were all women."

Micah nodded again. "There were a few men who wore the robes, but not many. The young king hated them all. Man or woman, he hanged them or sold them off."

"He died without an heir," Sadima said, repeating what Charlie had told her, just to say something. She never thought about the city of Limòri or its royalty.

Micah nodded. "I don't suppose you remember Nick Kulik?"

She shook her head.

"He had cousins here in the city. They said the young king was simple-minded and it was his chancellors writing the decrees. I can't see how they could. But yes or no, the magicians are gone and good riddance."

"There are still herb merchants, aren't there?" Sadima asked, hoping to distract him from more talk about magicians. It made her uneasy.

"A few," he said. "They keep it quiet."

Sadima nodded. "The one I met said she was an Eridian."

"That's all just women's foolishness." Micah waved one hand like he was shooing flies. "The packets and draughts are almost all made by the Gypsies back in the hills east of Ferne. Curatives, they call them. But they used to claim they were magic. No one claims that now, and no one has for a long, long time." He looked her. "They hanged three in Ferne, in the middle of the market square. Papa would have cheered. I did. We all did."

Sadima clasped her hands in her lap. Charlie had told her, but she hadn't really thought about it. *Hanged.* She knew what it meant. Maybe they deserved it, if they were like the woman who let her mother die. "The Eridian herb seller I knew seemed kind."

"Stay clear of the Eridians," Micah said. "They say this new king the chancellors dug out of the woodpile hates them as much as he hates the magicians. Two brothers and a few cousins have died over the past few years to cobble his road to the throne. He'll need to spill more blood to convince the royal half of his family to leave him be. The

Ferrins always have to fight. But if he can kill people who hate kings, so much the better."

"The Eridians hate kings?" she asked.

"So they say. Kings and magicians, both."

Sadima nodded, feeling like a child pretending to understand something she did not. She didn't know the new king's name, or how old he was, or anything about him. For a long time, she had talked only to Charlie; now she talked only to customers and Tapio. And her customers were all in a hurry to buy cheese and get out of South End.

"I won't make it here again," Micah said. He sighed. "Laran feels like a burden if I ask one of the boys to stay with her, and I don't want her alone."

"Maybe one day I can come visit you," Sadima heard herself saying. She didn't mean it, but this man was her brother, even if she couldn't remember him. And the smile that lit his face made her glad she had said it. She gave him a quarter-wheel of a rich, soft cheese Charlie had labeled Grrur because the dog had loved it. Customers thought it was a foreign word, something interesting and exotic. Micah laughed when she explained.

He repeated the directions to Ferne three times before he finally went out the front door, and even then, he turned back. "Please do come visit," he said. "Laran would so like to see you again. Her mother loved you like you were her own." He shook his head. "Everyone in Ferne misses Mattie Han. She was our mother's closest friend."

Sadima nodded and smiled.

He reached out and lay his hand on her cheek. Then he

turned and walked away. She watched him go down the street, leaning on his cane every other step. Then she went upstairs and found the narrow box in a cupboard in the little kitchen. She looked long and hard at herself in the mirror, then put it away and went downstairs. She could hear Tapio turning the ripening cheeses.

In the years that followed, Sadima watched Tapio grow into a good man. He found a wife, a hardworking girl with big, dark eyes and an easy laugh. They had three little girls, and Sadima adored them all. They all worked hard in the shop. People from all over Limòri sent their servants to buy Sadima's cheese.

The customers thought, as the girls grew, that she was their eldest sister. Then they grew past her and began to get small wrinkles around their eyes. When Sadima noticed some of the older customers staring at her, she began to work more in the back, letting Tapio's daughters run the shop. Eventually people assumed one of the girls was her mother, that she was Tapio's granddaughter. He just smiled his sunny smile and never talked to her about it. Not once. Nor did his wife or his daughters. Or his Eridian auntie. Sadima loved them for it. The girls married and Tapio got old. And when they told her they were all moving out of South End to begin their own shop, Sadima was glad for them all.

That evening, for no clear reason, she remembered what she had said to Micah about visiting. She bit her lip—he must have been dead for more than thirty years by now.

She left the shop and walked down by the docks. When she saw a mountain of fruit crates, stacked high, waiting to be unpacked in the morning, she wedged herself between them, pushing them aside just enough to squeeze through, then turning sideways and working her way in a little deeper, until she could go no farther. Then she cried. But she was glad Tapio and his family were moving away. Eventually they would forget her, and she wouldn't have to watch them die, one by one.

48

I didn't say anything to Gerrard for a few days. I am not sure why, exactly. Maybe I just didn't want it to be true. But of course it was. Somiss was exactly the kind of bully who would force himself on someone and not care who he hurt.

Celibacy? Poverty? For all I knew, Somiss spit on all the Founder's rules. And there was nothing I could do about it—except what I wanted to do anyway. So I worked on the next three songs and ate twice, barely touching one finger to the stone. On the fourth day, I sat on the edge of my cot in the dark as Gerrard got settled for the night. He seemed calm and rested, or as calm and rested as any of us ever were.

"I saw something," I began. He looked up, and I started talking. I didn't say I had followed Somiss and Luke as far as I did. And I didn't mention the lake, even though I had thought about it a hundred times. Just knowing that the dark, still water was so close, that I knew how to get there, comforted me in a way I cannot explain. I didn't want him to tell me to stay away from it, or ask me to show him. Not yet.

I told Gerrard everything else. He listened to me without interrupting. Then he leaned forward and blew out the lamp on his desk. "I am glad it isn't Will," he said from the darkness on his side of the chamber. There was no surprise in his voice. None.

"You *knew*?"

I heard him exhale. "Somiss likes scaring people, hurting them. He always has. Franklin can't stop him."

"Luke was pleading with him. He was—"

"South End is full of orphans," Gerrard cut me off. "I had friends who went home with well-dressed men. Both boys and girls. For some, it was a choice. Sex was a way to earn a meal. It could be that for Luke. He's the only one who hasn't gotten bone thin once or twice."

I nodded, remembering how casually Luke had made food. I felt sick—and stupid. "But it isn't a choice for Luke," I whispered. "He was scared."

I heard Gerrard arranging his blankets; then his cot creaked. "Somiss might tell him to plead like that. Maybe it's a weird game. Somiss likes games."

"No, it was real. If it wasn't Somiss," I began, then stopped. "I mean, if it was just some man in Limòri, Luke would have fought. He would have run away."

"Somiss wanted you to think it was me," Gerrard said.

It was so obvious that I felt stupid again. "I did, at first. But they walked a long way. He never once looked back. He couldn't have wanted me to know . . . everything."

Gerrard shrugged. "Maybe."

"No," I said, and I was almost sure. "He just wanted me to think that you and Luke were talking."

Gerrard didn't answer.

"But this means Luke hates Somiss," I said. "He'll join the pact and keep it secret."

"No," Gerrard said quietly. "It means he'll *run* to tell Somiss."

I leaned toward him, even though it hurt a little, even though I couldn't see him in the dark. "Why would he? He must be—" Then I stopped, because I knew Gerrard was right. "Do you think he already tells Somiss about whatever he sees the rest of us doing?"

Gerrard's cot creaked again. "Yes. He probably just makes things up, too."

I lay there without answering. All this time I had hated Luke when I should have been pitying him. "But if he could join the pact," I whispered. "Maybe—"

"He can't," Gerrard interrupted before I could go on.

"He hates Somiss," I breathed. "So long as he knew we all cared about him and—"

"Hate is complicated," Gerrard interrupted me again.

"No, it isn't," I whispered, and he didn't answer me. He didn't need to. I knew he was right. Somiss might be promising Luke he would be the one to graduate; Luke had to know it was a lie. I lay down and turned over, determined to escape my thoughts and the nagging pain in my ribs. I listened for the thrumming, and when it was loud enough, I finally fell asleep.

When a wizard pounded on our door, I snapped awake and sat up. I could hear Gerrard shuffling and thumping in the dark before he lit his lamp. Had he brought his little book back? Was he hiding it? I had almost forgotten about it. I wrapped the cloth tighter around my chest and splashed water on my face. Then I peed and stood back.

"Ready?" Gerrard whispered when he was finished.

"Yes," I said, not because I was, but because it didn't matter.

I was standing just a little behind him, looking over his shoulder, when he opened the door. Jux stood in the corridor, making an impatient motion with one hand. "Not you," he said to Gerrard. "Just him." He pointed at me.

Gerrard moved aside.

Jux turned on his heel and walked away. I hurried after him, glancing back. Gerrard had already shut the door. My rib still hurt a little, but not too much, especially with the cloth wrapped tight. I looked down at my hands. The skin was pink and puckered in odd places, but other than one finger, the blister scabs were gone. I pushed up the sleeve of my robe. The kite ropes had left scars too.

Jux glanced back at me, and I let my sleeve fall. "Those are sacred scars," he said.

"Why do you have to put us through all this?" I asked him.

Jux laughed without looking back at me. "We don't."

Before I could stop myself, I reached out and grabbed his shoulder and jerked him around to face me. It hurt my rib, and I pressed on it with one hand. I had no idea what to say. I had a dim realization that I was as tall as Jux now. And then I was lying flat on my back and he was standing over me. My rib shot a knife-pain through my body when I tried to sit up.

"Stay down. Don't move," Jux said.

I looked up at him. His eyes were narrowed, like he was concentrating. Then he kicked me. Not hard, but in the exact place my rib hurt. I gasped, but it felt *better*. "What did you do?" I whispered.

"I fixed it," he said, and put out his hand.

I let him help me up. "Why?" I breathed.

"I want you to live long enough," he said.

"Long enough for what?"

He didn't answer; he just started walking again. I got up and followed him. But he didn't lead me up the incline to his forest. He started making turns, one after another. I had trouble keeping up, but I managed. By the time he finally stopped, I had composed six sentences, long ones.

"Recognize it?"

I looked around the chamber. There were tables and benches like the food hall. But there was no stone, and . . . my skin prickled. This was the chamber we had come into on our first day. I stared at one of the tables. *There*. I had sat there, beside my mother. And Somiss had spoken to us from the podium, that strange, disconnected little speech that startled all the parents—but not enough for them to grab our hands and take us home. My eyes stung and my hands closed into fists, at the same instant.

"Keep up," Jux said, and he started off again.

It was hard to make my feet move. The torches were dim, and I could just see the outline of the massive door. Outside it was the wide shelf in the cliff face where carriages landed, the flying ponies trotting smoothly as their hooves touched the rock. Limòri was out there. My friends. Their houses and the shops my mother loved. All the schools I had attended. And across the wide, marshy Limòri River, my father's house. And all the—

"This way." Jux turned abruptly and ducked through a stone arch that was barely high enough for me to pass through without bending over.

"Where are we going?" I asked him.

"To see the sky," he said.

The very idea of being outside left me breathless. I would pretend not to know how we had gotten here. I would beg Jux to help me find the way back. I would convince him. And then I would leave this place and never look back. Anyone who wanted to could come with me. Even Luke. Especially Luke. And Will, even if I had to carry him. And—

"Be careful," Jux said, and pointed.

I saw slender crystals of some kind, hundreds of tiny mineral knives rising up from the stone floor. One misstep would have lamed me. I moved my thoughts to my belly and focused. It would be stupid to hurt myself now and ruin the only chance I might ever get. "Will you lead me back?" I asked after six more turns. I made my voice shake, just a little, and only on the last word. He didn't answer.

After five more turns, he led me through another arch, and we were suddenly outside the cliff, standing in sunshine that blinded me. I felt Jux take my hand and I shuffled along, trying to slow him down until my eyes adjusted. I couldn't open them. I shaded my face with my free hand, but tears rolled out of my slitted eyes and wet my cheeks. I heard wind sighing in the trees and the cry of a marsh hawk. There were always three or four pairs of them in the woods behind my father's house. The air smelled sweet and clean, and the feel of it against my skin made me feel weak, giddy. I had gotten my wish. I was outside.

"Are you going to kill me?" I asked Jux.

"Not today," he said cheerfully. He came to a halt. I stopped with him, still blinking, still trying to keep my eyes open for more than a heartbeat or two at a time. Jux was quiet and just stood there, his hand on mine. For an instant, I felt my skin crawl. If he was like Somiss—

"You have nothing like that to fear from me," he said.

I rubbed at my eyes. "Can you hear my thoughts?"

"Of course not," he said. "It's forbidden."

I squinted and found I could make out his face in the glare. If he had heard my thoughts about escaping—I forced them into my belly, deep, muffled. But it was probably too late. "Why are we out here?"

"Because we needed a lot more room for today's class."

The hawk called once more, closer.

"Move your thoughts toward her," Jux said.

"The bird?"

"Yes."

I shook my head. "I don't want to."

"Look down," Jux said.

I rubbed my eyes. My bare toes, black and calloused from the stone, were just over the edge of the massive cliff. The hawk called again. "Please don't push me," I whispered.

"Move your thoughts into Sadie," he said.

"Sadie," I heard myself echo him.

"Do it now." Jux put his hand on my shoulder.

Shaking with fear, I waited until the hawk called again. When she did, I turned my head and shoved my thoughts toward the sound. An instant later I felt her wings, smelled the warm dust on her feathers. "I will help," Jux said. And then he pushed me forward.

I fell like a stone for eternity, the hawk diving beside me. Then she spread her wings and I could feel them, feel myself slowing. I opened my eyes. The pain of the sunlight was gone, the ground was rushing toward us. I was not afraid.

The hawk called again, and I turned to look at her. She was beside me. Her eyes were the color of winter tea, and she stiffened her auburn wings, staring at me. I obeyed. I lifted my arms and curved them, stiff and strong against the rush of air. I rose a little, sliding on the wind, skimming the treetops.

Sadie led me back along the cliff face, rising at a slow, smooth angle. When she flapped her wings, I lifted my arms, then lowered them, imitating her. I could feel her complete faith in the air to bear her upward, and I knew that certainty was a gift. A gift for me. She was calm, so I was. And I was enraptured, caught in the absolute physical beauty of flight.

We found a column of warm air rising and we spiraled with it, going higher and higher. I felt truly and completely alive. My heart was swollen with happiness. Joy filled every part of me. The city looked small below me, crouched opposite the cliff, out where the land bulged out against the river.

Market Square was green and full of people. To the south, the buildings ran down to the river and along it to the bay, tall at first, then smaller and closer together toward South End. I could see the huge expanses of various shades of green to the east that were the Eridian farms.

Sadie was leading me in a long arc. As we came back around, the Ferrin Hill mansions looked like candy boxes beneath us. We flew over them, staying high, high above the earth.

After a long time, Sadie made a wide turn, tilting her wings; I followed her, devastated. I never wanted to go back down into the smelly, airless tunnels again. Never. Sadie called to me and she sounded sad too, as I banked into a long curve to follow her. Would Jux let me fly again? He had to. I wanted to learn, to be able to do it on my own.

I heard my own thoughts and knew what had happened, what Jux had done to me. I was in love again. Twice now: certainty and flying. If I left here, or if I drowned myself, I would never feel the beauty of certainty again, or the rushing joy of flight. The wizards were so cruel. All of them.

– 49 –

Sadima worked out a pattern. She closed the shop every eight or ten years. When she reopened it, a season or two later, she told each batch of new employees her name was Sophie, or Mary, or whatever struck her fancy, and that she had just bought the shop from a woman named whatever had struck her fancy the time before. Her introductory speech remained the same. "I prefer to work in the backroom," she said, over and over. "Please tell our customers that the original owner's recipes are being used and that we take great pride in making the cheeses from recipes handed down to us by Charlie da Masi."

She bought the old building that had housed the sewing shop Mrs. Jenness had run so long ago. She had it gutted, then refitted with clean new walls and bigger windows.

She moved out of the apartment above the cheese shop and lived next door on the top floor, leaving the ground floor empty and quiet. She spent most of her time there, alone, happy.

Rebuilding the interior, she found wonderful things stacked in corners and behind partitions. A set of old bronze coat hooks that looked like dragon's heads held her shawls and the ring of keys she had made for the new door locks.

The main staircases were wide, set in the center of each of the three floors. After she was settled, she made one more change. She had another stairway built, small and winding in a spiral from the third floor to the first. She had a passageway built beside it that connected the two buildings. After that, she could come and go without people seeing her.

That summer, Sadima had one of the shop girls ask their uptown customers where painters bought their materials. She was not surprised to learn that the shop was far beyond the invisible line she couldn't cross. She paid one of the orphan boys to go buy her an assortment of brushes and pigments and papers. Painting was like cleaning and cheese making. The instant her fingers touched the brushes, she knew how to use them.

Every year that passed, Sadima kept more to herself. She bought a leather belt-purse and always had enough coins to buy several pairs of shoes at once, a dozen bars of soap, enough lentils and beans for a year of stews; she rarely had to shop. She had a carpenter build three clothes closets in her room. Each one contained a distinctly different wardrobe.

She cycled through them, changing every time she reopened the shop. And once every five or six years, she tried to cross the invisible line and was paralyzed with the terror that made her shake and sweat until she turned back.

Sadima sometimes wandered the streets, her hair covered with a hat or a scarf, listening. She didn't make deep, long-term friendships. It wasn't that hard to avoid. People came to Limòri through South End's port. The immigrants either got mired in South End's vices and died, or eventually went back to wherever they had been born, or found work in Limòri proper and moved their families out of South End.

Whenever she walked down the street, she heard women whose homes were on the other side of the oceans talking in broken Ferrinides. They dreamed of moving to Limòri's east side; it was full of old brick buildings divided into flats—cheap flats—and they were full of families. Children played in the streets in Limòri, they said—they didn't have to beg or steal food to live. Sadima saw the hope in their faces, and she envied them. They could leave South End.

Sometimes, when there was a better king, for five or ten years, South End would seem to be changing. There would be king's guards on the streets, keeping order. Shops would open, the cobblestones would get swept, uptown people would come to buy embroidered cloth, dyes, leather sandals, or baskets woven tight enough to carry water.

More artisans stopped loading crates and began to practice the arts of their homelands. South End became a quaint outing for women in expensive dresses. They walked the streets, buying art hammered from cast-off metal or statues of wild beasts carved from the tropical hardwood salvaged from packing crates stacked behind the coir and coconut dealers' warehouses. And when money came into South End, orphaned children became rare.

But somehow—local drought, distant war, cheap opium, another bad king—South End always sank back into being a port town. It did what it had always done—catered to the needs and vices of bored, lace-shirted young men and lonely, stir-crazy sailors who had been two or more years at sea. Sadima always hated watching things slip back to that.

This time the change-bringers were the Servenians, pouring into South End because of the bloody three-generation war in their homeland. Before them, it had been tall, straight-backed men from Volubilis, because of the plague there. Most of them had taken their pay and gone home when the sickness passed. The Servenians were bringing their families, and they were staying. Sadima saw hope for South End in their honest, eager faces.

When the cheese shop was closed, the sign taken down, Sadima was often bored, and even lonelier than usual. She spent the time painting, learning to embroider and sew, becoming a very good cook. This time she decided to learn Servenian. Tapio had told her stories from his sailing days, so, wrapped in her scarf and shawl, Sadima walked along the quay one chilly morning and offered a reward to several cabin boys she saw on the docks. They all said they knew Servenians who spoke Ferrinides, too.

Three women were escorted to the empty cheese shop that afternoon, but they spoke only a few words of Ferrinides—too few. It was not until nearly thirty days later that one of the cabin boys brought a girl to the shop. She was tall and lovely, almost a woman. Sadima explained that she wanted to learn both the language and their customs. The girl nodded somberly.

"What is your name?" Sadima asked her in slow, precise Ferrinides.

The girl looked at her steadily. "Sistra," she said, pronouncing it *sigh-strah*.

Sadima nodded. "How long have you been in Limòri?"

"That is not the proper question," the girl said.

Sadima smiled. "What question should I ask?"

"First, if my family is well. Then, what is the meaning of my name."

"Is your family well?" Sadima asked.

Sistra lowered her eyes. "My father and brother died on the ship coming here. My mother is better than she was at first, but my little sister has been hurt."

Sadima hesitated.

"You must ask the meaning of my name first," Sistra said. "Then you may ask how my sister was hurt."

"What is the meaning of your name?"

"A sistra is made from copper, covered with clatters and bells. It makes the rhythm for the dancers at the Celebration of Birth. For a girl it means grace, like the dancers."

Sadima remembered the herb seller. So this girl was an Eridian? The last thing Sadima wanted was king's guards coming into the cheese shop. "I am so sorry your sister was hurt. How did it happen?"

"A man," Sistra said. "A sailor."

Sadima exhaled, remembering. "How old is she?"

Sistra lifted her chin. "Nine." She lifted her chin higher. "I will be a very good teacher."

Sadima nodded. "I know you will. How did you learn to speak Ferrinides so—"

"There was a sailor on the ship," she interrupted, her head still high, her eyes steady. "An old man. He taught me. It is a long voyage."

Sadima nodded. "I have an extra room here."

"We have no money to pay for a room," Sistra said.

"Does your mother know how to make cheese?"

The girl nodded. "Cheese and kefir."

Sadima showed her the apartment above the cheese shop. Sistra's eyes widened at the little kitchen, the window that looked out over the street. Sadima was transported back to the first day she had cleaned it for Charlie, the first time she had slept in the extra bed, the wonderful feeling of safety the walls had given her.

"This would be very nice," Sistra said cautiously. "We can all three work to pay for living here and—"

"You and I can trade until I learn the language," Sadima said. "I intend to open a cheese shop," she lied, and it was so automatic that it didn't feel like a lie anymore. Sistra was staring at her, absorbing every word. "I will pay your mother and sister fair wages," Sadima said. "I don't know what kefir is, but I would like to learn how to make it."

Sistra looked around the apartment again, and she suddenly smiled in a way that told Sadima she was younger than she looked. "May I please go tell my mother and sister and bring them back here before dark?" she whispered.

"Of course," Sadima told her.

Sistra took two long steps, then stopped and spun back around. "You have not told me your name."

"Mattie Han."

"How is your family?"

Sadima started to lie, then couldn't. "They are all gone."

Sistra came forward and embraced her tightly, then stepped back. "I will carry as much of your pain as I am able."

Sadima had no idea what to say, so she said nothing.

Sistra lifted her chin. "May I ask what your name means?"

Sadima shrugged. "It was my mother's best friend's name. To me it means a kind heart."

"Then it is the perfect name for you," the girl said. "I will be back before dusk."

Sadima watched her patter down the stairs, then stood still until she heard the shop door open and close. Then she wept, for Sistra, for her sister and mother, for herself. And for South End and all the cruelty that lived within the invisible lines she could not cross.

That first night, Sistra's mother was quiet and wary. Sistra's little sister clung to their mother's skirt, dark shadows beneath her eyes. But as the days passed, with hot meals and comfortable, safe beds, the smell of the first batch of cheese coming warm and soft up the stairs, they all smiled more often.

Sistra bloomed, helping Sadima with all her business. The girl tutored her daily and translated for her mother as the shop's staff learned how to make kefir. Sadima stared at the odd white grains they would use to turn the milk, then strain out to use again. There was no logic to calling them "grains." They looked like miniature cauliflower, but they were soft and smelled a little like yeast. They were alive, Sistra said, colonies of tiny animals kept alive with spoonfuls of mother's milk on the long voyage. The women had divided them the day the sailors spotted land. The mothers who had given their milk had gotten the biggest share.

The finished kefir tasted both sweet and tart, and all kinds of summer fruit could be added for flavor. The patrons *loved* it. The wealthy ones told their friends, and Sadima began buying little glass bottles so they could see the pink from the crushed strawberries and the rouge-orange from the peaches. Her piles of coins grew, and she increased the pay she gave her employees. With Sistra and her family doing most of the chores and all the shopping, she could avoid the streets of South End almost entirely.

By the time winter was near, Sistra was making jokes in Ferrinides and Sadima was speaking fair Servenian. And toward the end of the next summer, Sistra asked if she could hold a meeting in the apartment—a meeting of Eridian women.

"I don't want the king's guards here," Sadima said.

Sistra looked puzzled. "There is no king now. And the chancellors don't care about us. I have heard the stories of the hangings and the arrests, but that was all long ago. We have our meeting in the street now, down by the farmer's market. No one bothers us."

Sadima caught herself staring and looked aside. Micah had told her to be careful. But how long ago had that been? She was so isolated that this girl probably knew far more about Limòri, both the city and the kingdom, than she ever had. "Yes," she said. "It's fine."

Sistra danced in a circle. "It will be on the seventh-day, always," she said. "You are so kind!"

Sadima smiled as Sistra left, but she knew it had nothing to do with kindness. It was selfish. She was starving for voices, for news of the city. No, it was worse than that. With Charlie gone, she was hollow. He had been her life. And she had spent far too long sinking into a self-pity he would have hated.

I walked back slowly. My feet, my whole body, felt heavy. I stood outside our chamber door for a long time. When I closed my eyes and didn't try to move, I felt like I was still flying, like the wind was still holding me aloft. My arms kept rising, of their own will; any position except shoulder height felt wrong to me. I thought I could hear Gerrard snoring lightly when I finally pressed my ear to the door. How long had I been gone?

I started to go in, then didn't. I still felt like a swimmer getting out of the water. It had never once occurred to me that birds felt that. But they do. When they drop a little, then swoop upward to grasp a branch with their feet, they feel weighted, wary, vulnerable. Vulnerable. That was another word I had learned in school and never used. I remembered the teacher saying it had come from an old word for "wound." It made sense.

I forced my arms down to my sides and began the third breathing pattern, trying to silence my spinning thoughts. When they were a little quieter, I opened the door just far enough to slide into the room. It was completely dark. Gerrard was snoring, very gently, but I could smell the sharp scent of the last wisp of smoke from his lamp wick. He had put it out not long before. Had he tried to wait up for me? I tiptoed to my cot and sat on the edge, trying to ignore the heavy sadness in my gut. I couldn't. It was all too obvious.

The wizards knew we all dreamed of escape. So they had let me fly, and now I would probably never fly again. I was almost certainly trapped, my feet stuck forever to stone and dirt. But knowing there was the slimmest of chances that I might fly again would keep me here, keep me alive. At least for now. And if we all made a pact, it would be a temptation, something they could promise in exchange for us betraying one another.

Was this how they got the wizards who led us around to stay here? Let them fly once? Or feel the beautiful certainty of the wasps? Or something else that I couldn't imagine yet that was even more addictive?

"Where were you?" Gerrard whispered.

My whole body jerked, and I found I could not speak. I realized my arms had risen up, and I tried to lower them. I was still feeling the wind, the freedom of the sky, but it wasn't that I wanted to keep it a secret—I just could not manage to utter words.

"The wasps again?"

I opened my mouth, but nothing came out. *Please leave me alone*, I thought, but I couldn't manage to say it. I reached for my blanket, to pull it back so I could get into bed, and realized my arms had drifted upward again. I heard Gerrard moving, then the sound of his striker. I flinched away from the light, my arms still straight out. I heaved in a breath, trying to lower them.

"Are you all ri—," Gerrard began as he lifted his lamp, then stopped when he glanced over his shoulder at me. His eyes narrowed as he turned to face me. "Did you fly?"

I managed a nod. There was a tiny tremor starting in my belly. A vibration. It was like the thrumming, but *inside* me. Hawks were meant to fly, just like the wasp was meant to help feed the babies in the nest. Sadie had trusted the air completely. She had been certain it would hold her. Did all animals know exactly what they were for? People didn't. I didn't.

I shivered, still mute, watching Gerrard pace three steps to the door, then back. His forehead was ridged and his lips were pressed together. It looked very strange after seeing only half-invisible expressions—or none—on his face for so long. I swallowed, and my head bobbed a little. I forced my hands down and gripped the edge of the cot to keep them there.

"You shouldn't be flying yet," Gerrard breathed. "None of us should. Or the kites . . ."

I wanted to ask him how he could possibly know, but I couldn't speak and I knew he wouldn't answer me anyway.

I heard the wind off in the distance, and the instant I noticed it, it got louder. I could see Gerrard's lips moving. I had to listen carefully to understand what he was asking me.

"A sparrow?" he repeated. "Was it a sparrow? Or a robin?"

I opened my mouth to tell him, but when I parted my lips, the cry of a hawk came out. It startled me, and the confusion in my belly congealed into a lump. *Congealed?* I was scared. I wanted to speak more than I had ever wanted anything, and I couldn't. Was I lost again? Was this a dream? If Franklin and Jux let me die this time, and I couldn't speak to answer their question, would they bring me back?

"Is it like the wasps?" Gerrard whispered.

I shook my head. It wasn't. I was mute, but I could see the walls, the lamp. I knew Gerrard was real. My cot. Myself. All real.

"You are probably getting better at it," he whispered.

I shrugged, but I wanted him to be right. I saw him glance at the door. I had left it slightly ajar. He stood up to close it, then came back.

"Are they just trying to kill us?" he said so quietly that I leaned toward him to hear better. He didn't even notice. He was talking to himself, the way I did. Maybe we all did. I looked up into the darkness that hid the ceiling, then lowered my arms again. My eyes slid down the stone wall, and a motion caught my attention.

Gerrard was rocking back and forth. I watched him, blinking slowly. After a moment, he whispered again. "We shouldn't be trying to undo stone or fly or any of this. Not for a long time yet." His hands were fists. I could tell how angry he was. I was angry too, but the wind was more important somehow. I sat on my hands, to anchor them.

The knock on the door startled us both.

"We're awake!" Gerrard shouted after a few heartbeats. The wizard knocked again, instead of going away.

Gerrard stood up. I could not move. A recitation class? Now? I couldn't. I felt sweat rise on my skin as he walked to the door. But it was Jux. He gestured at Gerrard, just him, not me. I was so relieved that my eyes filled with tears. I let them roll down my cheeks, unwilling to free my hand to wipe them away.

"I want to wash up and piss," Gerrard said.

I was amazed at the anger he allowed to pour into his voice. But Jux just nodded, then stood in the open doorway as Gerrard went through his morning cleanup routine. When he was ready, Jux stepped aside to let him pass, then leaned back in to wink at me. "Sleep. It helps."

Feeling strange, I stared at the closed door after they left, then got into bed. As soon as I could find a position that kept my arms from slowly rising upward, I realized that the pain in my rib was gone. Jux really had fixed it. I could turn over. I could take a deep breath. And I managed to fall asleep.

When I woke up, Gerrard wasn't in his bed. I washed, then sat on the edge of my cot. My arms still felt light and strange, but I could force them down. Was it morning? How long had Gerrard been gone?

After a long time, a wizard knocked, sharp and hard. I flinched like someone had thrown boiling water on me. I tried to yell the usual answer, but it came out an unformed cry. I held my breath and the pounding stopped. So it was morning. And there was no class. I tried to say the word "morning" over and over. I couldn't. I tried my own name and still couldn't. So I practiced the question I wanted to ask Gerrard when he got back. I finally managed to whisper it more or less clearly, and I lay back down to wait.

When the door finally opened, I sat up straight. "Did you fly?" I whispered.

"Fly?"

Gerrard glared at me like I was dog crap on his shoe. Then he got into his bed, turned over, and was snoring within twenty breaths. I watched; his arms did not seem to be rising without permission. Maybe he had been too afraid and Jux hadn't pushed him off the cliff. I got up and walked to the lake.

The walk seemed longer than before, probably because I wasn't scared, hiding in the shadows. The huge lake chamber was dark, and I didn't know how to light the cold-fire, so I stopped where the passageway's torches stopped. I just breathed in the scent of the water for a while. Then I felt my way forward until I came to the stony ground that surrounded the lake, glancing back to make sure I never lost sight of the torches in the passageway.

I could hear the wind and feel the stone thrumming around me, but it wasn't too loud. At least this time, if I started to feel crazy again, if I couldn't make it stop, I could come here. I could fill my robe-front with stones and knot the hem. Then I would wade into the lake, and my father and the wizards and Gerrard could all just fucking wonder for the rest of their lives where I had gone.

— 51 —

Sadima was nervous about the first meeting with the Eridian women. She got up even earlier than usual, long before the roosters woke, and helped Sistra arrange the mismatched chairs and stoke the fire in the little stove to soften the chill. Then, as the women came through the shop door, her fears dissipated. They were every color, size, and shape, a few of them old, a few very young. Many of them brought their card looms, their embroidery, their mending. Some of the younger women brought their children and sat on the floor with them. Some of the oldest women sank gracefully, cross-legged, onto blankets they carried. They all spoke at least some Servenian—the language was more common than Ferrinides in South End's streets now. But many spoke a little Ferrinides in addition to their own language.

Translating for each other, repeating things in five or six languages, they talked about cooking, their children, the weather, Servenia, the Orchid Coast, Graudan, Tipora, and all the places they had called home before they came to Limòri's South End. They talked about why they had come, and they held hands and promised to carry as much of each other's sorrow as they could.

Sadima was silent, but every word, every kind face eased her heart. Their lives had all been cut in two, like her own. How had she not understood until now that the immigrants were her sisters?

There were three other Ferrinides-born women in the group. Beth's hands were claws, broken by an angry husband who had found her with her lover twenty years before. Half her teeth were gone; her nose was an uneven glob of flesh. He had left her for dead, but she had crawled away and hidden in South End. And she had made a home here. She had a little store, built from planks she had found, by sailors who had pitied her. She sold embroidered linens, made by children she hired and fed and allowed to sleep on the floor of the shop. She had a dog, too, one of the half wolves with teeth that shone in the moonlight. The children loved him. Sadima visited a few times to make sure the dog loved them, too. He did. He regarded them as his cubs.

The second Limòri woman was named Faith. Her mother had been a Gypsy, she said, and her father a nobleman. She had a long scar across her throat that disappeared behind her ear. "It's the mark of half-royal blood," she said when she saw Sadima looking at it. Then she laughed. "My aunties said Ferrinides men have always indulged themselves with women, men, and children—and they have always hated complications. That's all I was to my father. A complication. My mother talked about it only once. She said he meant to kill me and failed—that she had tried to stop him and couldn't, but he didn't cut deep enough. She staunched the bleeding after he walked out."

"Or maybe he just meant to mark you," Sistra said.

The murmurs around the circle got louder as the discussion splintered. In Servenia, Sistra said, babies believed to be holy were scarred in thin parallel lines on their cheeks. In Tipora, a dark-haired woman told them, scars were signs of evil.

Many of the women had scars to show and stories to tell, both sad and happy. The third Limòrian was Karo, a serving girl with a big smile and a swelling belly. Her scars were stretch marks, a milestone of her pregnancy.

Sadima listened to them all, trying not to stare at Faith. There was something tickling at her, some connection. Finally, once they had all gone home, she remembered the young man who had come into the cheese shop so long before. Had he been some nobleman's cottage-child too? She sighed as she washed her hands and dressed for bed. Whatever he had been, he had died long ago.

The meetings became bigger and more intimate as time passed. All the women had stories. Sadima finally told her own, leaving out only her age and the gap in her memories. And she cried, talking about Charlie. The women held her hands that day and made the promise to carry what they could of her pain. During the fifth meeting, Faith asked for a Telling. Sadima listened to them all recount stories about Erides. The details changed, depending on the teller, but the lessons were the same ones that all good mothers tried to teach their children: sharing, patience, hard work, love.

At the seventh meeting, one of the women asked Sadima the proper way to say "thank you" in Ferrinides. Six or seven more had similar questions. After that, with Sadima and Faith as the teachers for Ferrinides and others for their native tongues, every meeting began with language lessons. Sadima found she had a gift for remembering odd words she had never heard before. When the meeting broke off into groups, she was the only one who could move between them, understanding most of what she heard.

During the tenth meeting, Karo sobbed the entire time. She had lost her child in a too-early birthing two days before. They all took turns holding her hands, pushing her hair back from her face. No one spoke. No one bothered to bring out the food they had in their bags. No one left until she had emptied her tears, and rested, and thanked them for carrying part of her sorrow.

The eleventh meeting was dominated by gossip about a magician and haircutting. Sistra's mother had been a professional in Servenia and had a pair of scissors better than any Sadima had ever seen. When she had finished trimming everyone's hair who wanted it, Faith spoke up.

She had overheard two men saying that there had been a magician in Market Square. He had only done tricks that made people laugh; he had sold nothing, promised no cures, no rain, no magic. But he had worn a dark robe. The magistrate's guards had tried to catch him, but they couldn't. People were saying he was crazy, that he laughed when he saw the guards coming, a happy laugh, like a boy playing a game.

Winter was cold that year, and when Sadima bundled up and walked down the street to do her errands, her friends and their families called out a hello as she passed. It made her so happy. But in the dark, at night in her bed before she went to sleep, she knew she could not be Mattie Han forever. It could not last. She would have to end these friendships sometime. But not yet. Oh, not yet.

Sadima painted Sistra's portrait one evening from memory. Then Faith's. Over time, she painted every woman in the group and hung the portraits on the walls of her third-floor parlor. For a while, it made her feel like her friends were always with her. Then it began to bother her, knowing she could not keep them close, and she took the paintings down and stored them in a box.

For the twentieth meeting, in the spring, they opened the window wide, to let the breeze in. And once they were all seated, with food and drink in reach, one of the Servenian women lifted her hands and said she was grateful to celebrate with such good friends. They all made the same gesture, so Sadima joined them.

Then Sistra's mother stood up. She sang a song in her

low, full voice. It wasn't in Ferrinides or Servenian, but in some strange language with impossibly long words. She sang it three times through, then the others joined in for a fourth. They all seemed to know it, no matter what their own language was. Sistra's mother waited for complete silence before she began to speak.

"We celebrate the Birth of Erides this day," she said, stretching out each word. Some of the women closed their eyes. "Long ago and all too near," she went on quietly, "the king in Servenia, like the old Ferrinides kings here, and all others elsewhere, feared her wisdom."

"They feared her!" Faith whispered, awestruck, and others repeated it.

Sistra's mother waited for quiet before she went on. "They feared for their own power. They feared for their very lives as people began to understand that there was plenty of food if no one wasted, plenty of land if none was left untended, and that there was knowledge beyond their dreams, hidden and guarded. *Owned.*" She paused again, and when she next spoke, her voice was louder. "When Erides stepped off the boat in her dark robe, there were men there, waiting to shackle her and lead her away."

The women made a humming sound, their voices pitched to blend several notes into one. Sadima glanced toward the door, wishing she had closed it. They had never done anything like this before. This had to be the Celebration of Birth.

"But they had no prison that could hold her," Sistra's mother whispered, then lifted her voice again. "They had no prison, no dungeon, no jail, neither brick nor stone, that could hold her."

A tall woman in the back of the room began the song again. Her name was Mary, and she had come from the cold country of the ice rivers to the north. Her hair was straight as corn silk and her voice was high. She warbled, more like a bird than a woman, and it was both grating and beautiful and the last note drifted upward, softer and softer, until it faded to silence. And the silence filled the room again.

"Erides walked through their brick walls," Sistra's mother whispered in her own tongue. Sistra echoed the sentence, and the ones that followed, in Ferrinides, the one language they all spoke now.

Sistra's mother stood up. "She walked through their stone."

Three or four women lifted their heads. "Yes, she did."

"Went through it like it was air."

"The guards were dumbstruck."

"They could not keep her and they could not silence her."

There were murmurs of agreement in four languages.

"Wise men understood her," Sistra said. "And women protected her. They hid her. They hung woven bags of food on their gateposts and waterskins from their yard trees in case she was thirsty."

"She stayed in Servenia for fifteen summers and fourteen winters," Sistra's mother told them. "And all of that time, she spoke with anyone who would listen. She taught them to share everything, everything, everything, *everything*. The work, the food, the land, the knowledge."

Mary sang again, and this time Sadima closed her eyes, imagining Erides walking with the children.

"She was never angry with her captors," Sistra's mother said when the song ended. "She could have killed them without ever touching them, but she did not. Some of them heard her words and put down their weapons and took off their uniforms. Many wanted to learn the magic, but she would not teach it. She knew it would ruin them, make them lazy and arrogant. She always said it was a fight for her, every day."

A murmur went around the room as Sistra's mother sat down. Then Sharee stood up. Her Ferrinides was improving. "I come from Graudan," she said. "Erides came to us next. Her words did not change with time. Nor her heart. She didn't fear our Elders. Many men followed her and helped protect her. Women were not used to other women leading the way. It took them longer to hear her in Graudan. But when they did, they joined their men and followed her. Erides said this: Share the work. Share the food. Share the knowledge. Share the land."

She sat down, and another woman stood. Her name was Girta, and she was blushing and shaking her head. "I am from Stutger. My Ferrinides very poor. But I work for it. Very much." There was a respectful silence as she gathered herself. "Erides did no come Stutger. She had not enough years. But we love her too." She sat down, then stood up again, still blushing. "She say, everyone must work. Share food, share wisdom, share land. She say all that needs be to say." Once Girta had finished, no one else got up. The silence settled into the corners of the room again. After a long time, Sharee pulled her bag closer and took out a loaf of bread. All the women stirred then, unwrapping what they had brought.

Sadima went downstairs to get the half round of cheese she had set aside for the meeting. On her way back across the shop, just when she was about to start up the stairs, she heard a man shout close by, out in the street. Her heart skipped one beat, then began again, faster, heavier, when she heard more yelling. But the voices dimmed, and she carried the cheese to the women upstairs.

The women were standing in a half circle before the window. Faith turned to Sadima. "We saw a man run past, then guards, chasing him."

"They sometimes chase thieves here—," Sadima began, but Faith shook her head, breathless, her eyes wide.

"No. This man was wearing a dark robe that fell to his ankles. Both guards had their swords out. It was him—the one people talk about. He was laughing at them."

52

Sometime before morning, I woke in silence. I lay still, hoping to fall asleep again, but I could feel my day-dreams pulling at me. The darkness was an unbroken black mass that pressed against my eyes and my heart—and it made a perfect backdrop for the images my mind began to create. I exhaled, wishing I could stop. How many times had I bullied and threatened and murdered my father in my imagination? How many times would be enough?

When I heard the sound of the wind rising inside my skull, I pushed myself upright and got out of bed. I found my lamp and striker by touch and went out into the cor-ridor, so I wouldn't wake Gerrard in case it was the middle of our night.

Between the cold-fire torches and my lamp, there was

enough light to push my daydreams away, but as I paced back and forth, the wind got louder. I shook my head, hard, to make it go away, then realized I was holding my arms almost straight out.

I lowered them, whispering my own name over and over. I kept talking—nonsense, whatever came into my mind—until I was sure I could speak if Gerrard woke and came looking for me. Then I slipped back into the room, intending to get the song book. Imagining the songs had gotten easier, but I still had to concentrate, and studying them was a refuge; the effort left no room for anything else. But fumbling in the dark, I picked up the history book instead and was back out in the corridor before I realized it.

It had been so long since I had read it that it took a while to find the place where I had left off the last time. Once I did, I read slowly, trying not to hear the wind or think of more ways to kill my father. Or Somiss. Or myself.

The first section was a basic recounting of the child-hood of Erides, the one every Limòri student has heard. The prophet was a noblewoman who had lived hundreds of years before, when the city was a tiny seaport kingdom. The Kings' War had killed most magicians long before Erides's birth. There was little magic left in the world dur-ing her lifetime. But as a child she knew an old man—some believed he was a jester in her father's court, oth-ers thought it was her father himself, or an uncle—who taught her magic tricks, then real magic. Before he died, he made her promise to teach it. But when she was fifteen, she began telling anyone who would listen that magic was dangerous, corrupting, and that it should never be taught to anyone.

In her twenties, Erides began performing magic in Market Square to draw crowds. Once hundreds—or sometimes thousands—of people were there, she told them that the real magic lay inside them. She said that if they shared food, land, and knowledge, and if they did their work, whatever it was, as a sacred task, they would be happy, free of most of the miseries of humankind, that kindness would overcome cruelty in homes, in streets, in kingdoms, in the world.

That much was familiar. But the rest of what the history book contained wasn't. I had been taught that Erides went to Servenia, then came back to Limòri and began the "meetings" that some Eridians still observed on the seventh-day. The book made it sound like she had traveled half her life or more, preaching that knowledge should be shared, while refusing to share her own. She often met those who needed her skill, the book said. She never used it, not even to stop a flood or to save the life of a child. Kings, merchants, peasants, they had all tried to capture her, to force her to teach magic. But she could walk through walls. She could fly. She always escaped and went on to preach her poisonous doctrine. Only a few fanatics followed her. They persuaded the simpleminded and the poor to believe that magic was the source of their poverty, their unhappiness, and that it somehow caused wars. They kept to themselves and taught their children to hate anyone who did not follow Eridian teachings. Their faith in the doctrine of lies was unshakable, even when their own children were dying and could have been cured by magic.

I looked up at the cold-fire torch across from me. The information in the history book always seemed exaggerated. Eridians and their beliefs about magic sometimes annoyed my father, but he did business with them—almost all the big farms outside Limòri were owned by Eridians. I had heard rumors that there were families on the farms who were very strict and used no magic at all. But I had never met an Eridian who was anything like what the book described.

They held some of their meetings and their annual Celebration of Birth in my father's park. The rest of the time, they were like anyone else. Everyone in Limòri knew the Eridian Doctrines, more or less. All the Eridians I knew celebrated Winterfeast as well as the Celebration of Birth. They all went to the wizards for help with illness or injury. Everyone did, if they could pay for it.

I looked down and read the next heading: "The Murderous Eridians." Riots and murder? Why weren't we taught any of this in school? Could it be true?

The book said that many generations after Erides died, an army of a thousand Eridians surrounded the Founder's childhood home. He was a preternaturally intelligent boy who was, even then, studying magic. The Eridians feared a challenge to their prophet's teachings and had come to kill him. Much blood was spilled when the king's guards came, swords flashing, riding armored warhorses.

I turned the page, but heard footsteps and looked up. A

wizard was coming up the passageway, his torch held high. I went inside, laid down the book, and stretched out on my bed, hoping he would walk past. But he pounded on the door, and I shouted that we were awake. He pounded again. I waited until Gerrard was ready, then opened it.

Franklin's class was in the food hall this time. He told us all that it was safe to eat, then stood back. "And if you can make food without touching the stone at all," he added quietly, "do it that way now, please. If you have experimented with other breathing patterns, use them if you wish."

I glanced around. Gerrard was the only one who didn't look surprised. I got in line, but I still had the sound of wind in my head—distant, but still there. So I was even more afraid to open my mind to the stone.

Luke did it. So did Levin and Jordan. All three of them stood far back from the stone, their faces set with concentration. Their food appeared on the pedestal. They all retrieved their plates and sat at separate tables. When Franklin noticed, he asked them to sit together, then nodded at Will.

Stiff and nervous, Will tried twice and nothing happened. So he walked close enough to touch the stone. Gerrard didn't even try. He touched the stone to make his fish stew, yams, and bread—and this time, an apple, exactly like the ones from my father's orchards. He glanced at me on his way to sit down. I went last, and I touched the stone too.

We ate like a family again, with Franklin at the head of the table. No one talked, but it still felt wonderful to me. No one's eyes were bloodshot anymore, so they had solved the lamp problem somehow, unless they were always studying here in the food hall. Once we were finished eating, Franklin motioned for us to get rid of our dishes. Then he faced us.

"The next part of your education begins today. It is time to imagine things you are not familiar with, that don't come from your memories." He glanced at me, and I wondered if he knew about the lamp wicks or Gerrard's soap. He reached into the folds of his robe and pulled out a black cloth sack, closed with a drawstring. He undid it and dumped six objects in the center of the table. There was a broken hearth broom, a cream-filled pastry, a dead lizard, an intricate gold necklace, a goblet with a copper jacketband set with gems, and a raveled piece of silk woven of at least a dozen colors.

"Choose one," Franklin said.

Everyone hesitated, then we all reached at once. I grabbed the necklace because it was closest to me. Gerrard got the goblet, Will the broken broom. Levin tried for the goblet and ended up with the pastry. Luke held up the cloth and smirked to let us all know that the silk was what he had wanted and the best thing in the pile. Jordan laughed as he picked up the dead lizard by its tail and set it before him. It was good to hear him laugh, to hear anyone laugh.

"Look at the thing you have chosen," Franklin said. "Examine it very carefully, with your whole mind, your whole body. Touch it, taste it, smell it, and see it."

We all glanced at Jordan, and he made a face. No one laughed. Franklin stepped back from the table. "Your ability to imagine vividly has been more important than accuracy in what you have made so far. Now I want you to make accurate copies of your objects. You can practice as needed. But you will not be able to make food again until you have done it perfectly. When you have, tell Jux and we will have our next class."

And then he was gone.

We sat at the table, glancing at each other. We were afraid to talk, but no one got up. Even Luke sat with us as we turned our objects this way and that, examining them.

"I have never been this academically motivated," Jordan whispered. He held the lizard up with one hand and pinched his nose closed with the other. We all laughed; it just burst out of us. But it lasted about two heartbeats and an eyeblink before we fell silent again.

I looked down at the necklace and saw for the first time that the clasp was broken, and that several of the links were very slightly distorted, as though someone had tried to pull it apart. I glanced around the table. The goblet was missing a gem. "Everything is broken," I whispered.

There was a little murmur as they all noticed what I had. "Why?" Will breathed.

"To make it harder," Gerrard answered, so quietly that I wasn't quite sure I had heard him. I was pretty sure no one else had. I watched their faces and no one's changed, not even a little. But he was right, of course. I looked down at the necklace clasp. The gold was dented and scratched, and the clasp was bent in an odd way. There were tiny scratches going in two directions.

I looked up. One corner of the cloth was frayed, a complex, random mass of threads. The lizard was rotting, its scales uneven, its eyes sunken; the goblet stem was chipped, the copper band was old, discolored. It was shaded from pink to green-black. The pastry had one corner pulled off, exposing hundreds of tiny air pockets, each one different in shape, and the wooden broom handle had splintered along an oblique line. *Oblique*. Another Professor Doohan word.

"Somiss could be watching us right now," Luke said. He stood up and walked out.

"I think Somiss isn't here," Will whispered once Luke was out the door. "Maybe it's summertime out in the world and he's traveling to the Orchid Coast."

"Have you been there?" Levin asked quietly.

"Yes," Will whispered back. "The beaches have black sand."

And then we all fell silent. I don't know what anyone else was thinking, but I was remembering my life at home, not my father and his rages, but the dinners, the pleasure trips to Limòri's mountains, and the voyage to Suluk, a snowbound island far north of Servenia. My father had paid dearly for constant high wind, so it had taken only sixty days. My brother and I had learned to climb the rigging. Our tutor had been seasick most of the time, so we had barely studied. I glanced at Gerrard and wondered where his thoughts took him when he thought about home.

"How can we *do* this?"

It was Will, staring at the tiny strands of curled wood that edged the broken broom handle.

I looked down at the necklace. I had practiced imagining things whole for a long time—to learn the songs—and I had made the lamp wicks. But this was different. There was no real pattern to the scratches. Or the bent clasp.

Levin sighed. "I don't even know how to begin."

I leaned forward. This was the chance I had hoped for. If we worked together even a little, and no one got killed, it would be a first step to having a pact among us. And Luke was already gone, so we didn't have to worry about him telling Somiss. This was perfect. I took a breath to speak, but Gerrard got up abruptly, without saying a word. He started toward the entrance, almost running.

Levin followed him. Then we all stood up, and we spread out, too, from habit, walking toward the same arched entryway from five different angles, all of us staring into the shadows between the cold-fire torches. I knew they were all wondering what Gerrard had seen, if Somiss had been watching. I was almost sure he hadn't seen anything at all, that he had gotten up to keep me from speaking. Either way, it was over. No one spoke, no one exchanged a single glance. We were afraid again.

I followed Gerrard back to the room, staying well behind him. I wanted to knock him flat and make him bleed for this. But I knew it would do far more harm than good. He was the one I had to convince first. That was the first step.

53

"Will you come?" Sistra was fiddling with a strand of her little sister's hair. She had cut it again, Sadima noticed. Jadia hated brushing her coarse, curly hair, so the shorter it was, the better. She wasn't smiling. She almost never did. Sistra looked at Sadima. "Will you?"

Sadima smiled without answering. The water was pinging, coming close to a boil. She put wood into the little stove, then adjusted the chimney draft before she turned to look at Sistra again. "It's in a meetinghouse?"

Sistra nodded. She had gotten taller over the past seven years, and even prettier. But Sadima could see the pain behind the excitement in her eyes. Sistra had watched her mother die of a fever and her sister shrink into herself, consumed by sadness.

"A woman in Market Square told me about it," she said. "It's not too far."

"Today?"

Sistra nodded. "Please come with us. We're all going to walk together. Even Beth. She has someone to watch her store."

"I have a lot of work to finish here," Sadima said. She poured the scalding water over a crock of peaches, then set the kettle back on the stove.

"Jadia and I can help," Sistra told her. Her sister was staring at the wall and gave no sign that she had heard.

Sadima smiled and nodded, but while the peach skins loosened, she bent over the crock, hiding her face. She had bought a little tin of kohl to start darkening the skin beneath her eyes. She tried to remember to wear long sleeves and skirts, as older women often did now, too. It was easy in the winter, of course. But when the weather warmed up, she sometimes forgot. Sadima knew that Sistra was observant and smart. It would not be long before she noticed. Or one of the others. It was almost time to start over. Again.

Sadima knew it would be harder this time. She had broken all her rules. She had made friends. South End had gotten safer, cleaner, so people stayed longer before they moved on. She sighed. She would have to find a way to disappear for a generation, then reappear. She dreaded it.

Sadima picked up her tongs and took a peach out of the water. The skin split and slid off in one piece. Sistra set down her market bag. She and Jadia washed their hands, then, without saying a word, they worked as they often did, in unison, staying out of each other's way, their hands flying. Before long they had peeled, pitted, and pureed enough peaches to add to the last batch of kefir.

"Whose house is it?" Sadima asked as they washed up, and was surprised that she had said it. She had come to treasure the meetings above the cheese shop. But it was time to end these friendships, not deepen them.

"It's not a house," Sistra told her. "It's an old warehouse somewhere up by the marsh, at this end of the bay. Faith says the family that owns it has been Eridian for generations. They made a fortune on the silk trade way back when. The great-great-grandson is holding meetings every seventh-day. They sing and—"

"I need to finish turning the cheeses," Sadima interrupted, almost wishing she could go. She turned her back on Sistra for a moment, pretending to adjust the flue again. It had been a long time since she had been anywhere but the cheese shop's backrooms or her rooms next door. But if this warehouse was up around the marsh that edged the bay, it might be across the invisible line and she would have to pretend to be sick or say she had forgotten something she had to do. And there were memories up that way, too. She carried the crock to the washbasin to hide her sudden sadness. She still had some pieces of the silk she had brought to Charlie's that first night. Some were in a box, never washed, because even now, they smelled faintly of Charlie. The rest were in his grave. She still missed him every day. And Grrur.

"Please come," Sistra was saying. "There are whispers that two of the magistrates have been studying magic. This man says that—"

Startled, Sadima turned. "But it was the magistrates who—" She stopped herself, realizing that she was remembering the young king's chancellors who ordered the hangings. They had all been dead many years. She felt off balance for a moment, then recovered. "Has the man in the black robe been seen again?"

"In Market Square last spring, two or three times, then again seven days ago," Sistra said. "If it was the same man. I have been staying out of Limòri." She glanced at her sister, who was sitting on the floor, staring at nothing. "Jadia and I had to push our way through the orphans last time," she told Sadima in a low voice. "Some of them cut themselves with tin, deep enough to bleed, so people will stop and try to help. Then they grab bracelets, buttons, parcels, anything they can."

"I saw intoxicant sellers," Jadia said quietly.

Sistra glanced at Sadima. "Opium is everywhere in the city now. I want her to know who to stay away from."

Sadima turned away again, uneasy. Limòri had always been much better than South End. Everything was changing. Again.

"Will you come?" Sistra asked again, when Sadima said nothing more. "Please?"

Sadima nodded. Then she was sorry she had. "I felt a little sick this morning," she lied. "But I will try."

Sistra hugged her. "I am going to go meet the others

by the old lumberyard. Then we'll come here for you."

Sadima forced a smile. "I'll be ready."

As soon as Sistra left, she washed up, then pulled on a long dress and tied a scarf over her fuzzy hair. She dabbed on the kohl, squinting hard as she blotted her skin with a cloth, blurring the lines, before she put on her belt-purse. She would pass shops she had never seen, she was sure. If she came back alone, she might buy a dress or two—something very different from what she was wearing now. As much as she dreaded it, it *was* very nearly time to start over. She didn't want to close the shop and disappear, but this was the price of making close friends who would notice, eventually, that she wasn't aging. Especially Eridian friends, who hated magic.

It was a longer walk than she remembered. And it was very different now. Most of the abandoned warehouses had been reopened, some with small stores and kiosks partitioned in long rows. The cobbles had been swept clean and repaired in many places, and there was a new dock that ran along the edge of the wide river. She smiled. The Servenians had brought their families and their ambitions.

Sistra knew someone to wave at or shout a greeting to every five or six steps. Faith and Beth chattered about everything under the sun, and the others joined in when something caught their interest. Karo was still quiet, her eyes darkened with her sorrow, but she was talking more and more as the days passed.

Sadima was grateful that they all left her to walk a few paces behind with Jadia. She had felt no dread, no panic, so they were still inside the invisible line—but she knew the strange and terrible fear could come at any moment. She walked a little slower, ready to feign a bellyache if it did. Jadia slowed with her, staring into the shop windows.

Sistra finally turned back and pointed. "There it is!"

Sadima nodded. There were groups of people standing outside a huge brick building at the next crossroad. And the closer they got, the surer she was that it was where she had slept with Grrur, where she had found the silk. There were good glass windows now, one on the second floor that was bordered in squares of colored glass. The brick was still the same color. And as they turned the corner, she saw the cypress tree. It had been slender back then. Its trunk was as wide as a wagon now.

Jadia ran to catch up with Sistra as they went in. Sadima walked slower, looking around. The building had been gutted and cleaned. The stairs had been widened and carpeted and weren't as steep. But the whole second floor was still one huge room. At the far end, there was a stage with a massive brass lamp hanging above it and a huge, tufted chair with odd, bowed-out legs carved from some dark wood.

Sadima felt uneasy as the room filled up, and she stayed near the back as Sistra, Jadia, and Karo made their way to the front to stand beside Faith and the others. When Sistra looked back, gesturing for her to join them, Sadima put her palm on her belly and made a face, then gestured toward the stairs. Sistra nodded.

"Thank you all for coming!"

Sadima was startled by the man's voice. He was tall, with brown hair that fell in a cascade that brushed his shirt collar. His eyes were so dark they stood out against his pale skin, and they were full of something so intense that she looked aside for a moment, then back. He was young, but was sitting in the chair, a stout cane across his lap, facing the people standing in loose rows before him. He waited, smiling, as two more big groups came through the wide doorway and found places to stand. They were all dressed in their best; everyone was scrubbed clean.

"My name," he began, then paused for the room to quiet. "My name, as most of you know, is Thomas Marsham."

There was a rustling in the crowd. He laughed. "Yes. Marsham. Not all of us are criminals—though most of us have a great-uncle or a grandfather who did things he shouldn't have." People laughed, and he waited before he went on, raising his voice. "The worst years are long behind us, and we are determined, as you are, to claim our birthright as followers of our sister Erides."

The crowd closest to the stage exploded into a cheer. He looked into their faces and waited again. When the noise subsided, he smiled. "Ladies. Thank you for bringing your friends, and your men."

The women laughed, and the men smiled a little. Sadima felt odd, uneasy. Then she realized why. Marsham—of course. Chee Marsham.

". . . and I asked our sisters to bring their brothers and husbands and sons and fathers," he was saying, "because Erides came to both men and women with her message.

And she warned against separating women from men." He paused again, then lowered his voice a little. "I see the men wondering, so let me say that I mean no disrespect, sitting while you stand before me. I was hurt as a boy, and while I can walk well with a cane, it is painful to stand still for very long."

Sadima watched Sistra and the others. They were not exchanging glances. They had heard this before.

"My great-great-great-grandfather ran ships during the silk trade days," Thomas Marsham said. "He collected fancy chairs from all over the world. Until I was hurt, no one in the family knew what to do with all of them."

Everyone laughed at that, and he smiled. "But I did not ask you to bring your men to talk about old chairs," he said. "I asked you to bring them so that I could tell them something astonishing, something that will change them as it has changed me."

Thomas Marsham lifted his hands out to his sides, then brought them down slowly, like a seabird flying in a strong wind. He made the gesture again, even more slowly, and then stared at people, one at a time, his eyes moving from one face to another. The silence deepened.

"There was a time when men and women could fly," he whispered into the quiet. "Like a hawk. Like a sparrow. Like a hummingbird."

A murmur went through the crowd. Some of the men's smiles widened a little as they waited for him to make a joke out of it. But he didn't. He stood up and walked to the edge of the stage, his cane tapping the planks. "This knowledge was kept secret by generations of Ferrinides kings here in Limòri, but Erides spoke of it. Who knows the story?"

About half of the women raised their hands. Sadima looked at them. Most of them had skin the color of honey.

"Our Orchid Coast friends teach it to their children," Thomas Marsham said, raising his voice again. "Erides learned magic from one of the last magicians. Some claim she flew, twice, to prove that she could. She never taught anyone else how, and she let the knowledge of flying and a thousand other kinds of magic die with her." He walked, his step timed to the movement of his cane, uneven and slow, to the other side of the stage.

"As she meant to do," he added quietly. "For very good reasons." He paused again. "But this story leaves me with questions. How can it be that some men knew how to fly in a time when others could barely walk beneath the weariness of their daily toil? And is it better that some men now eat candied grapes and roast pheasant while others eat rice or beans or barley or lentils—without butter or salt—every day of their lives?"

"It is not right," a man in the back called out.

Thomas Marsham paused, and Sadima glanced around. Everyone was silent, watching him. "Is that what Erides taught?" he asked. "No. She said we must share everything."

The crowd murmured.

"Injustice!" he shouted, startling them all. Then he

dropped his voice. "Injustice was the reason Erides left her family's wealth and the comfort of their royal home. It was the reason that even though she had learned magic herself, she never taught it. She knew what would happen. The rich would hoard it the way they hoard everything. Their children would learn magic. Not yours. They would eat well and heal their sick and fly and have the light that gave no heat—and the poor would starve." He looked into the crowd again, and Sadima could tell he was meeting the eyes of one person after another. "And that," he said slowly, "is wrong. It is what Erides wanted to end, once and for all."

There were shouts and cheers. When Thomas Marsham spoke again, it was in a voice so low it was almost a whisper. "And when she died, at ninety-nine years of age, she was buried in a secret place so that no one could claim to own her body. So that no one could build a shrine. So that the worms could reduce her to garden soil."

He took a long, audible breath. "Erides knew it was wrong for some to play at flying while children were being sold and starved. She knew it was wrong for men to break their backs lifting cargo crates full of fancy goods brought over the ocean to feed the whims of kings and noblemen and rich merchants, then go home to their hungry children." He paused again, shaking his head, a look of disgust on his face. "Kings and wizards. Wizards and kings. They have warred against each other for time beyond counting. And now that most of the kings are gone, the merchants and magistrates have taken their place. They are all brothers in their hearts.

Merchants in Limòri live like kings of old now. They have servants who bring them sweets and wash them in the bath, and turn down their soft bedclothes at night. All these men and the women who are their consorts and companions and the mothers of their children—they all love comfort and power, not justice."

The crowd exploded into cheers. A few of the women made a high, ululating sound that cut through the rest of the noise.

"There are generations-old rumors," Thomas Marsham said slowly, turning in a half circle to include everyone there. "Rumors that boy children in Limòri sometimes disappear." He was shaking his head, his hands balled into fists. "Who knows that story?"

This time half the crowd responded.

Thomas Marsham smiled. "Erides told the Servenians that when the magicians rose again, they would steal the knowledge of the herbalists and the simple farmers and work their changes on it, and they would hide to study their corrupting arts." He looked at the ceiling. "Erides said they would begin to shun women and steal boy children in the night, charming them so they could not scream." He shook his head. "How hard must a man's heart be to do that?"

The room went still.

"And she said that when those stolen boys learned magic, they would no longer be their mother's sons," he continued. "Magic turns decent men into savages and hardened men into monsters. It erodes human hearts until nothing gentle is left there." He waited for the murmurs to stop, then lifted his head. "Erides told many stories of the fight that raged inside her because of the magic she was taught. She warned us all that one day it would come back." He hobbled to the chair and leaned on it, waiting for complete, absolute silence. "That day," he finally whispered, "has come."

54

The songs were getting longer, and it took three or four tries for anyone to pass, except Gerrard, of course, but he pretended that it did. Jux seemed to have stopped his own classes now that he had taken over Somiss's. I was grateful. He never told us we had done well, he never made us feel a little safer like Franklin did. But he never looked pissed off if we passed or happy when we failed. There were no fancy chairs, and for a while at least, we didn't have to worry about bears and snakes and kites.

I tried endlessly to think of a way to convince Gerrard we should get everyone to help each other, and I couldn't. He had known I was about to say something when we were all sitting around one table—he left abruptly to remind us that it was dangerous to talk.

Was it true? Did they watch us? Everywhere? All the time? The more I thought about it, the sillier it seemed to me. Certainly Somiss and Franklin had more important work—and Jux and Mabiki. So who was watching? The men who led us to class? That seemed silly too. They weren't allowed to talk to us at all, they seemed incapable of magic, and more and more of them were old men. Gerrard seemed sure that the wizards watched us, except in our rooms. And even though he talked to me more often now, he usually whispered. We all did.

One morning, lying on my cot, awake, waiting for the wizard to pound on the door, I listened to my thoughts chase themselves in circles and wanted to scream. Everything was becoming a complicated game.

Maybe, if I managed to copy the necklace before anyone else could do theirs, he would worry that I might help everyone *but* him if he refused. That might make him easier to convince. And if I figured out how to make the copy, at the least we might all end up around a single table again. I would have a second chance to try to talk to everyone all at once. So I began to study with a ferocity I had never felt before. Which was exactly what Gerrard had always done, for entirely different reasons.

The first time I went to the food hall to try to copy the necklace, I came close once, I thought. But when I walked back to the room and stared at the necklace again, handling it, smelling it, I started noticing more details. I worked at it until I was too tired to keep my eyes open, then started again the next morning. The longer I looked at it, the more

I knew it was going to be very difficult to copy. Maybe impossible.

At our next recitation class, Luke and Will arrived together, with one wizard leading them both. Luke had finally stopped walking a ways behind Will, or waiting for Levin and Jordan to walk past, then following them, or whatever he had been doing. I tried to catch Will's eye, but I couldn't, which probably meant that he was afraid of Luke. Will passed the recitation, and I was glad. But it didn't mean anything. None of us would dare try to make food until we passed Franklin's class.

The days seemed longer, then shorter again. I couldn't eat, and I barely slept. Gerrard rarely opened the song book now. He wasn't helping me anymore, and he had stopped pretending that he had to study the songs. He read the history book sometimes, but he spent most of his time staring at the goblet.

Imagining the songs took far less time than memorizing them had, and with each one, I understood the pronunciation patterns better. So I stared at the necklace most of every day, too, walking to the food hall at least once or twice. I always came back pissed off. It was harder to copy something real than it was to make it from memories. Much harder.

I wasn't sure why. I had managed it with the lantern wicks. The webbed pattern and the shape had been fairly simple—and I had used my own lamp to guess the right size and the way it should fit. I had done it in six tries. But the necklace didn't have one shape. It could be short or long, a circle, a mound, a serpentine, a jumble, and every one of those shapes revealed different surfaces, tiny bevels in the gold work. The stretched links never lay truly flat, but sometimes flatter than others, and the nicks and scratches were complex. The damage to the clasp was incredibly intricate. It should have been easier to make a perfect copy, having it on a table where I could look at it an instant before I touched the stone, but it wasn't.

At first I had pitied both Levin and Jordan. How could they possibly copy the details of something that was complex to start with and would rot—and change—as they worked at it? At least, I thought, the necklace wouldn't change. But it did. Some links were slightly thicker than others, and no two were identical. The scratches looked deeper if I moved the necklace farther from my lamp, and shallower if I moved it closer. The links were duller in the torchlight of the passageway than in the food hall. Which was the exact way to imagine it?

One day when he was out of the room, I picked up Gerrard's goblet and really looked at it. The bubbles in the glass were every bit as complicated as the air pockets in the pastry or the details of the necklace or the wood grain in the broken broom or the raveled silk or decomposing lizard.

We were all dead. It was true. They just wanted to kill us this time. I began to go back and forth between being so pissed off that I couldn't think and so scared that I couldn't think—both of which pissed me off even more. If the wizards were just waiting for us all to starve, I wanted to go to the lake and wade in. But a lot of what they'd had us do had seemed impossible at first. So I kept trying.

Every recitation class, we all looked a little worse. We were used to being hungry, but I could tell that everyone was skipping sleep, too; it showed in their faces. Will kept missing a lot of words, and his cheeks were almost sunken. He glanced at me every chance he got, his eyebrows raised enough to ask the question. I could only shake my head that tiny bit that Jux wouldn't notice, or at least that he couldn't quite be sure he had seen. And every time I had to admit to Will that I hadn't figured anything out either, I could see his eyes dim a little more. And that made me sad.

The next time I walked to the food hall to try to copy the necklace, Levin and Jordan were there. I sat quietly near the entrance and watched them try. The stone flashed and something appeared on the pedestal each time, but Jordan threw his results at the floor in a way that let me know he hadn't even come close. Levin tried fewer times, but he walked away from the stone and crossed the room to stare at the wall with his fists clenched after each attempt. They did not speak to each other, and they did not speak to me.

When they were ready to leave, Levin angled his path to walk past me slowly. He shook his head, a tiny, careful gesture, pretended to stretch, his hands wide apart, like a man lying about the size of a fish he had caught. Then he closed his empty hand into a fist, exhaled, touched his brow, and shook his head once more. Then he lifted his shoulders just enough to hollow his chest as he glanced down at the pastry in his right hand and closed his eyes for an instant and exhaled again. Then he went out.

It was almost as though I had heard his voice with each gesture: "I didn't even come close and I am pissed," he had told me. "I think about it all the time and have no idea why I can't do it. I'm so discouraged."

Alone in the food hall, I laid the necklace on one of the tables and looked at it for a long time before I tried to make a copy again. I used one finger on the stone the first three times, from habit, without thinking. All three times the necklace appeared, but in some terribly misshapen way. The links were fused the first time. The next time they weren't joined. I dropped all the copies on the floor and watched them sparkle and disappear.

The time after that most of the links were joined, but the scratches weren't there at all. I closed my eyes and imagined the necklace ten different ways, then twenty, then thirty, and I knew none of the images would work. Some showed the clasp, others emphasized the scratches. I picked up the necklace and turned to walk out, then saw Luke coming in.

I was pissed off enough to keep walking straight toward him. He lifted his chin and squared his shoulders, and when we were within a single step of running into each other and I was sure he wouldn't step aside, I did. He won.

And he laughed. It was an ugly, mean-hearted laugh, and I couldn't stand it. I reached out and shoved him, and he shoved me back. I hit one of the tables and lost my balance, and the necklace came out of my hand. It made a tiny sparkle and then it was gone. I waited for Luke to burst into laughter, but he didn't, and when I looked up, I saw him by the stone. He had just kept walking. He hadn't seen the necklace fall.

I stood there, panicked, unable to believe I had done something that stupid. I scuffed my calloused foot on the stone, trying not to scream. What would I do? What could I do?

I glanced back toward Luke and he smiled, a big, exaggerated expression as he showed me a large plate of food he had made. He wanted me to wonder why he could eat. But I already knew. I limped out of the food hall, pretending that his shove had hurt me. And it had, it had. That one shove would probably kill me. It was just going to take a little time.

55

Sistra and Faith—and all the others—had talked about the meeting the whole way home. Faith and Karo each knew a different version of how Erides had learned magic— and they all argued over which was the real one.

"They are all real!" Sistra finally shouted to stop four separate arguments at once. "Whether her uncle was the last magician or her father or the man she would have married if she hadn't been called to teach—does it matter?" And that had set off another discussion about caring about details and differences more than the core teachings.

Then, as they turned up a street lined by farmer's kiosks, Karo had run a few steps forward, then turned to face them all, walking backward as she spoke. "But if magic could be used just a little, and only for good things, wouldn't it be wonderful?"

That had stopped the whole group, forcing people to walk around them. Everyone knew what she was thinking. Her baby could have been saved, perhaps.

"Magic could be used for good," Faith said, adjusting the scarf that covered most of her scar. "It *was* used for good in her village, my grandmother said. Long ago and all too near."

Sistra was shaking her head. "But it never stayed that way. All the meetinghouse stories back home taught us that. People always think they can just use it a little, but they can't."

Karo looked close to tears. "But everyone knows the stories now. They would be careful. Or maybe just one or two or three in every generation should be allowed to learn it, and they—"

"Stop!" Beth interrupted. "Think about it. Some man gets jealous, or a woman is angry at her sister, or someone has great need."

Sistra nodded. "A dying child, a sick father, a drought that goes on for years and everyone's children are hungry, a flood . . ."

Beth was nodding. "It would be impossible to decide whose need was grave enough."

And then there was a silence, because if Beth could not imagine wanting magic to heal everything that had been done to her, none of them should consider it for an instant.

"But some things are grave, plain and simple," Karo interrupted. "I am not saying use magic for jealous people or angry people. But for the terrible things."

There was another silence. Who could blame Karo? Surely losing a child was a grave matter.

"But there is no way to control it," Sistra said. "It has been proven a hundred times. Erides said she restrained her own magic all of her days in order to never do harm. She was the only one who ever could."

Sadima listened for a while. Then she dropped back to walk with Jadia and talk about small things. And when the others decided to look for bargains in the shops they were passing, she left them, saying she had work to do.

The next morning she woke feeling like there was something she needed to finish. She almost never had dreams, and when she did, they evaporated the instant she opened her eyes. But the remnants of this one hovered just beyond her reach. She remembered running. Being out of breath. That much was clear. Out of breath because . . . and it was gone.

Later, sitting by her third-story window, looking out at the sky, she sipped her tea and thought about the Eridian meeting and the argument on the way home. Maybe that was what her dream had been about, she thought as she got dressed. Maybe she had been dreaming about all the friends she'd soon have to leave. Starting over was harder every time. And the worst thing was that there was no one she could talk to about it. Her friends loved her, she knew that. But they didn't know the single most important thing about her, and if they did, they would both fear and hate her. They were true Eridians. And it had to be magic. What else could it be?

Sadima set down her tea, breathing slow and deep and trying to keep the uncertain feeling from climbing from her belly into her heart. She had no business going to Eridian meetings. She stood and carried her cup to the washbasin, then opened what looked like a pantry door and pattered down the steep, winding stairs and into the narrow passageway that connected her two buildings. When she opened the door to the cheese shop, she pulled in another long breath, filling her lungs with the sweet-sour smell of the fermenting milk. The kefir had added a slightly different fermentation odor, and the lovely sweet notes of the fruit she mixed into every batch. Charlie would have loved kefir. Sadima blinked back tears. She missed him so much. He had known her secret and hadn't hated her for it—or for anything else. Charlie had loved her, deep and true, the way she had come to love him.

Standing in front of the washing trough, glad it was too early for anyone to come through the door, Sadima wished, with all her being, that she could have died with Charlie. Or that his life could have been as long as hers. Then they could have started over together every time.

As she worked the curds, Sadima admitted to herself that she loved not being alone, buried inside herself all the time. When someone at the meetings promised to carry a friend's sorrow, they meant it. Sistra had, even as a girl. Sadima knew she could call on any of them for help of any kind, for solace, or just for company. But none of the Eridian women would ever really understand her. No one could.

Sadima pumped water, watching the whey bucket fill up. There had to be others like her somewhere. Not in South End, or she would have noticed them—and they would have noticed her. But somewhere. She wanted to know why she was the way she was. If she could have one or two friends who understood how weary she got, how suffocatingly familiar the simple, repetitive acts of living had become . . . Her best memories—of her years with Charlie—were so far in her past now. They weren't fading— but they were buried beneath the unnatural weight of too many newer ones.

Carrying the buckets from the trough to the presses, Sadima wished, as she had a hundred times, that she had at least tried to go see Micah, that she had looked for the man Micah named, the magician named Conklin. Had he somehow destroyed her memories and left her here—and made her stay inside the invisible line? Was he the reason she hadn't died a long, long time ago? Was he still alive too? If he was, he hadn't cared enough to find her, to make sure she was all right, to explain anything.

Sadima started a fire in the stove and went to get the baskets of strawberries from the cool, dry backroom Charlie had used to store empty crates and bottles. By the time her employees came to work, she had the day's pressing done, a batch of kefir started, and the strawberries cleaned and crushed. She left them to open the shop and went back upstairs. Then she sat in front of her easel and tried to paint Conklin. She let her hand take over, that feeling of knowing how to do something she had found with painting and cheese making and cleaning.

The portrait came out well enough, but it was a stranger; a thin-faced man with eyes so light they looked almost like bottle glass was staring back at her from the canvas. Was it him? It bothered her to look at it. She went back to work.

The next morning she sipped her tea and made a decision. South End was her home. But she needed another one. Or maybe two. Being able to start over in new places was the only answer. She could make friends, make a life, then be able to live elsewhere for her next life—and make friends again. It was the best she could do.

She washed, put on her plainest dress, left her scarves all hanging on their hooks, and carried the half-dry portrait downstairs. She started the day's fire with it. Then she walked toward the alleys that led out of South End. Her stomach was in a knot that tightened with every step. By the time she stood at the end of the alley, her pulse was slamming at her wrists and her temples. But whatever Conklin had done to her, too many people knew her now. She had to be able to do this. She had to.

Sadima took one step forward. Her heart went faster. Her breath came quicker too, as though she had been running. She tried to take another step and couldn't. She felt dizzy and wondered if her heart would burst in her chest. She stood still, refusing to take a backward step, asking herself if she cared—and the truth was she didn't. She didn't want to live longer if it meant being trapped, doomed to watching Sistra and Karo get old and die. And someone would tell the Eridians eventually. Someone would notice. Sadima imagined Sistra, torn between her beliefs and their friendship, and managed to take another step.

A cold sweat rose on her skin like dew in a meadow. She forced one more step out of her rigid knees before she began to see black, ragged shadows at the edge of her vision, narrowing it. She swallowed a mouthful of bitter saliva.

A man was shouting behind her, saying something over and over, but she was afraid to turn, afraid of giving up the two steps she had taken. Then she heard the hoofbeats.

"Make way!" he was yelling. "Look out!"

Sadima turned and saw a panicked bay cart horse, her eyes rimmed in white, galloping hard. A jumble of images poured into Sadima: a snarling dog; the smell of snake mixed with the smell of fear; the farmer screaming at someone. He was half standing now, the reins taut, but the mare was terrified and frantic to get farther and farther away from whatever had scared her.

The alley was too narrow to step aside, so Sadima stumbled forward, out onto the boardwalk, making her legs work well enough to fall to the side as the bay mare jumped the walk, then went to her knees when the cart wheels hit the raised planks.

"Are you all right?"

Sadima turned, her breath still ragged and quick. It was Thomas Marsham. He was hurrying toward her, pivoting his weight on his stout cane with every step. He bent and got one arm around her waist and pulled her to her feet, then walked her across the street, his free hand still on his cane. "I remember you," he said once they were on the other side. "From the meeting."

Sadima's heart was slowing. Her vision had cleared. She looked up at the sky. It seemed impossibly blue.

"May I ask your name? I would be happy to walk you home."

She looked at him again and hesitated, unable, for an instant, to think of the name she was using. "Mattie Han," she said. "Are you going into Limòri?"

"I am," he said. "Are you?"

She tried to smile. "Yes."

He nodded. "It is safer for you not to go alone. May I walk with you?"

She looked back across the street. The mare was up, shaking her mane, standing square on all four legs. She was upset, but not hurt. Sadima turned to Thomas Marsham. "I would appreciate it," she said. "Thank you."

56

For the next three days—which seemed very short again—I worked on a song and tried to stop thinking about the necklace. But every time I closed my eyes, I could see it falling, see the quick twinkle of torchlight on the gold as it dropped, the way the links fell into a hummock, with one end in an ungraceful curve, then the sparkle of the floor. Then I felt the sickening weight in my belly I had felt as it disappeared.

Stupid, stupid, stupid.

Why had I tried to pretend that Luke didn't scare me?

I went back a day later and made a replacement, of course. It wasn't that hard to make a copy that would fool Luke just in case he had seen it drop. That became ridiculously important to me. I made five or six of the necklaces and kept the one that came closest to having all the dents and damage of the one I had lost. I could see the perfect images in my mind; still, I just couldn't put them together into one image to give the stone when I touched it. There were too many.

I carried the necklace to our next recitation class and made a point of walking just a little ahead of Luke coming out. I tossed it, catching it a few times, before I lengthened my stride and walked faster, without looking back. I didn't hear him laugh, so maybe he believed it. Or he had never seen me drop it.

Every night, trying to sleep, I listened to my thoughts go in circles. It was maddening, but I couldn't shut them off, and I really didn't want to. The few times I had managed to silence them, I could hear the thrumming or the wind, and that was worse. My dreams were strange, and a lot of them woke me, full of odd thoughts and dreading something I couldn't name.

When it went on long enough, I got up and went out into the passageway to study the next song. I passed the recitation on the first try. Everyone else failed. They all stared at me because they thought I was working at copying the necklace, too. I wasn't. There was no point in studying an imperfect copy.

Two nights after that, my belly aching with hunger, I slept for a while, then woke up and worked on imagining the pages of the next song out in the passageway. Twice I almost fell asleep sitting up, my back propped against the wall. The next night I tried to study the history book. Maybe everything in it was true and there would be a test soon. But it was hard to read about the man who had made this place what it was. I hated studying his life, like he was some kind of hero.

One night, the history book facedown beside me on the stone, I started a new daydream. In this one I met the Founder, in his twenties, when his father had wanted to kill him, not save him from the Eridians. In the daydream, I helped run him down and stood back, cheering, when a swordsman lopped his head off. Then I helped dig a grave so deep no one would ever find his bones. There were a hundred boys, all fighting for a turn with the shovel. And somehow, that helped me go back to bed and sleep.

The next day Gerrard sat on his bed cross-legged, holding the goblet, running through the breathing patterns I knew and making up his own, like he had been doing for a long time. He was skinny as a fence rail. His shoulder blades looked like knife tips through the cloth of his robe now.

At our next recitation class, I passed again. But it meant nothing to my belly, so it meant nothing to me. Will looked like shit. Levin was so thin he looked frail, and Jordan had begun whispering to himself, practicing the songs constantly, even while we were sitting in recitation class. He passed too, and I was glad for him. But I knew what the constant whispering meant. He was trying to silence something else inside his head. Luke passed too. He had barely lost weight, but he was quiet and didn't mock anyone or try to start a fight.

As we stood up to leave, I swayed on my feet, and it scared me. If no one managed to make a perfect copy, we would all die. Had I been right? Was that really what they wanted? After everything they had put us through, maybe they had finally decided that none of us was good enough. Maybe this was their way of putting an end to a bad class. I took a long breath. Fuck them.

"I made a perfect copy of the necklace," I said. Then I cleared my throat and said it louder. Everyone turned to look at me. Their faces were hollow, their eyes wide.

"I will tell Franklin," Jux said.

We shuffled out and went back to our rooms. I lay down on my cot and closed my eyes, intending to get up and go to the food hall to make a copy of the copy, so I would have two necklaces. Franklin would probably look at only one of them. But even if he realized I had lied, at least he would see how weak we all were. If anyone was going to help us, it would be him.

A wizard banged on the door.

Gerrard turned, and we ended up looking at each other.

"Did you really do it?" he whispered.

I didn't know what to say so I didn't say anything, I just stood there wishing I had gone straight to the food hall, furious with myself. Now my lie would be obvious, and I had no idea what Franklin would do. I picked up the fake necklace from my desk. Gerrard brought his goblet, and we walked behind the wizard to the food hall. And it wasn't Franklin. It was Somiss. Everyone else was already there.

I stopped and stared at him. Why? Where was Franklin?

I exhaled, my hands clammy. This was it, then. I would die on their terms, not my own. I could only hope that no one else would be hurt because of my lies and stupidity.

"Which one of you is it?" Somiss asked.

"Me," I whispered, and forced myself to take a step forward.

"Go first," he said.

First? He was going to make everyone try? I wanted to help us all, and I had hurt everyone. Again. I looked up at the darkness overhead and struggled not to cry.

"Now!" Somiss shouted.

Everyone jumped.

I walked to stand in front of the stone and glanced at the necklace in my hand, then looked away from it. I might do better if I just tried to remember. I knew where some of the mistakes were, I had memorized most of the scratches, but the clasp was—

"Now!"

I could hear the others lining up. I glanced back and saw Will behind me. I felt sick. There was an odd pressure from the images in my mind. They were crowding each other, jostling, like a hundred people trying to pass through the same door. It was painful. Really painful.

"Go to the end of the line," Somiss rasped. I flinched, but I shut my eyes again and remembered the smell and the feel and the taste of the gold, and was about to add a single image to it, one of the necklace lying flat, the way it would on the pedestal, but I couldn't. Maybe, I thought desperately, if I left my hands on the stone long enough, it would know which image was closest to perfect and use that one. Or would it just burn my hands to the bone?

I heard Somiss say something, then Luke's laugh.

Shaking, I imagined the images like pages in the song book, stacked, lined up, and I hoped the stone could choose one, but the pain only increased. It felt like someone was hammering a nail into my head. No. It was as though the hammer was inside my skull and the nail was about to emerge through the skin between my eyes. I bit my lip and tasted blood and put both hands on the stone and leaned my weight forward so I couldn't flinch if it burned me.

I felt the pressure ease a little as the first image moved into the stone. Then the second image did the same thing, the third, the fourth, and all the rest, quick as leaves in the wind. It was dizzying. The necklace flew past: A mound, a circle, in the bright light of the food hall, in the soft light of my lamp, and all the rest. It only took three or four heart-beats, and nothing happened until the last image flickered from bright to dim. Then there was a sound I had never heard before, a flash of light, and the necklace lay on the pedestal.

Breathing hard, unsteady, I shoved myself upright, turn-ing just as Somiss picked it up. He bounced it on the palm of his hand, staring carefully at the clasp. He turned it over and watched the links moving. I waited, breathing through my mouth.

Somiss finally nodded and dropped it on the floor. Then he pointed to the one I had left on the table, and it was gone too. "Good enough. Go sit down."

I tried to walk to one of the tables, but I was so dizzy after a few steps that I sank to the floor and sat still, breathing in and out. Just that. Breathing. It was all I could do.

"Next."

I heard the stone make its usual wind-through-the-trees sound, then Somiss's voice again.

"No. Go sit down," he said. Then he must have turned and seen me. "You too. Go sit down!"

I tried to get up and couldn't. Then, suddenly, Will was beside me, helping me, hitching my arm around his shoulder, staggering as he walked me to the nearest table. I slid onto the bench and he gripped my shoulder, then went on, sitting at a table even farther from the stone.

My thoughts slowed, and I swallowed the blood in my mouth. I could feel the cut with my tongue. I had bitten out a little chunk of flesh. And I was smiling. Good enough? Somiss had said, *Good enough.*

"No! Next!" I heard him shout.

Then, a single heartbeat later, he repeated it.

Levin walked past me, then Jordan. Neither of them looked at me. It wouldn't have mattered if they had. I was lost in my own disjointed thoughts.

Will had helped.

Me.

He had helped me.

In front of everyone. In front of Somiss.

"No! Next!"

Luke walked past, then Gerrard, then we all sat, scattered over the tables, waiting for Somiss to scream at us, insult us, kill us all. Except maybe me? I looked at Gerrard. He was staring at the far wall. Then I closed my eyes again.

Will, I thought. The pact would begin with Will. Then Levin and Jordan. Gerrard could join us or not. And Luke last, because by then he would be able to see that we had a chance and he wouldn't be so afraid of Somiss.

I opened my eyes. Somiss was gone. No one else had moved yet.

I staggered to the stone and made a lot of simple food. It was all I could manage. Cheese and apples and bread, enough for everyone. I took what I needed and walked out, one heavy step at a time. I didn't look back. And I couldn't stop smiling.

57

Walking into Limòri, Sadima felt suspended between
terror and joy. She felt free, wonderful, almost silly with
happiness. This time, she had not cowered. She had not
run back to the center of South End. She had crossed the
invisible line! But would the fear come back?

She ticked her foot on a cobblestone and stumbled.
Thomas Marsham held out his free hand. "I am steadier
than I look," he said. "And if I am not, we can at least fall
together."

Sadima smiled at him. And in that instant she remembered that she hadn't worn a scarf, had barely washed her
face. Without meaning to, she touched her hair.

"Why do you keep it that short?" he asked her. "It's a
beautiful color."

She felt herself blush and opened her mouth to answer, but nothing came out.

He squeezed her hand gently. "It is, perhaps, none of my business?"

"No, I just . . . ," she began, then stopped again.

He turned to look at a rattling freight wagon coming up behind them and guided her off the cobblestones onto the hard dirt path that ran alongside the street. They walked in silence for five or six blocks, and Sadima was glad not to have to talk. She tried not to stare at everything they passed. The houses were better than anything in South End. There were old oak trees that shaded the path. The gutters were full of leaves, not offal.

There were children in the streets, almost as many as there had been in South End long ago. But they weren't as thin, and she saw some of them playing a game with sticks and pebbles. People here had more coins and more food to give them, she was sure. And they probably found more and better things to steal.

At the next corner, while they waited for a carriage to pass, he leaned close. "My youngest sister spends endless hours with her hair," he said. "I admire a woman who doesn't." Sadima laughed, and he glanced at her. "Fiona will be furious if you ever repeat that."

"I won't," Sadima promised.

He thanked her, smiling, then they fell back into silence for another eight or ten blocks. At the next corner, he lifted his cane to point. "There it is, a perfect example of what is happening in this city. It's a marvel, isn't it? And only half-finished."

Sadima turned to follow his gesture and caught her breath. A stone building, taller than anything she had ever seen in her life, rose in the middle of a grassy square. She took a quick breath.

"Haven't you seen it before?"

She shook her head. And when she turned back, he was looking at her closely. "You are the woman who owns the little cheese shop, yes?"

Sadima nodded.

"And you have never walked twenty blocks past it?"

She shrugged. "I am not from Limòri, and I work every day. . . ." She trailed off, realizing how silly it sounded.

He smiled. "Your Servenian friends told me about your kindness, your generosity. They said you are a living example of Eridian teachings."

Sadima shook her head. "They are the kind ones. They're the best friends I have ever had." And as soon as she said it, she turned away so that he couldn't see the emotion on her face.

"You are a most interesting young woman," he said. "One day, when you know me better, I would love to hear how you came to South End."

"It isn't an especially interesting story, Mr. Marsham," she said, then looked back at the dark stone building and counted the windows. It was seven stories tall. "Do they really mean to make it fourteen floors?"

"Thomas," he said.

She turned to look at him.

"Not Mr. Marsham. Please call me Thomas."

She could feel herself blushing again and nodded, then turned to look back at the building. She saw now that the top floor had gap-toothed edges, but there were no stone setters working on it. "Will people live there?"

He shook his head. "I was joking. King Daniel began it seventy-five years ago—he intended it to be offices for his chancellors so they could work within the city they were to help him govern. When he died, the chancellors murdered his brothers and Limòri was finished with kings." He pointed at the building. "It's shrinking, not growing. Half the houses in Limòri have what is called a king-stone table or a king-stone courtyard bench."

Sadima was astonished. "Why didn't someone finish it?"

Thomas shrugged. "The magistrates they elected back then didn't want a monument to any king in the city. Now? No one cares. It's quaint, and as I said, it's shrinking." He tapped his cane on the ground. "I think magicians have been among Limòri's wealthy for a long time, Mattie," he said. "I think they helped defeat the Ferrinides families who clung to the idea of royalty. A few merchants have become remarkably wealthy. I wonder if they've had help." He reached out and cupped her cheek with one hand. "I apologize. Fiona says I am too serious all the time."

They walked on, talking a little, mostly silent, and Sadima realized she was enjoying herself. Thomas was funny and kind. He pointed out the oldest oak tree in the city—a massive one that shaded three houses—and a tiny grove of peach trees behind a building he said was a theater. She nodded as though she knew what the word meant.

"I have a favor to ask you," he said when they stopped at a corner.

Sadima looked at him.

"I want to start a women's meeting. In addition to the one we are having now on the seventh-day."

She nodded to let him know she was listening, but she knew she would have to make some excuse to keep from having to attend it.

"I want you to consider being the speaker."

Sadima stared at him.

"Let us pass, please?"

Sadima stepped backward to let two girls dressed in silk go by, then met his eyes. "I couldn't possibly do that," she said.

He didn't respond for so long that she felt awkward. Then he said this: "You can't possibly refuse."

Sadima shook her head. "I must. I have too much work every day," she said.

"But Erides is calling you to teach."

She shook her head. "Thomas, no. I wouldn't be any good at it anyway."

"You're wrong about that," he said. "Your heart shines in your eyes. You would be a very good teacher."

She had no idea what to say to make him stop. He was looking into her eyes so intently that she had to look aside. "Fiona says I am far too insistent," he said.

"Fiona is right."

He burst out laughing.

A shout made them both turn and look down the block. Ten or fifteen boys were running toward them, jumping flower beds, racing each other. "There's a magician!" one of them shouted as they sprinted past.

"Where?" Thomas called after them.

"Market Square," the boy yelled over his shoulder. Sadima started to ask Thomas if he wanted to see the magician, but he hooked his arm through hers and followed the crowd, pulling her along. She glanced at him; his face had turned to stone.

— 58 —

We had no classes at all for two days—and the days felt a little longer to me than they had been. I felt shaky for most of that time. I slept and ate and slept and ate again. And every time I made food, I made a lot and left it on the tables, then waited to see if Somiss would come kill me for it. He didn't. Maybe he never would. Or maybe he was about to knock on the door. Or he was gone again and Franklin was with him and neither one of them gave half a shit what any of us did.

Gerrard was stiff and quiet and I knew he was angry at me for making extra food. I didn't care. I was preoccupied with other things. The way the images had poured out of me into the stone made perfect sense now that I wasn't sick, sweating, and weak from hunger. No single image could have worked. It wasn't like the food and the soap and the other things I had made.

I knew what the underside of a piece of roast chicken looked like without a single conscious thought. I had seen hundreds of roasted chickens in bright light and candlelight and sunlight, half-cooked, with gravies, plain, herbed. It was true of soap, too. All the images must have gone into the stone along with the one I was trying so hard to make perfect, without me even being aware of them. Or maybe the stone remembered things. Wizards had made so many dinners for so many centuries that maybe the stone had its own library of roast chicken images to use.

But we had to *memorize* enough accurate images of something we had never seen before in order for the stone to work. It took all the angles, all the different lights, all the shapes, as well as my memories of the smell, taste, feel, weight—every bit of that and probably things I hadn't figured out yet—to make a good copy of something new. And I was sure my copy of the necklace had been good, not *perfect*. Maybe perfect wasn't possible.

I almost explained it to Gerrard. Then I decided not to. Not yet. I wanted to help Will first, for two reasons: Will had helped me, and if he was the next one to tell Jux he had managed a perfect copy, maybe Gerrard would realize that he'd be left out if he didn't agree to involve everyone. I listened to him practicing. He was moving his thoughts and getting better at it, because I had helped him. His help on the songs had kept me alive, and his refusal to continue helping had been a gift. I would repay him.

But for now, we were almost back to where we had been before the stone had turned into mist beneath our feet. One thing had changed. I didn't need his help as much. And for now, he needed me. I knew it wouldn't last. It never had.

I was two songs ahead—which was wonderful, because I felt weak and unsteady for a long time after Somiss's class. Eating helped. I passed the next recitation. So did Will and Jordan and Levin. Luke and Gerrard missed a few words. Not many. Everyone looked a little better. So they had been eating what I had left for them. I was glad.

After class, I waited for Will to leave, then followed him down the passageway. Luke was behind me somewhere, but I refused to turn and look. I walked just fast enough to pass Will a quarter stride at a time, allowing us a long moment to communicate silently. He told me, without speaking, that he could move his thoughts, was getting much better at it. I let him know I was glad for him and whispered, hardly moving my lips, "Meet me later." I touched my belly to tell him where. He gave me a barely visible nod, and two steps later, I was ahead of him.

I stopped at my own chamber and read the history book for a while. The next section was about the Founder and his accomplishments. He had taken ancient magic, apparently, and bent its use to the problems of the city. When the streets were dangerous, he had begun teaching ponies what birds knew. When storms sank ships, he took the old magic of raising storms and reversed it to quell them. He had made inert metal magical, so that water spigots knew that when they had been touched it was a request to open the valves. The Founder had made rain fall only into the lowlands, creating lakes, instead of seasonal floods. And Limòri had grown and prospered.

Reading that reminded me that my mother and her friends were somewhere sipping mint tea, laughing. My school friends were trying to decide whether to work for their fathers or strike out on their own. Ships came and went, and South End still stank of rotting fruit and dead fish and sailors' piss. People died of cold and hunger there. Magic was in all my friends' houses. Their fathers were happy to pay for it. And none of them had any idea what it really cost.

I went out into the corridor and almost stumbled over Gerrard. He was sitting with his back against the wall, the goblet in his hands. He looked up at me, and I saw both confusion and fear in his eyes for an instant before he hid it from me.

"It looks completely different in this light, doesn't it?" I asked him, then walked away, feeling like an asshole, and enjoying it a little. He had always known what was going on before any of the rest of us. How many times had he refused to answer my questions? I would explain it to him soon. Just not first.

Will was waiting for me. We walked down a passageway neither of us had ever been down before. I had no idea if it was safer in any way, but it *felt* safer not to be in a place the wizards would expect us to be. We ended up standing between torches, facing each other, four or five paces apart, but offset so he could keep watch one way and I could see past him in the other direction.

"Do you know where Levin and Jordan's room is?" I asked him, breathing the words so low I was afraid he might not have heard. But he nodded.

"Can you tell them how to do it too?"

He nodded again.

"Making the copy is simple," I whispered. "It isn't one perfect image."

He arched his brows a little as I explained how it felt, the stack of images, the way the stone had seemed to pull them out of me.

"I imagine the songs now," he said. "I can see the pages and turn them. Are the images like that? A stack of pages?"

I nodded. "Memorize a lot of images," I whispered, then I held out one hand palm up, palm down, sideways, vertically, close, at arm's length over my head. "Every angle, bright light, dim light, over, under, every which way. Stack them up, then just touch the stone like you would if you were about to make something."

He gestured a thanks. "Did Jux tell you about imagining the songs?"

"No," I said. "Franklin."

"Jux told me. Are they helping everyone?"

I shrugged. "I don't know."

And for the first time, I wondered if Will had flown, or tried to see inside the wasp's nest. I would have asked him, but I saw him tilt his head, listening—then I heard footsteps. I looked up the passage. A wizard was coming out of a side tunnel. He turned toward us. Will and I both started walking, as though we had simply crossed paths, coming from opposite directions. Will curved his lips and touched the center of his chest to thank me again, no matter what happened next. Then we were past each other.

The wizard was a man I had never seen here, but I knew his face. He had come to my father's house a few times. He nodded, a real, visible nod, as we passed, but he didn't slow his stride or look at me like he recognized me, and he didn't seem to care at all what Will and I had been doing. It unnerved me. I had never seen any wizard here besides the teachers and the silent, empty-eyed men who led us to class. Where did they live?

When I passed the food hall, I turned on an impulse and went in. I wasn't hungry, but I made some fruits—ripe figs and peaches—and put them on the tables nearest the back wall, in case anyone came looking. I was setting down the last peach when Luke walked in. I looked up and nodded at him, then turned to leave.

"Wait," he said.

I didn't really want to talk to him, but I stopped, thinking that if he was going to be part of the pact someday, it would be better if he didn't have one more reason to hate me. He motioned for me to go out into the hall and keep walking; then he followed me, staying five or six paces behind. "If you help me," he whispered, "I can make sure Somiss lets you live."

I shrugged and was glad that he couldn't see my face. Luke might think that Somiss cared about him and would do him a favor, but I was almost certain he was wrong.

"If you don't help me, I'll tell him about you leaving food for everyone to find."

"He must already know," I whispered.

"No," Luke said. "He isn't here most of the time."

"Where's Franklin?"

There was only silence except for his footfalls. Then he said this: "If you don't help me, I'll kill your little friend Will."

"I will help you if I can," I whispered over my shoulder. "But if you hurt Will you will be sorry." My whisper was steady but my gut was tight.

I heard him spit before he answered. "Tomorrow, after they wake us up, meet me in the food hall, or you won't ever see him again."

And before I could think of what to say, he shoved me hard from behind. I fell to one knee as he ran past me. I got up and forced myself not to chase him down. He turned into the next passageway, and I heard his footfalls for a moment, then he was gone. I was shaking with rage. We might all have a chance. We might, but Luke could take it away. And for the first time, I wondered if Gerrard was right. Maybe we would never be able to trust Luke.

Gerrard wasn't in the room when I got back. When he finally opened the door and came in, I could tell that something was wrong. He met my eyes and fumbled with the handle trying to close the door behind him. Then he went straight to his bed and lay down.

"What happened?" I whispered so quietly that I expected him to ignore me, but he put his hands over his ears like a little kid and started rocking.

"Gerrard?"

He lowered his hands and looked at me.

"Wasps?" I whispered, just a little louder.

"I thought I knew," he said. "But it's . . . how did you . . . ?"

I went to sit beside him on his cot. "This is real. I'm real. It'll help if you sleep. And if you wake up, I'll still be here, and I'll tell you what's real and what isn't. I promise."

He started to cry. I helped him get under his blanket, then lay down on my cot and closed my eyes.

Why now? I needed him. Did they know that?

In the middle of the block, Thomas guided her off the path and down a slope between two houses that led to a much narrower path—one with no one else on it. Thomas could not run, but he walked remarkably fast. He cut through yards and knew where there were doors that saved them half a block by walking through buildings instead of around them. Finally he led her into a cobblestone street that ran along the edge of a tree-lined market. She blinked. This had to be Market Square.

There were carts full of vegetables and kiosks selling clothing and racks of leather bags and stalls full of grain bins and linens and everything else in the world. It was much bigger than she had imagined it. And it was full of people. Most of them were running through the kiosks and stalls, shouting.

"In case we are separated," Thomas said, "this is Market Street." Then he pointed with his cane. "That's da Masi Street. If you follow it straight back, you will eventually come to the alley where we met."

Sadima nodded, surprised. "I knew someone named da Masi," she said.

Thomas nodded. "It's common in South End. Remind me to tell you the story." He let go of her arm and led the way beneath fig trees so tall and so old that their limbs formed a ceiling of leaves that stopped the sunlight completely. Thomas was breathing hard, his lurching gait more pronounced on the grass than it had been on the cobblestones. Sadima stayed close, and halfway across the square he took her arm again.

When they got closer, she saw hundreds of people standing in a loose circle, twenty deep or more. It was impossible to see anything. Thomas led her to one side, walking at an angle into the crowd. Instead of trying to get in front of people, he simply walked past them, keeping the angle, spiraling inward, so that by the time they had gone around the circle, there were only five or six people between them and the man in the black robe. They could go no farther. The last few rows were a solid wall of bodies.

Sadima tried to find a place where she could see. Thomas was stretched up to his full height, staring, his face still stony. Sadima rose onto her tiptoes and managed to peer over the shoulder of the man in front of her.

The magician was turned away, talking to someone she couldn't see. Then he stepped back and was hidden behind the onlookers. "My grandma needs your help!" a child's voice rang out. "Please?"

The man in front of Sadima stood taller and leaned, trying to get a better look, and blocked her view completely. Then someone pushed him, and he lurched to one side to keep from falling. In the instant before he stood straight again, Sadima saw the old woman, bent almost double, pain narrowing her eyes, and the magician with his arm extended, his hand on her head.

"If I help her," Sadima heard the magician shout, "will you watch for the magistrate's guards?"

The crowd roared back at him, shouting, jostling. Sadima dragged in deep, quick breaths, fighting a strangling tightness in her chest and throat. If the magician who had left her in South End had done to himself what he had done to her, this could be him, he could still be alive. Desperate to see, she knelt and saw the magician's bare feet, through the forest of legs, his robe hem swinging as he turned. The crowd shifted and the glimpse was gone. She staggered up and felt Thomas's hand on her waist as she found her balance.

Sadima could hear the magician talking, but she could understand only a word here and there. His voice was so low and rough that it didn't carry far. Was he healing the woman? Could he? She glanced at Thomas. His face was full of hatred, full of murder. Sadima could feel his rage boiling in her own stomach. No, not just his. It was coming from every direction and from inside her, too. Even if this magician healed the old woman, it was just a way to seduce people into believing that magic was good. It wasn't.

Sadima clenched her fists. A magician had left her to starve, to die—or to live so long that life would become a misery. Whoever he was, whatever his reason had been, what he had done was despicable.

Sadima realized Thomas was watching her.

"It is right to hate them." He reached out and touched her cheek.

"You must be quiet!" the magician roared. The jumble of voices stopped, instantly and completely.

In the sudden silence, everyone who could not see tried to inch forward. Sadima braced herself against the woman behind her and tried not to bump up against the man in front of her. Thomas put his arm around her shoulders and pulled her in front of him, her back against his chest.

There was a sudden gasp, then a tangle of low voices from the people closest to the center. Sadima saw them turning to look at each other, their faces full of wonder.

"He did it!" a man shouted, turning halfway around. "Her back is straight. He did it! She says the pain is gone."

"Erides hated magic!" a man shouted.

A few people cheered.

"Be quiet!" a woman yelled.

"She forbade us to learn or use it!" the man shouted. "Erides was wise!"

"She didn't forbid *me*," another woman yelled, and the crowd laughed.

"Yes, she did!" someone called out. A few people echoed the shout, and a ragged rhythm began, a three-word chant that got louder and louder. Then a woman's scream from the center of the circle made them all falter and stop.

"He's gone!" she shrieked. "I wanted help for my baby and now he's gone!"

Her sobs grated at Sadima's anger, sharpening it. Of course the woman with the baby would feel cheated, furious. Whatever her child suffered after this day would seem worse. The old woman would feel guilty that she had been healed while a baby had not been. This was what Erides had said. It was what Thomas said. Magic could never be fair, and it came at a terrible price, always. Her own long, hollow life was perfect proof.

The voices around her rose again. Sadima heard one man demanding to know how the magician could be gone, but she couldn't hear anyone answer him—if anyone did. Women began to argue and weep, and a shoving match started between two men in the front row. Thomas put his left arm around Sadima and held her close.

"Guards coming!" someone yelled, and people began to run in every direction. Thomas grabbed Sadima's wrist and held her still for a moment. Then, when most of the crowd had scattered, he offered her his arm and she took it. "Smile," he said. "Laugh."

Then he began to walk, leaning toward her and laughing as though she had just said something funny. He tipped his head and spoke in a low voice. "Pretend we are good friends. Don't look around, just at me. And pretend I am amusing. Laugh."

Sadima heard hoofbeats and managed a small laugh.

"Louder," he said, smiling at her.

Sadima laughed again, much louder this time. Thomas smiled wider. The rage was still in his eyes as the hoofbeats came a little closer. Sadima knew the horse was a mare and that she was uneasy. She hated to have so many people around her—she didn't trust them.

Sadima wondered what Thomas would think of her if he knew she had lived nearly four lifetimes already, she could almost talk to animals, and she had run away from home to be with a magician. She glanced up at him.

"You are a beauty," he whispered. "And very brave. The perfect follower of Erides." He spoke close to her ear. "Just stay calm and we will be fine."

She smiled, and it came without trying. She liked Thomas Marsham and the way she felt around him. The rest didn't matter. There was no reason to tell him her secrets.

"Have you seen a magician here today?" the guard called.

"Tell him no," Thomas whispered. "Tell him we just got here."

"No, we haven't," Sadima called out, turning to face the man on the uneasy mare as he reined in. "But we just walked in off da Masi Street."

The rider nodded curtly and called out the same question to two young men leaning against one of the huge tree trunks, talking as though nothing had happened here.

"I wonder why the guards are wearing red tunics," Thomas said as the man rode off. Then he looked at Sadima. "They have always worn blue. Maybe the magistrates are splitting into factions?"

Sadima had no idea what to say. She only hoped that what was happening in Limòri would leave South End alone. Things were better now than they had ever been, in all her lifetimes there.

"Mattie Han, you are a joy," Thomas said.

She smiled at him.

"Erides is calling you. I only hope you will listen," he said.

And then he kissed her. Lightly. On her cheek. His lips were warm and his breath was sweet. She nodded. "All right. I will be the speaker."

"Can we keep this secret for a while?" he asked. "I want to tell everyone, all at once, next meeting."

"Yes," she said, and he kissed her hands.

— 60 —

Gerrard woke up over and over. I left one lamp burning so that every time he opened his eyes, he could see where he was, could see that I was there if he needed me. For a long time, I reminded him about the wasps and then just listened. It was strange to hear him talk so much. Mostly he described being inside the wasp's nest and how he had felt so safe, so perfect when he was there. Just hearing it woke my longing for certainty.

"Now that you can move your thoughts," I said softly, "you can—"

"I didn't," he interrupted me, whispering. "Neither did you. Not with the wasps. When you opened your first gate, trying to push your thoughts out toward them, theirs came *in*."

I exhaled. That was exactly what it had felt like. Why was it so different from the hummingbirds and the snake?

"Hives," Gerrard said. So he *could* hear my thoughts? "Hive creatures are one big mind. They don't even notice whatever you are thinking because they can only hear the majority. Is there a bear?"

"In here?"

He nodded. "By the tree."

"No," I told him. "And there's no tree. It's just you and me. We're lying on our cots, here in our chamber." I turned my head so I could see him. His face was half-lit by the lamp on my desk. He looked exhausted. "No bears," I said.

He nodded and closed his eyes.

I took four or five long breaths. It made perfect sense. With the wasps, my thought-voice had been one in thousands, drowned out by the perfect agreement of all the others. That's why I had gotten lost and why Gerrard was so confused now. Every one of Jux's first-year classes proved the point. The hummingbirds had listened to me. So had the snake. But the ants hadn't. Not until I put my thoughts in the honey, and then they had warned each other. Nests, hives, colonies of any kind must be that way.

"It's more complicated than that," Gerrard whispered without opening his eyes. "But not much more."

Was I pushing my thoughts into his mind? Or was he just lying there with his first gate still so wide open so that he could hear them?

"Both," he said.

Then we were quiet for a long time. "How do you know all this?" I finally asked him.

He shook his head. "Can't tell." He stood up and paced to the door and opened it, then closed it again before I could react.

"Are you afraid someone's listening?"

He nodded and got back into bed.

I lay still, thinking about everything I had seen after I had been inside the wasp's nest: Somiss and Franklin in the food hall, laughing together, the woman, the weird light, my father, Franklin bending over me saying that I had to learn what the songs were for.

"We could," Gerrard said. "But it's dangerous."

"Do you understand the language?" I asked him, but he ignored me and rolled over.

I lay awake, trying to figure out if I had put my thoughts into the hawk's mind, or if I had just experienced what she was thinking and feeling because her thoughts were coming into me. I remembered looking down at the city, the air rushing past. I had not felt lost, and except for the first few moments, I had not felt like I was in Sadie's body. I was almost sure I had been in my own. "Did you fly?" I whispered.

Gerrard turned onto his back. "No. Jux put me in an enclosure with a lion that day. A stupid lion, an old, sleepy one. He wanted to make me worry that you were getting way ahead of me. Sometimes he helps Somiss."

"Helps Somiss?" I echoed. Then, for an instant, I wondered if it was true, if I really was ahead of Gerrard. I caught myself and was ashamed.

"We all think like that," he said.

I sat up. "Why do they do all this?"

He stretched, and I could hear him breathing a pattern I didn't know for a long time before he spoke again. When he did, his voice was steadier. "To win. But there's never just one reason. Jux hoped I would pretend I had flown to worry you. Or that you would assume I was lying if I told the truth. But he didn't let me fly, so I would still hate you for getting ahead of me, no matter what else happened." He paused, then I heard him sigh. "It's like that shit when Franklin says he's been waiting for you. He tells that to almost everyone."

I held very still. During our first year, I thought Franklin had meant it. It had helped keep me alive. Gerrard's breathing deepened and slowed. I wanted to ask him more questions, but I knew how fragile he was.

I dozed until I heard him at the basin, drinking water in big gulps. "It's so hot I'm dizzy," he said, staring at me when he turned and saw that I was awake. "I have sand in my teeth."

"You aren't in a desert," I said quietly.

He looked puzzled. "No?"

"No," I assured him. "But that's really water, and it won't hurt you to drink as much as you want."

He thanked me and turned back to the basin. I stared upward into the darkness the lamplight couldn't reach and hoped that Jux had not hurt him. I barely slept, and told him again and again what was real and what wasn't. I led him back to reality each time, hoping that by morning, he'd be able to stay.

When Gerrard slept, I tried to decide what to do about

Luke. If he had threatened me, I could have ignored it, or I could have told him I knew about Somiss and promised not to tell anyone else if he joined us. But he hadn't threatened me. And I wasn't at all sure that everyone else would agree to a pact anyway.

It took me all night, in fits and starts, but I finally came up with a plan I thought might work, without anyone getting hurt. At least for now. I woke up early and washed up quietly, then waited.

Gerrard was more or less making sense by the time a wizard pounded on the door. I shouted that we were awake and the pounding stopped. I was relieved. I had no time for classes today. Gerrard was staring at the stone wall, his head tipped to one side.

"Are you hearing something?"' I asked him.

He nodded.

"A humming sound, like inside the wasp's nest?"

"Yes. It's beautiful."

"It's in the stone," I told him. "It gets dimmer and dimmer. But it never goes away."

He looked back at me. "Good."

"If we all help each other, we can learn faster," I said. "We could hide that we're doing it."

He was shaking his head before I was halfway through. "Someone will betray us," he said.

"Not me," I whispered. "Not you, not Will, and not Levin. I don't know Jordan that well. I don't think he would either. Levin will know for sure. We are all going to die the way it is now."

"Maybe not you," Gerrard said.

I had been ready to keep arguing, but that stopped me. I shook my head. "I have been lucky, and some of this is easy for me. But who knows what they will expect us to do next?"

"Disappear," he said evenly. "Then most of us will have to . . ." He trailed off, shaking his head. Then he rubbed his hands over his face, and I heard his stomach growling.

"You need food," I said.

He looked up at the ceiling, then back at me. "I do. Yes."

"Will you be part of this? Of all of us helping each other?"

He looked past me, and I wondered if he was seeing bears again, if he was understanding me, if he could even find his way to Will's room. He finally exhaled and nodded. "But you have to promise. We will kill all the wizards. Not one left alive when we are done."

"The ones who lead us to class are—"

"You don't know what they are," he interrupted.

"How many are there?" I whispered.

"Ones who can fight back?"

I nodded.

"Fewer than you think. But they all have to die."

What I saw in his eyes scared me, and I tried to hide my reaction. I explained my plan, such as it was. He stopped me twice and we changed things a little, but mostly he agreed. When I was finished, he nodded and recited the turns to Will's room. "Memorize them if you haven't," he said. I recited them back, but he wasn't looking at me. His eyes were crawling up the wall, then down again. I waited until he looked back at me. He was listening to the thrumming, I could tell.

"Yes," he said. "I am. But I can hear you."

"Luke will do better. He feels shut out now because—"

"He's lazy and stupid?" Gerrard interrupted. Then, without warning, he came close, clamping his hand on my throat, just below my jaw. He squeezed a little and I jerked free. "You can kill anyone like that," he said. "Be quick. Dig your fingers in and bring your knee up at the same time, sudden and hard, then don't let go when they fall—not until they are limp."

I stared at him.

"I learned that when I was five years old," he said. "It took both hands the first time."

I stared at him, wondering if he was making it up to see if I would believe it. If he could hear my thoughts, he didn't answer.

"Are you sure you can do this now?" I asked him.

He recited the turns to Will's room once more. Then he nodded. "My part is easy. You're the one they will want to kill if this falls apart." He smiled at me and left.

I stood there long enough to be sure that Luke wouldn't see us leaving close together in case he was watching, and a little longer to stop shaking. Then I started for the food hall.

At the next meeting, Thomas began by asking how
many had heard about a man in a black robe running from
the guards, laughing. Sadima and her friends all raised their
hands. "We saw him," Faith called out, and many other
voices echoed her.

Thomas nodded and waited for the noise to subside. His
chair this time was made of a light blond wood, carved into
patterns like the veins in a wasp's wing. "Erides said that one
day we would have our own lands," he said. "How many
know that prophecy?" Almost every hand went up. "Now,
I am no defender of kings," Thomas said. "Even the kind-
est kings were bad. The cruel ones were monstrous. Weak
ones invited the selfish influence of chancellors, sycophants,
seductive or disloyal servants, wealthy merchants, their

cousins' cousins—anyone who could catch their eyes and ears. But hear me: The magistrates are no better."

Thomas stood up and walked to the front of the stage. Sadima winced at how slowly he moved. His limp seemed worse. Had he hurt himself hurrying to Market Square?

"The Marsham family has almost as many stories as the Eridians do," Thomas said. "Because I could not play with other children, I learned them all from my grandfather and great-grandfather. They taught me that almost every line of kings begins with one man. He raises an army from hungry, angry, desperate people and kills all his rivals. It is nearly always that simple. This was true of the Ferrinides dynasty. They ruled Limòri and all the lands around it until five generations of weak and stupid kings ended their reign. Daniel was the last to wear the crown." Thomas paused, then peered at his listeners. "Do you know how many of our current Limòri magistrates are Ferrinides?"

There was a murmur in the crowd, but no one answered. "More than half," Thomas said. "Seven of the twelve. And I am told that two of them are studying magic using their hidden libraries, and that they have been buying magic for nearly a generation from magicians who have come to their homes dressed like any businessman. The rest of us are just now seeing these magicians as they finally don their black robes." He shook his head. "But they have been among us for many years, making friends. Wealthy friends. Powerful friends. How many of you can read?"

Not a single hand went up except his own. Thomas leaned forward. "Under every Ferrinides king, all the way back to their defeat of the da Masi kings, knowledge was not shared. It was hoarded. There was a time when anyone without royal blood was hanged for learning to read. Now the schools are so expensive commoners can't pay the price. The result is the same. Only the children of the wealthy learn to read."

Thomas walked heavily to the far side of the stage, and Sadima saw heads turn in slow unison to follow him. He was leaning hard on his cane. "Magicians could destroy the city and everyone in it," he said, and snapped his fingers. "A single storm, a generation of drought, fire, lightning, flood, sickness, famine. All the things they can prevent, they can cause."

Most of the people in the room nodded.

"Our magistrates know this," he said. "They have built up the force of the guard lately. Have you noticed the red tunics? I have not found anyone who can explain to me why they have chosen this color, who is paying for the new uniforms . . . but I can tell you this: If the magicians promise to let the magistrates keep their beautiful houses and their gold coins, the guards will stop chasing the magicians. I think the Ferrinides magistrates are behind these new red-tunic guards. They are showing the magicians their power."

He rammed his cane against the planks of the stage and everyone jumped. "We could be the generation to become what Erides taught us to be," he said. "Free people with our own lands. Without royalty, without Ferrinides noblemen calling themselves chancellors or magistrates, to rule us. We could kill magic once and for all. We could share the work, the food, the knowledge, and the land, and force the lazy heirs of kings and wealthy merchants to do the same."

The people burst into cheers, some of the men raising a fist over their heads. The cheers became a roar. Sadima shouted with them. Thomas finally walked back to his chair and sat down. Only then did the shouts thin and soften, and finally stop. "Free," Thomas said, "governed only by Eridian teachings. Imagine it."

No one made a sound. No one moved. Sadima closed her eyes. Magic was exactly what Erides had described: amazing and beautiful, and dangerous beyond words.

"Will you come up here, Mattie?"

Her eyes flew open, and she saw Thomas beckoning her from the front of the stage. She felt her heart speed up as he lifted his voice. "Mattie and I saw a magician a few days ago."

People turned, looking for her. Startled, blushing, Sadima shook her head, but Sistra nudged her from behind. When she took only one step, Faith took her hand and pulled her forward.

There was a little laughter, but it was warm, not unkind. Sadima saw people smiling, encouraging her. She could feel it. They all understood. None of them would want to climb up on the stage either, but they were hoping she would, because they were all curious about the magician. Sadima let go of Faith's hand and managed to walk forward, each step a little longer than the one before it. Thomas helped her up the steps, and she was careful not to pull him off balance.

"Mattie and I met by chance on Market Street and went walking in Limòri," Thomas said, facing her for the first three or four words, then looking at the crowd again. "Some boys ran past us, and one of them yelled that there was a magician in Market Square. So we went to see if it was true." He paused to look at Sadima again. "And it was."

Another round of murmuring rose. Sadima took a deep breath. They would all remember her face. It would be a generation or two, or three, before she could be invisible in South End again.

"There were at least two hundred people, running in from all directions," Thomas said. "By the time we got there, they had made a circle around a man in a black robe." He smiled at Sadima. "I am taller than our Miss Mattie, and I probably saw a little more. But I would like her to tell you what she saw and heard first."

He made a gesture, and Sadima felt her mouth go dry.

"We all walked here together today," Faith called out from where she stood. "I can't believe you didn't tell us, Mattie!"

People laughed, and Sadima felt the warmth again. "Thomas asked me not to," she said.

"I did," he told everyone. "Erides always asked people to save their stories for the meeting. We are a family, a big family. And this is our house." He stepped back and sat down again, leaving Sadima alone at the front of the stage.

She swallowed and took a deep breath. "I couldn't see much—I tried, but there were too many people standing in front of me." She paused and turned to look at Thomas.

"Tell it from the beginning," he said, so quietly no one else would be able to hear. "Like a story, so everyone can see what we did."

Sadima started over, with the boys who had raced past them. She described how almost everyone in the street had reacted the same way, running to follow. She told them about some of Thomas's shortcuts and the river of people pouring across the square, how the circle was already formed when they got there.

"It was almost impossible to see the magician from where we stood," she said, "and Thomas managed to get us fairly close." She described the glimpses she had caught. "There were Eridians there," she went on. "They shouted out, reminding everyone that magic was forbidden." She shook her head. "Some people mocked them, but they were proven right."

As she spoke, telling everyone exactly what she had seen and heard, Sadima realized that she *liked* telling the story, having the people looking at her as she spoke. And when she described the healing—and the bitter woman whose child was not helped—she paused while they looked at each other, then back at her. "And then he was gone, in an eyeblink," she said. "I didn't see him disappear, but he either used magic, or he somehow slipped into the crowd and had everyday clothes under his robe, or—"

"It was magic," Thomas interrupted her quietly. "I could see his shoulders, his head. He was there, and then he wasn't—just that quick."

"Did you see the woman get healed, Thomas?" a man

called out from the back of the room. Thomas nodded. "Just barely, but yes, in glimpses, like Mattie's. She was very old and she was bent in half, crippled with knotted joints like a lot of old women. The magician whispered something, and he touched her like this." Thomas stood and came to lay his hand on Sadima's head. Then he stepped back and sat down again. It was clear his leg was causing him pain. "The woman stood up straight, smiling," he said. "It was astounding. Then someone called out that the guards were coming, and the magician disappeared."

"My grandfather is bent like that," a man near the front said. No one else spoke up, but there was a murmur across the room.

Thomas hit the stage floor with his cane again. Sadima watched him struggle to his feet. "You must not long for magic," he said, very quietly. "I understand the temptation, perhaps better than many of you do." He shook his head, and there was sorrow in his eyes. "Magicians do not really heal. They close one wound and open ten. Imagine that old woman's lifelong friends who are also in pain from age. They will try to be glad for her. They will try hard."

Sadima watched Thomas let that sink in before he swept one hand into the air and went on. "And the child who was left to his illness? His mother will be bitter now and forever. Imagine her thoughts. What if she had asked first? What if the Eridians hadn't started shouting? Would the magician have stayed and healed her child if the guards hadn't come? She will wonder and she will hate us, herself, the guards, the magicians, her brothers and sisters, her husband, and anyone who questions her right to the hatred that will now poison everyone close to her." Thomas paused again, then lifted his head. "Who knows the story about Erides disappearing?"

Almost everyone raised a hand. Sadima knew it too. Sistra had told it, beautifully, at one of their meetings. She turned to Thomas. "Sistra tells it well."

He smiled at her, then looked up, scanning the crowd. "Sistra?"

It took more nudging from Faith, but once Sistra began speaking, the silence was immediate and deep. Sadima listened, as entranced as all the others. Erides had walked through walls, in front of many people. She had stood in bright sunlight in open fields and simply disappeared, too, to prove that she could do it.

As Sistra spoke, Sadima found herself wishing that Karo could be right, that magic could be learned and used for those with great need. Used fairly, kindly. She watched Thomas and wondered how he remained committed to the Eridian principles. Surely he would rather walk on two good legs. He was such a strong-willed man, such a brave one. He met her eyes and smiled, and she blushed a little, turning quickly to hide it.

That night Sadima lay down on her bed and thought about Thomas, the almost weightless touch of his hand on her head when he was telling what he had seen, the fierce sincerity in his eyes and his heart. Maybe one day she could tell him her own story.

She turned over, jerking at her bedclothes. What had

been done to her had caused her so much pain and would cause more, she was sure. Thomas would probably hate her for having been involved with a magician so long ago, and for her long, strange life. Or would he? Charlie hadn't.

Sadima sat up and put her feet on the floor. Thomas would notice eventually. If she wasn't going to disappear, she would have to tell him. She might manage to fool her friends a while longer if she used the kohl, wore long, loose clothes, and taught herself to walk slower, imitating the onset of age. But she would never be able to fool a man who slept beside her, a man who touched her.

Sadima sighed. It was silly to think about Thomas like this. If the Eridian meetings were a family, he was the father. She knew he liked her. But he liked everyone at the meetings. Any unmarried woman there—and probably some of the married ones—would be glad to have his attention.

Sadima looked upward, into the darkness that hid the ceiling. She had worked so long and so hard at being invisible, at learning to be alone. Now she wanted to love someone again. She wanted to be loved. Without meaning to, she imagined herself holding a baby.

Unsettled, she got up and lit her lamp, then carried it into the room she used for painting. It was black outside the window, and her lamp could not light her easel enough to see the colors. But she drew on the canvas with a stick of charcoal, sketching what she would paint later. It was a portrait of Thomas. She was amazed at how easily she could picture the angle of his shoulders, the shape of his eyes, his hands, the curve of his mouth.

— 62 —

Luke was waiting for me. He was pacing back and forth in front of the stone. I stood just inside the door until he noticed me. When he did, he came toward me, walking fast, an ugly look on his face. I thought about what Gerrard had showed me and felt a wild urge to sink my talons in his flesh. The feeling came and went like a gust of wind, but it made me shiver.

Luke saw it. "Are you sick?"

I stared at his throat, wondering if I could do it. "Stay back," I said. My heart was pounding, and my voice cracked from angry to scared. I cleared my throat. "You aren't going to hurt Will, or anyone else."

"It's up to you," Luke whispered. "If you help me, he'll be fine. If you don't, he won't." When I didn't answer him,

Luke flexed his arms and lifted his shoulders. "Did you figure out a way to kill me?" He spoke the last few words in a singsong voice.

"I didn't have to," I said evenly. "Gerrard showed me how. He will be here soon." I refused to glance at the entrance, but I was listening, hoping Gerrard would hurry, that he hadn't gotten lost in a daydream along the way. Or changed his mind.

Luke laughed. "Liar. That bastard wouldn't help anyone do anything."

"I think we should all help each other," I whispered.

Luke's mouth opened, and he stared at me. "What?"

"If we help each other, maybe no one else has to die."

"That's stupid," he whispered. "Somiss will find out and—"

"Not if you don't tell him," I cut him off. And I looked into his eyes and watched his anger turn into fear, then back.

"No one will have to tell him," Luke said, looking past me at the far wall. "He knows everything."

I didn't answer him. Luke would hate me if he knew what I had seen, no matter how much I despised Somiss for it. Gerrard was right. Hate was complicated.

"I don't want to die here," I said.

Luke's shoulders went up a notch, but his eyes were shiny. He didn't speak.

"We can destroy this place," I breathed. "Kill them all."

The change in his eyes was immediate and astonishing, and I knew his anger had found a place to live. Mine too. I wanted to hate the people who had earned it. "Think about it," I whispered. "All of them dead. Gone."

He looked away, but I saw his hands tighten.

"And then we take the magic out of this place and give it to everyone," I said. "The magistrates and our fathers and every skinny orphan in South End. Everyone."

"Give it away?" he whispered, looking back at me.

I took a step toward him, glanced around, then took another step. "We will be heroes, Luke. They'll have a procession, like the old kings, with people cheering when we go by."

"My father would be proud of that," he said in a voice so low I could barely hear him.

"Mine too," I whispered, feeling soiled. I wanted all this to be true, but I knew I was probably lying. I did it anyway. I had to. I noticed the sound of the stone thrumming and realized I had been silent too long. Luke was looking at me. "I'm sorry if my father cheated yours," I said. "I know he can be an asshole."

Luke nodded at me, then leaned in so close that I found myself squaring up on the balls of my feet and looking at his throat. "So you and Gerrard would teach the rest of us—"

"No," I interrupted him, keeping my voice as low as his had been. "Whoever figures things out first shows the rest. But we have to hide it. Sometimes we'll have to starve for a while to keep the wizards from getting suspicious. We can take turns pretending to fail."

Luke nodded, his brow wrinkled in thought, and I

watched him piecing together what I had said. I hoped that his memory was quicker than his thoughts. Gerrard had said nothing was ever simple with the wizards. So maybe they had chosen Luke for other reasons. There was the obvious one, if Somiss had been involved, but I was sure it was more complex than that.

Luke was tall and broad shouldered, a bully, angry—and his father hated mine. He had played a big part in keeping all of us off balance. I looked up to find him staring at me.

"Everyone helps everyone?"

I nodded, using a tiny gesture from habit, then I realized that he hadn't seen it. I nodded again, more deeply. "We will make a pact. Can we trust you, Luke? I have to know that."

"Somiss talks to me sometimes," he said. "If you let me be part of the pact, I can find things out. I could tell you what he says."

"Give me your word you won't tell Somiss about this, or anything else we do. No matter what happens."

"I promise," he said solemnly.

I put out my hand.

Luke just looked at it for a long moment before he finally clasped it. "I get to kill Somiss," he whispered.

I had been ready to promise him anything just to get him to be part of the pact and uphold it, but I had lied enough. "I think everyone might want to help," I breathed. "And it might take all of us, even once we've learned all the magic. And we have to do that first, Luke. It could take years."

He smiled, and I knew he hadn't heard the last part. "You five can hold him down," he whispered. "I have been trying to make a knife. The stone makes a different noise."

"Don't try anymore," I said. "Maybe Somiss can tell what we make."

He nodded, his eyes wide. He had never thought of that.

And at that moment, I heard footsteps. Gerrard and the others came in, one at a time—they had spread out in the passageway so that if any of the wizards were walking the corridor, they wouldn't be as likely to notice or follow. "I wanted everyone to agree, all together," I whispered to Luke. Then I spoke my hope again, even though I knew it was probably impossible. "We have to be loyal, like brothers, if it is going to work." He nodded solemnly.

Gerrard's eyes were still wild, and I was glad when Jordan went to stand by him. I had thought of twenty or thirty reasons to give them for forming a pact, but I had barely started when they all began to whisper. They were all as scared and angry as I was.

"I think something is going on in the city," I said. "It feels like the wizards don't have time for us, like they are making us go too fast. Does it seem like that to anyone else?"

"How could we know?" Levin whispered. "Maybe it's always like this."

I glanced at Gerrard, hoping he would say something, but he was staring at his left foot. I had no idea how he had managed to get everyone here, as distracted as he was, and I was grateful enough for that.

I looked back at Levin. "It just seems too fast, like they

don't care if we all die. And no one can really keep up with everything."

Levin shrugged. "I don't think they ever cared."

"Franklin did," Gerrard said, looking up. "But he's a coward."

"We can be the last class," I whispered. "We can be heroes if we learn the magic, then—"

"We can give magic away to everyone in Limòri," Luke interrupted.

"But we will have to kill them all first," Gerrard said.

No one spoke. Jordan walked to the entrance, went out, looked both ways, then came back. "I agree. You have my word."

Will nodded. "Me too."

They all agreed; Gerrard hesitated, then nodded.

"Thank you," I said. Then I told them the truth. "When they pound on the door, this has been my reason to wake up, my reason to stay alive." I looked into their faces and knew they all understood.

And that was it. Levin put out his hand, and I covered it with mine, then the others came forward to huddle like street boys playing a game of Soldiers and Kings.

"No lies, no cowardice, no betrayals," I said, and was amazed when Will began to repeat my words slowly and carefully, and they all joined in, speaking together.

We left, one at a time, careful not to walk too close. I stayed behind Gerrard, making sure he didn't turn the wrong way or get scared at whatever he was seeing.

63

At the next seventh-day meeting, there were so many
people that there was barely room to stand. Thomas sat on
a chair with carved wooden snakes that looked far too real.
Sadima hadn't seen him since the last meeting, and she was
startled into blushing when he asked her to join him on the
stage again.

"Mattie is holding meetings for her neighbors, something Erides encouraged all of us to do," he said as she
came up the steps and stood beside him. Then he looked at
her. "How did you get started?"

Sistra was smiling at her from the audience, and Faith
and Karo were hushing everyone around them. Sadima
did what Thomas had told her to do the last time. She
started at the beginning and tried to make people feel as

though they had been in the little apartment above the cheese shop, hearing her language lessons; then she told about the meetings, the translations, the shared sorrow and laughter.

"And did you learn to speak our tongue?" a tall woman asked in Servenian.

"Yes," Sadima said. "And others." She repeated Erides's famous words about sharing in four languages, and the meeting room rang with laughter and cheers.

Sistra cupped her hands around her mouth. "I am proud to be her sister!" she shouted in her perfect Ferrinides, then again in Servenian. Mary, Sharee, and Karo called out, and some of the others, too, in different tongues. The laughter in the room was so warm, so kind. Sadima felt herself smiling, a wide, easy smile that felt both foreign and wonderful on her lips.

She glanced at Thomas. He was clearly pleased. She started to go back to her place in the crowd, but he stepped forward and put his arm through hers. "And I am proud to be Mattie's friend." He turned to her. "How old were you when you first heard the name of Erides?"

Startled, Sadima could only stare at him. She had heard the name from the herb seller. But how long ago had that been? A hundred and fifty years? More? There were no herb sellers in the alleys now and hadn't been for a long, long time. Thomas met her eyes, then lifted his cane and jabbed it at the ceiling. "I envy the ones who learn about Erides when they are so young that they can't remember the first time."

Sadima looked at him, grateful, hoping he would never ask her why she had hesitated. "Where did you come from, Mattie Han?" someone called out. "Are you a child of Limòri?"

"A farm near Ferne," she said, as firmly and clearly as she could. "My mother died birthing me, and my father became stern and unkind." She paused, as Thomas so often did. "So I ran away to Limòri." It was true, from what Micah had told her, and it *felt* true as she said it. True and sad.

There was a soft sound as people exhaled, sharing her sorrow. She felt a weight deep in her belly dissolving. She hadn't known it was there until it eased. These people cared about her. And she cared about all of them.

"My mother was very cruel," a woman in the back of the hall said. "I ran from home too, back in Servenia. It is a hard way to begin a life."

Four or five more people spoke out, saying their parents had been neglectful or unkind or worse. To each one, Sadima said she would carry as much of their sorrow as she could. She meant it with all her heart.

"Erides was unselfish," Thomas said. "We who follow her must try to be. How many of you know the story about unburdening?"

Almost everyone raised a hand. Sadima had never heard the story—it hadn't ever been told in the meetings above the cheese shop.

"How many of you have done it?" Four hands stayed up. Only four.

A few people laughed uneasily. Thomas nodded, smiling.

"Nor have I." He lifted his cane again, waggling it at the crowd. "The unburdening story is simple and short. Erides chose a friend and asked her to listen. Then Erides talked honestly about her own failures, her vices, her petty angers, her shameful secrets, her lies, her meanness, all the things we usually hide. She told her friend everything, everything, everything. And she said she felt free afterward, as though she had laid down a burden."

He twirled his cane and smiled at the audience. "I know some of you have never been here before. But many of you have become a family. And the family knows what I am going to ask of them. Don't you?"

There was another round of laughter.

"Before next meeting," Thomas said, "please, each one of you, tell your whole truth, without pride or shame, to at least one person you can trust." He walked from one side of the stage to the other, his eyes brushing across a hundred faces before he spoke again. "Leave nothing out. Add nothing false. It is a sacred act, Erides said." He paused. "Sacred. It's an old word, from long ago and all too near. It means doing something that lifts us beyond ourselves." He was silent for a moment, then spoke again in a somber voice. "Listeners, remember. The story belongs to the teller. Do not judge or advise, and never repeat any of what you hear."

People looked at each other, then away. There was tension in the room, something Sadima had never felt before at the meetings. She was angry at Thomas for causing it, then realized how many people shared her fear. She could imagine the beauty of unburdening; she just couldn't do it.

"We must all consider this," Thomas was saying. "If we are to become the kind of family that Erides believed we could, we must follow in her footsteps. I am going to unburden myself. Who will join me?"

"I will!" a woman shouted. Immediately thirty or forty other voices rang out.

"These are our leaders," Thomas said. "Will you have the courage to follow them?"

A second round of voices was louder and lower—the men were responding now.

Thomas asked everyone with the courage to tell the truth about themselves to sing a song with him—it was the one the women had sung at the cheese shop on Erides's birthday. Sadima listened to the voices get stronger as the song went on, saw joy come into the eyes of the singers.

"Mattie?"

It was Thomas, speaking from his perch on the edge of his chair. "Will you say a few words to end our meeting today?"

She was startled out of her thoughts and blushed, knowing that she was a liar, the least worthy to say even one word. But Thomas smiled and winked and made a small gesture that included everyone in the meeting. She understood. He wanted her to make people feel even more like a family, if she could.

"The first day I met Sistra," Sadima began, "she asked about my family, and I told her they were all gone. Sistra was a girl then, with terrible sorrows of her own, and she still promised to carry as much of mine as she could. She has kept her word. All the women who come to our meetings have become my sisters."

She glanced at Thomas; he was watching her closely, a little smile touching his mouth. "I will find out who has time and heart to listen to me," she heard herself saying. Was she lying to please Thomas?

"Come back in seven days," Thomas said. "Come back to your family." He paused, then said one more word. "Unburdened."

Sadima had been watching him, but when he looked at her as he spoke the last word, her heart fluttered.

That evening she sat before her easel a long time, then drew a picture of Charlie. "I will never love anyone the way I loved you," she said as she worked. "But I want a family, Charlie. I want a baby. I want my life to mean something." And before she went to bed, she opened the trunk that held the silk bedcovers from so long ago and pressed the fragile fabric against her body for a long time. Then she put them away, her decision made.

Three days later she walked to the alleyway. This time she went straight down it, walking fast, and across the street with only a hitch in her stride when the fear hit. It hit her hard, but she knew it would subside, and it did, faster than she had dared to hope.

Sadima followed the path, watching other women who passed her, examining their clothing. She hoped to make Thomas see her differently than he saw the rest of his

Eridian sisters. She wanted him to hear her story and she wanted to hear his.

A few blocks on, she saw a woman in a blue-green dress made of silk. It flowed with her stride, making every movement graceful. Sadima took a deep breath and waited until the woman glanced at her. "May I ask you where you bought your dress?"

The shop was on the far side of Market Square, with a lettered sign because it catered mostly to royals. Sadima thanked her and started off. There were no crowds today, no magicians, and it was easy to spot the round black sign with light blue lettering. The dresses were all beautiful, and she bought a simple one, paying enough to have bought twenty dresses at the little stores in South End.

Halfway home, daydreaming, hoping Thomas's face would light when he saw her, she heard clattering hooves and looked up. Men in red tunics were riding abreast, trotting toward her. One of them carried a brass bell, and he was ringing it and shouting, his voice raw and gruff.

It wasn't until the horses were closer that Sadima felt how nervous they were, how tired of the clanging bell, how thirsty and weary. And a moment after that, she understood what the man with the bell was shouting, over and over. "Go home and stay in your houses! Clear the streets! Go home!"

"These are our streets!" a man's voice ran out. "Tell the magistrates Eridians can rule themselves."

Sadima spotted him just as he threw the rock. It hit a guard's horse, and the startled gelding reared. Another stone came from behind a hedge, and the guards all reined in. One of them drew his sword. He galloped across the cobblestones and chased the rock thrower across a lawn, killing him from behind with a single wide slash across his neck. Then he reined in, looking for the others, but they had disappeared into the bushes. "We'll get you all before this is over!" he shouted, then cantered back to the street. The guards rode on.

Sadima waited until they had passed, then began to run. She told her employees what she had seen and sent them home to their families. Then she helped Sistra find Faith and Karo and Beth and Sharee and everyone else they could. The families gathered in Sistra's apartment over the cheese shop, sitting so close that their legs and shoulders touched. They listened to Sadima's story, rocking their babies and comforting their children.

Then they waited, whispering, wondering where Thomas was, if they should go to the meetinghouse. But if the guards were looking for Eridians, that seemed foolish. One family left, apologizing, explaining that they were new to Eridian teachings and just wanted to leave Limòri, if they could. Everyone wished them well.

The sun went down and still they heard no shouting, and Sadima began to hope. But not long after dark, they heard hooves on the cobblestones.

64

Our next recitation class was with Somiss. I had been hoping that he would be gone a long time, to give the new pact a chance. Luke worried me. Twice I saw him staring at Gerrard, and I saw him push Will in the passageway—just hard enough to make him take one wide step to keep his balance. If Somiss wanted him to be the bully, maybe Luke was just trying to pretend nothing had changed.

Somiss's chair was narrow and tall, made of a milk-colored wood that was grained with black streaks. I had never seen anything like it. Somiss wasn't smiling, but there was something different in his expression that made me uneasy. He wasn't as distant. He was watching us.

"You," he said, and pointed at Luke, then me, then Levin, and so on. We all passed. So everyone was imagining the songs now—maybe even Luke.

When Will had finished, Levin looked up. "I made a perfect copy of my pastry."

Somiss didn't answer him. He just said this: "We will recite again in the morning. Have the next song ready." And then he and his chair burst into flame. We all gasped and stepped back, then stood, glancing at each other after Somiss, his chair, and the flames disappeared. The fire had been real. I had felt the heat. Or, maybe, if Franklin was right, I just expected to feel it.

"Yes."

We all turned and saw Franklin through the arched opening of the chamber. He was looking straight at me. He smiled. "You may go." He looked at the others. "The rest of you, follow me."

I watched them leave, then stood for a moment, wishing I could have gone with them. I was staying two or three songs ahead, so the extra study time really wasn't welcome. I walked out of the chamber and turned to go back to the room. Jux appeared in front of me.

"Follow me."

I couldn't help hoping that he was going to let me fly again.

"Not today," Jux said over his shoulder.

He had heard my thoughts. "The history book says silent-speech is forbidden," I whispered.

"It is," he said aloud. *But it's the only way to do this*, he added without speaking, his voice clear inside my head. Then he lengthened his stride.

He was walking so fast that I had to run a few steps to get close enough to whisper again. "The only way to do what?" I asked aloud. Then I tried to do what he had, to put my words into his mind. He didn't answer or react in any way. I fought an impulse to grab his shoulder and make him turn around and face me as we started up the long incline.

When he got to the door, he opened it and went through, leaving it wide open for me. I slowed just enough to be sure there were no cliffs. There weren't; just the grassy slope and the forest beyond it. I ran to catch up again, and Jux led me into the trees without saying another word— silently or aloud.

I was nervous, as I always was in Jux's classes. I kept trying to see ahead, expecting a glass enclosure or the old lion Gerrard had told me about, or a lake full of snakes, but there was nothing but trees. Jux didn't say anything more, and he didn't look back. He went faster and faster, until I was running to keep up. And then all of a sudden, he was gone.

I stopped, breathing hard. Then I turned in a circle and realized that the whole time I had been looking ahead and wondering what the lesson would be, I should have been paying attention. The assignment was probably to find my way back.

"Not yet," a voice said.

I whirled around to see a wizard in a white robe. He was pale-skinned and young, like Somiss, but his eyes reminded me of Franklin's. There was a little kindness left in them. Or at least the pretense of kindness.

Pretense, he said, except that his lips didn't move. *Open the first gate in your mind.*

I looked around to see if Jux was close, or Franklin. The wizard repeated it out loud. "Open the first gate."

I looked for something to try to push my thoughts into so that the gate would open and—

"No," he said. "Close your eyes."

I took a step backward, without thinking, and I saw him smile. "Close your eyes," he insisted. I did it, but every muscle in my body was tight.

"The gates all look different," he said. "Yours will probably be a gate or a door that comes from an early memory. Usually the entrance to someplace you felt safe."

I opened my eyes. He was still standing two paces back. "Got it?"

I shook my head and closed my eyes again. The door to Celia's kitchen. When she could tell that I had been crying, she would often close it. That meant I would have at least a little warning if my father came looking for me. And once I was under the pastry table, my back pressed against the wall, Celia would lie and say she hadn't seen me. The door was made of heavy oak, hung on hinges as long as my boyish forearms. When it closed, there was a solid sigh-click sound. I could see the scratches in it, the places where the inside was dented from years of waiters carrying wide trays passing through it.

I opened my eyes.

"Over here," he said from behind me.

I turned around.

"Did you see it?"

I nodded.

"It's always closed unless you open it. Imagine opening it, as you would in reality. Use your hands."

I closed my eyes and imagined myself standing before the door, reaching to turn the handle. I pushed it hard and it swung open. "Franklin explained this in our first-year classes," I said when I opened my eyes.

Really? the wizard said inside my mind. *He usually saves it for later.*

I stared at him. His lips hadn't moved.

Once you open the gate, he said silently, *you can hear the thoughts of anyone close enough to you who has also opened the first gate. You can hear me, yes?* He lifted his eyebrows slightly, like we all did, and I nodded, a tiny movement to tell him I understood.

Most people can't open their first gate—or any other, he said silently. *Some do it now and then by accident or with intoxicants. The stone usually opens it for you. But only a few can do what you just did.*

I kept staring. I could hear his voice inside my skull. It was perfectly clear, and he had not said a single word out loud. Franklin had spoken to me like this once or twice the first year, but I had convinced myself that I had been stupid with hunger, imagining things.

It's the breathing patterns, the wizard said. *At first they calm you so much that the gate just falls open. The wasps open two gates, usually. Sometimes three, which can kill you.*

"I died," I said aloud.

I know. But you can see the advantage of this, the wizard said inside my head, as he pulled an orange from his pocket and began to peel it. He separated it into fourths and handed me one. *Can you still hear me?* he asked.

I nodded. "But this is silent-speech," I said aloud. "It's forbidden."

"Eat," he said.

I put the orange in my mouth.

"Where are you from?" he asked me.

How can he not know? I thought. *Everyone is from Limòri.*

"Everyone is?" he asked me, and I realized he had heard me thinking.

He kept feeding me oranges and asking me questions. "Having your mouth full helps at first," he said. "You need to slow your thoughts, form them, and learn not to think what you don't want someone else to hear."

Why are you telling me all this? I thought, asking him without uttering a sound.

"Because it will help you with the pact," he said.

I started to pretend I didn't know what he was talking about, but he shook his head.

"If the door is open, anyone can hear what I am thinking?"

Gate, he answered silently. *No matter what it looks like, it's called a gate. And no. If the other person's gate is closed, they hear nothing.*

"All wizards can do this?"

"Most of Franklin's choices can," he said. "They hide

it, of course. Somiss can't. His applicants usually can't."

"His appli—," I began, about to ask which boys had been Somiss's choices, then I stopped. "*Somiss* can't?" My heart leapt, and the wizard laughed, shaking his head.

"Oh, this will be a good one," he said aloud.

And then he was gone.

I stood there, feeling more hope than I had ever felt for two or three heartbeats, and then it all collapsed. *A good one?* What the fuck did that mean?

I started back, wandering in the trees for a long time before I finally found the round door. I would have told Gerrard everything and asked him what the wizard had meant, but when I got back to the room, he was sound asleep, his lamp out. Could it be night already? How short were our days now?

That night I had a dream. I was older, walking on longer, stronger legs through Market Square on a Saturday morning, watching pretty girls go past. One of them touched her friend's arm, then pointed at me. They both smiled and I tried to talk to them, but my mouth would not open. It was as though my lips had been sewn shut. I woke up in a cold sweat and whispered to myself in the dark to make sure it had been a dream.

It took me a long time to go back to sleep.

65

Sadima opened the window a little to hear better as the red-shirted guards rode past. "Stay inside!" one man was shouting. "Stay inside! Anyone found in the street will be arrested."

After the guards had passed, Sadima stood back, listening to the people behind her trying to figure out what was happening, what they should do. She had no idea what to tell them. She finally sat down with the others and watched the women going through the bags they had brought, touching their children's clothing, their wooden combs, their sewing shears, needles and thread, their homemade remedies, the gifts friends had given them—the things they needed and the things they did not want to lose.

The conversations got heated, then stalled, then stopped.

They had said everything there was to say. No one knew enough about what was going on to make a decision. The children went to sleep and the adults dozed, then woke again to listen. And when the sky was rouged with sunrise, they heard shouts again.

Sadima went to the window and stood with her back against the wall, looking out at an angle. At first she saw riders and people milling in the street, and her heart eased. The guards were probably just telling people they could go to work, to the markets. But then the crowd came closer and she saw that the families were walking stiff-kneed with fear, being driven along like cattle by the guards riding behind them.

She looked up the street again and slowly began to understand. The red-shirted guards were emptying the buildings, one by one, and herding the people away. She turned to the frightened faces behind her and explained.

"Where will they take us?" Sistra whispered.

Sadima shook her head. "I don't know."

"What can we do?" Faith asked.

Sadima turned. "They're searching every room of every building, I think."

She turned back to the window. Down the block, she saw a guard come out the front door of a little sweets shop. He shook his head, and the captain blew a shrill whistle and the guards all came one building closer. They stood at the ready as two men went inside a four-story brick building of apartments. The residents came out all at once, the guards behind them. Then two guards went back in. When they came out, they had four more women, one of them weeping. The guards shoved them into the crowd. Then ten guards on horseback came down the street, swords unsheathed, faces blank and grim. The crowd was forced to march forward.

It was horrible to watch. Some of the women and most of the children were beginning to cry. The men looked furious and helpless. Sadima stood, her hands clasped tight, as three men broke ranks and tried to drag one of the guards off his horse. Swords flashed and the horses whinnied at the sudden smell of blood. Sadima could feel their fear as the men's bodies fell limp on the cobblestones. The guards closed ranks and spurred their horses forward to keep any of the people from trying to go back to where the bodies lay.

"Oh, no," Sharee breathed from behind her. "Oh, no."

"But it isn't just Eridians," Sistra said.

"Maybe they will separate us later," Sharee's husband said quietly. "Perhaps the others will be let go?"

"How will they know us?" Sadima asked.

"The Servenians all have the tattoo," Sistra said.

Sadima stared at her. "Tattoo?"

Sistra turned her back and unbuttoned her bodice to bare her shoulders. The tattoo was faint, a lightening of her skin, barely visible: a row of three small stars, separated by crescent moons.

"Those from the Orchid Coast and the southern lands are bound by a vow," a man said quietly. "We cannot deny that we follow Eridian teachings if we are asked."

Sadima breathed a long, slow breath, trying to think. She wasn't bound by an oath and she didn't have a tattoo, but she had given her word to carry sorrow for her friends. She leaned against the wall, feeling helpless, watching the guards move to the next building. They went in and brought everyone out, then two guards checked a final time. Not long after that, the horsemen arrived and the guards moved on to the next building. She caught her breath. "I know what we can do," she said.

The whispering behind her stopped. She explained about the passage she had built. "There is only one bed next door, a small stove, it looks like a place where one person lives. The rest of the building is empty. They will assume I am gone, that I have run away. The stairwell door just looks like a pantry. I can stack things in it so they won't notice the stairs." She paused, working it out, then went on. "We will wait until they have searched it, and then go over there, before they start to search here. If we carry all of our things with us, this place will look like an abandoned cheese shop, not a dwelling house."

They all began to nod, and she saw hope in their eyes.

"What about the passage door on this side?" Beth asked.

Sadima exhaled. "It's in the cheese shop, and it opens inward. We can stack crates in front of it, ten or twelve deep, eight or ten high, leaving just enough space to slide along the wall. They won't see it."

Sadima pointed at Sistra. "The men can help you move the crates out of the backroom into the curding room. Leave enough space for the biggest man to pass, walking sideways, not a bit more. Bring cheeses out onto the work counters. The guards are tired and hungry. It will distract them."

Sistra nodded and said something in Jadia's ear, then left, five or six men following her down the stairs.

"As they get closer, we should stay away from the window," Sadima said. "Gather your things now, so that we can leave in an instant, with nothing left behind to make them think anyone has been here. Explain to your children so they know what to do." She tried to smile. "I am going to go next door, to hide the stairs. I'll be back as soon as I can."

As the families began rebundling everything they had opened in the night, sweeping up crumbs, gathering the small toys their children had brought along, Sadima went down the stairs and looked around the shop. There was nothing amiss, there were coins in the drawer, clabbered milk ready to press in the morning. It was just a cheese shop, abandoned by frightened workers.

She went into the backroom and saw that Sistra had the men in a line, tossing the crates one to the next, while four men stacked them. The job was more than half done. Sadima slid along the wall and went through the door, taking the steps two at a time.

In her apartment she used a shawl to carry the few things she could not bear to leave behind, then built a false wall of grocery crates to hide the stairs. She filled them with her kitchen goods, potatoes, flour sacks, nothing that could be eaten without preparation, nothing that would tempt a guard to go through the crates. She left a pan on her woodstove, full of the soup she had meant to eat for supper. She tousled her bed and left the hall door ajar, dropping a single shoe just outside it. Then she went back down to the cheese shop to wait with the others.

They had all finished their tasks. Sadima stood by the window, watching, as the guards came closer. "Almost," she whispered. "They have just gone in next door. Line up." She heard people moving behind her, hushing their children and gathering their belongings.

Her heart pounding, Sadima waited until she saw the guards come out, shaking their heads. The guard captain waited for two more to look. The instant they reappeared, she turned.

"Now!" she whispered.

The families behind her filed down the stairs, none of them crowding or hesitating, and in ten heartbeats, they were gone. Sadima glanced around the room, looking for anything dropped, anything forgotten, then she ran to follow them. She was the last through the hidden door, and she closed it carefully and quietly just as she heard the voices of the guards discovering the cheese.

Upstairs, in her third-story refuge, all her friends were waiting, tense and scared. She slid along the wall to see out the window. There were three guards this time, all of them carrying chunks of cheese to hand to their companions as they came out of the shop. And then they went on, without a single backward glance. Sadima turned, tears in her eyes, and nodded. Sistra kissed Jadia's forehead, then came to hug Sadima. Families stood in small circles, relieved, jubilant, and silent.

They were careful to be quiet all day, and ate cheese and water for supper to avoid the tiniest hint of smoke from the cookstove chimney. They used all her bedclothes and whatever each family had brought to make pallets to sleep on, then divided up the watches.

It was the second watch, the one before midnight, that fell to Sharee's husband. And he woke them all with three words. "I smell smoke." No one moved, no one spoke. They all heard careful footsteps on the stairs. Sadima's heart stopped.

"Mattie?" It was almost a whisper, but she would have known the voice anywhere. Thomas appeared in the doorway. He was breathing hard. "Gather your things," he said. "We all have to leave here now."

– 66 –

When a wizard woke us the next morning, I shouted,
but the pounding didn't stop. Then I remembered—Somiss's
class. I heard Gerrard get up, but I lay still, wondering if
Somiss had known Jux would take me to the pale wizard.
Almost certainly not. Silent-speech *was* forbidden.

For an instant I was afraid that it had been a dream.
Why wasn't the pale wizard worried that I would tell
Somiss? The question answered itself: because he knew I
would want to use silent-speech for my own reasons, for
the pact. I pushed my hair back and noticed the smell of
oranges on my hands. It had been real.

A wrinkled, dour wizard led us to a weird little chamber
that had a ring of curved benches carved from the stone.
Gerrard had brought his goblet. As the others arrived, I was

happy to see that they had all brought their objects. Jordan set his lizard carefully in the corridor, against the far wall, where he could see it but not smell it for a while.

Then the pale wizard appeared, startling all of us—especially me. He made no sign of recognition, so I didn't either. And he had apparently graduated from the Somiss School of Common Cordiality, because without the slightest attempt at politeness, he jabbed his index finger toward me.

"You."

I recited and passed, then sat listening to the others. It made me uneasy when the wizards changed things around like this. Where was Somiss? When Will finished, I glanced up. The wizard nodded at me, the almost unnoticeable nod we all used. He curved his lips into a nearly invisible smile.

Did he know our language of gestures? Had his class done something similar? When he glanced at me again, I touched my chest, then my ear, then brought my hand down over my throat in one heartbeat, tracing the shape of Jux's scar as I pretended to be pushing my hair back. *Thank you for what you told me in Jux's forest.*

The wizard nodded, an even smaller gesture than we were using, but I was positive I had seen it. And then he didn't look at me again.

Will passed. Gerrard passed. Luke got four or five words wrong, but the wizard just nodded and pointed at Levin to go next. I looked down to hide my reaction. Had they been passing Luke like that all along and I had never noticed? I felt sorry for him. He was so far behind the rest of us, and he was going to hate us all when he realized it. He would be dangerous as part of the pact, I knew that, but he would be even more dangerous if we had kept him out.

Jordan recited last—accurately—and the wizard nodded again. He stood up, and I was afraid he was going to disappear before anyone could speak, but Jordan stepped forward. "We are supposed to tell Somiss or Jux when we can make a perfect copy," he said.

The wizard looked a little annoyed. "And you can?" Jordan and Levin both nodded.

"Go to the food hall," he said. "All of you." Then he winked at me. An instant later he became a snake, then a lion, then a bear. And then he was gone. We all just stood there, dumbstruck, for a few heartbeats before we followed each other out into the passageway, exchanging glances, afraid to talk as always.

I was pissed at him for winking. Did he want me to have to explain it? Was he making sure I would tell the others about silent-speech, or was he trying to make them suspicious of me when I tried to tell them? I could only hope everyone thought the wink was for all of us.

Gerrard walked far to one side as usual. I wondered if he could make a copy of the goblet yet, or at least come close. Abruptly, he turned his head to stare at me. I looked down, but I knew I hadn't been quick enough. He had been watching me, waiting for me to glance at him. Why? I hoped that it wasn't the wink. Gerrard had just started to trust me again. I was careful not to look at anyone else the rest of the way.

Franklin was back. I was glad not to see Somiss—or Jux or the pale wizard. We filed in and sat at separate tables. Would

Gerrard be able to do it this time? I hoped so. I glanced at him, and he was looking at me again. I looked away.

Will, Jordan, and Levin passed. Gerrard made a lopsided goblet, and Luke couldn't produce anything that even suggested frayed silk.

"Are you all able to move your thoughts now?" Franklin asked. Everyone nodded. "The four who have passed," he said, pointing at me, Levin, Will, and Jordan. "Your next assignment is to copy these." He lifted a big box from beneath a table and opened it. He set four little cages on the tabletop. "Feed them," he said, "and they will need water. When you can do it, tell whoever is teaching your recitation class." Then he disappeared. I glanced at Gerrard. He was staring at nothing. I was afraid to look at Luke.

The four of us walked to the table, staring into the cages. Then Levin reached for one, so we all did. Mine contained a mouse that peered out at me, its whiskers trembling. Astonished, I looked around. I couldn't see what Will had, but Levin's cage was chirping, and Jordan bent to look into his, then jerked back. I noticed Luke staring at me, desperation on his face. I glanced around. Gerrard was leaving; I hurried to catch up with him.

Back in our chamber, Gerrard looked angry as he settled into his usual position to study, his back stiff and straight. I set the mouse cage on my desk and started talking, explaining where Jux had taken me, repeating everything the wizard had said. "So if we can all learn how to form our—"

"Did the wizard explain to you how to close the gate?" he cut me off. He turned to face me. "Did he?"

Startled, I shook my head. "No."

"So you are about to teach everyone to open the first gate and use silent-speech. Perfect. Then all Franklin has to do is listen to every thought we have in class, tell Somiss, and he will kill all of us."

I sat down on the edge of my cot, shaking my head. "The wizard said the first gate is closed unless we open it," I whispered.

Gerrard looked disgusted. "It opens on its own every time you move your thoughts, or even just try hard enough to move them. Then it closes again. The wasps open the first gate and usually the second one, too. And the gates close again after a few days. But once *you* open it yourself, intentionally, it remains open until you close it again."

"How can I close it?" I whispered, hating the arrogant look on his face, terrified that I had made it so the wizards could hear all my thoughts. "If there isn't a way, then it's too dangerous for any of us to—"

"Any of us?" He shook his head. "If you would stop trying to save everyone, you and I might have a chance."

There was so much anger in his voice that I stood up, afraid he was going to hit me. But he didn't. "You're just a spoiled little rich fuck," he said. "But you want to be a hero. Why do you think you were the one who was led up into the forest for a private class with a wizard you had never seen before?"

I was shaking. "How could I possibly know that?" I shouted at him. My voice rang against the rock and startled me into whirling around to look at the door.

"Closing the gate is easy," Gerrard said wearily. "You just imagine it, reversing whatever you pictured when you opened it."

"Why are you such an asshole?" I asked him. "I never know whether to believe you or—"

"Believe this," he said. "You can't imagine how long wizards have been teaching magic. You can't begin to realize how many boys have died trying to figure out what we are trying to figure out. You can't possibly understand how bored Somiss and Franklin are with every possible variation of every possible effort to survive that boys like us have made here."

"Then *help* me," I said. "Whoever you are and whatever you know, just help. Will and Jordan and Levin are doing their best. So am I."

"And Luke?" Gerrard asked me. "Do you think he won't run to Somiss to tell him about the wink, about anything else he notices, to repeat whatever you say to him?"

I exhaled and didn't answer for a few heartbeats. "I wasn't going to tell him about this. Not until I helped him catch up," I said. He just shook his head. I looked at the wall, then back at him. "Could Franklin hear me thinking in class today?"

Gerrard nodded. "If he opened his first gate, yes. If not, no."

"That's why you kept looking at me."

He nodded again. "I couldn't hear anything from Franklin today."

I sank onto my cot and shut my eyes, so relieved I felt half-sick. I pictured Celia's kitchen door and there it was, still standing open. I imagined myself closing it and suddenly saw myself, little, pale, wearing knee pants, reaching up to hold the handle. I shoved it closed and heard it latch, the same little sigh-click sound.

"Wizards always have at least three reasons for everything," Gerrard said.

"Like the wink," I whispered.

"Exactly."

"Was it true about Somiss? That he can't hear thoughts?"

Gerrard hesitated, then nodded. "I think so. But it's better to assume he can, that they all can."

"How close do you have to be to someone?"

He shrugged. "Ten paces. Or less. And if you are in a crowd, or just walking in the city, you can sometimes hear four or five people at once—and animals."

I nodded and paced to the door and back, thinking. "I'll meet with Will, Levin, and Jordan soon and get them all practicing on opening and closing the gate," I said.

"Tell them to keep it from Luke," he whispered. "Or no one will be alive tomorrow."

"I will. But I wish Luke—"

"I do too," Gerrard said. "The pact is probably our best hope."

"I'll help Luke," I said. "I am good at a lot of this."

He nodded. "Most of it. And I hate you for it."

"Try not to hate me."

He looked straight into my eyes. "I am trying."

"Then try a little fucking harder," I said.

And he smiled. He *smiled*.

"Be very quiet. Wait for me at the bottom," Thomas was whispering over and over, guiding people down the stairs to the first floor of the building. Sadima was the last to leave. She had on her belt-purse full of coins and carried a flour sack that held her paints, her clothes—including the new dress—her sturdiest shawl, and the silk blankets that had warmed Charlie.

"Ready?" Thomas asked.

She nodded.

As they came down the last few steps, Thomas made a low hissing sound, and everyone turned to look at him. "We are going to the meetinghouse," he whispered. "I know a way out of Limòri from there."

Sadima heard people murmuring, mothers telling

their children what was going to happen. For the hundredth time, she marveled at Thomas Marsham. No one was afraid now. They trusted him. She smiled at him and mouthed, *Thank you*. He leaned close and kissed her on the cheek, then walked to the front door. Everyone turned to watch him.

He made the long hissing sound again, then he spoke, very quietly. "Follow that sound. Keep walking until you hear this: *Sst-sst-sst!* Then stop immediately." He looked at them. "Stay close together, but not so close that you're in each other's way. No talking, no stumbling, no babies crying, no children running off. There are guards all over South End, but they are half-asleep in their saddles. We can do this." He paused. "Is there anyone who is not ready?" There was no answer.

Thomas made the barely audible hiss, then started walking. Sadima waited for all the families to file ahead of her, then she came last, her eyes wet, saying good-bye in her heart to her only home for all her many lives, Charlie's home, Grrur's, too: South End.

It was chilly outside. The moon was a crescent, high and small, giving just enough light to trace the edges of the buildings. The streets were empty, the still night air hazy with smoke. And all the familiar noises of South End were silenced.

Thomas kept the pace fast. Sadima carried a sleepy two-year-old for a few blocks while her father worked at retying a bedsheet bundle into a sling to put over his shoulder. When he could, he took the child back and

Sadima went a little faster, walking to one side, trying to see if anyone else needed help.

Thomas somehow found a route through the maze of buildings that avoided almost all the red-shirted guards. Only twice did they see mounted men. Both times, Thomas signaled them to stop in deep shadows, all of them holding their breath, mothers' hands over their babies' mouths, until the riders passed.

At the meetinghouse, Thomas led them inside without lighting a single lamp. They walked in near-perfect silence, not a whisper from the children, only the sound of his cane quietly clicking on the steps. Sadima stayed back again, making sure that everyone was inside and safe before she went through the door; then she closed it quietly behind her.

As strange as South End had felt, darkness and silence made the meetinghouse even stranger. Instead of leading them up the steps to the big room Sadima had come to love, Thomas stayed on the ground floor, turning down a long hall that ended in a storage room. He made the sound to stop, and everyone waited in the dark as he and two Servenian men whispered, figuring out how to move something heavy out of the way.

Sadima heard it scrape against the floor planks, but didn't realize what it was until Thomas finally lit two lanterns. He set one on the floor to light the stone stairway that had been hidden by a false wall. He carried the other, leading people down a long, steep set of steps. Bringing up the rear, Sadima saw the grand chairs Thomas had used at the meetings stacked along the walls. Passing the one with carved snakes, one child made a tiny, startled sound and was shushed by his mother.

Sadima stood at the top of the stairs, waiting for Thomas to come back. When he did, he let her help him swing the heavy trick door back into place. Then he handed her the second lantern and motioned for her to follow him. At the end of the line she stopped, holding the lantern high as he made his way back to the front.

Sadima heard people fidgeting, moving uneasily. It was odd to be underground, but somehow it didn't scare her. She found herself taking deeper breaths, her shoulders sinking, the stiffness of fear leaving her legs. She felt safe here.

Thomas lit two more lanterns that stood ready along the wall, with strikers beside them. After that, he spoke in an almost normal voice. "Most of our families came to the meetinghouse before the guards could stop them," he told everyone. "I walked these passages with them earlier, then came back to get you. They are waiting for us."

Quiet voices rippled along the line, and Sadima smiled. They were going to be all right. Thomas knew what to do.

"My ancestors were thieves and smugglers in Limòri for three hundred years," he said, raising his voice a little more so all could hear. "They built these tunnels over lifetimes, and whatever their purpose once was, the passages will carry us to safety. Mattie? Can you hear me?"

She stood straighter. "Yes."

"Make sure no one falls behind."

"I will, Thomas, and thank you," she said. He didn't

answer, but she heard him make the little hissing sound and the line moved forward.

The passages were narrow and twisting. And the walls changed as they walked. At first they were plain dirt; then she began to see patches of dark stone here and there. Not long after that, there was dark stone underfoot and overhead. It gave way in places to old, chipped brickwork and big gray blocks of stone. Sadima wondered who had made these passages, and she marveled at what they had done.

Three times she spotted what looked like faces chipped out of the stone. They were menacing. Who had taken the time here, underground, to make them? And why?

Thomas veered from one tunnel into another, then passed several more. As he led them through what had to be an enormous maze, she began to wonder how long it had taken him to learn his way. Then, at the next junction, she noticed a little stack of stones and just above it, three wavy lines, one above the next, scratched deeply into a crooked wall of old red brick. Sadima had no idea what the stacked rocks or the wavering lines meant, but their purpose was obvious. Someone had worked out a way not to get lost, and Thomas understood it.

When he finally brought them up out of the passages, he asked the lantern bearers to snuff their lights and leave them against the wall. Then they all felt their way up a long set of steep steps and out into the night. The air was cool, and there was a little breeze blowing, sliding across Sadima's skin like a stranger's touch, almost unwelcome after the still air underground.

She shivered, not from cold, but fear. It was so dark. There was no smell of smoke here, at least. She heard the hissing sound and followed with the others, her eyes slowly adapting, the massive shadows ahead becoming the ancient fig trees of Market Square.

"Run!" someone screamed.

Sadima stopped, confused, bumping into the people ahead of her. One of the babies began to cry. Somewhere, someone whistled, and a hundred lanterns were unshrouded, all at once. Sadima turned, seeing the row of red-shirted guards standing almost shoulder to shoulder in an enormous circle.

"You will sleep here tonight," a man said, pitching his voice into a shout. "In the morning all but one of you will be free to leave Limòri forever."

Sadima tried to see which guard was speaking, tried to understand what was happening. All but one? Would they hang Thomas? All he had done was help families save their children. She turned again, looking for him. But it was too dark. Only the faces of the guards were lit, seemingly bodiless and grotesque in the yellow lantern light.

"There is a woman among you," the man shouted again. "She has dark red hair, cut short. Keep her close. If she disappears tonight, you will all die here when the sun rises."

— 68 —

There was no class the next day, so I went to the food
hall and brought back a loaf of brown bread and a tiny glass
dish for the mouse's water. After I fed it, I talked to it a
little, and Gerrard turned around to laugh at me.

"Shut up."

"Make me," he said, turning back to the wall.

"I probably can't."

"Probably?"

Then I sat on my cot, looking at his back. "Thank you,"
I said, very quietly.

He didn't answer, but he turned his head slightly.

"For going along with the pact," I said. "I know you
think it's stupid."

"I do," he whispered. "Are you going to show them?"

"Yes, all but Luke."

"Be careful."

I went out into the passageway, and walked fast, following the route I had worked out. I met with each one in a different place, for just long enough to explain silent-speech, including everything Gerrard had said. I helped them open and close the first gate a few times. Then we tried to talk silently.

It was strange, hearing their thoughts, their voices, like that. "Practice," I told each one of them, "but only when you know no one is within twenty paces or so. Never use it in class. Never." And then I warned all of them about Luke and explained that he would need help to catch up.

No one asked me how he had been managing to eat all this time. Maybe, I thought, Somiss had made sure I wasn't the only one to know about Luke. Or it could have been an illusion, like Gerrard making food without touching the stone. I shut off my thoughts with the fifth breathing pattern and tried adding four quick breaths in the middle of it, and a half breath at the end. It helped.

I talked to Levin last.

"Are you eating?" I asked him after we had gone over everything else.

He nodded. "I think Somiss was testing us."

I nodded, but didn't ask him what he meant. We could talk for days about all the things that didn't make sense. "Is Luke—?" I began, then stopped because I didn't know how to say it.

"He goes back and forth between our room and Will's now," Levin said. "We let him—to give Will a break." Levin hesitated, then leaned close. "Do you really think we have a chance?"

I shrugged. "Sometimes."

He smiled. "First thing, when we get out of here," he said, reaching out to grip my shoulder, "let's go find a good roof."

Then he walked away. I watched him until he turned up a branching passageway, my heart lighter than it had been in a long time. I knew they would all practice hard and it wouldn't be long before we could talk—really talk, without being afraid. Maybe we could live through this, all of us.

Back in the food hall, I made a huge meal and ate slowly, staring at the entrance. I was hoping Luke would come in. It was time to find out exactly what he could and couldn't do. Franklin's class was only going to get harder, and the songs were getting longer and longer. Had Luke ever been to one of Jux's classes? I exhaled, all my optimism seeping away. It was hard to imagine Luke studying, working constantly to catch up.

"Hahp."

I looked up. Gerrard was standing just inside the wide arch. He tipped his head, just enough for me to see, then went back out, turning toward our room. I counted to fifty, then followed. When I got there, I opened the door and then stopped, astounded.

Luke was sitting on my cot. No, not sitting. His hands were tied behind him with strips of Gerrard's blanket. His feet were tied together, and there was a rolled-up wad of cloth in his mouth. He tried to talk and couldn't, then tried to stand and couldn't do that, either. His feet weren't just bound together—they were tied to the cot frame.

I looked at Gerrard. "What are you—"

Gerrard held up a knife, then jerked his robe aside for me to see a deep cut across his collarbone. "I went out. When I came back, he was waiting, just inside the door."

"With the knife?"

"He meant to kill me. Or you. Whoever came in first."

Luke was struggling, but the knots were too tight. I stared at him, furious, my teeth locked, my hands clenched. How could he do this now, *now* when we might actually have a chance? "How could you be this stupid?" I hissed at him.

Gerrard got in front of me, whispered something to Luke, then pulled the cloth out of his mouth. Luke looked up at me, his eyes full of fear. "Somiss said I had to." His voice was shaking. "He said he wouldn't let me eat any-more if you were both alive when he came back. At least one, he said. I had to." Luke looked at Gerrard, then me, then back at Gerrard, his face contorted. "You would have done it," he said. "If Somiss said you had to."

Gerrard looked over his shoulder at me. "He was so ter-rified he might miss one or two meals while we all figured out what to do, he used the stone to make this." Gerrard hefted the knife, and Luke shrank backward.

"Please, no," he begged. "I promise. I'll make something up for Somiss. I'll think of something. Please. Look, I know I haven't—"

"Shut up," Gerrard whispered, and Luke closed his mouth. His face was beaded with sweat, and I could smell his fear. And I had no idea what to do. No idea at all.

Gerrard pointed the knife at Luke's face. "Make one

sound, I will cut you. If the knots are looser when I come back, I will cut you." Then he went out the door and I followed him, leaving it just a little ajar.

"Shit," I whispered. "What can we do?"

Gerrard shook his head. "I know what I would do. But you're the leader of this pact. Not me."

I was shaking. "Maybe he means it. Maybe he will tell Somiss a lie that—"

"Hahp?"

I met Gerrard's eyes. "The pact might have worked," he said. "It still might."

I paced away from him, then walked back. "Do we have to kill him?"

Gerrard didn't answer me. After a long silence, he shrugged. "Somiss is gone. So is Jux, I think. Wren showed you silent-speech because he is playing some side game, trying to make Somiss angrier at Franklin. Tonight might be the only chance. Ever."

Side game? I wanted to ask Gerrard how he knew the pale wizard's name. I wanted to ask him a hundred things, but there was no time, and what came out of my mouth was this: "I hate this fucking place."

He nodded.

"It has to be all of us," I whispered, my throat tight. "If there is going to be anything good left afterward, it has to be."

Gerrard nodded again.

I turned and ran, feeling strange inside my body, like I was running in a dream, something terrible behind me, and something even worse up ahead.

69

Sadima could hear the whispers. They began close to her, then spread in a widening circle. She stood very still, her thoughts stumbling over each other, her hands and feet suddenly ice-cold. Why her? She turned, scanning the circle, and still couldn't spot Thomas. But he had to be here. He had come out of the tunnels first and . . . she shivered. Maybe they had taken him prisoner already. Maybe he had been dragged off in the confusion. And if whoever was leading the red-shirted guards had sent someone to the meetinghouse to spy, they had seen two people on the stage. Thomas, and her.

"Mattie?"

It was a barely-there whisper, but she knew the voice instantly. "Sistra? You and Jadia, just stay away," she hissed. "Tell Sharee and Faith and Karo and all the others. Don't let anyone see you close to me." She turned her back and walked a dozen paces, careful to skirt the families trying to lay out blankets for their children on the grass. People glanced up at her as she passed.

She found a place to stand, alone. Had they already arrested Thomas? Or killed him? The only reason the guards weren't trying to find her now was the darkness. They were afraid of a fight, not because they thought they might lose, but because any kind of struggle in the dark might give her and others a chance to slip away.

Sadima wiped her eyes when she noticed she was crying. Tears were not going to help her, Thomas, or anyone else. And it was only fair that she be killed if someone had to die. She had spent more time alive than anyone should. Until she had met Sistra and Thomas, she hadn't cared at all about living any longer. Now? Now it didn't matter what she cared about. She would not try to run, even if she somehow had a chance. How could she? There were children here. Old people. Whole families. And many of them were her friends.

It was just sad that she had been about to tell Thomas her secret, to see if he could come to love her, to try to have a real life, not just a long one. *Thomas.* How like him to risk his life for the rest of them. No matter where they had taken him, if they had not yet killed him, he would be thinking about the people here, in Market Square.

"Mattie?"

She turned and saw Sistra and Faith standing behind her.

"I told you to—," Sadima began, but Sistra reached out and grabbed her wrist.

"Don't talk. Sit down." She sank to the grass and pulled Sadima with her.

"What are you—," Sadima began, then saw the vague glint of polished metal. For an instant she thought they were going to kill her, then she saw the curved handle.

"My mother's shears," Sistra whispered. "Hold still or Faith and the others will sit on you."

Sadima looked up, then wrenched around to look behind her. Women were standing in a loose circle around them, whispering, talking, hiding them. "It won't do any good to cut my hair," Sadima said.

"You don't know that," Sistra said. "Sit still."

Faith and Sharee sat on either side of her, arguing with her, and finally pinning her arms down, holding her hands out of the way. She still wriggled, shaking her head until she felt the sharp edge of cold metal touch the back of her neck. Someone behind her reached over her shoulders and covered her mouth with both hands. The women standing around them whispered a little louder, just enough to hide the clicking of the scissors.

Sistra was both careful and quick, working by feel. When she was finished, and they finally freed Sadima's arms, she rubbed her hands over her scalp; it was almost perfectly smooth.

"This was stupid," Sadima whispered. "They will know it's me, trying to hide. Or they will think I am gone and hurt all of you. Either way it's not going to—"

"Hush, Mattie," Faith said. "If it doesn't help, it doesn't, but we had to try something."

"I'm going to tell them who I am."

None of them answered her, and Sistra got up and left without saying another word. Faith stayed by her and asked her if she had been able to see what had happened to Thomas. Sadima shook her head.

"Will you let me unburden myself to you?" Faith asked. "If we are all going to die, I would like to leave this life lighter, with fewer sorrows locked in my heart."

Sadima let out a long breath. "Yes. If you will listen to me."

They sat close together, to see each other's faces in the scant moonlight. Faith began with her earliest memories and described her mother's terrible cruelty. Sadima could not imagine a mother who would forget to feed her child, who would hit her and scare her. "She had me very young," Faith said. "I think she had foolish hopes that my father would marry her, in spite of his royal family." She shook her head, and Sadima saw her lift one hand to touch her terrible scar. "But she hated me," Faith whispered. "And even though she said my father tried to kill me, I have always wondered if it was her." Sadima felt her eyes fill with tears, as Faith went on.

After a time Sadima looked up and realized that most of the women around them had paired off and were standing close together, talking, and she knew that at least some of them were unburdening themselves. She was glad, as she listened to Faith, that they had all found a way to pass what was left of the night, a way to still their fears. And she knew Thomas would be proud of their courage.

When her turn came, Sadima started with her first day in South End, her terror, the way the children had chased her, the terrible pain of the bruises from their sticks.

"And you had no memories?" Faith interrupted quietly.

Sadima shook her head. "Not one. I had no idea where I had come from."

"But you told us about the farm at the meeting."

Sadima nodded. "My brother came and found me, and he told me about our parents, and about myself as a little girl." She repeated almost everything that Micah had said, because it comforted her to remind herself that even if she lived only until sunrise, at least she knew something about her family now. "But before that," she said, "I met Charlie. He helped me stay alive and eventually, he came to love me." Sadima could hear Faith's breathing quicken as she talked about the best years, and finally about Charlie's death.

When Sadima finished, she hesitated, wondering how to begin the strange part, how to explain to Faith what she didn't understand herself. She glanced up and caught her breath. The stars were gone, the sky was graying in the east. She heard birds high in the trees and listened. They were sleepy, and delighted the night was waning. Their hearts always rose with the sun.

Sadima heard people whispering, and she sighed. "No one has slept at all."

Faith yawned. "The little ones have, or we would have heard them by now."

Sadima smiled, glad for the interruption in her unburdening. What right did she have to give Faith a gift of anger and sadness on this night of all nights? Sadima reached out to touch Faith's cheek. "Maybe we should rest a little?"

Faith nodded and they lay down, ending up back-to-back for warmth. Sadima closed her eyes and listened to the last of the night. The birds would start singing soon, but for now, they had put their heads back beneath their wings.

Sadima did not realize that she had dozed until she heard the guards shouting. She jerked upright and stared, blinking at the rouged eastern sky. Sunrise had begun. Faith was no longer beside her.

"Erides taught us many things," she heard Sistra call out, high and clear. "To be kind. To carry our friends' sorrow when we can."

Sadima tried to spot her, but there wasn't enough light yet. "Is that so different from what your mothers taught you?" Sistra asked.

A few of the guards laughed. Two or three shouted at her to shut up. "There are babies among us," another voice rang out. "How have these babies harmed you?"

"We just do what we're ordered to do," one of the guards answered.

"Why?" Sistra shouted. "Because your comrades would kill you if you didn't? And why do they obey? Because they fear you?"

There was a round of nervous laughter from the guards.

"Silence!" a man shouted from somewhere outside the circle. His voice was deep and strong and loud.

Sadima could hear the guards shuffling, standing straighter, adjusting their swords. In the long silence that followed, she heard muted voices, all men, and she knew they were waiting only for better light. But when the sun finally came above the horizon and the dawn became morning light, they stared, dumbstruck, at the people they had held prisoner all night.

Sadima glanced behind herself, then turned, staring. She teetered at the edge of laughter, even though it was a terrible thing Sistra had done.

Everyone was bald: men, women, and children.

The ground was littered with piles of hair.

70

Luke was rocking, his eyes closed. Gerrard had stuffed the cloth back in his mouth. We stood in a half circle in front of him, all but Will. He was at the door, listening, peeking out, over and over. It was the middle of our night. No one would be coming to lead us to class, no one would be walking the passageways.

Levin was pale and sweating. Jordan's face was hard, and when he leaned close to whisper to Luke, his teeth didn't separate. "You stupid shit."

Luke made a little sound, like a kicked dog.

"We could just keep him tied up somewhere," Levin said for the third time. No one answered him. "I know," he said, glancing at the rest of us. "I know."

We had been through it over and over. No one had a

solution. We had all closed our first gates, by agreement, but I knew what was in their hearts, because it was in mine. Gerrard was right. We had no choice.

If we let Luke live, none of us would be able to sleep, ever again. None of us would ever walk down a corridor without being even more afraid than we already were. If Somiss decided to teach Luke silent-speech, we couldn't even keep our plans from him. Somiss would think of endless ways to use Luke.

I tapped Gerrard on the shoulder, then Levin, and led everyone out into the passageway.

"I don't want to be a murderer," Will whispered, before anyone could say anything.

"I don't think we have a choice," Jordan said quietly. He lifted his head. "But how would we do it?"

Will was shaking his head. "None of you has had to listen to him like I have. He's mean and dangerous and everything else we've said. But he's pathetic, too. He's so scared all the time."

I swallowed. Will was right. But it didn't matter. There was a weird, bitter taste in my mouth. "No one wants to do this," I whispered. I looked up the passageway, then down it. I saw everyone fidget; we were all terrified to be standing together like this, in one place.

"It has to look like suicide," Gerrard whispered.

"We could cut his wrists," I heard myself say. Then I swallowed again.

Will's face was wet with tears, but his breathing was even and steady and I knew he wasn't going to argue with us anymore.

"Where would *he* do it?" Levin whispered. "In the food hall so everyone would have to see him?"

Will shook his head. "He wouldn't kill himself. He would do what he did. He would kill any of us, all of us, whoever Somiss told him to kill."

There was a silence after that, because we all knew it was true.

"What if Gerrard had just killed him instead of tying him up?" Levin asked. "Would Somiss care?"

No one answered, because no one could even guess. But I knew something none of the rest of them knew—maybe, anyway. I argued with myself for a long moment before I spoke. And when I did, I said it in very few words, explaining what I had overheard, and about seeing the blood-dark bruises on his legs. "But maybe that was one of Jux's classes."

"He's never gone to Jux's," Will said quietly. "He told me that."

No one spoke for a long time.

"He has to be miserable," Jordan said. "He knows none of us can stand him, that we notice when the wizards pass his recitations with mistakes. He has to know he can't possibly catch up."

"He might kill himself," Will said slowly. "He is very proud. He hates being wrong about anything." He paused, then whispered, "I feel so sorry for him."

There was another silence.

Levin finally leaned forward to whisper, "I was exploring once, down past the food hall. I saw Somiss with a girl about our age. She was scared, shaking. I ducked back and hid until they were gone. I was afraid to—"

"He came to our house once," Jordan interrupted. "There was a stray dog barking at him when he left. He just lifted one hand, and its teeth were gone. It starved."

"Somiss is the one we should kill," I said.

"We will," Levin whispered. "But first we have to—"

"Where would Luke do it?" Gerrard asked.

"I know," I whispered, and explained about the lake. "Somiss would look there, I think."

They all nodded, and I knew we had decided.

"We can't carry him that far," Jordan whispered.

Gerrard took a long breath and let it out. "We won't have to. I'll tell him that one of us found a way out and that Hahp is going to show him."

"He'll recognize it," I breathed. "Who knows how many times Somiss—"

"It won't matter," Will cut me off. "We can blindfold him. We can tell him we don't want him to ever find his way back."

"Gerrard and I could do this alone," I whispered. "We're the ones Somiss wanted dead."

They all shook their heads.

Gerrard looked at me. "The lake, then?"

"Yes." My voice sounded steady.

Levin nodded, then Jordan. Then Will. And together, we figured it out.

I taught everyone the turns. Levin and Jordan started off, both carrying their study lamps and strikers. Will would wait, then go after them, carrying his. Gerrard would come behind me and Luke, to make sure no one followed us. And he would bring the knife.

Luke was trembling when I tied the blindfold. Maybe he could feel my hands shaking. I tried to keep my voice steady. "I found a way out of the cliffs," I told him. "We don't want you to see, so you can't find your way back in. You have to promise. You have to run and keep running and never come back."

He made a sound so full of anguish and hope that I dropped the knot and had to start over. Once the blindfold was on, I undid his feet and rested my hand on his forearm. "I'll guide you," I whispered.

The walk seemed eternal. Luke shuffled, sliding his feet, scared that I was going to shove him over a cliff, probably. When we came to the long downward slope, I felt him taking even shorter steps. I could smell the water, and I was sure Luke could too. He couldn't run, blindfolded and hand-bound, but he could refuse to walk. Gerrard was behind us somewhere, I knew, with the knife.

"I found this place by accident," I whispered. "There's a passage on the far side of a big lake." His steps lengthened. I wondered if Luke was afraid Somiss might follow us, and that we'd all get caught before he could escape. I gripped his forearm, guiding him as well as I could. "Not too much farther," I said in a low voice when I felt the stones under my feet. Then I pretended to stumble and staggered a little, the stones clicking and rolling beneath my feet. Down by the lake I saw three lamps sputter, then glow. I led Luke toward them.

"Here," I said to him when we were at the water's edge. "Sit down here and rest a little."

He shook his head, but when I tugged at him, he gave in and bent his knees, collapsing sideways when he lost his balance. I helped him sit up. Then I stripped off my robe and laid it aside.

After a few heartbeats, Luke heard the others walking closer, then Gerrard coming across the beds of stone. He hung his head. They were already naked. It took all four of us to hold Luke still, to keep his arms outstretched. Gerrard leaned over Luke's shoulder, stretching forward to make the cuts, elbow to wrist, one much shorter than the other.

"I am so sorry," I heard Will whispering, and then we all repeated it, over and over, as Luke struggled, stopped, then slumped. Gerrard laid the knife down and eased Luke to the stones. Gently. Then he cut the cloth ties and freed Luke's mouth to sigh.

Time stopped.

Then it started again.

Levin was the first one to wade into the shallows. We followed, going in chest deep, rubbing at our hands and arms, washing the spattered blood off our faces, out of our hair, sluicing each other's backs. After a long time, we waded out a little ways from Luke's body, silent, dripping and shivering. We used the flat of our hands to whisk the droplets off our skin. When we were damp but no longer wet, we dressed and left in the order we had come, leaving only the knife behind, near Luke's right hand.

Gerrard and I didn't say a word to each other as we pretended to study a little, rubbing at our hair until it was dry. Then we went to bed. I could not sleep. I was afraid of the dreams that waited for me, and scared to my bones of the day that would soon begin.

But when the wizard pounded on the door, he walked us to class. Somiss just sat in his circular, auburn-wood chair and pointed at us one after another. I tried to hide my fear and managed to recite with only a few missed words. Will did about the same. So did Levin and Jordan. Gerrard passed.

"Good," Somiss said, and we all lifted our heads to stare at him as the chair rose into the air and he disappeared.

"Good?" Will echoed, whispering. "Did he want us to do it?"

No one answered.

Gerrard waited for me at the entrance, and we started back to our chamber only a few paces apart. Halfway there, he dropped back and we went on, walking shoulder to shoulder.

71

The sun got brighter and brighter. Sadima watched the guards; they were restless, standing their posts, but glancing at each other. Sistra had made them think. Then Sadima caught a glimpse of black robes. She shivered.

"Prisoners!" the loud voice roared. "Stand up!"

Everyone obeyed, and by instinct a circle formed; men on the outside, the grown women next, then women with babes in arms, children at the center. Looking through the heads and shoulders of the men in front of her, Sadima could see the guards glancing at one another. And she saw a man in a dark robe moving behind them. Why weren't the guards arresting the magicians? Was Thomas right? Had they made some agreement with the magistrates?

Sadima gathered her courage. If the guards didn't identify her—and didn't move aside to let them all go— she would step forward. If Thomas wasn't already dead, perhaps they could die side by side. There would be some small happiness in that for her.

"Eridians! Four lines!" the loud voice shouted. "Four lines. Women and children in these two. Men over there." He pointed. "Now!"

Sadima rose on her tiptoes to see. There were four men in black robes, positioning themselves, at one end of the circle of guards. One of them nearest her turned and glanced at the crowd. He was tall and his eyes were pale and cold in the slanting light of morning.

"We want that one," Sistra said from behind her, leaning over Sadima's shoulder to point at a slight young magician. His shoulders were back, his head was high, and he was scanning the crowds. "He's kinder," she whispered. "He smiled at me."

"Line up!" a guard shouted. "Women and children, this side! Line up!"

Sadima was herded along by Sistra and the rest of her friends. As the Eridians formed lines like people waiting to board a ship, the guards moved closer, the circle shrinking as they made a new perimeter, much smaller, two men deep, the red of their tunics an unbreakable barrier.

"Single file!" the shout came as the lines began to inch forward.

"Get away from me," Sadima whispered to Sistra. "All of you should."

"No," Sistra said, and she put her hand on Sadima's shoulder.

"Don't stand close and don't talk to me," Sadima whispered. "Mind your sister."

Sadima stepped forward each time the line moved. She could see the wizard looking into each face, asking a question or two, then letting each woman move on, into another enclosure formed by magistrate's guards. The men were being let into it as well, and families were gathering, standing together. Sadima strained to see, trying to spot Thomas, but she couldn't.

The line continued to inch forward. When they finally got closer, Sadima heard a guard telling the women to quiet their children, stand straight, and look up, showing their faces.

Breathing deep and slow, Sadima watched the magician wait for an old woman who was placing her feet carefully before she tilted her face up. He spoke a few words to her and smiled. The line moved forward. The next woman was young and very pretty, even without her hair. The magician let her pass. Five more women and their children were allowed through, and then it was Sadima's turn.

Trying not to tremble, she took a step forward and looked up at the magician. There was a terrible scar across his throat. It was like Faith's, or worse—and she knew his face. But he couldn't be the young man who had come into the cheese shop all those years ago. Sadima caught her breath. Unless he was like her.

The magician looked into her eyes, smiled, then leaned

close. "Don't come back to Limòri, Sadima. Not ever."

He waved her past and she stumbled forward. Was this Conklin? She wanted to talk to him, ask him . . . everything. He had saved her life by not identifying her. Or maybe he had just condemned all of them.

Sadima heard shouts. She turned to look. The last few women were being let through, but the magicians weren't giving up. Thomas was being marched toward them. They were going to make him do this. Sadima walked to the edge of the crowd before Sistra or any of the others could react. She stood apart from the others, to make it easy for Thomas—and everyone else.

But he didn't point her out. He looked right at her and gave no sign that he recognized her or anyone else. One of the guards shoved him, and Sadima took a half step forward, thinking he would fall, wishing she could steady him. But he didn't fall. Instead he danced backward a few steps, quick and graceful. Then he caught his balance and leaned on his cane.

Sadima stared at him, suddenly understanding. Thomas had made an agreement. He had delivered all of them into the hands of the magistrates and the magicians, and he had asked for only one thing in return. The guard shoved him again, but Thomas was ready this time, pretending to need the cane as he always had. Behind him, a group of men stood close, talking. Sadima saw black robes among the red tunics, and men dressed like merchants.

A command was shouted and a dozen guards stepped back, breaking one side of the circle. Hesitating, then hurrying, people began to walk. Sadima moved forward with the other women, weak with relief, smiling back at Sistra. Faith was pale, her eyes big and full of joy. Two or three women began to sing.

Then, sudden shouts made Sadima pivot and look back just in time to catch a glimpse of Thomas running, his cane held out to one side as he jumped over a bush and made it across the street, disappearing into a yard full of trees and plum thickets. The guards chased him, then slowed, looking in different directions. Two of them beat at the plum branches with their swords, then stood back, calling for help. More guards ran toward them. Sadima knew they would never catch Thomas now. And she would never see him again.

Sadima faced front, almost smiling when she saw all the bald heads before her. Sistra had saved her life. So had Thomas. And the magician. All three were willing to die for her. She had debts to pay, and she would, if ever she could.

Twenty guards walked with them until they came to the wide dirt road that led away from the city. Then they turned back. The Eridians kept walking. But once the red tunics were far behind them, people began to look around anxiously, whispering a little. They slowed, then stopped.

Scared, but knowing it was part of her debt, Sadima made her way to the front. "Are there farmers among us?" she asked, lifting her voice so all could hear. People glanced at one another, then answered, a murmur of voices coming from a hundred mouths.

"I know how to make cheese!" she yelled.

"And kefir!" Sistra called out from the back of the crowd. "I brought the grains, all we need is a cow." There was laughter.

"I know dairy work," a man said, then raised his voice and said it again, much louder.

A woman near the front turned and waved both hands above her head. "I can sew clothing, ship's sails, corn sacks for harvest, anything!"

Then five or six people shouted at once, saying what they had to contribute, and the shouts swelled, mixing into a cheer. When it quieted, there was a little laughter. Sadima set off again at a quicker pace, and when she glanced back, they were all following her.